SPELL of the
HIGHLANDER

Also by Karen Marie Moning in Large Print:

Beyond the Highland Mist
The Dark Highlander
The Highlander's Touch
The Immortal Highlander
To Tame a Highland Warrior

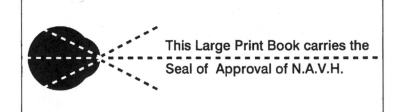

SPELL of the HIGHLANDER

Karen Marie Moning

Thorndike Press • Waterville, Maine

Published in 2005 by arrangement with The Bantam Dell Publishing Group, a division of Random House, Inc.

Thorndike Press® Large Print Basic.

The tree indicium is a trademark of Thorndike Press.

The text of this Large Print edition is unabridged. Other aspects of the book may vary from the original edition.

Set in 16 pt. Plantin by Ramona Watson.

Printed in the United States on permanent paper.

Library of Congress Cataloging-in-Publication Data

Moning, Karen Marie.
    Spell of the Highlander / by Karen Marie Moning.
        p. cm.
    "Thorndike Press large print basic" — T.p. verso.
    ISBN 0-7862-8071-9 (lg. print : hc : alk. paper)
    1. Americans — Scotland — Fiction. 2. Women archaeologists — Fiction. 3. Highlands (Scotland) — Fiction. 4. Immortalism — Fiction. 5. Time travel — Fiction. 6. Large type books. I. Title.
    PS3613.O527S64 2005b
    813'.6—dc22   2005020969

This one's for my husband,
Neil Sequoyah Dover.
Were not there you — I'd be not too.
I love you.

As the Founder/CEO of NAVH, the only national health agency solely devoted to those who, although not totally blind, have an eye disease which could lead to serious visual impairment, I am pleased to recognize Thorndike Press* as one of the leading publishers in the large print field.

Founded in 1954 in San Francisco to prepare large print textbooks for partially seeing children, NAVH became the pioneer and standard setting agency in the preparation of large type.

Today, those publishers who meet our standards carry the prestigious "Seal of Approval" indicating high quality large print. We are delighted that Thorndike Press is one of the publishers whose titles meet these standards. We are also pleased to recognize the significant contribution Thorndike Press is making in this important and growing field.

Lorraine H. Marchi, L.H.D.
Founder/CEO
NAVH

* Thorndike Press encompasses the following imprints: Thorndike, Wheeler, Walker and Large Print Press.

Dear Reader —

When I am uncertain how to pronounce certain words in a book, it makes my brain stutter each time they occur in the text, jarring me from the immediacy of the moment. Toward that end, I have attached this brief key of significant names:

Cian: *Key*-on, with a hard C.

Dageus: *Day*-gis, with a hard G.

Drustan: *Drus*-tin, U like drum.

The Draghar: Druh-*gar,* U like drum, hard G.

Tuatha Dé Danaan: *Tua* day dhanna

Aoibheal: Ah-*veel*

Synchronicity: 1. The simultaneous occurrence of two or more meaningfully but not causally connected events; 2. The coinciding or alignment of forces in the universe to create an event or circumstance; 3. A collision of possibles so incalculably improbable that it would appear to imply divine intervention.

FIRST PROLOGUE

Aoibheal, queen of the Fae, stood in the catacombs beneath The Belthew Building, concealed by countless layers of illusion, a formless projection of herself, beyond any *Sidhe*-seer's vision, beyond even her own race's perception.

In the dimly lit labyrinthine tombs, Adam Black was pacing furiously, holding his ears and cursing a wailing Chloe Zanders.

But it was not Adam's plight that concerned her now.

It was her own.

Tonight she'd wielded the formidable magic of the Queen of the Tuatha Dé Danaan to destroy the Druid sect of the Draghar.

But it was not for that purpose alone she'd done it. As ever, she had motives within motives. Her use of the full power of the High Queen of the Seelie Court of the Light had caused a blackout of all mortal magic throughout Britain, part of Scotland and a fair portion of Wales.

It had shattered wards humans believed unbreakable, voided protections spells, and temporarily leeched all sacred mortal relics of any power they possessed.

Closing her eyes, Aoibheal turned her far-vision outward, analyzing the weft and weck of the fabric of her world. She'd pulled a thread here, tugged a thread there, and the infinitesimal changes she sought had begun.

Somewhere in Tibet an ancient sorcerer was seeking the unholiest of Dark Hallows.

Somewhere in London a thief was casing a wealthy residence reputed to contain unimaginable treasures within.

Somewhere a Keltar was biding his time, waiting for a vengeance long overdue.

Ah, yes, it had begun. . . .

SECOND PROLOGUE

Some men are born under a lucky star.

Showered with female attention from the moment of his highly anticipated birth into a family of seven lovely wee Keltar lasses, but, alas, no sons — his da dead to a hunting accident a fortnight earlier — Cian MacKeltar came into the world, at ten pounds three ounces, already laird of the castle. Heady stuff for such a wee bairn.

As he matured into a man, he inherited the typical Keltar looks: wide-shouldered and powerful, all rippling muscle, topped by the dark, savagely beautiful face of an avenging angel. His noble Celt bloodline, true to its aggressive warrior–aristocracy heritage, also bequeathed him a lion's share of sexuality; a simmering, scarce-contained eroticism that shaped his very walk, underscored his every move.

At a score and ten, Cian MacKeltar was The Sun, The Moon, and The Stars.

And he knew it.

He was a Druid, to boot.

And unlike the vast majority of his broody, overly serious ancestors (not to mention the veritable plethora of broody ones yet to be born), he *liked* being a Druid.

Liked everything about it.

He liked the power that hummed so potently in his veins. He liked cozying up with a flask of whisky among the collection of ancient lore and artifacts in the underground chamber library of Castle Keltar, studying the arcane knowledge, combining a chancy spell with a risky potion, growing stronger and more powerful.

He liked walking the heathery hills after a storm, saying the ancient words to heal the land and the wee beasties. He liked performing the rites of the seasons, chanting beneath a fat, orange harvest moon, with a fierce Highland wind tangling his long dark hair, and fanning his sacred fires into pillars of flame, knowing that the all-powerful Tuatha Dé Danaan depended upon him.

He liked bedding the lasses, taking their sweet lushness beneath his hard body, using his Druid arts to give them such wild, mindless pleasure as — it was whispered — only an exotic Fae lover could bestow.

He even liked the brush of fear with which much of his world regarded him, as a Keltar Druid and heir to the ancient, terrifying magic of the Old Ones.

The laird responsible for the continuation of the sacred Keltar legacy in the late ninth century was devilishly charming, darkly seductive, and the most powerful Keltar Druid ever to live.

None nay-sayed, none challenged, none ever bested Cian MacKeltar. Verily, the possibility that someone or something one day might, never even occurred to him.

Until that cursed Samhain of his thirtieth year.

Some men are born under a lucky star.

Cian MacKeltar was not one of them.

Shortly thereafter, the underground chamber library was sealed off, never to be mentioned again, and all record of Cian MacKeltar was stricken from the Keltar written annals.

It is highly debated among surviving Keltar progeny whether or not this controversial ancestor ever even existed.

And none know that now — some eleven

hundred years later — Cian MacKeltar still lives.

Sort of . . . in a hellish manner of speaking.

PART 1

CHICAGO

1

FRIDAY, OCTOBER 6TH

The call that changed the entire course of Jessi St. James's life came on an utterly unremarkable, dateless Friday night that differed in no particularly significant way from any other unremarkable, dateless Friday night in her all-too-predictable life, which — she was in no hurry to discuss — were a *lot* of Friday nights.

She was sitting in the dark on the fire escape outside the kitchen window of her third-floor apartment at 222 Elizabeth Street, enjoying an unseasonably warm autumn evening. She was being a shameless voyeur, peeping around the corner of the brownstone to watch a crowd of people that, unlike her, had time to have a life, and were talking and laughing out on the sidewalk in front of the nightclub across the street.

For the past few minutes she'd been riveted by a leggy redhead and her boyfriend — a dark-haired, sun-bronzed, muscled hottie in jeans and a white T-shirt. He kept backing his girlfriend up against the wall, stretching her hands above her head, and kissing her like there was no tomorrow, getting into it with his whole gorgeous, rippling body. (And would you just *look* at that hip action? The way he was grinding against her — they might as well be doing it right there in the street!)

Jessi sucked in a sharp breath.

God, had she ever been kissed like that? Like the man couldn't wait to get inside her? Like he wanted to devour her, maybe crawl right inside her skin?

The redhead's hands slipped free, down to the hottie's ass, fingers curving into his muscled butt, and Jessi's hands curled into fists.

When the hottie's hands skimmed up the redhead's breasts, his thumbs grazing her nipples, Jessi's own went hard as little pearls. She could almost imagine she was the one he was kissing, that she was the one he was about to have hot, animalistic —

Why can't I have a life like that? she thought.

You can, an inner voice reminded — after *your PhD.*

The reminder wasn't nearly as effective as it had been years ago as an undergrad. She was sick of being in school, sick of being broke, sick of constantly racing from her classes to her full-time job as Professor Keene's assistant, then home to study, or if she was really lucky, snatching a whopping four or five hours of sleep before getting up to do it all over again.

Her demanding, tightly organized schedule left no time for a social life. And lately she'd been feeling downright sulky about it. Everywhere she turned lately there were couples, and they were busy coupling and having a wonderfully couplelicious time of it.

But not her. There was no time for coupling in her life. She wasn't one of the lucky ones that had a free ride through school. She had to scrimp and save and make every moment and penny count. In addition to working full-time and taking a full load of classes, she taught classes too. It barely left her time to eat, shower, and sleep.

On the infrequent occasions she'd tried to date, the guys had gotten so fed up with how seldom she could see them and how low on her list of priorities they seemed to be and how unwilling she was to fall right in bed with them (most college guys seemed to think if they didn't score by the third date there was something wrong with the *woman* — puh-*leeze*), that they'd soon sought greener pastures.

Still, it would all be worth it soon. Although some people didn't seem to think being an archaeologist and playing with old, dusty, or, frequently, dead things for the rest of one's life was a particularly exciting thing to do (like her mom, who hated Jessi's choice of major and couldn't understand why she wasn't married and blissfully popping out babies like her sisters), Jessi couldn't imagine a more thrilling career. It might not top other people's lists of dreams, but it was hers.

Dr. Jessica St. James. She was so close she could taste it. Another year and a half and she'd be done with her course work for her PhD.

Then she might date like the Energizer Bunny, making up for lost time. But right now, she'd not worked so hard and gone into so much debt to go screwing everything up just because she seemed to be stuck in some kind of hormonal overdrive.

In a few years, she consoled herself, staring down at the busy street, the people hanging out at that club would probably *still* be hanging out at that club, their lives completely unchanged, while she would be traveling to far-off places, digging up remnants of the past, and having grand adventures.

And who knew, maybe Mr. Right would be waiting for her out there at some future dig site. Maybe her life just wasn't scheduled to take off as fast as everyone else's. Maybe she was just a late bloomer.

Holy cow — the hottie was slipping his hand inside the redhead's jeans. And her hand was on his — oh! Right there in front of God and everybody!

Behind her, somewhere in the cramped and crowded apartment that desperately needed to be cleaned and have the trash taken out, the phone began to ring.

Jessi rolled her eyes. The mundaneness of her existence always chose the most inconvenient moments to intrude.

Ring! Ring!

She gulped another fascinated look at the unabashed display of sex-on-the-sidewalk, then reluctantly boosted herself inside the kitchen window. She shook her head in a vain attempt to clear it, then pulled down the shade. What she couldn't see, couldn't torture her. At least not much, anyway.

Riiiiing!

Where was that blasted phone?

She finally spied it on the sofa, nearly buried beneath pillows, candy wrappers, and a pizza box that contained — *eew* — something fuzzy and phosphorescent green. As she gingerly pushed aside the box, she hesitated, hand suspended in midair above the phone.

For a moment — the briefest, most peculiar of interludes — she suffered the inexplicable, intense feeling that she shouldn't pick it up.

That she should just let it ring and ring.

Maybe let it ring all weekend.

Later, Jessi would recall that feeling.

Time itself seemed to stand still for that odd, pregnant slice of time, and she had the weirdest sensation that the universe itself had stopped breathing and was waiting to see what she would do next.

She wrinkled her nose at the ridiculous, egocentric thought.

As if the universe ever even *noticed* Jessi St. James.

She picked up the phone.

Lucan Myrddin Trevayne paced before the fire.

When employing a sorcerer's spell to conceal his true appearance — which he

22

did whenever he wasn't completely alone — he was tall, in his early forties, handsome, powerfully built, his thick black hair dashed at the temples with silver. He was a man who turned women's heads, and made men take an instinctive step back when he walked by. His mien said one thing: *Power — I have it, you don't. And if you think you do — try me.* His features were Old World, his eyes cold gray as a loch beneath a stormy sky. His true appearance was far less appealing.

He'd amassed tremendous wealth and power in his lifetime, which had been considerably longer than most. He held controlling interest in many and varied enterprises, from banks to media to oil. He kept residences in a dozen cities. He retained a select group of uniquely trained men and the occasional woman to handle his most private affairs.

To his left, seated in a deep armchair, one of those men waited tensely.

"This is absurd, Roman," Lucan growled. "What the hell's taking so long?"

Roman shifted defensively in his chair. He was aptly named, his features as classically handsome as those on an ancient coin, his hair long and blond. "I've got men on it, Mr. Trevayne," he said with the trace of a

Russian accent. "The best men we've got. The problem is, they went in a dozen different directions. They were sold on the black market. No one has names. It's going to take time —"

"Time is the one thing I don't have," Lucan cut him off sharply. "Every hour, every moment that passes, makes it less likely they'll be recovered. Those damned things *must* be found."

"Those damned things" were the Dark or "Unseelie" Hallows of the Tuatha Dé Danaan — artifacts of immense power created by an ancient civilization that had passed, centuries ago and quite erroneously, into Man's history books as a mythical race: the *Daoine Sidhe* or the Fae.

Lucan had believed there was no better place to safekeep his prized treasures than in his well-warded private residence in London.

He'd been wrong.

Critically wrong.

He wasn't certain what had happened a few months ago while he'd been out of the country pursuing a lead on the Dark Book, the final and most powerful of the four Unseelie Hallows, but something had transpired somewhere in London — its epicenter in the east side, he could feel the

24

lingering traces of power — that had rever-berated through all of England. An im-mense and ancient power had risen for a brief time, so strong that it had neutralized all other magic in Britain.

Which he wouldn't have cared about since whatever it was had departed as swiftly as it had come, except for the fact that its rising had shattered formidable, al-legedly unbreakable wards that protected his most prized possessions. Protected them so well that he'd found the notion of a modern-day security system laughable.

Not so laughable now.

He'd had a state-of-the-art system in-stalled, with cameras in every room, sweeping every angle, because while he'd been away, a thief had broken into his mu-seum of a home and stolen artifacts that had belonged to him for centuries — in-cluding his irreplaceable Hallows: the box, amulet, and mirror.

Fortunately the thief had been spotted by neighbors while hauling away his loot. Unfortunately, by the time Lucan's select staff had managed to identify and track the bastard, he'd already sold the artifacts to the first in a series of elusive middlemen.

Artifacts such as his, fabulous and ut-terly lacking provenance, inevitably ended up in one of two places: with the legal authorities of one country or another after being intercepted in transit, or sold for a fraction of their worth on the black market before disappearing, sometimes for hundreds of years before so much as a whispered rumor was heard of them again. They'd gotten few names — and those, obvious aliases — from the thief before he'd died. For months now, Lucan's men had been chasing a deliberately and cunningly muddied trail. And time was growing critical.

". . . though we've recovered three of the manuscripts and one of the swords, we've learned nothing about the box or amulet. But it looks like we might have a solid lead on the mirror," Roman was saying.

Lucan stiffened. The mirror. The Dark Glass was the one Hallow he needed urgently. Of all the years it might have been stolen, it'd had to be this one, when the tithe was due! The other Dark Hallows could wait a bit longer, though not long; they were far too dangerous to have loose in the world. Each of the Hallows conferred a gift upon its possessor for a price, if the possessor had the knowledge and the power to use it. The mirror's Dark Gift was immortality, so long as he met its conditions. He'd been meeting its conditions for over a thousand years now. He intended to continue.

"A shipment rumored to fit the bill left England for the States via Ireland a few days ago. We believe it's headed for some university in Chicago, to a —"

"Then why the fuck are you still sitting here?" Lucan said coldly. "If you have a lead, any lead at all on the glass, I want you on it personally. *Now.*" It was imperative he recover the mirror before Samhain. Or else.

That "or else" was a thing he refused to contemplate. The mirror would be found, the tithe paid; a small quantity of pure gold passed through the glass every one hundred years — in the Old Ones way of marking time, which was more than a century by modern standards — at precisely midnight on Samhain, or Halloween as the current century called it. Twenty-six days from today the century's tithe was due. Twenty-six days from today the mirror *must* be in his possession — or The Compact binding his captive to it would be broken.

As the blond man gathered his coat and gloves, Lucan reiterated his position where the Dark Hallows were concerned. "No witnesses, Roman. Anyone who's caught so much as even a glimpse of one of the Hallows . . ."

Roman inclined his head in silent concurrence.

Lucan said no more. There was no need. Roman knew how he liked things handled, as did all who worked for him and continued to live.

Some time later, shortly after midnight, Jessi was back on campus for the third time that day, in the south wing of the Archaeology Department, unlocking Professor Keene's office.

She wondered wryly why she even bothered leaving. Given the hours she kept, she'd be better off tucking a cot into that stuffy, forgotten janitor's closet down the hall, amid mops and brooms and pails that hadn't been used in years. She'd not only get more sleep, she'd save on gas money too.

When the professor had called her from the hospital to tell her that he'd been in a "bit of a fender bender" on his way back to campus — *a few inconvenient fractures and contusions, not to worry,* " he'd assured her swiftly — she'd been expecting him to ask her to pick up his classes for the next

28

few days (meaning her sleep window would dwindle from four or five hours to a great, big, fat nil), but he'd informed her he'd already called Mark Troudeau and arranged for him to take his classes until he returned.

I've a wee favor to ask of you, though, Jessica. I've a package coming. I was to accept a delivery at my office this evening, he'd told her in his deep voice that, even after twenty-five years away from County Louth, Ireland, had never lost its lilt.

She *loved* that lilt. Couldn't wait to one day hear a whole pub speaking it while she washed down a hearty serving of soda bread and Irish stew with a perfectly poured Guinness. After, of course, having spent an entire day in the National Museum of Ireland delightedly poring over such fabulous treasures as the Tara Brooch, the Ardagh Chalice, and the Broighter Gold Collection.

Hugging the phone between ear and shoulder, she'd glanced at her watch, the luminous dial indicating ten minutes past ten. *What kind of package gets delivered so late at night?* she'd wondered aloud.

You needn't concern yourself with that. Just sign for it, lock it up, and go home. That's all I need.

Of course, Professor, but what —

Just sign, lock it up, and forget about it, Jessica. A pause, a weighty silence, then: *I see no reason to mention this to anyone. It's personal. Not university business.*

She'd blinked, startled; she'd never heard such a tone in the professor's voice before. Words sharply clipped, he'd sounded defensive, almost . . . well, paranoid.

I understand. I'll take care of it. You just rest, Professor. Don't you worry about a thing, she'd soothed hastily, deciding that whatever pain meds he was getting were making him funny, the poor dear. She'd once had Tylenol with codeine that had made her feel itchy all over, short-tempered and irritable. With multiple fractures, it was a sure bet he'd been given something stronger than Tylenol 3.

Now, standing beneath the faintly buzzing fluorescent lights in the university hallway, she rubbed her eyes and yawned hugely. She was exhausted. She'd gotten up at six-fifteen for a seven-twenty class and by the time she got home tonight — er, this morning — and managed to fall back into bed, she would have put in another twenty-hour day. Again.

Turning the key in the lock, she pushed open the office door, fumbled for the light

30

switch, and flipped it on. She inhaled as she stepped into the professor's office, savoring the scholarly blend of books and leather, fine wood polish, and the pungent aroma of his favorite pipe tobacco. She planned to one day have an office of her own very much like it.

The spacious room had built-in floor-to-ceiling bookcases and tall windows that, during the day, spilled sun across an intricately woven antique rug of wine, russet, and amber. The teak-and-mahogany furniture was formally masculine: a stately claw-foot desk; a sumptuous leather Chesterfield sofa in a deep, burnished coffee-bean hue; companion wing chairs. There were numerous glass-paned curio cabinets and occasional tables displaying his most prized replica pieces. A reproduction Tiffany lamp graced his desk. Only his computer, with its twenty-one-inch flat screen, belied the century. Remove it, and she might have been standing in the library of a nineteenth-century English manor house.

"In here," she called over her shoulder to the deliverymen.

The package hadn't turned out to be quite what she'd expected. From the way the professor had spoken of it, she'd imagined a bulky envelope, perhaps a small parcel.

But the "package" was actually a crate, and a huge one at that. It was tall, wide, about the size of a . . . well, a sarcophagus or something, and proving no easy matter to navigate through the university corridors.

"Careful, man. Tilt it! Tilt it! Ow! You're smashing my finger. Back it up and angle it!"

A muttered "Sorry." More grunting. "Damn thing's awkward. Hall's too frigging narrow."

"You're almost here," Jessi offered helpfully. "Just a bit farther."

Indeed, moments later, they were carefully lowering the oblong box from their shoulders, depositing it on the rug.

"The professor said I needed to sign something." She encouraged them to hurry. She had a full day of working and studying tomorrow . . . er, today.

"Lady, we need more than that. This here package don't get left 'til it's verified."

" 'Verified'?" she echoed. "What does that mean?"

"Means it's worth *boo-koo* bucks, and the shipper's insurer's got to have visual verification and release. See? Says so right here." The beefier of the two thrust a clipboard at her. "Don't care who does it, lady, so long as somebody's John Hancock's on my paperwork."

Sure enough, *Visual Verification and Release Required* was stamped in red across the bill of lading, followed by two pages of terms and definitions detailing shipper's and buyer's rights in pedantic, inflated legal jargon.

She pushed a hand through her short dark curls, sighing. The professor wasn't going to like this. He'd said it was personal.

"And if I don't let you open it up and inspect it?"

"Goes back, lady. And let me tell you, the shipper's gonna be plenty pissed."

"Yeah," said the other man. "Thing cost an arm and a leg to insure. Goes back, your professor's gonna have to pay the second time around. I bet he's gonna be plenty pissed too."

They stared at her with flat, challenging gazes, clearly disinclined to wrestle the awkward crate back up on their shoulders, squeeze it back down the hall, reload it and return it, only to end up delivering it again. They weren't even talking to her breasts, a thing men often did, especially the first time they met her, which told her how deadly earnest they were about dumping their load and getting on with their lives.

She glanced at the phone.

She glanced at her watch.

She hadn't gotten the professor's room number and suspected that if she called the main desk, they'd never put her through at this hour. Though he'd insisted he wasn't badly hurt, she knew the doctors wouldn't have kept him if he hadn't been seriously injured. Hospitals these days spit people out as fast as they took them in.

Would the professor be more upset if she opened it — or if she refused the delivery and it cost him a fortune to have it reshipped?

She sighed again, feeling damned if she did and damned if she didn't.

In the end it was the constantly-broke college student in her who flipped the coin and made the call.

"Fine. Let's do this. Open it up."

Twenty minutes later the deliverymen had secured her wearily scribbled signature and were gone, taking the remains of the crating with them.

And now she stood, eyeing the thing curiously. It wasn't a sarcophagus after all. In fact, most of the packaging had been padding.

From deep within layers and layers of cushioned wrapping, they'd unearthed a mirror and, at her direction, propped it carefully against the east wall of bookshelves.

Taller than she by more than a foot, the mirror's ornate frame was a shimmery gold. Shapes and symbols, of such uniformity and cohesion to imply a system of writing, were carved into every inch of the wide border. She narrowed her eyes, pondering the etchings, but linguistics was not her specialty, and the symbols were nothing that, without searching through books or notes, she could identify as a letter, word, or glyph.

Inside the gaudy gilt frame, the outer edges of the silvery glass werc marred with a cloudy, uneven black stain of somc sort, but aside from that, the glass itself was startlingly clear. She suspected it had been broken and replaced at some point and would ultimately prove centuries younger than the frame. No mirror of yore had achieved such clarity. Though the earliest artificial mirrors discovered by archaeologists dated back to 6200 B.C.E., they had been fashioned of polished obsidian, not glass. The first glass mirrors of significant size — roughly three-by-five-foot panels —

hadn't been manufactured until the 1680's by Italian glassmaker Bernard Perroto for the Hall of Mirrors at Versailles, commissioned by the extravagant Sun King, Louis the XIV. Exceptional glass mirrors of the size of the one before her — an impressive six and a half feet tall — generally proved to be a few hundred years old, at most.

Considering this one's pristine silvering, it was likely less than a century in age, and no one had gone mad or died from slow mercury poisoning making it. Hatmakers, or "hatters," hadn't been the only ones to suffer from the toxic fumes of their trade (though, for some reason Jessi'd never been able to figure, the idiom "mad-as-a-mirrormaker" had never quite caught on).

Eyes narrowed thoughtfully, she scrutinized it. The archaeologist in her itched to know the piece's provenance, wondered if the frame had been accurately dated.

She frowned. What did the professor want with a mirror, anyway? Such an item wasn't at all in keeping with his usual tastes, which ran toward replica weapons and reproductions of ancient timepieces such as the sixteenth-century German astrolabe adorning his desk. And how could the professor possibly afford something worth *"boo-koo* bucks" on his teaching salary, anyway?

Fishing the key from the pocket of her jeans, she turned to leave. She'd done as he'd asked. Her work here was finished.

She flipped off the light and was just stepping through the doorway when she felt a chill. All the fine hair at the nape of her neck lifted, tingling as if electrified. Her heart was abruptly pounding against the wall of her chest, and she felt the sudden, terrifying certainty that she was being watched.

In the manner that prey was watched.

Flinching, she turned back toward the mirror.

Dimly illumed by the pale blue glow of the computer's screen saver, the artifact looked positively eerie. The gold appeared silvery; the silver glass, smoky, dark and deep with shadows.

And in those shadows something *moved.*

She sucked in a breath so fast she choked on it. Sputtering, she groped for the light switch.

Overhead light blazed down, flooding the room.

She stared into the oblong glass, a hand pressed to her throat, swallowing convulsively.

Her reflection stared back.

After a moment, she closed her eyes. Snapped them open. Stared into the glass again.

Just her.

The hair at her nape continued to bristle, icy chills rippled up her spine. The pulse at the hollow of her neck fluttered frantically beneath her palm. Eyes wide, she glanced uneasily around the room.

The professor's office, precisely as it should be.

After a long moment, she tried for a laugh but it came out shaky, uncertain, and seemed to echo unpleasantly in the office — as if the room's square footage and actual occupiable space didn't quite coincide.

"Jessi, you're losing it," she whispered.

There was nothing, no one with her in the professor's office but her overactive imagination.

With a dismissive toss of her head, she turned, flipped off the light again, and this time pulled the door shut behind her hard and fast and without a backward glance.

Hurrying down the corridor, she dashed out into the back parking lot, kicking up a swirl of red and gold leaves as she hastened to her car.

The more distance she put between herself and the building, the more ridiculous she felt — really, getting all spooked alone on campus at night! One day she would be working on excavations in the middle of nowhere, quite likely late at night and sometimes alone. She couldn't afford to be fanciful. At times, though, it was hard not to be, especially when holding a twenty-five-hundred-year-old Druid brooch, or examining a fabulously detailed La Tène period sword. Certain relics seemed to carry lingering traces of energy, the residue of the passionate lives of those who'd touched them.

Though not *anything* like what she thought she'd just seen.

"How weird was that?" she muttered, shaking off a lingering shiver. "God, I really *must* have sex on the brain."

Watching the hottie and his girlfriend earlier had apparently done quite a number on her. That, coupled with exhaustion and the low lighting, she decided firmly as she unlocked her car and slipped behind the wheel, must have pushed her over the edge, into a brief, eyes-wide-open kind of hallucination/fantasy.

Because for a moment she actually thought she'd seen a half-naked man — an

absolute sex-god of a man, no less —
standing in Keene's office, looking back at
her.

*A trick of the light, strange shadows
falling, nothing more.*

A towering, muscle-ripped, darkly beautiful man, dripping power. And hunger.
And sex. The kind of sex nice girls didn't
have.

*Oh, honey, you so need to get a boy-
friend!*

Looking at her like she was Little Red
Riding Hood and the big, bad wolf hadn't
been fed in a long, long time.

Definitely a trick of the light.

Looking at her from *inside* the mirror.

In a place that was not a place, yet was
place enough to serve as an inescapable
fortress prison, a place to terrify, to drive
the common man stark raving mad, six feet
five inches of caged ninth-century Highlander stirred.

A hungry animal sound rumbled deep in
his throat.

Just as he'd thought: He smelled *woman*.

2

A FEW DAYS LATER . . .

When next Jessi unlocked the professor's office — late on Monday night — a distant part of her brain noted something askew, some tiny niggling detail, but she failed to process it, as she was currently the guest of honor at her own festive and highly enthusiastic pity-party.

That she turned the key, and back again, actually locking *then* unlocking the door, eluded her utterly.

Had she not been busy muttering beneath her breath about the depressingly huge stack of freshman papers that had been dumped on her in the professor's absence, that she might have actually gotten time to work on grading if he hadn't left her a message last night with a list a mile long of periodicals and sources he wanted her to collect from a dozen different places and bring to the hospital so he could flag notes for the book he was writing while laid up recuperating, she might have been cognizant enough of her surroundings to have reconsidered walking through the door.

Maybe closed it again, locked it for real, and gone and gotten campus security.

Unfortunately, enthused celebrant of her own misery, she didn't notice a thing.

She paused with the door slightly ajar, puffed a few strands of hair from her face, and shifted the crammed-full backpack on her shoulder so her textbooks would stop gouging the back of her ribs.

"A hundred and eleven essays? Would somebody just shoot me and put me out of my misery?" She'd counted them in disbelief when Mark Troudeau, smirking openly, had handed them over. There went any hope of sleeping for the next few days.

Hey, I agreed to teach Keene's classes, Jess, and you know how tight my schedule is. He said you would grade.

She knew exactly why Keene had said she would grade. Because, no doubt, Mark had called him over the weekend and "suggested" she grade. Mark had been a shit to her ever since last year, when he'd hit on her (unsuccessfully) at the department Christmas party. She couldn't stand men who talked to her breasts, as if there was nothing above them worth noting, and he was one of the worst. She didn't go around talking to men's crotches.

Sure enough, the professor had left her *another* message while she was in class, bringing his total in the past twenty-four hours to five (would somebody please either take that man's phone away or knock him out with sedatives?), and thanked her for being *"such a lovely assistant and helping out. Mark really does have his hands full, and I told him you would be happy to assist."*

Right. As if anyone had given her a choice. And as if Mark's hands were any more full than hers. But the world of academia was, like the rest of the world in many ways, still an Old Boys' School, and anytime Jessi began to forget that, life invariably gave her a refresher course.

Nudging the door open with her hip, Jessi pushed inside, leaving it ajar. Skirting the desk, she headed straight for the wall of bookshelves. She didn't bother turning on the light, partly because she'd organized the office herself and knew exactly where to find the two books on Celtic Gaul that Professor Keene wanted, and partly because she was determined not to get distracted by the mirror, and the slow, relentless burn of questions it had ignited in her mind.

She'd made peace with that weird little trick of the eye she'd suffered on Friday — a product of nothing more than low light and exhaustion. But she was dying to know if the mirror was a genuine relic. How had the professor come across it? Was its origin provable? Had any valid dating been done? What *were* those symbols, anyway?

Jessi had a sticky memory — a useful ability in her field — and several of the symbols had gotten embedded in it from her single, cursory inspection. She'd been subconsciously pondering them since, wondering why they seemed so familiar, yet somehow . . . wrong. Trying to pinpoint where she'd seen something similar before. Her specialty was the archaeology of Europe from the Paleolithic to the "Celtic" Iron Age. Though the mirror was clearly of recent manufacture, she was titillated by the possibility that the frame might actually date to somewhere in the late Iron Age.

She knew herself well enough to know that if she took another look at the relic tonight, curiosity would get the best of her and the next thing, she'd be digging through the professor's reference books trying to determine what the symbols were and doing her best to guesstimate a date. *Been there, done that,* she thought wryly. Blew an entire night without even realizing it, poring over one artifact or another, especially on those rare and glorious occasions the university was briefly entrusted with a collector's piece for study or verification. She always paid for it double the next day. With that infernal stack of papers waiting for her, she couldn't afford to waste any time. In and out, swift and efficient, was her plan and she was sticking to it.

She was just reaching up to pluck the two thick volumes from the shelf when she heard the soft *snick* of the door closing behind her.

She stiffened, froze midreach.

Then snorted and pulled the first book from the shelf. A draft. Nothing more. "No way. I am *not* getting all freaked out on campus again tonight. That blasted mirror is *just* a mirror," she told the bookcase firmly.

"Actually, it's not," a smooth, faintly accented voice murmured behind her. "It's far more than a mere mirror. Who else knows it's here?"

Jessi gasped and turned around so fast that the book went flying from her hand, hit the wall with a solid *whump,* and slid to the floor. She winced. The professor was going to kill her if she'd spindled the spine; he was funny about his books, especially his hardbacks. Across the office, in the dim light afforded by the computer, she could just make out the silhouette of a man leaning back against the door, arms folded across his chest.

"Wh-what — wh-who —" she stammered.

Light flooded the room.

"I startled you," the man said softly, dropping his hand from the wall switch.

Later Jessi would realize he'd merely noted a fact, not apologized.

She blinked against the abrupt increase in wattage, taking him in. His arms were crossed again; he leaned casually against the door. Tall and well built, he was extremely attractive. Longish blond hair was pulled back from a clean-shaven, classic face. He wore a dark, expensive tailored suit, a crisp shirt, a tasteful tie. His accent held distinct Slavic undertones, perhaps Russian, she mused. A young professor visiting from abroad? A speaker engaged by the university? "I didn't realize anyone else was still in this wing," she said. "Are you looking for Professor Keene?"

"The professor and I have already had our time together this evening," he replied with the ghost of a smile.

An odd way of phrasing things; his comment passed through her mind absently, as she was still hung up on his opening gambit. She pounced on it, pursuing it eagerly: "What did you mean, 'it's far more than a mere mirror'? What do you know about it? Where is it from? Are you here to authenticate it? Or has it already been? What are the symbols? Do you know?"

He stepped away from the door, moved deeper into the room. "I understand it was delivered this past Friday. Has anyone else seen it?"

Jessi thought a moment, shook her head. "I don't think so. The deliverymen opened it up, but other than that, just me. Why?"

He glanced around the office. "There's been no cleaning crew in since then? No other persons such as yourself with a key?"

Jessi frowned, perplexed by the direction of his questions. And getting irked that he wasn't answering any of hers. "No. The cleaners come on Wednesdays and the only reason I have a key is because I'm Professor Keene's assistant."

"I see." He eased forward another step.

And that was when Jessi felt it.

Menace. Rolling off him. She'd not picked up on it right away, disarmed by his good looks, curious about the artifact, peripherally distracted by her own brooding. But it was there — a wolf beneath the sheep's clothing. For all his seeming civility, there was something cold and dangerous beneath that elegant suit. And it was focused on her.

Why? It didn't make any sense!

And suddenly the tiny niggling detail that had eluded her when she'd turned the key in the door swam up from the murky waters of her subconscious: It had already been unlocked! He must have been inside the office, concealing himself behind the door when she'd pushed it open!

Keep him talking, she thought, fighting panic. She drew a careful, deep breath. Adrenaline was kicking in, upping her heart rate, making her hands and legs feel shaky. She concentrated on betraying no sign of her belated recognition of danger. Surprise might be the only advantage she had. Somewhere in the office was something she could use as a weapon, something more threatening than a book. She just had to get her hands on it before he figured out she was on to him. She snatched a surreptitious glance to her right.

Yes! Just as she'd thought, there lay one of the professor's replica blades on a nearby curio table. Though a reproduction piece, fashioned of steel not gem-encrusted gold, it was every bit as lethal as the real thing.

"So how old is the mirror, anyway?" she asked, donning her best wide-eyed, I'm-not-the-brightest-bulb-in-the-box look.

He moved again. Smooth, like a well-muscled animal. A few more steps and he'd be past the desk. She eased right a tad.

It seemed he was pondering whether or not to answer her for a moment, then he shrugged. "You would probably place it in the Old Stone Age."

Jessi sucked in a breath and for just a moment, the briefest of instants, fear fell by the wayside. The Old Stone Age? Was he *kidding?*

Wait — of course he was. He had to be! It was patently impossible. The earliest forms of writing, cuneiform and hieroglyphics, weren't even in existence until the mid to end of the fourth century B.C.E.! And those etchings on the mirror were *some* kind of writing.

"Ha, ha. I'm not that stupid." Well, today, she ceded dismally, she certainly seemed to be, on just about all fronts, but normally she wasn't. Normally she suffered only one or two stupid fronts, not this all-encompassing, blanket idiocy. "That would put it at pre-ten-thousand B.C.E.," she scoffed, as she stole a few more inches. Had he noticed what she was doing? If so, he was giving no indication.

"Yes, indeed it would. Considerably 'pre.' " He took another step forward.

She considered screaming but she was nearly certain there was no one else in the south wing this late at night, and suspected it would be wiser to conserve her energy to defend herself with. "Okay, I'll go with this a minute," she said, inching, inching. *Just a little farther. Keep him talking.* Dare she make a leap for it? "You're claiming the frame is from the Old Stone Age. Right? And the carvings were added later, and the mirror inserted in the last century or so."

"No. The entire piece, in sum, Old Stone Age."

Her jaw dropped. She snapped her mouth closed, but it fell open again. She searched his face, detected no sign of jest. "Impossible! Symbols aside, that's a *glass* mirror!"

He laughed softly. "Not . . . quite. Nothing about an Unseelie piece is ever . . . quite what it seems."

" 'An Unseelie piece'?" she echoed blankly. "I'm not familiar with that classification." Her fingers curled, she braced herself to dive for the blade, doing a mental five-count . . . *four . . . three . . .*

"Not many are. It denotes relics few ever see and live to tell of. Ancient Hallows fashioned by those darkest among the Tuatha Dé Danaan." He paused the space of a heartbeat. "Don't worry, Jessica St. James —"

Oh, God, he knew her name. How did he know her name?

"— I'll make it quick. You'll hardly feel a thing." His smile was terrifyingly gentle.

"Holy *shit!*" She lunged for the dirk at the same moment he lunged for her.

When one was afraid for one's life, Jessi observed with almost serene, dreamlike detachment, events had a funny way of slowing down, even though one knew events were really rushing toward one with all the velocity and surety of a high-speed train wreck.

She noted every detail of his lunge, as if it unfolded in freeze-frames: his legs bent,

51

his body drew in on itself, coiling to spring, one hand dipped into a pocket, withdrew a thin wire with leather-wrapped ends, his eyes went cold, his face hard, she even noticed the whitening around the edges of his nostrils as they flared with a terrifying, incongruous sexual excitement.

She was aware of her own body in a similar dichotomous fashion. Though her heart thundered and her breath came in fast and furious gasps, her legs felt made of lead, and the few steps she managed seemed to take a lifetime.

His lips curled mockingly and, in that sharp-edged smile, she saw the sudden stark certainty that even if she managed to arm herself with the small blade, it wouldn't matter. Death waited in his smile. He'd done this before. Many, many times. And he was good at it. She had no idea how she knew, she just knew.

As he closed in on her, wrapping the leather-cased ends of the wire around his hands, the silvery glint of the mirror, leaning against the bookshelves beyond the table, caught her eye.

Of course — the mirror!

She might not be able to best him in a physical struggle, but she just happened to be smack between him and what he wanted!

And what he wanted was *highly* breakable.

She practically fell on top of the curio table, shoved aside the dirk, and closed her hand instead around the heavy pewter base of the lamp next to it. She whirled to face him at dizzying speed, backed up against the mirror, and hefted the lamp like a baseball bat. "Stop right there!"

He stopped so abruptly that he should have fallen flat on his face, which spoke volumes about how much lethal muscle was under that suit — oh yes, she'd be dead if he got his hands on her.

"Take one more step and I'll smash the mirror to smithereens." She brandished the lamp threateningly.

Was that the sound of a sharply indrawn breath *behind* her? Followed by a muttered curse?

Impossible!

She dare not turn. Dare not take her eyes off her attacker for even a moment. Dare not give in to the sob of fear that was trying to claw its way up the back of her throat.

His gaze darted over her shoulder, his eyes flared, then his gaze latched back on her. "No, you won't. You preserve history. You don't destroy it. That thing is priceless. And it *is* as old as I said it was. It is conceivably the single most important relic any archaeologist has ever laid eyes on. It debunks thousands of years of your so-called 'history.' Think of the impact it could have on your world."

"Mine personally? Gee, like, uh, *none,* if I'm dead. Back off, mister, if you want it in one piece. And I think you do. I think it's not worth a thing to you broken." If he was going to kill her, she had nothing to lose by smashing it into a gazillion silvery little pieces; no matter that her inner historian violently protested such sacrilege. If she was going down, she was taking whatever he wanted with her. If she was going to be dead, by God, he was going to be miserable too.

A muscle worked in his jaw. His gaze skidded between her and the mirror and back again. He tensed as if to take a step.

"Don't do it," she warned. "I'm serious." She shifted her grip on the lamp, prepared to swing it into the mirror if he so much as breathed wrong. If nothing else, maybe they'd struggle atop the shards of glass; he'd slip, cut himself, and bleed to death. One never knew.

"Impasse," he murmured. "Interesting. You've more spirit than I'd thought."

"If you are wishing to live, lass," came the deep, rich purr of a brogue behind her, "best summon me out now."

A chill shuddered through her entire body, and the baby-fine hair at the nape of her neck stood up, quivering on end. Just like on Friday, the room felt suddenly . . . wrong. Not quite the size and shape it was supposed to be. As if a door that by all conventions of reality couldn't possibly be there had suddenly opened, skewing the known dimensions of her world.

"Shut the hell up," her assailant clipped, his gaze fixed over her shoulder, "or I'll smash you myself."

Dark, mocking laughter rolled behind her. It made her shiver. "You wouldn't dare and well you ken it. 'Tis why you've not rushed her. Lucan sent you with precise instructions. Bring it back intact, nay? The mere possibility that the mirror might be shattered makes your blood ice. You know what he'd do to you. You'd be begging for death."

"Huh-uh, no way," Jessi whispered, eyes going wide. She could feel the blood draining from her face, knew she'd gone white as snow. "Not believing this." She took a shaky little breath. "Any of this."

Logic insisted there couldn't possibly be

anyone behind her. And certainly not anyone *inside a mirror,* for heaven's sake!

But her gut was of a different opinion.

Her gut sensed "Man" with a capital "M" behind her, and he was throwing off all the heat of a small, fiery forge at her back. Enough that it made the sides and front of her feel abruptly cold. Made her neck ache with the effort of keeping her gaze fixed firmly on her would-be murderer, and not turning to gape at the looking glass. She could *feel* him behind her. Something. Someone. Caged power. Caged sexuality. Whatever was behind her was formidable.

"Doona turn, woman," he — it — whatever it was — counseled. "Keep your eyes on him and speak after me —"

"I'd advise against that," the blond man warned, locking gazes with her. "You've no idea what you'd be letting out of that mirror."

Jessi took another shallow breath. She could sense the blond man's tightly leashed fury, knew if he thought, for even a split second, that she might not actually break the mirror, she was dead. She was afraid to so much as blink, afraid he would lunge during that brief moment of vulnerability. And there was something behind her that couldn't possibly be there, at least not according to any laws of physics *she* understood. Admittedly, there were many laws of physics she didn't understand, but she felt confident enough of those she did to protest faintly, "This is crazy."

" 'Crazy' would be letting him out," the blond man said. "Step away from the mirror. Do as I say and I'll see to it he doesn't harm you."

"Oh, like I'm believing that. Now you're my *protector?*"

"Summon me out, woman. *I* am your protector," came the command at her back.

"This isn't happening." It couldn't be. None of it. Her mind was incapable of processing it, and the sensation of dreamlike detachment was increasing exponentially. She felt as if she were standing, bewildered, on a stage set, as actors played their parts around her, and if somebody had a playbill with one of those helpful little plot synopsis thingies, she sure hadn't gotten to see it.

"He *will* kill you, lass," rolled the deep Scots burr behind her, "and you know it. You doona ken the same of me. Sure death or a mayhap death, 'tis a simple choice."

"And that's supposed to be reassuring?"

she snapped over her shoulder, to whatever it was that was there that couldn't really be there.

The blond man smiled coldly. "Oh, he'll kill you, and far more brutally than I. Step aside and I'll let you live. I'll collect the mirror and leave. I give you my word."

Jessi shook her head from side to side, once. "Leave. Now. And I won't smash the mirror."

"He won't leave, lass, 'til you're dead. He cannot. He is bound to serve one who would punish him were he to leave you alive now that you've seen the Dark Glass. I've no means to convince you to trust me. You must hang your bonnet on faith. Him. Or me. Choose. Now."

"He was imprisoned in such a fashion because he is a ruthless killer that couldn't be contained any other way. He was locked away for the safety of the world. It took the power of formidable Druids —"

"Woman, choose! Repeat this: *Lialth bree che bree, Cian MacKeltar, drachme se-sidh!*"

Jessi echoed the strange words without missing a beat the moment she heard them.

Because she finally understood what was going on.

She was right — none of this was happening.

What was happening was that she'd let herself in Professor Keene's office and, rather than going to the bookshelf as she'd thought, she'd sat down for a moment on the plush leather Chesterfield sofa to rest her eyes. But she'd ended up getting too horizontal. And she was currently snoozing soundly away, having the most bizarre of dreams.

And everyone knew nothing mattered in dreams. One always woke up. Always. So why not let the man out of the mirror? Who cared?

She echoed the odd incantation twice, for good measure. Brilliant golden light flashed, the heat behind her increased markedly, and the room suddenly seemed too small for all that was in it. The sensation of spatial distortion increased almost unbearably.

The lamp was plucked from her limp grasp and placed elsewhere. Strong hands closed on her waist from behind. Lifted her from the floor and swept her aside. Deposited her behind him, sheltering her with his body.

She caught scent of him then — God, had she ever smelled such a scent? The female muscles deep in her lower belly clenched. He bore no chemical traces of aftershave or deodorant. Nothing artificial. Just pure man: a blend of sun-warmed leather on skin, a kiss of something spicy like clove, a touch of sweat, and the raw, unspoken promise of sex. If male sexual dominion had a scent, he reeked of it, and it worked on her like the ultimate pheromone, bringing her nipples and groin to intense, painful sexual awareness.

She glanced up. And up.

It was the same towering, gorgeous, muscle-ripped man from her Friday-night fantasy, his long dark hair a tangle of dozens of braids bound with gold, silver, and copper beads, falling halfway down his back. His bare, oh-so-beautiful, velvet-skinned back.

"Whuh," she breathed. In all her voyeuristic forays, she'd never seen a man so savagely, splendidly masculine. Figured he existed only in her subconscious.

It occurred to her then that since it *was* her subconscious at work, it was high time she transformed her id's twisted little everyone's-trying-to-kill-Jessi-today dream into something more to her liking: one toe-curling, scorchingly hot sex-dream.

Usually even the most intractable of bad

dreams needed only a tiny nudge.

Nudge she would. With this fantasy man? Happily. Blissfully, even. She slid her palms up that perfect, powerful back, gliding over the ridges of muscle.

Fisted her hands in all that magnificent dark hair. Rubbed up against him, molding herself like Saran Wrap to his muscular, deliciously tight ass.

And licked him.

Slipped her tongue right up his spine. Tasted the salt and man and heat of him.

His entire body jerked with a violence that she would have found frightening, were she awake and any of it real. He sucked in a sharp breath between his teeth, a long, tight indrawn hiss, as if he were in exquisite pain. He went completely still, and made a guttural sound deep in his throat.

"You try me, woman," he hissed.

He tossed his head — hard — yanking his braids free of her hands. In two strides he was through the door, slamming it behind him.

Only then did Jessi realize her assailant, too, was gone. He must have fled the moment she'd freed the man from the mirror.

With a gusty sigh, she went and slumped down on the couch. After a moment, she lay down, stretched out, and folded her arms behind her head.

She crossed her legs. Uncrossed them. Rubbed her eyes. Pinched herself experimentally a time or two.

God, she was horny. She couldn't remember ever being so horny. The instant she'd pressed up against him she'd felt the strangest . . . well . . . *jolt,* for lack of a better word, sizzle through her entire body, and she'd gotten instantly ready. Panties-slick, ready-for-sex, no-foreplay-necessary ready.

So this *is a wet dream,* she thought with a little snort of amusement.

A worrisomely vivid, detailed wet dream, but a dream nonetheless.

She was going to wake up any minute now.

Yup. Any minute now.

3

Jessi awakened stiff, cold, and with the beginnings of what promised to be a perfectly vicious headache.

Her neck was crinked from sleeping funny and she must have pushed her pillow off the bed in the middle of the night, because there was nothing remotely downy beneath her head. She opened her eyes and pushed herself up, intending to take some Advil, retrieve her pillow, and lie back down for a few minutes, but the moment she opened her eyes, she had to add utterly-perplexed-as-to-her-current-location-in-the-universe to her list of complaints.

Unfortunately, her cranky, sleep-muddled respite from reality was far too brief. As soon as she sat up, she discovered she was not in her bed as she'd thought, but on the sofa in Professor Keene's office, and the events of last night sledgehammered back into her brain.

Groaning, she dropped her head forward

and clutched it with both hands.

Impossible events: a stranger in the office who'd tried to kill her; an absurd tale that the mirror was Old Stone Age; a man inside the mirror whom she'd freed — allegedly a ruthless killer.

Insane events.

Face buried in her palms, she whimpered, "What's *happening* to me?"

But she knew what was happening to her; it was painfully obvious. She was losing it, that was what. And she wouldn't be the first graduate student to crack under the strain of an overly ambitious load. Hardly a term passed without one or two dropping out of the program. The survivors always shook their heads and gossiped mercilessly about how so-and-so "just couldn't take the pressure." She knew; she'd been among them.

But I can *take the pressure! I'm doing great; look at my GPA!* she protested inwardly.

Right. Uh-huh, logic countered flatly, *so what other explanation is there for the crazy hallucinations — or dreams — or whatever they are — that you've been suffering for the past few days?*

She sighed. There was no denying it; in the past few days she'd had two distinct bouts of . . . well, something . . . during which she'd not only been incapable of distinguishing reality from fantasy, she'd not even been in charge of her own fantasy.

Which hardly seemed fair, she thought, biting back a bubble of near-hysterical laughter. If a girl was going to lose her mind, shouldn't she at least get to enjoy it? Why on earth would she conjure the perfect male specimen, the most incendiary of hotties, then make herself the hapless victim of some bizarre murder plot?

"I just don't get it." Gingerly, she rubbed the pads of her index fingers in small circles on her throbbing temples.

Unless it had actually *happened*.

"Right. Uh-huh." A man in a mirror. Sure.

Still holding her temples, she raised her head, peering about the dimly lit office, seeking clues. There was no indication that anyone but she had ever been there. Oh, the lamp was on the floor, rather than in its usual perch on the table, and a book was lying on the rug near the wall, but neither of those things could be construed as conclusive evidence that someone else had been in the office with her last night. People were known to sleepwalk in the midst of highly vivid dreams.

She forced herself to look in the mirror. Directly into it.

Hard silvered glass. Nothing more.

Forced herself to stand up. Walk over to it. Place her cold palms against the colder glass.

Hard silvered glass. Nothing more. No way anything had come out of that.

Squaring her shoulders, she turned her back on the relic.

Moving stiffly, she retrieved her backpack from the floor, scooped up the books the professor wanted, stuffed them into her bag, let herself out, and locked up the office.

For the first time in the entire history of her academic career, Jessi did the unthinkable: She ditched classes, went home, took some aspirin, tugged on her favorite *Godsmack* T-shirt, crawled into bed, pulled the covers up over her head.

And hid.

She never gave up. Never abandoned her plans and schedule. Never failed to meet things head-on. As tight as her schedule was, if she let a single thing slip or fall behind, a dozen others were affected. One tiny lapse could initiate a wildly entropic downward spiral. Ergo, everything had to be tackled and completed as planned.

Last winter, she'd trudged to class in the middle of one of Chicago's most brutal snowstorms, trembling from head to toe with violent flu-chills, so sick that all the millions of tiny pores in her skin stung like little needle pricks. She'd lectured on more than one occasion while bordering on laryngitis, forcing her voice only with the aid of a disgustingly vile tea of orange peel, olive oil, and varied unmentionables she still shuddered to think about. She'd graded papers with a fever of a hundred and two.

But craziness wasn't something one could tackle and complete, moving on to the next project.

And she had no clue how to deal with it.

Figuring chocolate was a start, as soon as she stepped through the door of her apartment, she grabbed a bag of Hershey's Kisses she kept stashed away for emergencies (i.e., bad hair, severe PMS, or just one of those good old men-are-stupid-and-suck days) and in her warm cocoon beneath the blankets, began making short work of the decadent, melty little morsels.

After devouring the entire bag, she fell asleep.

She slept straight through until nine o'clock that night.

Upon awakening, she felt so much better that it occurred to her perhaps all she'd really needed was a good, solid ten hours of uninterrupted sleep. That perhaps, now that she was getting older — after all, she wasn't a freshman anymore, she was twenty-four years old! — her frequent all-nighters exacted more of a toll than they used to. That perhaps she should start taking vitamins. Drink more milk. Eat her vegetables.

She wasn't crazy, she thought, shaking her head and smiling faintly at the sheer absurdity of the notion. Those two intensely vivid dream/hallucinations she'd suffered had been merely an isolated occurrence of stress coupled with lack of sleep, and she was making a big deal out of nothing.

"I was just exhausted," she told herself with a perfunctory, optimistic little nod.

Chocolate and sleep had buoyed her spirits. Fortified her to begin anew.

She was ready to start all over again, to face the day, or night, as it may be, and prove to herself that there was nothing wrong with her.

At least that was how she felt *before* she turned on the TV.

Vengeance.
'Twas the possibility that had kept Cian

68

MacKeltar from going stark raving mad during the past 1,133 years of his incarceration in the Dark Glass.

From without, the glass looked to be little more than an elaborate mirror. From within, it was a circular stone prison, fifteen paces across at any point one chose to walk it. And he'd walked it a lot. Counted every bloody stone. Stone floor. Stone walls. Stone ceiling. Gray. Drab. Cold.

He'd stayed heated over the centuries by one thought only, burning like liquid fire in his veins.

Vengeance.

He'd lived it, breathed it, *become* it, caged and waiting, ever since the day Lucan Myrddin Trevayne, a man he'd once counted his closest friend and boon companion in the arts, had bound him to the Dark Glass, thereby securing immortality for himself.

Given the extent of the binding spells Lucan had used on him — coupled with his powerlessness within the glass and his inability to exit it, unless granted a brief freedom by the chanting of a summoning spell by someone beyond it — some might have dismissed his hope for vengeance as an impossibility.

But being a Druid, and a Keltar at that,

Cian understood things that seemed impossible rarely were.

What impossible truly meant was "hasn't happened *yet*."

A fact that had been demonstrated well enough when, three and a half months ago, a thief had broken into Trevayne's London stronghold — an impossibility in itself — and carted off half the bastard's most prized relics, including the Dark Glass, scant months before the tithe that bound Cian to the Hallow was due.

Chance had favored him at long last. Lucan had lost possession of the mirror just when he needed it the most.

Now it was the tenth day of the tenth month, and Cian need only stay out of Lucan's hands for a mere twenty-two more days — until just after midnight on All Hallows' Eve, the anniversary of his original binding — in order to satisfy his millennium-old lust for vengeance. And bloody hell, he was starved for it!

Now that Lucan had a solid lead on the Dark Book, the most dangerous of all the Unseelie Hallows, it was even more critical Cian shatter the cursed Compact imprisoning him. Fulcrum for some of the deadliest black magyck known to man, the Dark Book in the hands of any man was a recipe for cataclysmic destruction. In the hands of Lucan "Merlin" Trevayne, it could brew the end of the world as the world knew it. Lucan could rewrite history, change time itself, if he managed to decipher some of the intricate spells therein. Cian *had* to stop him from getting the book. He had to defeat his ancient enemy once and for all.

He'd thought success within his grasp, had believed, given how many hands the Dark Glass had been passed through, and how far it had been sent, that Lucan would never find it in time, but yesterday had illustrated otherwise. He'd indeed been found, and his time had run out.

He'd recognized the Russian assassin the moment he'd slipped into the office last eve. He'd glimpsed him several times in the past when Roman had visited Trevayne's London residence, where Cian had hung high on a wall in Lucan's private study, being taunted by a view out a wall of windows that overlooked a busy London street in a world in which he would never live again.

At least he'd had a view. Had Lucan hung him *toward* the wall, he wasn't certain even lust for vengeance would have kept him sane. Nor would it have afforded

71

him the opportunity to test the mirror when his gaoler was away and learn to summon in inert objects that were within his line of vision. In such a fashion, he'd kept up with time's fierce trot forward, devouring every book, periodical, and newspaper that passed through Lucan's study over the centuries, occasionally even seeing a bit of television, while his view beyond the window metamorphosed from a sweetly rolling meadow to a small town, and finally to a sophisticated, bustling city.

Much like this "Chicago" in which he'd walked last eve.

Free, sweet Christ, he'd walked free again for a time! He'd felt the crush of grass beneath his boots, savored the wind in his face!

There were days inside the mirror when he felt he might willingly cut off his right arm for a single deep breath of a peat fire heaped with sheaves of fragrant heather, or a few lungfuls of briny air on Scotia's wild shore. Or to sprawl on his back atop a high ben, as close to the heavens as one could get only in the Highlands, and watch the gloaming take the sky, streak and smudge it with violet and crimson, then turn it to a black velvet canopy sprinkled with starry diamonds.

He'd not seen his beloved Scotia in eleven hundred and thirty-three years. That was hell right there for a Highlander, to live exiled from his motherland.

Though Lucan had occasionally granted him freedoms in exchange for aid with a particularly difficult spell or a dark deed he wanted done — the bastard had stayed on intricately warded ground the entire time, so Cian couldn't touch him — the last had been over a hundred and twenty years ago, and such freedoms were agonizingly brief. The Dark Glass's magic always reclaimed him after a time, despite his resistance. It didn't matter how fast or far from it he fled, didn't matter what Druid wards he wove about himself, after a time — and it was never the same interval; once, an entire day; another time, no more than a single hour — he was simply no longer wherever he'd been: one moment free; the next, back in his prison.

It had taken him some time last night to track Roman and, because he'd been concerned the mirror might reclaim him before he'd succeeded, he'd focused single-mindedly on the task. He had no doubt another of Lucan's men would soon be coming. And another and another, *ad infinitum,* until the mirror had been collected and all trace of any who'd so much as glimpsed it, eradicated.

It was the way of men of their ilk — men of magycks, light and dark, those who practiced *draiodheacht* — to conceal such things as the Hallows from the world. Cian — because common man should not be troubled by the existence of such things. Lucan — because there were many other sorcerers out there (scrupulously staying off one another's radar) who would stop at nothing to steal the coveted, dangerous Dark Hallows, were they to learn he had them. Contrary to what many thought, sorcerers and witches were a flourishing breed.

A Keltar Druid would have worked a complex memory spell to harmlessly — if properly and painstakingly done — erase the forbidden knowledge from the minds of any who'd encountered it.

But not Lucan. Simpler to kill: minimum effort, maximum pleasure and gain. Lucan thrived on power over life and death. He always had.

Cian smiled bitterly. Anyone in his path was expendable, and the woman was in his path. She was in mortal danger that she couldn't possibly begin to fathom or hope to survive.

His thoughts both gentled and grew fiercer as they turned toward her. Fiery, determined, courageous, she was a stunning woman, with short glossy black hair curling softly back from a heart-shaped, delicate-featured face, and the most perfect, bountiful, lusciously rounded breasts he'd ever seen. A delectable ass too. He'd seen in great detail each intimate curve in her low-slung blue jeans and snug peach sweater. He'd even glimpsed part of her panties — which couldn't have covered more than a fraction of her generous bottom, fashioned as they were from little more than ribbons — peeking up from the waistband of her jeans. The orange lacy stuff had been adorned by a bright pink butterfly at the base of her spine, making it seem her panties had been designed to slide up from her jeans to taunt a man's eye. *Men must be paragons of restraint in this century,* he'd thought, staring fixedly at the scrap of frothy fabric rising from between the twin globes of her ass, *or a bunch of bloody eunuchs*. Creamy sun-kissed skin, eyes of jade, mouth of a temptress, Lucan's assassin had called her Jessica.

As Cian had anticipated, she'd endeavored to convince herself that none of last eve had happened. On those infrequent occasions he'd been glimpsed by the uninitiated, they blamed everything and anything to deny the possibility of his existence.

He, on the other hand, would replay over and over a single moment from last eve, convincing himself it had indeed happened.

She'd rubbed up against him and tasted him. Crushed those round, heavy breasts to his back, nipples hard and poking him through the fabric of her woolen, and *licked* him.

As if she'd hungered for the salt of his skin on her tongue.

His cock had shot up so painfully erect that his balls had jerked and his seed had nearly exploded out of him right then and there.

The feel of her against his body had caused a thing he'd never before experienced: a violent jolt that had speared straight to the core of his soul. It had been all he could do to force her hands from his hair and pull away. It had taken every ounce of his will to not simply turn on her, drop her to the floor, and spread her for his pleasure. Forget about her assailant entirely. Bury himself inside her and stay there until torn from her body by Dark Magyck.

But nay, not only wouldn't he let her life be snuffed like some frail candle flame caught in a deadly tempest not of her own making — he needed her.

"Twenty-two days," he murmured. After more than a millennium of biding time, his vengeance was now dependant upon a laughably finite number of days.

Jessica St. James didn't know it yet, but she was going to help him get them.

If not willingly, then by means of every Dark Art he knew.

And he knew a lot of them.

Had practiced most of them. And excelled at all of them.

Lucan wasn't the only one who'd wanted the Dark Glass.

4

CASTLE KELTAR — SCOTLAND

"You'll ne'er believe this, Drustan," Dageus MacKeltar said, glancing up as his twin brother, elder by three minutes, strolled into the library at Castle Keltar.

"I doona think much would surprise me after all we've seen, brother, but try me," Drustan said dryly. He crossed to a handsome mahogany serving bar, artfully crafted into a section of bookshelves, and poured himself a tumbler of Macallan, fine, aged, single-malt scotch.

Dageus flipped through a few more pages of the scuffed leather tome he held, then placed it aside and stretched out his legs, folding his hands behind his head. Beyond tall velvet-draped windows, violet smudged a cobalt sky and he paused a moment, savoring the beauty of yet another Highland gloaming. Then, "You know how we've ever thought Cian

MacKeltar naught more than a myth?"

"Aye," Drustan replied, moving to join him near the fire. "The legendary and terrible Cian: the only Keltar ancestor to ever willingly cross over to the Dark Arts —"

"Not quite true, brother. So did I," Dageus corrected softly.

Drustan stiffened. "Nay, you acted out of love; 'twas a vastly different thing. This Cian — who, like as not, is pure fable crafted to reinforce our adherence to our oaths — did so out of unquenchable lust for power."

"Mayhap. Mayhap not." Cynicism shaped the edges of Dageus's smile. "I would place no wagers on what our progeny might say of *me* a thousand years hence." He gestured to the tome. " 'Tis one of Cian MacKeltar's journals."

Drustan stopped, halfway down into a chair, tumbler nearly to his lips. Silvery eyes, glittering with fascination, met his twin's golden gaze. He lowered his glass, sank slowly into the chair. "Indeed?"

"Aye, though a great many pages have been torn out, the notations were made by one Cian MacKeltar, who lived in the mid–ninth century."

"Is that the journal you said Da found in the hidden underground chamber library, last you went through the stones with Chloe to the sixteenth century?"

The hidden underground library was the long, narrow chamber hewn of stone that stretched deep beneath the castle, wherein the vast majority of Keltar lore and relics, including the gold Compact struck between Tuatha Dé Danaan and Man, were housed. It had been sealed up, the entrance concealed behind a hearth, more than a millennium ago.

Over time, the existence of the chamber had been completely forgotten. Vague tales that once the Keltar had possessed much more in the way of lore existed, but few believed and fewer still had searched for it, and those to no avail. It wasn't until the castle housekeeper, Nell — who'd later wed their da, Silvan, and become their next-mother — had inadvertently triggered the opening mechanism while dusting one day, that it had been found again. Still, she'd said naught about it, believing Silvan knew, and would be upset if she had knowledge of his clan's private doings. She would likely never have mentioned it to Silvan had Dageus not been in such desperate straits.

Their da had briefly opened that chamber in the sixteenth century, but had resealed it in hopes of not altering events that had already transpired between the sixteenth and twenty-first centuries. Drustan had recently agreed to make it again accessible for future generations. Since reopening it, Dageus had been translating the most ancient of the scrolls therein, recopying the fragile documents, and learning much more about their ancient benefactors in the process. And now, about one of their ancient ancestors.

"Nay. That journal was but a record of recent events: handfastings, births, deaths. This journal deals with his studies into the Druid arts, much of it in cipher. 'Twas hidden beneath a cracked flagstone o'er which Chloe tripped. She suspects there may be more concealed about the chamber."

Dageus's wife, Chloe, an avid historian, had set her heart on systematically cataloging the contents of the underground repository and, as Dageus couldn't bear to be parted from her for any length of time, he'd resigned himself to spending a great deal of time (meaning, probably until the very moment his lovely, pregnant wife was about to deliver) in the dusty, subterranean compartment, hence the scribing task he'd assigned himself.

He smiled. Better a dank chamber with his cherished Chloe than the sunniest Highland vista without her. *Och,* he amended fiercely, *better Hell with Chloe than Heaven without her.* Such was the depth of his love for the woman whom he'd taken captive in his darkest hour, who'd pledged her heart to him despite his actions, despite the evil within him.

"So what does it tell us of this ancestor of ours?" Drustan said curiously, jarring him from his thoughts.

Dageus snorted, disgruntled. He'd hoped for much more, and planned to dig deeper in the chamber to see what else he could uncover about their epic ancestor. He believed an understanding of the past was necessary to ensure a bright future, that those who forgot the past were condemned to repeat it. "From the parts I've managed to decipher, little more than that he was, in truth, a man, not a fable, and that the chamber was not forgotten but deliberately hidden from us. Da believed there'd been a battle or illness that had taken many lives abruptly, including all those who knew of the chamber. But 'twas not the case. The final entry in the journal is not his, but a warning about the use of magycks. Whoever made the entry also made the decision to seal the chamber, altering the rooms above to forever conceal it."

"Indeed?" Drustan's brows rose.

"Aye. So many pages have been torn out, I doona ken what Cian MacKeltar did that was so terrible, or what became his fate, but the last entry makes it plain that the chamber was secreted away because of him."

"Hmm," Drustan mused, sipping his scotch. "It makes one wonder what a man might have done to cause such drastic measures to be taken — the separating of all future generations of Keltar from the bulk of our knowledge and power. 'Twas no small thing to divide us from our heritage."

"Aye," Dageus said thoughtfully, "indeed, it does make one wonder."

"Can you frigging believe it, man? Somebody broke the guy's neck and left him there on the commons, dead as a doornail!"

"Great. That's just what we need. More crime. The university'll use it as another excuse to put the screws to us and raise tuition again."

Jessi shook her head, pushed her way

through the group of undergrads loitering at the coffee bar. As she placed her order, she wondered if she'd ever been so young, or so faux-jaded. She hoped not.

Campus was abuzz with gossip. The police had released few details, so everyone was pretending to know something. Funny thing was, she really *did* know something about the blond, well-dressed "John Doe" found dead on the campus commons yesterday, and she was the only one *not* talking.

And she wasn't about to.

When she'd flipped on the TV last night, only to discover the local news featuring a story on the murder of one of the two men she'd spent most of the day convincing herself weren't real, she'd sat, stunned, staring blankly at the screen long after the segment had ended.

The police were investigating the blond man's murder. He'd carried no identification and they'd issued a statement asking anyone who might know something about him to come forward.

All of which begged the questions: If the rest of the world could see the blond man, too, did that mean she wasn't crazy?

Or did it mean that the blond man was real, but she'd still hallucinated the man in the mirror and accompanying events?

Or did it mean she was so-far-gone crazy that now she was hallucinating news programs in a sick (though — if she had to say so herself — admirably determined and impressively cohesive) effort to lend credibility to her delusions?

Ugh. Tough questions.

She'd mulled over such convoluted thoughts for hours, until finally, in the wee hours of dawn, she'd achieved a measure of calm via a firm resolution: She would approach her current predicament the same way she would approach an archaeological inquiry, by applying the meticulous methods of a scientific analyst.

She would gather all the facts she could and, only when she had everything she could dig up, would she endeavor to piece the facts together into the most accurate representation of reality she could achieve with them. There would be no further talk of crazy, nor thoughts of it, until she'd completed her investigation.

Critical to her investigation: a talk with Professor Keene. She needed to ask him questions about the relic she'd come to wish she'd never laid eyes on — like where the heck it had come from?

Maybe it wasn't a relic at all, she

thought, briefly buoyed by the possibility, but a gag-relic of some kind, a special-effects prop from a *Stargate* episode or some other SciFi channel program. And maybe it had state-of-the-art, highly technical, cleverly hidden audio/visual feeds hooked into it somehow. And it all powered some really tiny, extraordinarily sophisticated projection screen system.

Which . . . er, didn't exactly explain the interaction between attacker and man in the mirror, but hey, she was just working up possibilities, devising and discarding.

Possibility: Maybe it was . . . uh, well, uh . . . cursed.

That thought made her feel inordinately foolish. Didn't sit well with her inner analyst.

Still, better foolish than mad-as-a-mirrormaker.

She'd phoned the professor last night, using the direct line to his room that he'd left her in one of his gazillion messages, but he'd not answered. She'd tried again first thing this morning, but no luck. Still sleeping, she supposed.

Bottom line, she was a pragmatist. She'd not gotten this far in her life by being illogical or prone to whimsy. She was a what-I've-got-in-my-hand kind of girl. And after intense reflection, she decided that she didn't feel crazy. She felt perfectly normal about everything except for this idiotic on-going mirror-incident.

Maybe she *should* smash it, she thought peevishly. End of problems. Right?

Except, not necessarily. If she *was* crazy, her illusory sex-god would probably just take up residence in some other inanimate object (that certainly brought to mind a few intriguing ideas, especially something in her bedside table drawer). If she *wasn't* crazy, she could conceivably be destroying one of the most pivotal, dogma-shattering relics in recent human history.

"Looks like I'm stuck fact-finding." She puffed out an irritated little sigh.

Rummaging in her pack for her cell phone, she withdrew it, flipped it open, and glanced down at the screen. No messages. She'd been hoping the professor would call her back before she got tied up in classes all day.

Too late now. She turned off the phone, tucked it back in her bag, grabbed her coffee from the counter, paid the cashier, and hurried off.

She had classes back-to-back until 4:45 p.m., but the second she was done she was heading straight to the hospital.

★ ★ ★

5:52 p.m.

The Dan Ryan Expressway at rush hour was a level in Dante's Hell.

Jessi was hopelessly gridlocked in stop-and-go traffic that was *way* more stop than go — so much stop, in fact, that she'd been working on homework for the past half hour — when her cell phone rang.

She tossed aside the notes she'd been taking, crept forward a celebration-worthy eighteen inches, whipped out her phone and answered, hoping it was the professor, but it was Mark Troudeau.

The statement was just forming on her tongue that there was no way she was taking on even *one more paper to grade* when he ripped all the words right out of her mouth by telling her he was calling to let her know the campus police had just informed him that Professor Keene was dead.

She started shaking, clenched the steering wheel, and exhaled a sob.

"And get this, Jess, he was *murdered,*" Mark relayed in an excited rush, clearly fascinated and clearly oblivious to the fact that she was crying, despite the wet snuffling sounds she was making. Men could be so dense sometimes.

Dimly, she realized traffic was creeping forward again. Eased her foot off the clutch. Dragged the sleeve of her jacket across her face.

"The cops are talking like he got mixed up in something bad, Jess. Said he recently pulled a lot of money out of his retirement and mortgaged his house big-time. I guess he owned some land somewhere in Georgia that he just sold too. Cops have no idea what he suddenly needed so much money for."

Belatedly realizing the car in front of her had stopped again, she hit the brakes and came to an abrupt halt a bare inch behind the rear bumper of the car in front of her. The guy behind her honked angrily. Not just once, but *laid* on it, complete with assorted hand gestures. "Right," she snapped through tears, making a gesture of her own in the rearview mirror, "like it's *my* fault traffic stopped moving again. Get over it."

Traffic was the least of her concerns. She closed her eyes.

The cops might not know why the professor had needed the money, but she did.

It would seem the mirror was a bona fide relic, after all, albeit one that had come — she was now willing to bet serious money — hot off the black market.

The professor had indeed gotten mixed up in something bad.

"Garroted," Mark was saying. "He was actually garroted. Nobody does that anymore, do they? Who does that kind of thing?"

She palmed the microphone on her cell, stared unseeingly out at the sea of stopped cars. "What on earth is going on?" she half-whispered.

Mark continued talking, a distant, chafing din.

The professor and I have already had our time together this evening, the blond man had said. And she'd pushed the comment brusquely aside, too wrapped up in her own petty concerns and interests.

And now the professor was dead.

Correction, she thought, a little chill seeping into her bones, according to what Mark had just told her — time of death 6:15 p.m. Monday — he'd been dead before she'd even gone to pick up his books that night.

The whole time she'd been standing in his office he'd been dead.

"And get this," said Mark, still blathering away, "Ellis, the department head, tells me I'm gonna have to take the professor's classes for the rest of the term. Can you

90

believe this shit? Like they can't afford to hire —"

"Oh, grow *up,* Mark," Jessi hissed, thumbing the OFF button.

When finally she managed to escape the tenth level of Hell, Jessi made a beeline for side streets and headed straight back to campus.

Thoughts tumbled in disjointed confusion through her mind. Amid them all was a single clear one, drawing her like a beacon.

She had to see the mirror again.

Why — she had no idea.

It was simply the only thing she could think of to do. She couldn't bring herself to go home. In her current state of mind she would climb the walls. She couldn't go to the hospital; there was no longer anyone to visit. She had a few close friends, but they tended to work as much as she, so dropping by unexpectedly wasn't the coolest thing to do, and besides, even if she did, what would she say — *Hi, Ginger, how have you been? By the way, either I've gone insane, or my life has taken on distinct shades of Indiana Jones, complete with mysterious relics, foreign villains, and spectacular audiovisual special effects.*

When she got back to the office there was police tape across the door.

That stopped her for a moment. Then she noticed it was campus police tape and tugged it aside. Violating university procedures didn't seem quite as felonious a felony as breaking a law in The Real World.

As she jiggled the key in the lock, making sure it really *was* locked this time, she asked herself just what she thought she was going to do once she was inside.

Strike up a conversation with a relic? Lay her hands on the glass? Try to summon a spirit? Make like it was a Ouija board or something?

As fate would have it, she didn't have to do a thing.

Because the moment she opened the door, a shaft of light splintered in from the hallway, straight onto the silvery glass.

Her feet froze. Her hands clenched on the door. Even her breath stopped midinhalation. She wasn't certain, but she fancied her heart paused a long, ponderous moment, as well.

The towering, half-naked, absolute sexgod of a man standing inside the mirror, glaring out at her, snarled, " 'Tis high damned time you came back, wench."

5

When Jessi was seventeen years old she'd almost died.

She'd gone to one of those indoor rock-climbing gyms (because her best friend had called to tell her that the football player she had a crush on was home from college that weekend and he and his friends were supposed to be there) and taken a horrible fall, breaking multiple bones and splitting her skull.

She'd missed the best parts of her senior year in high school, recuperating at home with her head shaved from where they'd inserted a metal plate to piece her skull back together, listening to other people's stories of proms and parties and graduations.

And the guy she'd been so crazy about hadn't even been at the climbing gym that day.

She'd learned a few things from the experience. One: the whole "best laid plans of mice and men" adage was absolutely true — she'd not gotten to rally her football team to the State finals the *only* year they'd made it in the past seven; she'd not gotten to wear the scrumptious pink prom dress that still hung in her closet; she'd not tossed her cap; she'd not attended a single senior party. And two: Sometimes when things got bad, a sense of humor was a person's only saving grace. You could either laugh or you could cry, and crying not only made you feel worse, it made you look worse too.

It occurred to her as she stood there, staring at the thing in the mirror that couldn't possibly be in the mirror, in a room where a recent attempt on her life had been made — said room's previous occupant having been murdered recently himself — that events of the past few days certainly qualified as bad, even by conservative standards.

She started to giggle.

She couldn't help it.

The sex-god's dark eyes narrowed and he scowled. " 'Tis no laughing matter. Get in here and close that door. *Now.* There is much of which we must speak and time is of the veriest essence."

She giggled harder, one hand to her mouth, the other clutching the doorjamb.

Time is of the veriest essence. Who talked like that?

"For the love of Christ, wench, summon me out," he said, sounding exasperated. "Someone needs to shake you."

"Oh, I don't think so," she managed between giggles. Giggles that were starting to sound just a tiny bit hysterical. "And I am not a wench," she informed him loftily. And giggled.

He growled softly. "Woman, you summoned me out the other eve and I did you no harm. Will you not trust me again?"

She snickered. "I thought I was sound asleep and dreaming the other night. It had nothing to do with trust."

"I killed the man who was trying to kill you. Is that not reason enough to trust me?"

She stopped laughing. There it was. He was the one who'd snapped the blond man's neck and left him lying dead on the commons. Though a part of her brain knew it had to have been him — whether such events had transpired in a delusional world or The Real One — his remark drew her gaze to his hands. Big hands. Neck-snapping hands.

After a moment's hesitation, she stepped warily into the office. Another pause, then she slowly closed the door behind her.

The giggles were gone. A thousand questions were not.

Jamming her hands into the front pockets of her jeans, she starcd at the mirror.

She closed her eyes. Squeezed them shut hard. Opened them. Tried it twice more for good measure.

He was still there. *Oh, shit.*

"I could have told you that wouldn't work," he said dryly.

"Am I crazy?" she whispered.

"Nay, you're not daft. I am here. This is indeed happening. And if you wish to survive, you must credit what I tell you."

"People can't be inside mirrors. It's not possible."

"Tell that to the mirror." He thumped his fists against the inside of the glass for emphasis.

"Funny. But not convincing." Oh, that was weird, seeing him pound on the mirror from the inside!

"You must resolve your own mind on the matter. Best do so before another comes to kill you."

His blasé response argued his case to her. Said he knew he was real, and if she was too dense to figure it out, it wasn't his problem. Surely a delusion would endeavor to self-persist, wouldn't it?

But *how* could he be real?

She had no precedent for dealing with the inexplicable. *Fact-finding. All I can do is explore what's happening, and reserve judgment until I know more.*

Toward that end, shedding light on things, she reached for the wall switch and flipped on the overhead.

And got her first truly good look at him.

Crimeny, she thought, eyes widening as if to drink in even more of him. The two prior times she'd caught glimpses of him, they'd been briefly snatched and the room had been heavily shadowed. She'd absorbed only a general impression of him: a big, dark, intensely sexual man.

She'd not seen the details.

And what details they were!

Stunned, she looked down. Up. Down. Up again. Slowly.

"Take your time, lass," he murmured, so softly she scarcely heard him. His next comment was deliberately beyond her audible range, a silky "I plan to with you."

He was tall, stuffing the mirror from top to bottom of frame. Powerfully built, with wide shoulders and rippling muscles, he wore a fabric of crimson and black around his waist — an honest-to-God kilt, if she wasn't mistaken — glittering metallic wrist cuffs, and black leather boots.

No shirt. Wicked-looking black-and-crimson tattooed runes covered the left side of his sculpted chest, from the bottom of his rib cage, up over a nipple, across his shoulder, and to the edge of his jaw. Each powerful biceps was also encircled by a band of tattooed crimson-and-black runes. A thick, silky trail of dark hair began just above the navel on his ripped abs, slid down into the plaid.

Oh, God, was it tenting? Was that a bulge lifting the tartan?

Her gaze got stuck there for an awkward moment. Her eyes widened even further. Sucking in a shallow breath, she jerked her gaze away. A flush heated her cheeks.

She'd just ogled his penis.

Stood there, blatantly eyeing it. Long enough that he *had* to have noticed. Something was just not right with her. Her hormones had somehow gotten seriously out of whack. She was an artifact-ogler, not a penis-ogler.

She forced her gaze up to his face. It was as sinfully gorgeous as the rest of him. He had the chiseled, proud features of an ancient Celt warrior: strong jaw and cheek-bones, a straight, aristocratic nose, flaring arrogantly at the nostrils, and a mouth so sexy and kissable that her own lips instinctively puckered, then parted, just looking at it, as if sampling a kiss. She wet them, feeling strangely breathless. Dark shadow stubbled his sculpted jaw, making his firm pink lips seem even more sexual against all that rough masculinity.

His hair wasn't black as she'd thought in the dark, but a rich gleaming mahogany shot with shimmering strands of gold and copper. Half of it was caught in dozens of narrow braids, banded at the ends with glittering metallic beadwork. His eyes were burnt-whisky, his skin tawny-velvet.

He dripped primeval, elemental power, looked as much a relic as the mirror itself, a throwback to a time when men had been men and women had Done As They Were Told.

Her eyes narrowed. She couldn't stand men like that. Chauvinistic, domineering men who thought they could order women around.

Too bad her body didn't seem to be of the same mind. Too bad her body seemed downright intrigued by the various orders possible, like: *Take off your clothes, woman; let me get the taste of you on the back of my tongue . . .*

It didn't help that he looked like the kind of man who wouldn't take "no" for an answer, who would tolerate zero inhibitions on a woman's part; the kind of man that, once he got a woman in bed, didn't let her out again until he'd done everything there was to do to her, had fucked her so thoroughly that she could barely walk.

"Summon me out, woman," came the tight, low command laced by that sexy Scots burr. His voice was as incredible as his appearance. Deep and rich as hot, dark buttered rum, it slid down into her belly, pooling there in a slow burn.

"No," she said faintly. No way she was letting all that . . . whatever it was, too much testosterone by far . . . out again.

"Then I bid you, woman, cease looking at me like that."

"Like what?" she bristled.

"Like you wish to be using your tongue on me again. And on more than my back." He caught his lower lip between his teeth and flashed her a devilish smile.

"I didn't *mean* to lick you," she snapped defensively. "I told you, I thought you were a dream."

"Any dream you wish, woman. You need

but summon me out." His gaze raked over her, burning hot, lingering at her breasts and thighs.

Heat suffused her skin where his gaze skimmed. "Not. Going. To. Happen."

He shrugged, powerful shoulders bunching and rippling. "Have it your way, wench. Die needlessly. Doona say I didn't offer my aid."

He turned in the mirror then. The silver encasing him seemed to ripple, the black stain around the edges flowed and ebbed as if the surface were suddenly liquid, then she was beholding a mere looking glass.

"Hey, wait!" she cried, panicking. "Get back here!" She needed answers. She needed to know what was going on. What the mirror was; how any of this was even happening; who was trying to kill her; would there really be more assassins sent after her?

"Why?" His deep butter-rum voice resonated from somewhere within the glass.

"Because I need to know what's going on!"

"Naught in this world is free, woman."

"What are you saying?" she asked the smooth silver surface. She was conversing with a mirror. Alice in Wonderland had nothing on her.

" 'Tis plain enough, isn't it? I have something you need. You have something I want."

She went absolutely still. Her breath caught in the back of her throat and her heart began to hammer. She moistened suddenly parched lips. "Wh-what?"

"You need my protection. You need me to keep you alive. I ken what's going on, who's coming after you, and how to stop them."

"And what do you want in return?" she asked warily.

"Och, myriad things, lass. But we'll keep it simple and start with freedom."

She shook her head. "Uh-uh. No way. I don't know the first —"

"You know all you need to know," he cut her off flatly. "You know you'll die without me. Think not to constrain me. I've been stuck in this bloody frigging mirror far too long for civility. This glass is the only prison I'll suffer. I'll no' be allowin' ye to be buildin' another for me, woman."

His brogue thickening, he spat the final words. She swallowed. Audibly. Her mouth had gone so dry that she heard tiny things crunch as her Adam's apple rose and fell. She cleared her throat.

Suddenly there he was in the mirror

again, looking at her, silver rippling like diamond-spiked water around him.

That sexy, arrogant mouth curved in a smile. If he'd meant it to be reassuring, she thought, shivering, he'd missed the mark by a mile. It was a smile full of leashed power and chained heat. Barely leashed. Barely chained.

It occurred to her then that, had she gotten a good look at him the other night, she would probably never have released him, whether she'd believed herself to be dreaming or not. The killer she'd thought so terrifying was no match for this man. They weren't even remotely in the same league. Breaking the blond man's neck had probably been as easy for him as absently swatting a fly. Whatever he was, he had something *more*. Something normal people just didn't have.

She fumbled behind her for the doorknob.

"Let me out," he said, low and intense. "Say the words. I will be your shield. I will stand between you and all others. 'Tis what you need and you ken it. Doona be a fool, woman."

Shaking her head, she turned the knob.

"Will it be nay, then? Prefer you to die? Over me? Just what is it you fear I might do to you that would be so terrible?"

The way his heated gaze was lingering on certain parts of her made quite clear *some* of the things he was thinking about doing to her.

Which of course made her think about them, too, in great detail. And there she was, wet-pantied again. What on earth was wrong with her? Had her ovaries somehow gotten stuck in a permanent ovulation cycle? Were her eggs firing indiscriminately and constantly — and in some perverse, inversely proportionate fashion — with greater enthusiasm the *worse* the man seemed for her?

Yanking open the door, she backed out into the hall. "I need to think," she muttered.

"Think fast, Jessica. You've not much time."

"Great, just great. Every-freaking-body knows my name." With a fierce little scowl, she slammed the door so hard the frame shuddered.

"The next one he sends after you may arrive any moment," came his deep burr through the door, "and will be more sophisticated than the last. Mayhap it will be a woman. Tell me, lass, will you even see death coming?"

Jessi gave the door an angry little kick.

"Doona venture far. You're going to need me."

She gritted something rude at the door that he shouldn't have been able to hear, but he did. It made him laugh out loud and say, "A physical impossibility, woman, or, believe me, most of us 'asshole men' would."

She rolled her eyes and didn't bother locking it this time.

As an afterthought, she plucked off the rest of the police tape, balled it up, and stuffed it in her pocket.

Maybe she'd get lucky and somebody'd steal the damned thing and get it out of *her* hair.

OPTIONS

1. Go to police. Tell all and request protection.
2. Get in touch with original delivery company, ship mirror back, hope that fixes everything.
3. Flee country.
4. Check self into mental hospital and trust, with lockups and padded walls, they're safer than regular hospitals.

105

Jessi finished the last of her coffee, pushed aside the mug, stared down at her pathetic little list, and sighed.

She was still feeling shaky in the pit of her stomach, but compiling her list of options had calmed her a bit and forced her to take a realistic look at a completely surreal situation.

Number four was out: it reeked of casting one's fate to the wind and, when all was said and done, if she had to be in a car wreck, she'd prefer to be the one driving when it happened — control of one's own destiny and all that.

Number one was out. The police would laugh her right out of the station if she tried telling them she knew who'd murdered their John Doe: a tall, dark, and broody sexgod who was after his freedom, who just happened to be inside a ten-thousand-year-old-plus mirror, who might also be a ruthless criminal that had been . . . er, paranormally interred inside said mirror for the . . . er, safety of the world.

Uh-huh. Wow. Even *she* thought she was nuts with that one.

That left numbers two and three as potential solutions. The way she figured it, fleeing the country and staying out of it forever — or at least until she was reasonably certain she'd been forgotten about — would cost a whole lot more than trying to ship the thing back, even with the exorbitant price of insurance figured in, and Jessi had to believe that if she just returned the relic, whoever was after it would leave her alone.

After all, what was she going to do? *Talk* about it, for heaven's sake? *Tell* people about the impossible artifact once it was gone? Totally discredit herself and ruin any chance she might one day have of a promising future in the field of archaeology?

As *if*.

Surely she could persuade them of that, whoever they were. Anyone with half a brain would be able to see that she'd never, in an Ice Age, talk.

She glanced around the university café; the cushioned wood booths were sparsely populated at this time of night, and no one was sitting near enough to eavesdrop. Pulling out her cell phone, she flipped it open, dialed Info, and got the number for Allied Certified Deliveries, the name she'd seen emblazoned on the side of the delivery truck.

At 8:55 p.m., she didn't expect an answer, so when she got one, she sputtered for a moment before managing to convey

107

the purpose of her call: that she'd gotten a package she wanted to return, but she'd not been given a copy of the bill of lading, so she didn't know where to ship it back to.

Making no effort to mask her irritation, the woman on the other end informed her that the office was closed for the day, and she'd only answered because she'd been talking to her husband when their call had been dropped, and she thought it was him calling her back. "Try again tomorrow," she said impatiently.

"Wait! Please don't hang up," Jessi exclaimed, panicking. "Tomorrow might be too late. I need it picked up first thing in the morning. I've got to return this thing *fast*."

Silence.

"It was really expensive to ship," Jessi shot into the silence, hoping money would keep the woman on the line and motivate her to be helpful. "Probably one of the more expensive deliveries you guys have done. It came from overseas and required special handling."

"You going to pay to reship, or you trying to stick it to the shipper?" the woman asked suspiciously.

"I'll pay," Jessi said without hesitation.

Though she loathed the thought of spending money on something she would end up with nothing to show for, at least she'd be alive to pay it off. She had a downright scary amount of credit on her Visa; it never ceased to amaze her how much rope banks were willing to give college students to hang themselves with.

"Got an invoice number?"

"Of course not. I just told you, I don't have the bill of lading. Your guys forgot to give me a copy."

"We never forget to give copies of the BOL," the woman bristled. "You must have misplaced it."

Jessi sighed. "Okay, fine, I misplaced it. Regardless, I don't have it."

"Ma'am, we do hundreds of deliveries a week. Without an invoice number, I have no way of knowing what delivery you're talking about."

"Well, you can look it up by last name, can't you?"

"The computers are down for the night. They go off-line at eight. You'll have to call back tomorrow."

"It was an unusual delivery," Jessi pushed. "You might remember it. It was a late-night drop. A recent one. I can de-

109

scribe the guys who brought it." Swiftly, she detailed the pair.

There was another long silence.

Then, "Ma'am, those men were murdered over the weekend. Garroted, just like that professor man that's been all over the news. Police won't leave us alone." A bitter note entered her voice. "They been acting like my husband's company had something to do with it, like we got shady dealings going on or something." A pause, then, "What did you say your name was again?"

Feeling like she'd just been kicked in the stomach, Jessi hung up.

She didn't go straight to him.

She refused to do that.

The thought of such a swift show of defeat was too chafing.

The past few days had been a study in humility for her. Not a single thing had gone according to anything remotely resembling The Jessi St. James Plan For A Good Life, and she had the bad feeling nothing was going to for quite a while.

So she stubbornly toughed it out in the university café until half past midnight, sipping still more coffee that her frazzled nerves didn't need, savoring what she suspected might be her last moments of near-normalcy for a long time, before caving in to the inevitable.

She had no desire to die. Crimeny, she'd hardly even gotten to live yet.

Life is what happens to you while you're busy making other plans. Her friend Ginger had given her a coffee mug with that quote on it a few months ago. If you spun it around, the other side said: *When did having a life become an event you had to schedule?* She'd stuffed it way in the back of her cupboard and not looked at it again, the sad truth of it shaving too close to the bone.

No, she certainly wasn't ready to die. She wanted at least another sixty or seventy years. She hadn't even gotten to the good parts of her life yet. Problem was, she didn't suffer any illusions about her ability to, as he'd so succinctly put it, "see death coming." She was a college student, an archaeology major, at that. People were not her forte. Not living ones, anyway. She was no slouch with the dead ones, like the Iceman or the Bog People, but that wouldn't get her very far with an assassin. Sad fact was, Death could probably stalk up to her wearing a hooded black robe and toting a scythe, and she'd get all distracted wondering about the age, origin, and composition of the scythe.

Ergo, like it or not — and dear God, she didn't — she needed him. Whatever he was. The professor was dead. The deliverymen were dead. She'd been next. Three out of four down. She felt like one of those ditzy heroines in a murder mystery, or one of those fluffy romance novels, the loose end that needed tidying up, the one the psychopath kept coming after. The helpless, girly girl. And she'd never considered herself helpless in her entire life. Girly, maybe, but not helpless.

Now, standing outside the door to Professor Keene's office yet again, she stiffened her spine, mentally preparing to fling herself upon an impossible being's mercy.

Either he would protect her as he claimed, or he really was some cosmically evil villain, justly imprisoned and lying through his teeth, who planned to kill her — the way things had been going for her lately — gruesomely and with much blood, right there on the spot.

If that was the case, she was damned if she did and damned if she didn't, her demise a mere bit of squabbling over place and time, so she should probably just buck up and get it over with.

She glanced at her watch — 12:42 a.m.

Good-bye life as she knew it, hello

chaos. Hopefully not just good-bye life.

She pushed open the door and stepped into the office. "Okay," she told the silvery surface with a sigh, "I think we can make a deal."

He was there before she'd even fully formed the word "think." She finished the rest of the sentence a bit breathlessly.

A slow, exultant smile curved his lips.

"Deal, my ballocks. Get me the bloody hell out of here, woman."

6

"Don't give me excuses," Lucan snarled into the phone. "Roman is dead. I need Eve in Chicago *now*."

He rose and stood before the tall windows of his study, staring out at the London dawn as the first faint streaks of sun burned off the fog. The sky beyond was still dim enough that he could also see his own reflection superimposed on the tinted glass. Alone, he did not bother with a spell to conceal his appearance.

His entire skull was a miasma of crimson-and-black runes, his tongue flickered black inside his tattooed mouth when he spoke, and his eyes were feral crimson.

It was Thursday morning. He had twenty days.

He turned his gaze to the darker spot on the silk wallpaper where the Dark Glass had hung for so long. Cian's captivity had been a constant source of amusement to him — the legendary Keltar, the most powerful of all Druids ever known, ensorcelled by one Lucan Myrrdin Trevayne.

His hands fisted, his jaw clenched. That empty spot *would* be filled again, and soon. Returning his attention to the conversation, he snapped, "The St. James woman knows she's in danger now. There's no telling what she'll do. I need her taken care of immediately. But first, I need that damned mirror back. Roman said it was in the professor's office. Have her ship it to my private residence the moment she arrives. Then get rid of the girl and anyone else who's seen it."

Damn Roman. The police were asking too many questions, and he suspected at least one or two officers had seen the Dark Glass, which meant retiring a few members of law enforcement, and *those* cases never closed. In the past he'd not denied Roman his preference for strangulation, so long as he went in, disposed of all problems before the police found any bodies, and got out fast, before an investigation was even opened.

But he hadn't. He'd failed with the woman and ended up dead himself.

Which gave Lucan no small amount of pause.

How had Roman ended up on the commons with his neck broken? He could think of one man that possessed the deadly strength and skill to snap the Russian's neck as if popping chicken bones: Cian MacKeltar.

And if that were the case, someone had let him out of the mirror. Not good, not good at all.

The only person he could fathom might have done so was the St. James woman. According to Roman, when he'd last checked in, there were four people in Chicago who'd seen the Dark Glass or, like Dr. Liam Keene, had possessed critical knowledge of it, and Jessica St. James was the final one to be dispatched. Lucan knew well the Keltar had a way with women.

His upper lip curled. So much wasted on a primitive mountain-man, a Highlander, no less. Not just looks, strength, and charisma, but wild, pure magic. The kind of power Lucan had worked dozens of lifetimes to achieve a mere fraction of, the Keltar had been born with a hundredfold.

If the St. James woman had indeed been seduced to the Keltar's bidding, then Lucan was sending Eve to her death. He'd have his answer soon enough. If Eve went missing, he'd know he had a far more serious problem on his hands than he'd thought.

"Tell her to put her other contract on hold. I need her now." A pause. A growl. "I don't believe you have no way of reaching her. Find one. Get her in Chicago today or else."

He listened a moment, holding the phone away from his ear. After a long pause he said tightly, "I don't think you understand. I want her there now. I'd advise you to pass on my orders to her and let *her* decide." He punched off the phone, terminating the call. He knew what she would do. She trafficked in death for a living, and feared little, but she feared Lucan. They'd had a liaison a few years past. She knew his true nature. She would obey.

He rubbed his jaw, eyes narrowed. Samhain was too swift approaching. For the first time in centuries, he felt a whisper of unease. He'd been untouchable, virtually invincible for so long that, he didn't quite recognize the feeling.

At least he knew exactly where the mirror was. That alleviated much of his unease. Still, if it weren't in his possession within a very short time, he would have no choice but to go after it himself.

He greatly preferred not to.

On those rare occasions he'd freed the

Keltar from the Dark Glass, he'd stayed on heavily warded ground that had neutralized the Highlander's immense power until the mirror had safely reclaimed its captive. The complex, intense warding necessary to keep Cian MacKeltar's power suppressed required painstaking ritual and time.

Could he and his men manage to ward the university's grounds around the mirror?

Possibly. It would be risky. Many things could go wrong. They could be seen. There could be other magic, both old and new, on the grounds that might create conflicts. People didn't know it, but magic was all around them. Always had been, always would be. It merely concealed itself with greater sophistication now than it had in days of yore.

Dare he confront the Highlander with his full powers intact on unwarded ground?

Surely, after a thousand years, he'd surpassed Cian MacKeltar and was the greater sorcerer at last!

He turned away from the windows, wishing he felt certain of that. It had not been his superior sorcery that had put the Keltar where he was. It had been wellplayed deceit and treachery.

Perhaps the Keltar hadn't been freed.

Perhaps Roman had fallen prey to another assassin. They did that sometimes, went after each other for money or glory or the challenge of it.

He'd know for certain in a day or two. Then he'd decide upon his next move.

Cian stood, hands fisted at his sides, waiting. He'd known she would return. She was no fool. She'd been wise enough to identify the mirror as her most effective weapon when Roman had threatened her; he'd not doubted she'd see the wisdom of his offer. He'd just not been certain how long it might take her, and time was everything to him now.

Twenty days.

'Twas all he needed from her.

'Twas not, by far, all he *wanted* from her. All he wanted from her would bring a blush to the cheeks of even the most practiced whore.

Standing a few feet beyond his prison, staring at him, her dark green eyes were huge, her lips softly parted, and those dream-come-true breasts were rising and falling with each anxious breath she drew.

He couldn't wait to taste them. Rub back and forth, teasing her nipples with heated swirls and flicks of his tongue. Suckle her, firm and deep. Breasts like that made a man want babes at them. *His* babes. But not too often, or there'd not be time enough for him.

He tossed his head, beaded braids clattering metallically, drawing tight rein on his lustful thoughts.

The moment she summoned him forth, he would use Voice on her.

His skin was crawling with the need to escape the place Lucan surely knew he was by now. He'd killed the assassin in the wee hours of Tuesday morn. A full twenty-four hours had passed since then. Though he'd not walked free in the world for longer than he cared to recall, from his purloined books and papers and view in Lucan's study, he had a fair notion of the weft and weck of the modern world. It was both horrifyingly larger and shockingly smaller than ever it had been, with billions of people (even a Keltar Druid felt a measure of awe at those kinds of numbers), yet telephones that could span continents in mere moments, computers that could instantly retrieve all manner of information and connect people on opposite poles, and airplanes that could bridge continents in under a day. It was confounding. It was fascinating.

It meant they had to move. *Now.*

Voice, the Druid art of compulsion, was one of his greatest talents. As a stripling lad on the verge of manhood — the time of life when a Keltar's powers became apparent and often fluctuated wildly while developing — for nigh a week he'd strolled about the castle using Voice on all and sundry without realizing it. He'd caught on only because he'd grown suspicious as to why everyone kept scrambling to please him. He'd learned to be careful, to listen to his own tones for that unique layering of voices. Only a bumbling fool, or a novice with a death wish, wielded magyck inadvertently.

When free of the mirror, on unwarded ground, there was none alive but Lucan himself who could withstand his command of Voice — and only because 'twas Cian who'd taught the bastard the art. In the practice of Druidry, mentor and pupil developed resistance to each other during the process of training.

She would heel nicely. Women did. It wasn't their fault nature had designed them to be so malleable. They were softer all around. He would command her to lead him to a safe place where they could go to ground. And once there — och, once there, he had centuries of unsated lust for things other than vengeance, and this

121

woman with her ripe curves and creamy skin and tangle of short glossy hair was the answer to all of them!

What better way to spend the final twenty days of his indenture than feeding his every sexual hunger, indulging his deepest desires and most carnal fantasies with this sensual delicacy of a woman?

At that moment, the sensual delicacy of a woman notched her chin up.

Stubbornly.

There might even have been a glint of fire in her eyes.

"I'm not letting you out until you answer a few questions," she informed him coolly.

He snorted with impatience. Of all the moments for her to get contrary! Women certainly knew how to pick them. "Wench, we have no time for this. Lucan has no doubt already dispatched another assassin who is drawing ever nearer as we speak."

" 'Lucan'?" she pounced. "Is that who wants the mirror back?"

"Aye."

" 'Lucan' who?"

He shifted his weight from foot to foot. Crossed his arms. "Why? You think you might know him?" he snapped sardonically, one dark brow arching. When her nostrils flared and her chin tipped higher, he sighed and said, "Trevayne. His name is Lucan Trevayne."

"Who and what are you?"

"You called my name when you released me the first time," he said impatiently. " 'Tis Cian MacKeltar. As for the what of me, I'm but a man."

"The blond man said you were a murderer." Her voice was poison-apple sweet. "Remember him? The one you murdered."

"Och," he said indignantly, "and there's the pot calling the kettle black."

"He said you were locked away for the safety of the world."

"Hardly. Your world, Jessica, would be far safer with me in it."

"So why are you in a mirror?" She brightened, as if at a sudden cheerful thought. "Are you, like, a genie? Can you grant wishes?"

"If you mean a *djinn,* even the feeblest of bampots know they doona exist. Nay, I doona grant wishes."

"Yeah, well, everyone also knows men in mirrors don't exist. So how did you come to be in one?"

"I was tricked. How else would a man end up in a mirror?"

"How were you tricked?"

" 'Tis a long story." When she opened

123

her mouth to press, he said flatly, "And not one of which I care to speak. Leave be."

Her eyes narrowed like a cat's. "That blond man also said the mirror was an Unseelie piece. I looked up 'Unseelie' on the 'Net. It's not a classification of artifact. It's a classification of *fairy*" — she sneered the word. "What, I ask you, am I supposed to make of that?"

"That 'tis an exceedingly rare artifact?" he suggested lightly. "Woman, we've no time to discuss such matters now. I'll answer all your questions once you've freed me and we're on the move."

The lie spilled easily from his tongue. He would silence her concerns with a simple command laced with Voice the moment she let him out. He planned to immediately toss a few other commands her way, as well. He was a man who'd been without a woman far too long, and his hunger was immense. Contemplating the erotic orders he would give her stiffened his cock and drew his testicles tight. *Bring that sweet ass over here, Jessica. Open that lovely mouth of yours and lick* this. *Turn around, woman, and let me fill my hands with those splendid breasts while I bend you over the* —

"Why would someone want to trick you into a mirror?"

Jarred from the lustful stupor of his thoughts, he stepped back, drawing silver around his lower body to conceal the rising of his kilt. He doubted such blatant proof of his intentions would serve as persuasion to free him. Bloody hell, he should have used Voice to get himself some modern clothing when he'd dispatched Roman the other eve! Those tight blue jeans both men and women favored would likely hold down a shaft of even his size. "Because by binding me to it, the one who tricked me gained immortality. Each Unseelie relic offers a Dark Power of some sort. Living forever, never aging, never changing, is the Dark Glass's gift," he growled. By Danu, what was it going to take to get her to let him out of the blethering glass?

"Oh." She stared at him blankly for a moment. "So let me get this straight: You're telling me that not only are there people inside mirrors, and fairies somewhere busily crafting artifacts endowed with paranormal attributes, but there are also immortals skulking around my world?"

He nearly snarled aloud with frustration. "I very much doubt they 'skulk,' woman. And, to the best of my knowledge, the Fae haven't crafted aught in millennia, not since they withdrew to their hidden realms. And doona be facetious. I'm merely answering your questions."

"Impossible answers."

"Docs not the maxim still hold that once a thing occurs, 'tis impossible, 'tis impossible, ergo, 'tis possible?"

"I've never seen an immortal, and I've certainly never seen a fairy."

"You split hairs. You've seen me. And best hope you never do see either of *them*."

"Why — ?"

"Jessica," he said softly, menacingly, infusing her name with the promise of infinite dangers, "I am going to count to three. If you permit me to reach that number without having begun the chant to release me, I will rescind my offer. I will not so much as lift a finger when the next killer comes for you. I will sit back and watch you die a slow and heinous death. I'm beginning now. One. Two —"

"There's no need to get pissy," she said pissily. "I planned to say it; I just wanted to clear a few things up first —"

"Thr—"

"All right, I'm saying it! I'm saying it! *Lialth bree che bree* —"

"Bloody hell, wench, *finally!*"

126

7

"— Cian MacKeltar, drachme se-sidh!" Jessi
finished breathlessly.

Heart hammering inside her chest, she
eased back nervously, her gaze riveted to
the mirror.

The silver went smoky and dark, boiling
with shadows, like a doorway opening onto
a storm. Then the black stain around the
edges expanded, swallowing up the entire
surface. Simultaneously, golden light
blazed from within the engravings on the
frame, painting fiery runes across her
clothing, the furniture, the walls of the
office. The disconcerting sensation of spatial distortion in the room increased to a
nails-on-a-chalkboard degree, rasping over
her nerve endings.

Then, as abruptly as it had begun, the
light dimmed and the black cleared, revealing a watery silver that rippled and
danced like the surface of Lake Michigan
on a windy day.

One booted foot pushed through, then a powerful thigh, as the one-dimensional image crossed some kind of fairy-tale threshold and transformed from a mere reflection into a three-dimensional man, bit by bit.

It was impossible. It was terrifying. It was the most thrilling thing she'd ever seen.

Out came those kilt-clad hips, that six-pack abdomen, followed by his sculpted upper body rippling with those wicked-looking crimson-and-black tattoos.

Last came that sinfully gorgeous dark face, his white teeth flashing in an exultant smile, his whisky eyes glittering with triumph.

He gave a regal, full-of-himself toss of his head, beaded braids tinkling, as he fully exited the mirror.

The sensation of spatial distortion eased and the glass went flat silver again, reflecting his tight ass and beautifully muscled back.

Jessi braced herself, trying to console herself with the thought that if she was going to die now, at least she'd gotten one final heaping helping of eye-candy. This man belonged in the RBL Romantica Braw and Bonny Beefcake Farm. Crimeny, this man probably *owned* the farm or, if not, had stood stud to the mothers of half the other members.

Though he'd looked massive enough inside the glass, outside it, he seemed even larger. The man had presence, that elusive quality that made some people lodestones, drawing others, even against their will. And he knew it.

From the looks of him, he'd always known it.

Arrogant, cocky prick.

But was he a murderous one? *That* was the important question.

"If you're going to kill me, I'd appre—"

"Cease speaking, wench. You will bring that sweet ass over here and kiss me now."

Jessi gaped, mouth open, midword. Snapped her mouth closed. Opened it again. Her head suddenly itched just beneath the skin, above her metal plate. She rubbed at her scalp. "As *if*." She meant to hiss it indignantly, but it came out more of a squeak. Sweet ass? He thought she had a sweet ass? They could form a mutual admiration society of two.

"Remove that woolen, woman, and show me your breasts."

Choking on an inhalation, she sputtered

for several seconds. Numerous were the men who'd tried to go there — even she knew she had exceptional breasts — but none quite so obviously and without exerting even an ounce of seductive effort. She clamped her hands over them defensively. "Oh, I so don't think that's going to ha—"

"Cease speaking," he roared. *"You will not speak again unless I tell you to."*

Jessi drew back like a cobra, scratching her scalp again. He couldn't be serious!

He certainly looked like he was.

After a moment's stunned silence, in a voice sweet enough to cause cavities in porcelain caps, she said, "You can go fuck yourself, you great big domineering Neanderthal. Wake-up call: Guess what? We're not in the Stone Age anymore."

"As I pointed out earlier, a physical impossibility. And I ken full well what epoch it is. *Come here, Jessica St. James. Now.*"

Jessi blinked at him. A sudden thought occurred to her; one that would explain much about this man. "How long have you been inside that mirror?" she demanded.

A muscle worked in his jaw. "I told you to *cease speaking.*"

Despite his persistent asininity, her

temper was decreasing as her suspicion that she was correct was increasing. "Well, duh, clearly I'm not going to, so you may as well answer my question."

His eyes narrowed, that whisky gaze swept her from head to toe intently. "Eleven hundred and thirty-three years."

Whuh. She sucked in an astounded breath. That would place him in — no! The ninth century? No way. A living, breathing, ninth-century man, right here in front of her, somehow trapped in an ancient relic and cast forward eleven centuries?

Chills rippled across every square inch of her skin. Even the hair on her head felt as if it werc trying to rise. *"Really?"* She nearly squealed the word, she was so delighted. The remnants of her hot temper collapsed into a pile of ash.

Oh, the things he might be able to tell her! Had the legendary King Cináed mac Ailpin been his contemporary? Had he lived through those mighty battles? Had he seen the unification of the Scots and Picts? Were those incredible wrist cuffs genuine ninth-century work? What were those tattoos, anyway? And those runes on the mirror — was it possible they comprised a previously undiscovered language? Holy *shit!* For that matter, was it really from the Stone Age? How could that be? Where had it come from? Who'd made it? What was it made of? Now that she'd conceded the reality of his existence, she had a gazillion questions about it. They all collided in her mind, getting tangled up in one another, and she ended up gaping at him in stunned silence.

It took her several moments to realize that he was regarding her with exactly the same expression.

As if he couldn't quite believe *she* existed.

There they stood, in Professor Keene's office, ten feet separating them, each eyeing the other with blatant incredulity and suspicion. Now, that was just silly. What could he possibly find hard to believe about *her?*

"Say my name, wench," he thundered.

She shook her head, stupefied by all her questions, befuddled by his request. "Cian MacKeltar. Why?"

He looked mildly appeased. Then suspicious again. *"Scratch your nose, woman."*

"It doesn't itch."

"Stand on one foot."

She wrinkled her nose at him. *"You* stand on one foot."

"Bloody hell," he breathed, as if to himself, "it can't be." He gave her that intent scan from head to toe again, seemed to hold a brief but heated inner discourse with himself, then nodded toward the desk. *"Go sit in that chair."*

"I don't feel like it. I'm perfectly happy standing right where I am, thank you."

"Moisten your lips?" His gaze fixed on her mouth.

It took considerable effort not to moisten them while he was looking at them like that. It made her fixate on his own incredibly kissable mouth, made her want to not only wet her lips but pucker up and hike her "sweet ass" right over there. Maybe even show him her breasts, after all. She was appalled at the indiscriminatory nature of hormones — how awful that it was possible to actively dislike a man, have nothing in common with him, including not even existing in the same world — and still want to tear his clothes off and have hot animal sex with him.

Stoically, she resisted. "What's your deal?"

"Christ," he whispered slowly, "I've been in there for so long, I've lost it."

" 'Lost' what? Oh, you mean your mind. Yeah, well, not going to argue with you there."

He stared at her a long moment in silence, frowning. Then his brow eased and his eyes cleared. "Nay, my mind is still as extraordinarily superior as it has always been. No matter. There's more than one way to skin a cat."

God, he was arrogant. She marveled at the sheer, unmitigated cockiness of the man. Had all ninth-century men been that way?

In retrospect, it occurred to her that she should have seen it coming.

She was, after all, a fan of history, a studier of mankind, a ponderer of ancient civilizations. She knew what life had been like a thousand years ago for women.

Men had been Men.

And women had been Property.

And somehow, she *still* managed to be utterly unprepared when he ducked that sexy, dark head of his and charged her.

"*Oomph!*" Jessi grunted, as his shoulder made contact with her stomach.

Her feet left the ground, her world tilted precariously, and the next thing she knew, she was hanging upside down over his shoulder.

One of his muscle-bound arms banded her waist, pinning her to his shoulder. The other hand splayed firmly on her bottom.

She parted her lips and was just about to let loose a screech that would do a banshee proud, when his hand moved.

Possessively. Intimately. Dipping right between her legs.

He pressed strong fingers against the opening of her vulva through her jeans, his thumb expertly finding her clitoris at the same time.

Fire exploded red-hot inside her. Her mouth, open on an intended shriek of rage, released a soft, stunned exhalation of air instead.

His big warm hand rested there a moment, applying a firm but gentle, relentless pressure. Enough to bring every nerve ending brutally to life and awaken an aching hunger deep within her womb.

He said nothing. She said nothing, either, mostly because, at the moment, all she could think of to say was: Excuse me, but your hand seems to have slipped between my legs and if you'll move it just the tiniest bit, I bet I could come.

His hand was gone.

It returned, lower, banding her to him by the backs of her knees.

Reason returned also, accompanied by fury. The sad part was that what he'd just done had made her so instantly, incredibly horny that she wasn't sure if she was more furious at him for doing it in the first place, or for stopping when he had.

And *that* made her even more furious still.

"Put me down," she managed to hiss. So maybe it came out a bit more breathy than sibilant, but it was the best she could do upside down with her boobs in her face.

"Haud yer wheesht, woman."

"Hold my *what?*"

"It means 'hush,' Jessica. Just hush. Would it kill you to hush?"

"Probably," she snapped. "Put me *down*. I can walk."

"Nay. I've no desire for you to be master of your destiny in any manner, however small. You are too unpredictable."

"*I'm* unpredictable?"

"Aye."

She was speechless a moment. Then she pinched his butt, hard.

"Ow!" He smacked her bottom.

"Ow!" she yelped.

"Behave," he growled. "Tit for tat, lass. Remember that." The arm banding her waist relaxed, he repositioned her on his shoulder, then tightened his grip again, making her realize she probably couldn't get off his shoulder if her life depended on it. That single muscle-bound arm was as unyielding as reinforced steel.

The abruptness with which he shifted her jostled her backpack, still looped over her shoulders. Crammed with purse, laptop, assorted notepads, pens, pencils, and a four-inch-thick *Ancient Civilizations* textbook, it yielded to gravity, slid down, and *thump*ed her in the back of the head.

Hard.

"Ow!" she yelled again. "Shit! Put me down this instant, you brute!"

"Unbelievable," she thought she heard him mutter.

"Oh — *you* think so?" she snarled. "I'm the one flung over a primate's shoulder. *You're* the primate. I'm the one entitled to be saying 'unbelievable.' Not you."

"Unbelievable," he muttered again. He spun about so quickly that she nearly puked the five extra cups of coffee she hadn't really wanted but had drunk anyway in the café earlier, all over that magnificent butt she'd just pinched, and yes, like his arm, the man had buns of steel.

Plucking up the massive mirror, he tucked it beneath the arm he'd freed by shifting her, and turned for the door. Woman on one side, artifact on the other. Not even straining.

And she knew how heavy that mirror was. The two deliverymen had wrestled with its weight.

Stalking out into the corridor, he demanded, "Which way?"

She raised her head for as much clearance as she could gain with thirty-eight pounds of backpack — she'd weighed it once so she could factor the toting about of it into her daily caloric intake; it had earned her two Krispy Kremes every other morning — resting against her skull. "Why should I tell you?" she said snottily.

He bit her hip.

"Left," she gritted.

He turned left and took off at a trot.

The strain on her neck was too much. She put her head back down. Her breasts were in her face and, as she bounced against his back with each step he took, her backpack *thunk*ed her steadily in the back of the head. At least her face was cushioned against the repeated blows. She wasn't getting her nose hammered *rat-a-tat-tat* into his spine. Thank God for small blessings. Or two large ones, as the case may be.

"Where are you taking me?" she mumbled against her sweater.

"I am taking you to whatever manner of

transportation you have. You are then taking us to procure suitable lodgings."

"I am?"

"If you wish to live."

She wished. She mumbled directions to the lot in which her car was parked.

"You're mumbling, lass."

She mumbled again.

"What was that?"

She mumbled again.

"Did you just say something about your breasts?" he said warily. A pause, then a reverent "Och, Christ, they're in your face!" He stopped so abruptly her backpack *thump*ed the back of her head in double time: a soft *whump* followed by a solid *thwack,* dazing her.

When she felt his chest shaking, it took her a few moments to identify the motion. He was laughing. The rat-bastard was laughing.

"I *so* hate you," she told her breasts. Meaning not them, of course, but him.

As he continued to laugh, the fight went out of her, up in a puff of smoke. She was tired, she was freaked out, and she really just wanted to walk on her own two feet. "Would you *please* put me down?" she said plaintively.

She suspected he must have felt the diminishing of tension in her muscles, read her body language, and knew, mentally, she'd capitulated.

His laughter subsided. He bent and gently deposited her on her feet. His scotch-gold gaze glittered with amusement and sexual heat he made no effort to disguise. "Better?" He cupped her chin with one big hand, thumb brushing her lower lip.

She twisted her face away. "Better. Come on. Let's get out of here before someone sees us with the professor's —"

"What the hell do you think you're doing, Jess?" Mark Troudeau barked sharply behind her.

Jessi turned disbelievingly. What — had the mere thought been a self-fulfilling prophecy?

Mark's office was a few hundred feet down the hall from Professor Keene's. When she'd passed it earlier, there'd been no lights on. Didn't he have a life? What was he doing here so late?

Was nothing going to go right anymore?

Great, just great. This was just what she needed: Mark running off to tattle to anyone who would listen that not only had she crossed police lines and gone into the professor's office, but she'd made off with a priceless, mysterious artifact. If the police did the least bit of checking into things, they would discover that what she'd taken was what the (murdered) deliverymen had delivered to the (murdered) professor.

And she would be oh-so-incriminatingly on the lam, nowhere to be found, last seen in the company of a tall, dark, kilt-clad stranger, "stealing" the fabulously expensive black-market relic that three people had already died over.

Without getting the slightest chance to tell her side of the story and point out that somebody'd tried to murder her too.

As if anyone would believe her anyway.

Shit, shit, shit. When all this was over, she really wanted to be able to finish her degree at the university where she'd begun it, not via correspondence courses from jail. That kind of stuff just didn't look good on a resumé.

"Oh, for crying out loud, Mark, it's two in the morning! *What* are you doing here?"

"I believe I just asked you that." Close-set brown eyes behind rimless glasses darted from her to the half-naked, towering man toting the mirror, and back to her again.

What could she say? Dredging her mind,

she drew an empty net. Try though she might, she couldn't think of a single excuse for her current circumstances — convincing or otherwise. She would have been grateful even for an absurd one, but apparently her brain was done for the day.

As she stood there, staring at him like the biggest idiot, Cian MacKeltar took care of the problem.

"You will go back in that room from whence you came, and remain in there, silent, until well after we've gone. Now."

Mark turned and cantered dutifully back down the hall toward his office without so much as a neigh of protest.

Wow. Jessi blinked up at Cian MacKeltar.

"Hmm," he murmured softly, staring after the retreating grad student. "Mayhap 'tis only her."

" 'Her'? Do you mean me? What me?" Jessi said expectantly.

"Puny little man," he scoffed, as Mark obediently closed the door.

Was that it? Was that why Mark had slunk off — because he was puny and Cian MacKeltar was so big and forbidding?

She tipped her head back, eyeing him. At six and a half feet, and a good two-hundred-plus pounds of pure muscle, he dwarfed people. With those wild dark braids tangling

142

halfway down his back and those wicked red-and-black tattoos licking across his chest, up to the edge of that whisker-shadowed jaw, he looked downright primeval: an ancient, deadly warrior stalking the halls of the university. She supposed his mere appearance might have been enough to make Mark decide he clearly wouldn't be winning any arguments with this man, so there was little point in beginning any.

How nice it must be to have such an impact on the world! If reincarnation was the way of things, she wanted to come back as Cian MacKeltar. She'd like to be the asshole man, for a change, rather than subject to asshole men's dictates. And if she were going to be the asshole man, she'd like to do it up right and be the biggest and baddest.

"That was amazing," she said fervently. "He is *such* a pain in the butt. I can't tell you how many times I've wished I could get him to just go away like that. Like he had no choice but to obey me, or something."

"Come, Jessica." Cian MacKeltar closed a hand around her upper arm. "We must away ourselves."

They awayed.

8

An hour later they pulled under the canopy of the Sheraton in downtown Chicago.

Jessi had wanted to go home and get a few things, but Cian MacKeltar had immediately, vehemently vetoed that.

The next assassin could already be awaiting you there, woman, he'd said, and she'd shivered. How creepy to think someone might even now be lurking in her dark apartment, waiting to kill her. How odd to think she couldn't go home. Maybe not for a long, long time.

Maybe never again.

This was it, she'd realized while driving. She'd gone too far to turn back now. She was officially on the run. Her situation wouldn't have been so dire if Mark hadn't caught her leaving with the artifact.

But he had. That milk was spilt, and there was no point crying over it.

She glanced over at Cian, barely able to see him over the top of the huge mirror that was wedged sideways between the bucket seats of her car. A good quarter of the mirror was hanging out the open hatch-back, which was bungeed carefully around it, with various bits of her clothing — jackets and sweaters and T-shirts that tended to accumulate in her car as the seasons changed — wedged protectively between metal and glass.

Head flush to the ceiling, he looked miserably uncomfortable. It had been as difficult to cram him into the tiny car as it had been to finesse in the mirror.

They'd argued over the top of the looking glass the entire way downtown. He took backseat driving to a whole new level.

Cease ceasing movement so abruptly! Christ, woman, must you catapult *forward after each cessation? Are you certain you've strapped the mirror securely? We should stop and check it. By Danu, wench, try nudging this beast gently, not kicking it with both heels!* A silence, a slew of choked curses, then: *Horses! What the bloody hell is wrong with horses? Have they all been slain in battle?*

When she'd finally cranked up her favorite Godsmack CD in an effort to tune him out, he'd let out a roar that had rattled the windows in her car: *By all that's holy, woman, what is that hideous noise? Cease and desist! A battlefield at full charge could be no more cacophonous!*

Huh. She loved Godsmack. The man clearly had no taste in music.

Scowling, she'd stuffed in Mozart's *Requiem* — which she reserved for only her broodiest days, usually during finals week — and in moments, he'd been whistling cheerfully along. Cheerfully. Go figure.

"You're going to have to stay here," she informed him. "I'll get the room and come back for you."

"I doona think so," he growled.

"You don't look like the rest of us."

"Nay," he agreed. "I am bigger. Stronger. Better."

The look she gave him said she had something nasty on her tongue and couldn't scrape it off. "That's not what I meant. There's no way we'll be able to keep a low profile with you walking around dressed like that."

"Leave it to me, woman."

Before she could utter another word, he grappled with the handle, opened the door, and stepped out. Or rather uncramped and unfolded himself onto the pavement, closing the door behind him.

For a man from the ninth century, he

sure seemed to know a lot about modern-day things, she mused, though it seemed to be from having observed them, not from having interacted with them. When he'd first gotten in, he'd examined everything, twisting knobs and pushing buttons. He'd even eyed the steering wheel consideringly. Fortunately, he'd seemed to think better of it. Unfortunately, she didn't think his restraint would last long. He liked to be the one in charge.

"You will not look at me," she heard him say to the valets. *"You will see only her."* A silence. Then, *"And you will not look at her breasts."*

Jessi blinked and burst out laughing. The man was such a Neanderthal! Like her breasts were his or something! What did he think — that the valets would just dutifully obey him as Mark had?

She had news for him: He wasn't that impressive.

"You're not that impressive," she said, stepping from the car and casting a dry look across the roof.

Five valets stood around the car, looking at her, and only at her, and only at her face.

"May we take your luggage, ma'am?" one of them said, looking her dead in the eye.

Men rarely did that. At least not at first. She smoothed her pink sweater down and took a slow, luxuriatingly deep breath. That always worked.

Five gazes remained fixed on her face.

She glanced down; they were still there, round and perky and obvious as ever. Mystified, she said, "No luggage," and removed her car key from the key ring.

Cian moved to the rear of the car and began unstrapping the mirror.

"We can't take that in with us!" Belatedly, she realized it would have been much smarter to go to some seedy No-Tell Motel way out on the outskirts. But the Sheraton down on the lake was the only hotel she'd ever stayed in (during an archaeology seminar last summer), and when they'd left campus, she'd headed for it, driving on a sort of bemused autopilot, far too busy defending her driving skills to be thinking clearly. Getting him into a room without causing a memorable stir was going to be difficult enough. They needed to be inconspicuous. Taking the mirror in with them just wasn't possible. Then again, she thought, frowning, they could hardly leave it in the car, either.

Again, he merely said, "Leave it to me, woman."

It was then that she realized, with a sinking sensation in the pit of her stomach, that it was only a matter of time before the police came and arrested her.

As if a grim portent, a few blocks down the street a police siren began to sound.

She shivered.

Oh yeah. Only a matter of time.

He still had it. *Bloody hell, he still had it!*

There was nothing wrong with him. There was something wrong with *her*.

Mirror beneath one arm, the other wrapped around his woman, he steered her into the brilliantly lit, polished, and gleaming lodgings.

Christ, it felt good to walk free! And to walk free with such a beautiful woman on his arm? 'Twas heaven to be alive.

Even hunted. Even knowing what lay ahead. 'Twas far more than he'd thought he'd get at such a late hour in the game.

Her city seemed much like what he'd seen of London, with insignificant differences. Both enormous, both massively populated, frenetic with cars and people rushing to and fro, but her city had taller buildings than aught he'd glimpsed from Lucan's study.

He continued tossing out commands in

Voice as they strode into the lodgings she'd selected. *Doona look at us. Move out of my way. Do not notice the mirror. We are not here.*

Memory spells were extremely complicated and could cause terrible, irreversible damage if done wrong. 'Twas easier to turn eyes away than attempt to make people forget.

Still, nonspecific commands such as "we are not here" weren't truly effective. They served mostly to gloss things over a bit, make events seem dimmer. For Voice to be truly compelling, the commands needed to be concise, precise. Commands too vague or complicated could get messy. Orders strongly counter to a person's fundamental beliefs could cause intense pain.

"Why don't you just stand here and I'll go get a room?" She tipped her head back and looked up at him. "And you don't have to hold on to me," she added peevishly. "I don't have anywhere else to go."

He smiled. He liked that. "Where?"

" 'Where' what?"

"Where does one 'get a room'?"

"Oh. Over there." She pointed. "Wait here."

"You will cease attempting to give me orders, wench." He tried Voice on her

150

again, thinking perchance something in their earlier environment had conflicted with his use of magyck.

"*You* will cease *ordering* me to cease giving you orders," she said exasperatedly. "I'm just trying to help."

"The day I need help seeing to the needs of a woman is the day I may as well be dead."

She gave him a measuring look. "Actually, it'd be nice if more men felt that way. Of course, you still need to lose that whole me-Tarzan, you-Jane thing."

He had no idea what she was *havering* about, but it didn't matter. What mattered was the getting of a room.

He escorted her where she'd pointed, GUEST CHECK-IN, and propped the mirror carefully against the short wooden wall.

A trim, auburn-haired, fortyish man with a bristly mustache came over, looking as if he'd rather be anywhere else at this hour.

"You will give us a room. Now. And stop looking at me."

Beside him, Jessica said hastily, "You'll have to excuse him. He can be a bit heavy-ha— oh, for heaven's sake!" She changed both sentence and direction of her gaze midstream, frowning up at him when the desk clerk obediently, and without protest

151

whatsoever, averted his eyes and began processing the paperwork for a room. "People keep obeying you like you're some kind of . . . of . . . well, *god* . . . or something."

"Imagine that." *In my day, lass, I was.*

"I can't."

"I'm excruciatingly aware of that," he said dryly.

"Well, why do they keep doing it?"

"Mayhap, woman, they recognize a Man among men." He couldn't resist provoking her. "That would be Man with a capital 'M.' "

She rolled her eyes, as he'd known she would.

He bit back a smile. There was no point in explaining to her about Voice. She wouldn't understand; the wench was infuriatingly immune. Impossibly immune. His amusement faded. He narrowed his eyes, studying her for the hundredth time, trying to discern something — anything — different about her that might explain her condition.

He couldn't discern a blethering thing. Of all the wenches the Fates might have appointed to serve as his reluctant savior, the humorless bitches had sent him the only woman he'd ever encountered that he couldn't control.

"I'll just need a credit card," the man behind the counter was saying.

Cian opened his mouth to use Voice again, but Jessica was already handing the man something. He had no idea what it was. He shrugged. He didn't mind letting her feel useful. He knew women liked to feel important too. 'Twas but that he preferred to make them feel important in other ways.

Like as women. In his bed. While he was inside them.

And this one, och, this one did something strange to him. A subtler version of that electrifying jolt he'd felt the first time she'd touched him had been happening each time he touched her. It made it nigh impossible to keep his hands off her. The entire time she'd been over his shoulder he'd felt a gentle current sizzling through the length and breadth of his body. Wherever their bodies were touching, he felt as if heat lightning crackled just beneath his skin.

And he knew, though she pretended otherwise, that she felt it too. When he'd put his hand so blatantly on her woman's mound, he'd been prepared for indignation, outrage, a fierce tongue-lashing. He'd deserved it. He'd never treated a woman in such a possessive fashion — at least not until *after* they'd become lovers — bypassing any pretense of civility or seduction entirely. And yet somehow, at the same time, he'd known she wouldn't lambaste him.

It was as if his hand simply *belonged* there on her. And she knew it too.

You're getting fanciful, Keltar. Next you'll be thinking she's your one true mate.

According to Keltar legend, each Druid born into the clan was destined for a soul mate, a perfect match in heart and mind, as well as body, coming together with an explosive, incendiary passion that could not be denied. If the Keltar male exchanged the sacred Druid binding vows with his true love, and his mate willingly returned them, they could bind their souls together for all eternity, in this life and forever beyond. The vows linked them inextricably. 'Twas said if a Keltar gave the vows and they were not returned, he would be forever incomplete, missing a part of his heart, aching for the love of a woman he could never have, eternally bound to her, through this life and all his future existence, whether in the cycle of rebirth, heaven, hell, or even an eternal Unseelie prison. *If aught must be lost . . .* the legendary vows began, *'twill be my life for yours. . . .*

He snorted derisively. He had no life to give.

Very little left of a soul.

Not much honor, either, if one wanted to go further into the oath. Which he didn't.

"What?" she asked, wondering why he'd snorted.

He looked down at her. She was glancing askance up at him, her head tipped back. Her short glossy black curls glistened beneath the hotel lights, her creamy skin glowed with a kiss of sun-gold — the lass liked the outdoors — and the expression in her eyes managed somehow to be curious, irritated, worried, and determined, all at the same time.

Just looking up at him like that, she took his breath away. And he wasn't the kind of man that happened to easily. It was more than what she looked like that did it to him — it was the woman *inside* the lush package.

Jessica St. James was a handful of a woman; precisely the kind he'd so long ago hungered to find. Scholarly, learned, she possessed spine and sauciness and independence of will. In the ninth century it had gotten to the point where he would have positively welcomed a temper tantrum from a woman, even if it had been completely unfounded — he would have appreciated *any* show of backbone — but as laird of the castle since birth, and heir to the ways of Druidry, virtually all he'd gotten from the lasses from a tender age on was obedience, deference, and awe. *Aye, milord. If it please you, milord. How may I serve you, milord? Is the wine to your liking, milord? May I fetch you anything — anything at all — milord?* And it had only worsened as he'd aged and become a formidably powerful man, sorcerer, and warrior.

He'd found himself increasingly drawn to more mature women, like this one. He suspected she had a good quarter century to her name. In his century she would have, like as not, had three or four babes and lost a few husbands by this time in her life. He preferred women who'd lived a good bit, women whom the passage of years had deepened and made more interesting. He liked to toop — bloody hell, did he ever! — but he also liked to be able to talk when the tooping was at a temporary hiatus.

This woman was certainly interesting. Beyond his compelling. Feisty and sexy and looking up at him with an enticing sheen on her plump lower lip.

He ducked his head and tasted her.

She was soft, silky, and utterly delectable. He nipped her lower lip gently, then brushed his mouth lightly against hers, savoring the sweet friction. He didn't push to deepen the kiss; there would be time later for scorchingly intense kisses. He contented himself for the now with a purely hedonistic, lazy taste of her. Moving soft and slow, lulling her into him. When he felt her body melting forward, he pulled away with a slow, erotic tug of her lower lip.

She stared up at him with a startled, searching expression, her lips parted, the lower one slightly puffed out.

His mouth tingled from the touch. He wondered if she felt it too. Wondered what she was thinking, feeling.

He stretched his senses and probed, suspecting deep in his bones it wouldn't work. If Voice had no effect on her, he highly doubted deep-listening would.

Deep-listening was the Druid art of reading the minds and hearts of others, and was another of his greatest skills. Nay, that wasn't quite right. He excelled at all Druid skills. He always had.

He was an anomaly: the only Keltar ever to have been born with the full power of *all* of his ancestors, combined and compounded; an abnormality of nature; an anathema in an otherwise ancient, honorable, and predictable bloodline. While his da had excelled at healing, and his granda had been adept at predicting the seasons for the sowing and reaping, and his uncle had been highly skilled in both Voice and alchemy, Cian had been born with all those talents a hundredfold, plus abilities no Keltar had ever displayed before. 'Twas much of why he'd ended up trapped in the Dark Glass.

Too much power for one man. Pull back, Cian, his mother used to say, with troubled eyes. *One day you'll go too far.*

And indeed he had. He'd coveted the Dark Hallows himself, even knowing they bore the innately corruptive essence of black magyck, and that no man could own one and remain unchanged. Still, he'd hungered, just as Lucan had, for ever-greater power; but where Lucan had been perfectly willing to embrace evil, Cian's error had been that he'd arrogantly believed himself *incapable* of being corrupted or defeated by either man or magyck.

How wrong he'd been.

But that was another time, a long-ago story, and one best forgotten.

She was now.

He opened himself, focusing his senses, probed gently at her.

Nothing. He probed harder. Silence. Utter and absolute.

Centering, he *pounded* at Jessica St. James, a battering ram at the castle gates of her mind.

Not a hint of an emotion. Not a whisper of a thought.

Astonishing.

To test himself, he fired a questing arrow at the man arranging for the room. He flinched back hastily. The desk clerk was a miserable man. His wife had recently left him for one of his best friends. Cian swallowed, trying to scrape the foul taste of the man's despair from his tongue. Despair served no one well. He wanted to shake him and say, *Fight, you fool. Fight for her. Never cede the battle. Never yield the day.*

"Doona give up, man," Cian hissed.

The desk clerk glanced up, looking startled.

"You can't just let her walk away," he growled. "She's your *wife*."

The clerk's eyes narrowed, flickered uneasily. "Who are you? Do I know you?" he said defensively.

"What?" Jessica said beside him. "What's going on?"

"Nothing. Forget it." To the desk clerk he said, *"Be at ease."* It wasn't his place to save the world. Well, mayhap it was, but he knew what must be done, and it wasn't this.

With a soft snort of exasperation beside him, Jessica accepted a packet from the once-again submissive desk clerk, twitched that sweet bottom of hers, and stalked off toward two huge burnished-gold doors in the wall. She cast a glance back over her shoulder at him, and her expression could not have more clearly said: *Well, come on, you great, big, overbearing brute. I don't like you one bit, but we're stuck together.*

Cian admired the view for a moment, before picking up the mirror and loping off to join her.

Twenty days with this woman.

Mayhap, somewhere, some divinity in which he'd not believed, believed in him. Believed he would redeem himself and was rewarding him in advance.

She stopped at the doors. Yawning, she stretched her arms over her head, arched her back, and twisted from side to side as if stretching out her spine.

Bloody hell, the woman was a woman in all the right places!

Who cared the why of things?

She was *his* for the next twenty days.

9

Jessi sat at the cherry writing desk in room 2112, hooking up her laptop, scowling into the small wall mirror that hung above it, wondering why hotels always put mirrors above writing desks. Who wanted to look at themselves while writing? Apparently a lot of people must, because every hotel she'd been in had pretty much the same setup: closet inside the door on the left; bathroom inside the door on the right (or vice versa); first bed facing a writing desk with requisite mirror hung above it; a small table between the beds sporting clock radio and phone; second bed facing a TV armoire/dresser; and, at the far wall, a small table and two chairs sat before a wall of windows.

This room was no different, though a cut above some she'd been in, with merlot-and-champagne carpet, patterned with a gold diamond design, walls papered in textured ivory with gold embellishments at the moldings, beds topped with crisp ivory linens and champagne comforters, the windows hung with billowy wine drapes.

Behind her, Cian MacKeltar was taking a shower, beyond the closed bathroom door.

She'd closed the door.

She'd also closed her eyes when he'd dropped his kilt right in front of her. Which wasn't to say that she was a prude and hadn't stared at him through the glass of the shower enclosure when she'd firmly shut the door a few moments later. She had.

The moment they'd entered the hotel room, his gaze had gone instantly to the double king beds. So had hers, and there'd been one of those intensely tense moments where people either jumped on each other or got as far away from each other as they could.

She'd done a little crab-scuttle sideways, nearly sidling right back out into the hall. He'd smiled faintly, mockingly, at her, then stepped past her and thoroughly scanned the entire room before positioning the mirror against the far wall, facing the entry door. She'd not missed that it also faced the beds, but was refusing to ponder it overlong.

For a moment she'd thought he was

going to kiss her again, but, as he'd walked back toward her, his gaze had swept past her to the bathroom.

Christ, he'd exclaimed, *'tis a modern gardcrobe! I couldn't see beyond the door to the one in Lucan's study, though I've seen pictures. . . .* He'd trailed off wonderingly.

Is that where he kept you . . . er, the mirror hung? In his study? How strange his existence must have been inside a mirror! She couldn't begin to fathom it.

Aye. Though I've seen most modern inventions in books and the like in his study, I've not had the opportunity to examine the real things.

She'd been about to give him a quick demonstration — anything to get away from those beds — but he'd plunged right into things, just as he had in the car, taking command, twisting handles and turning knobs, squirting little bottles of shampoo and conditioner until the room had been a steam sauna, scented of perfumed toiletries.

Does this hostelry contain a kitchen and serving wenches, lass? he'd paused long enough in his explorations to ask.

She'd nodded.

Command us a feast, woman. I'm famished. Meat. Much meat. And wine.

When he'd unfastened his wrist cuffs, she should have gotten the hint.

Without further ado, he'd dropped his kilt. Had stood there, utterly unself-conscious, wearing nothing but a leather sheath strapped to one heavily muscled thigh, casing a heavily jewel-encrusted knife. Doffing that, too, he'd placed it high on the shower stall's edge and stepped beneath the spray.

Pulse suddenly jumping in her throat, she'd turned sharply away and squeezed her eyes shut.

She could still taste him on her lips. The kiss he'd given her in the lobby had stunned her.

And scorched her right down to her toes. He'd not pushed for tongue, or tried to grab a breast the instant hc'd thought he'd gotten her distracted with a kiss. No, he'd kissed her lazily, without touching her anywhere else at all, as if he had all the time in the world, brushing his firm, full, sexy lips back and forth over hers, gently sucking her lower lip.

She'd actually melted into the egotistical Neanderthal, had felt her lips parting.

Logic, reason, and awareness of current events had vanished from her mind as abruptly and completely as if someone had just vacuumed her brain out through her ear.

It was his gentleness that had gotten her, she'd decided on the way up in the elevator. It had surprised her, that was all. It was just that she'd not expected such a soft touch from such a hard-bodied, aggressive man. She'd not been prepared for it, any more than she had been for him to get butt-naked in front of her.

And, Crimeny, what a butt . . .

When she'd opened her eyes and turned back, she'd stared though the steamy glass at him — all six and a half magnificent naked feet of him.

Powerful muscles shaped his long legs and massive thighs, his ass was tight, perfectly formed, and packed with more sweet muscle. She loved a good butt on a man! Too many guys had none at all. Both legs and butt were dusted with fine, silky dark hair; he wasn't one of those lady-killer bodybuilders or models that shaved — he was a man's man, and proud of it. More dark hair dusted his forearms and beneath his arms.

He'd lathered himself up and begun scrubbing beneath the steamy spray. As his powerful hands moved over his body, prime, sleek muscle rippled beneath his slick, golden skin.

She'd been so engrossed, watching him wash himself, that when he'd squirted conditioner in his hand and closed a fist around himself, she'd continued dazedly watching. Not until he'd begun to rhythmically slip his hand up and down had she realized what she was watching him do.

Eyes snapping wide, she'd jerked her gaze to his face. His gaze had been locked on her face, his eyes narrowed, his gaze dark and hot. He'd flashed her a sexy, wicked smile that had been both invitation and challenge, catching the tip of his tongue between his teeth.

She'd backed hastily out and slammed the door.

The man was *seriously* hung.

An insane, utterly-uncaring-of-consequences part of her had wanted nothing more than to go right back in there, strip, get in the shower with him, push his hand away, and replace it with hers.

Get a grip, Jessi, she'd rebuked herself firmly. *And not on mirror-man's dick.*

After shutting him in the bathroom and gulping a few steadying breaths, she'd gone to the phone and ordered room service, putting it also on her credit card.

"Why not?" she muttered to her reflection over the top of her laptop. "I may as well charge with impunity." The way things were going, she probably wouldn't live long enough to have to pay it off anyway. She made a face at herself in the mirror. It had been a long day and she was showing signs of the strain. Her makeup was as good as gone, her stubborn cowlicks were acting up, and her clothes were rumpled.

Plucking a tissue from a box on the desk, she dabbed at the remnants of mascara smudged on her lashes and ran a hand through her short glossy curls.

People often told her she looked like a curvier version of the girl who'd played Virginia, the heroine in *The 10th Kingdom*, and she supposed she did — after Virginia had gotten her hair whacked off by the wolfman. After the gypsies had cursed her for setting their poor birds free. Jessi would have set the poor birds free too. Not that her hair looked like it had been whacked off or anything. She got it trimmed every six weeks down at the Beauty Training Academy, and they did a pretty good job for six bucks.

She narrowed her eyes at her reflection. Breasts. They were undoubtedly her best feature. Some people got great nails and hair, some people got beautiful smiles or pretty eyes, some people got skinny little perfect beach-butts, those disgustingly ideal ones that actually *stayed* in bikini bottoms. She'd gotten good breasts. It wasn't that they were so big. Frankly, she didn't think they were. It was just that they were really round and really high and really perky, and she had a short neck (which was why she wore her hair short — the girls at the Beauty Academy said it made her neck look longer), and sometimes even *she* thought her breasts looked fake in certain tops, but they weren't. They were real. Perhaps a bit too enthusiastically perky, but she figured she should enjoy that while she could, because she fully comprehended complex equations like gravity plus time.

The reflection of the glowing red face of the clock on the bedside table suddenly drew her attention, blinking as the hour rolled over.

4:00 a.m.

She stared at it in the mirror, aghast, realizing that in three hours and twenty minutes, classes would begin for the day. On Thursdays, she taught four one-hundred-level anthropology courses.

Or she'd used to. She certainly wouldn't be teaching any today.

She considered calling in sick, but decided it was wiser not to. When this was over, she'd figure out what kind of story to tell. She might be able to get away with claiming to have been forcibly abducted and fully exonerate herself. Which meant if she called in sick now, it would make her look like a liar later. *I know it's odd for a kidnapper to let his kidnappee call in sick, but he was an odd kidnapper.* Right. That would go over like a ton of bricks.

Exhaling gustily, she returned her attention to her laptop and plugged it into the hotel line. She'd decided to check her E-mail while he was showering, partly in a no-doubt-pointless bid for the comfort of routine, but also to keep her mind off sex, which, with him around, was like trying not to think about chocolate while sitting in a person-sized fondue pot of the dark, creamy stuff, surrounded by flowering cacao trees.

Her inbox was filled with the usual: newsletters to which she subscribed to stay apprised of significant developments in her field; E-mails from students in the undergad classes she T.A.'d, filled with impressively creative excuses as to why they should be the exception to the rule, forgiven their: a) absenteeism; b) failure to appear for an exam; c) late paper. The entertaining and inventive pleas for leniency were followed by spam spam and more spam, and finally, the one she liked best — the Naked Man of the Week pictures from her cyberfriends at RBL Romantica.

She made short work of her correspondence, shooting the newsletters to a suspend folder for later perusal, denying any and all excuses/pleas for extensions that didn't involve a death in the family, reporting the spam, and perusing the Naked Man pictures appreciatively before setting one of them as her desktop background.

She was about to log off when a new E-mail popped in. She scanned the sender's ID.

Myrddin@Drui.com.

She didn't know a *Myrddin@Drui.com* and had a phobia about viruses. If something happened to her laptop, a new one wasn't in the budget. There was no topic in the subject line, which meant, according to her stringent guidelines, there was no place for it but the Trash folder.

As she slid the pointer over it, she got an instant bone-deep chill. She whisked her fingers over the mouse pad, jerking the pointer away.

Slid it back again. An immediate, painful, bitter chill licked up her hand.

She shivered, jerked the pointer off.

171

Oh, that was just too weird.

She frowned, thinking about the way it had arrived. Had an E-mail *ever* just popped into her inbox when she'd been sitting idle on the inbox page?

Not that she could remember. Sometimes when she was refreshing a page, or reentering the inbox, new ones showed up, but one had never popped in like that when she was just sitting static on the page.

Gingerly, she slid the pointer back over the topic line: **NO SUBJECT.** Grimacing at the immediate sensation that her hand had been plunged, dripping wet, into a Subzero freezer, she *click*ed on it hard and fast and yanked her fingers from the mouse pad.

She pressed her palm shakily to her cheek. It was as cold as ice.

Wide-eyed, she stared at the screen. The E-mail contained three short lines.

Return the mirror immediately.

Contact Myrddin@Drui.com for instructions.

You have twenty-four hours.

That was all it said. There was nothing else on the screen but for a line of nonsensical symbols and shapes at the very bottom.

As she scanned them, a sudden shadow seemed to fall over the hotel room. The bedside clock dimmed, the overhead light in the little entrance foyer hummed, and the ivory walls took on a sickly yellowish hue.

And as clearly as if a man were standing in the room with her, she heard a man's deep, cultured baritone say:

"Or you will die, Jessica St. James."

Whipping around, she scanned the room.

There was no one there.

Beyond the bathroom door, the shower still ran, and Cian MacKeltar still splashed.

She sat perfectly still, brittle as glass, waiting to see if her disembodied guest had anything further to add.

The moments ticked by.

Her shoulders drooped and she stared morosely at her reflection.

He'd called her Jessica St. James. Freaking *everybody* knew her name.

Lucan removed his hand from the screen.

She was gone. But for a moment there, he'd had her.

Vibrant and young. By his measure, so very, very young.

Beyond that — an enigma. Concealed by

173

shadows he couldn't penetrate. Who was this woman with Cian MacKeltar?

Usually if he was able to secure a connection, he could deep-listen, probe, and get more than the general sense of her he'd gotten, which was why he'd attempted the contact to begin with. He'd wanted to see if there was anything he could learn about her and pass on to Eve so she could expedite matters.

People were so concerned about viruses and identity theft, and so oblivious to the true risks of plugging themselves into the World Wide Web, wiring themselves to any and everything that might be out there, hungry, waiting. They worried about cons and killers, sexual molesters enticing their children. They had no notion how thoroughly they could be violated, probed, and coerced by a skilled practitioner of the Dark Arts across a phone line.

Still, he'd not gotten far with this woman. The moment he'd pressed at Ms. St. James, he'd encountered some sort of barrier.

Flipping open Roman's file, which contained the dead assassin's thorough evaluation of his targets, including photos, addresses — both real and cyber — vehicle registration, birth certificate, passport, lines of credit, available funds, and other pertinent facts, he studied Ms. St. James's picture again.

Her driver's license supplied her vital stats. Twenty-four. Height: five feet six inches. Weight: 135 pounds. Eyes: green. Hair: black. Organ donor: no.

She was a lovely woman.

He had no doubt Cian MacKeltar wanted her. The Highlander would be as fascinated by her resistance to probing as was Lucan. He and the Highlander weren't quite as different as the condescending bastard liked to believe.

Closing the file, he punched in a series of numbers on his phone and conveyed a change in plans to Eve's associate: The mirror was still the priority, but make every effort to bring Ms. St. James in alive.

He'd enjoy cracking her open and studying her. He'd not been intrigued by a woman for a very long time.

He would do it while the Keltar watched from his powerless perch high up on his study wall.

"Oh, now *that's* just not going to work," Jessi said flatly when Cian stalked out of the bathroom. She hopped off the bed and moved to regard him from a safer vantage, over near the window. Sitting on a bed with that man in the room just didn't seem wise. "You go back in there and get dressed," she ordered.

Funny thing was, she'd just been placing bets with herself about what condition the archaic Highlander would exit in: kilt-clad and modest, in a towel and semimodest, or in-your-face nude and on the predatory prowl.

She'd decided on in-your-face nude. She owed herself five bucks.

He placed his thigh sheath and jeweled blade on the writing desk, wearing two towels: one at his waist and the other wrapped turban-style around his head. It was barely better than nude. In fact, it only made her want to peel those offending towels away.

As if reading her mind, he ducked his head and unwound the first towel, sponging the excess water from his dark mane. Righting himself, he tossed his hair back over his shoulders, metallic beads *clink*ing. Tiny rivulets of water ran down over his magnificent tattooed chest, a thin channel of it slithered over that tattooed nipple. Muscles bunched and rippled in his tattooed biceps.

She moistened her lips, wondering what

on earth was wrong with her. She'd never had such an intense reaction to a man before.

She had only to look at him to get all shaky-feeling inside. And it wasn't as if she'd never dated a good-looking man before. She had. Kenny Dirisio had been a Grade-A-Italian-Stallion-Extraordinaire. Even brainy Ginger, who was every bit as focused and driven as she was, had said, "Jessi-chick, take my advice, drop a few courses this term and hop on that one. They don't come along like that often."

But she hadn't — hopped on him, that was. In fact, she'd volunteered to teach another seminar and they'd broken up over it, and now she knew why. While her brain had appreciated Kenny's incredible looks, her body had just never quite kicked in. It never really had with any of the guys she'd dated.

With Cian MacKeltar, however, despite the fact that her brain wanted nothing to do with him, her body wanted to do everything with him that was possible between a man and a woman. Her body had done more than kicked in; it was stoking up the oven for the baking of little MacKeltar buns.

With a man that called a mirror "home." This was not good.

"Did you not send for food, Jessica?"

Jessi blinked again, trying to refocus her thoughts. "Yes, but it won't be here for a little while yet. Look, I've been thinking, what's your plan, anyway?"

"To bed you."

"No, I mean, your plan that might actually *work*." She bared her teeth in a cool masquerade of a smile.

"Ah, *that* plan. That would be to cross this room right now and kiss you until you start tearing off your clothing and begging me to f—"

"No, that's not the one I meant, either," she said hastily.

How in the world had he moved that fast?

One instant he was across the room, the space of two beds separating them; the next, one big hand was cupping her chin, tipping her head back, the other hot and possessive on her waist. The man was lethally fast. Which boded well for protection — from everyone but him.

He stared down at her with smoldering intensity. He lowered his mouth slowly, lazily, never breaking eye contact with her. Up close, he was beyond gorgeous. Those whisky eyes shimmered with golden depths and were framed by thick dark lashes. His skin was tawny-velvet, darkly stubbled. His lips were sensual, pink and firm, and curved in the hint of a smile.

"Tell me not to kiss you, Jessica. Tell me right now. And best you make me believe you mean it," he warned softly, a breath from her lips.

"Don't kiss me." She wet her lips.

"Try again," he said flatly.

"Don't kiss me." She swayed toward his body, a magnet to steel.

"Try again," he hissed. "And best 'ware, woman, 'tis your last chance."

Jessi took a deep breath. "Don't." Another deep breath. "Kiss me?"

He laughed, a cocky, rich purr of a sound.

Crimeny, she thought dismally, as he lowered his sexy dark head toward hers, even *she'd* heard the wrong punctuation there.

10

Even though she knew it was coming, Jessi wasn't prepared for Cian MacKeltar's kiss. *Nothing* could have prepared her for the mind-blowing, sizzling intensity of it.

This was no gentle brush of a kiss like the one he'd given her in the lobby. This was the real deal. Intense and demanding, it was every bit as raw and unapologetically carnal as it was seductive.

Gripping a fistful of her short dark curls, the ninth-century Highlander slanted his mouth over hers. He cupped her cheek with one big hand and pressured the corner of her lips with his thumb, nudging them apart. The moment she yielded, he sealed his lips over hers, opening wider, deepening the kiss, taking complete possession of her mouth, obliterating any lingering protest she might have thought to make.

It was a dominant kiss, an expert kiss, the kiss of a man who knew he was a man, liked being one, and knew exactly what he was doing. This was no college boy kissing her, no young grad student toeing the lukewarm line between desire and political correctness. This was a man who was one-hundred-percent okay with lust, who suffered no hesitation or inhibitions.

It was exactly the kind of kiss, she realized dimly, for which she'd always been waiting. But until now, she'd not been able to define exactly what it was she'd been missing, what she'd been holding out for. She was struck by the sudden realization that the problem with her boyfriends was that they'd been just that — boyfriends, with the emphasis on "boy."

Cian MacKeltar was a man — and a formidable force to be reckoned with sexually. She was, quite simply, out of her league with him.

She was struck by another sudden realization then: that she was going to be very, very lucky if she managed to walk out of that hotel room, at whatever point in the future they departed, the same way she'd walked in. A virgin, though she'd never admit it to any of her friends. Nobody was a virgin anymore, and peer pressure could get intense if people thought you were.

Personally, she'd never thought it was

anyone else's business whether or not she was. Only her own, and whatever man she chose to share it with. Her mom might liberally encourage baby-having, but she'd also encouraged a healthy degree of self-respect. *Pick carefully, girls,* Lilly St. James had advised her daughters. *There are a lot of duds out there.* As her mom was currently between husbands number four and five, Jessi figured she should know.

"Christ, lass, you taste sweet," he purred.

She shivered with pleasure as he sucked her lower lip into his mouth, nipped it, then closed his mouth hard over hers, plunging deep. He kissed like a man who hadn't had the luxury in — oh, maybe a thousand years or so — exploiting it for all it was worth, savoring all the subtle, sensual variations. Luring one moment, assaulting the next, and it made her crazy. He kissed like he wanted to devour her, maybe crawl inside her skin. He kissed like he was fucking her mouth, this sinfully gorgeous Highlander with his hot wet tongue and his hard, tattooed body. He kissed so thoroughly and possessively that she wasn't Jessi anymore, she was a woman and he was a man, and she existed because he was kissing her and if he stopped, she might stop being.

She had no idea how they ended up on the floor.

One moment she was in his arms, being kissed senseless — literally, apparently — and the next she was flat on her back beneath his still shower-damp, big, powerful body, her nipples so hard they were poking through both her bra and sweater against his bare chest, with the steely bar of his erection jammed against her stomach.

And she wasn't entirely certain, but she didn't think she was feeling a towel between them anymore. And holy cow, the man was huge.

Dazedly, she wondered what in the world she thought she was doing — even as she buried her fingers in the wet tangle of his hair.

More kisses, soft and slow, hot and hard. She was drowning in man, in the taste and scent and feel of him. Her hands slipped of their own accord down the thick column of his neck, over the muscled ridges of his shoulders.

She barely noticed when he shifted position so that his legs were straddling hers, until he fit himself snugly in the vee of her thighs, and his thick ridge nudged the inseam of her jeans against her clitoris with delicious friction. She jerked at the raw intimacy of it.

When he cupped a hand beneath her bottom, tilted her hips, and began a slow, erotic bump-and-grind that was as old as Mankind itself, a distant part of her mind began sounding a clamorous alarm. But with each slow, powerful thrust of his cock, that inner alarm grew fainter and fainter, as Jessi slipped irresistibly deeper beneath Cian MacKeltar's seductive spell.

When he rucked her sweater up to her ribs and began tracing a path from her bottom to her breasts, slowly, lingeringly, as if committing the subtle shape of each dip and turn to memory, she whimpered into his mouth, hungry to feel those big hands all over her bare body. Everywhere he was touching her, she felt as if a low-voltage electrical current was pulsing beneath her skin, jolting each nerve ending to delicious, tingling awareness. When he closed a hand over one of her breasts, heat shot straight down to her belly and lower still, and she dug her nails into his shoulders, arching hungrily up to meet his next thrust.

He sucked in a shallow hiss of a breath, and suddenly he was working at the fly of her jeans, and then the air was cool on her bare skin as he pushed her jeans and panties down. That faint alarm was sounding again, more loudly, but he was kissing her so heatedly, so passionately and —

— abruptly she was sucking air like a fish out of water.

Alone on the floor.

She blinked. Heavens, but the man could move fast! She sat up, looking dazedly around. "Where did you go?" she said breathlessly.

"Behind you, woman," came the tight, furious reply.

She glanced over her shoulder. He was inside the mirror, propped in the corner, breathing hard, like he'd been running a race. She was panting herself, she realized. Her lips were swollen, she had the sting of a rug burn beginning on her spine, and her nipples throbbed.

Why was he in the mirror? For that matter, *how* had he gotten in the mirror? She gaped at him, bewildered.

"It reclaims me after a time," he said flatly.

She continued gaping. "W-without pre-amble?" she stammered. "Just like that?"

"Aye. 'Twas not my choice to leave you in such a fashion." His gaze dropped sharply and fixed there. "Och, Jessica, you've a beautiful ass. Nigh worth living a thousand years to see."

His words drew her awareness to the fact that she was sitting on the floor, between the TV armoire and the bed, facing the entry door, her bare bottom pointed at the mirror, glancing over her shoulder at him, her sweater rucked up, jeans and panties down around her knees.

The cold reality of reason returned.

Oh, God, what had she almost just *done?* She gaped at the mirror, stunned.

In a matter of mere minutes, she'd been down on the floor, with her jeans and panties around her knees! A few heated kisses — and she'd been about to have sex with a man she barely knew. An arrogant, throwback of a man, at that. Who lived in a mirror. And in the midst of such dire straits, to boot!

This wasn't like her at all. Was she freaking *nuts?*

Shocked and appalled at herself, Jessi stumbled to her feet, tugging at her jeans. Her panties got twisted and her jeans got stuck partway up, just beneath her butt. She yanked but they didn't yield. Only her butt did — she felt it jiggle.

He made a choking sound. "Sweet Christ, woman, you're killing me!"

Cheeks flaming, she shot a scowl over her shoulder at him as she bunny-hopped, bare-bottomed, into the bathroom.

A groan followed her.

"Stop looking at my butt," she hissed fiercely.

She could hear his laughter, even through the closed door.

Hours later, Jessi awakened so hungry that her stomach was cramping.

Rolling over on the miserably lumpy hotel bed, she glanced at the clock. No wonder she was hungry — she hadn't eaten in over twenty-four hours!

The room service she'd ordered earlier hadn't come, for whatever reason: Either they'd tried to deliver it while she'd been stretched beneath Cian MacKeltar's rock-hard body, deaf, dumb, and blind to all but his erotic assault on her senses; or they'd lost her order; or it had arrived so late that she'd been sleeping. Since she rarely got a full night's sleep, she tended to drop off the moment her head touched the pillow, and slept like the proverbial dead, sprawled flat on her back, arms outflung.

After the near-sex-on-the-floor debacle, Jessi had gone in the bathroom and stayed in there awhile, cooling down and trying to think things through. But mostly cooling down — the man threw off serious sexual heat — because by then she'd simply been too exhausted to make much sense of anything.

When she'd finally come out, she'd stiffly informed the mirror to *go away and let me sleep and don't you dare wake me unless my life is in danger. And I do* not *want to talk about what just happened. Not now. Maybe never.*

He'd laughed softly. *As you wish, Jessica,* he'd replied.

Her stomach sounded a long, growling, painful protest.

Fumbling for the light switch on the wall sconce above the bed table, she turned it on, picked up the phone, and pressed the button for room service. As she was placing her order for a double cheeseburger, fries, and a large Coke, the mirror rumbled:

"Quadruple all of that. And if there's naught sweet, add something."

Shrugging, she did so, assuming he'd eat it whenever he was able to come out of the mirror again.

Until the mirror had reclaimed him, it hadn't occurred to her to wonder why he'd gone back in once she'd let him out that first night he'd killed the assassin. In her own defense, she'd had a lot of other things on her mind. Now she knew the answer. Apparently, he had no choice. Though he could be released from the mirror by the chanting of a spell, he couldn't stay out long.

That was a problem. Exactly how did he plan to protect her from behind a pane of silvered glass?

Replacing the phone in the cradle, she scowled at him. God, the man was beautiful. Every time she looked at him, he took her breath away. Made her forget all the important things she should be thinking about. She shook her head, striving for levelheadedness. It was time for more answers. "How often and for how long can you be released from that glass?"

He leaned back against something in the mirror that she couldn't see, folded his arms over his chest, and crossed his booted feet at the ankles. She narrowed her eyes. "Wait a minute, how did you get your clothes back in there?"

"I've had centuries to test the glass. Though the elements comprising it are beyond my fathoming, I've learned to exploit it after a fashion. 'Twas designed to hold humans, not inanimate objects, and I've learned to summon in inert items that reside in my field of vision."

She blinked, glancing around. Kilt — gone. Boots — gone. Even his thigh sheath and knife were gone. Apparently he'd drawn those items back in while she'd slept. Oh, she had a million questions about the nature of that artifact! But first things first: her continued survival. "So?" she prodded. "How often?"

He shrugged. "Try again now."

Jessi drew a deep breath. She really didn't want him out of the mirror at the moment. She wasn't prepared to deal with him in the flesh — all that rippling, sexy, horny male flesh, at that — just yet. Still, she needed to understand the parameters of their situation. She recited the chant to release him.

Nothing happened.

He inclined his head. "I didn't think so. I cannot answer your question precisely. I can tell you only what has occurred in the past. On occasion, when Lucan wished something of me, he afforded me a temporary freedom. Once, several centuries ago, he released me on four consecutive days. Each day I was allotted a different interval by the glass. One day I had but a few hours, another five or six, the fourth day I had the entirety of a day and a night. There is no predicting it."

"So, you can come out every day, for at least a while," she clarified.

"Aye."

"Which means you probably can't come out again until tomorrow morning?"

Another shrug. "I doona ken. You should continue trying at frequent intervals."

"How do you intend to protect me if you can't stay out of that glass?" she said peevishly.

"Lass, we need only evade Lucan for a number of days. Twenty more, to be exact. Scarce any time at all. I assure you, I will keep you safe and well until then."

" 'Twenty days'? Why only twenty?" That didn't sound so bad. She hadn't known there was a time limit to how long her life was going to be screwed up, and it was a relatively short one. Surely she could get her life back on track after only twenty out-of-control days, if things really would be resolved by then. She was grateful that she'd had the foresight not to call in sick. Her odds for survival and a return to normalcy were suddenly looking considerably brighter. One whopper of a good story might take care of things. It might not even have to be half as inventive as some of those her students tried to feed her.

"Because the Compact that holds me bound to the Dark Glass requires that a tithe of purest gold be passed through the mirror every century to reaffirm the Unseelie indenture. The next tithe is due this Hallows' Eve, on the thirty-first day of October, at midnight."

Crimeny. Tithes, Compacts, indentures: Anytime she began thinking about resuming a normal life, she was reminded that she was currently up to her eyebrows in a fairy-tale world of spells and curses.

And the scary part was that it was all beginning to sound somewhat reasonable to her. The longer she interacted with a man who lived inside a mirror, the more inured she became to the strangeness of subsequent oddities. His existence was so inexplicable in and of itself that it seemed pointless to squabble over further inexplicabilities. Though she never would have believed it, magic existed. There was proof of it right in front of her eyes. Arguments over, case closed.

Shaking her head wonderingly, she pushed off the bed — she'd slept fully clothed but for shoes and socks — and went to stand in front of the mirror. She studied the fabulous frame with its odd symbols, stroking the cool gold of it, trailing her hand down over the silvery glass.

Inside the mirror, Cian raised his hand, too, and traced the path of her passage, making it appear as though their fingertips met. She felt only cold glass.

When the tips of her fingers passed over the black stain at the edge, she snatched them hastily away. It had felt icy, just like that strange E-mail, and it had seemed to almost . . . well, kind of . . . *stick* to her skin like a psychic leech as she'd pulled away, as if reluctant to release her. She made a mental note to tell him about the Myrddin-guy and his goose-bumpy E-mail. But first, more questions.

" 'Tis because it is an Unseelie Hallow, lass," he said softly.

"What?"

"The chill. Dark power is cold. Light power is warm. A Seelie artifact exudes a gentle heat. Mere rubbings of a page from the Unseelie Dark Book suck the heat from a man's body. 'Tis said handling the Dark Book itself turns a man into something no longer human, day by day, robbing him of all remnants of inner warmth and light."

Jessi absorbed the information but refused to get sidetracked from the issue at hand. She needed to regain a measure of control that could only be achieved via a thorough understanding of her immediate situation, and as far as she could see, this Dark Book, whatever it was, had nothing to do with her problems.

"So, all we have to do is keep you away from this Lucan person until after the tithe is due, and the spell will be broken? We just need to hide for three weeks? That's all?"

"Aye."

"Then what — once the spell is broken and you're free?" Could he get rid of this man who wanted her dead? Assure her return to a nice, normal life?

He inhaled deeply, his whisky gaze gleaming with sudden, chilling brutality. When he spoke, his voice was hard. "Then you'll never have to worry about Lucan Trevayne again. No one will. This I swear."

Jessi stepped back, in spite of herself. With those words, he'd transformed from sexy man to savage beast, lips drawn back in a silent snarl, nostrils flared, eyes narrowed and not quite sane. Madness born of a thousand-plus years of captivity flickered in those whisky depths, shadowy and cold as the inky stain on the perimeter of the Dark Glass.

She swallowed. "You sound pretty sure of your ability to defeat him, considering that he's the one that stuck you in the mirror," she felt obligated to point out.

A wicked, feral smile curved his lips. "Ah, Jessica, I'll win this time. Of that you may be certain," he said with soft menace.

His words chilled her to the bone. There was such implacable surety in his voice, such savagery in his eyes, that she no longer entertained the slightest doubt whatsoever about Cian MacKeltar's ability to keep her alive.

She had a feeling the man had a few tricks up his proverbial sleeves. Even stuck inside a mirror. Tricks she probably couldn't begin to imagine. Again, she had that sense of something *more* in him.

Oh yes, one way or another, this man would keep her safe.

And how are you going to keep yourself safe from him?

Good question.

Twenty more days. And he could be released from the mirror for at least a portion of each day.

God help her, she had no idea.

Cian MacKeltar attracted her in a manner that defied logic or reason. Then again, she thought wryly, that shouldn't surprise her too much, because *everything* about her current situation defied logic or reason. She was chagrined by the sudden sinking suspicion that her intact hymen was probably due less to her impressive moral fiber than to the fact that she'd simply never experienced such intense, brainless chemistry before. If she had, she highly doubted she'd have lasted so long.

"Room service!" The cheery call was accompanied by a sharp *rap-tap-tap* at the door.

Brightening, Jessi turned away from the mirror. "Thank goodness," she said. "I'm starving."

Cian eased back, just behind the silver, where he could still see but couldn't be seen.

As Jessica walked toward the door, his gaze fixed on her luscious little ass. He'd had that silken-skinned, sweet bottom in his hands only that morning, a cheek of it in each palm. He'd been about to make her his woman, fill her with his cock and pump deep inside her. He'd touched those heavy, round breasts, kissed those full lips, tasted the honeyed sweetness that was Jessica St. James. And soon he would taste the sweetness between her thighs, while he lapped and nibbled and sucked her to shuddering orgasm after orgasm.

A soft growl built in his throat. Christ, he loved to watch her move! Her stride was determined and purposeful, yet graceful and sexy. With a body like that, she couldn't help but be sexy. Her short dark curls only made her seem more womanly, showcasing the delicate, creamy nape of her neck, the fine bones of her shoulder blades, and the sweet slender bow of her spine.

I do not *want to talk about what just happened,* she'd snapped.

Fine with me, woman, he'd thought with a silent laugh and a shrug. They didn't need words.

Their bodies spoke the same language, used identical vocabulary.

Desire. Lust. Need.

He looked at her and something hot and possessive flexed inside his chest.

It wasn't about *wanting* to bed her. It was about answering an ancient, undeniable call to mate.

It was about raw, animal passion. It was about —

Food. Bloody hell. His mouth began to water. He smelled meat.

"You can put it here," Jessica was saying, gesturing to the table by the windows.

A slender, thirtyish woman with shoulder-length brown hair wheeled a tray into the room, pushing it down the narrow aisle between beds and furniture.

Red meat. She'd not ordered fish or fowl, bless the wench! It had been over a century since he'd eaten, and he wanted meat with blood. The last time Lucan had freed him, he'd managed to wolf down a meal of bread, cheese, and ale. To his deprived palate it had been a feast of divinely varied flavors and textures, but it hadn't been rich, juicy, tender meat. That was a memory that had been tormenting him for more than 427 years.

Though inside the glass his existence was suspended and he suffered no bodily needs — no hunger, no thirst, no need to sleep or piss or bathe — that didn't mean he suffered no mental ones.

He hungered. Holy hell, did he hunger! He'd whiled away entire weeks at a time, conjuring the memories of the tastes and scents of his favorite foods.

Closing his eyes, he savored the aromas currently wafting past his mirror as the woman began unloading the cart.

He had no idea what tipped him off.

He decided later that mayhap the woman's intentions were so intense and finely focused that he'd inadvertently deep-listened, catching them even through the glass. Such had happened on occasion with Lucan, usually when his emotions had been strong because he'd been in a fury over one thing or another.

Whatever it was, Cian acted on it instantly, without hesitation.

His hand went to his thigh sheath.

Snapping his eyes open, he whipped his selvar free, hissed the chant to part the veil of silver.

And flung the eight-inch, razor-sharp blade, end over end, through the glass.

11

Jessi backed away from the room service lady, shaking her head from side to side, mouth open on a scream.

One moment she'd been making small talk with the hotel employee, the next something hot and wet and unexpected had sprayed her, splashing her face and hair, her sweater, even splattering her jeans. She'd squeezed her eyes protectively shut against it.

When she'd opened them, it had been to find the woman, standing, eyes wide and glazed, lips moving soundlessly.

With Cian MacKeltar's jewel-encrusted knife protruding from her throat.

Belatedly comprehending what had sprayed her, she'd almost thrown up. But when she'd opened her mouth, a scream came out instead.

"Jessica, you must stop screaming!" came the sharp command from inside the mirror.

She knew that, and she was going to any second now. Really.

The woman staggered back into the TV armoire, knocked her head against it with a solid *thud,* collapsed, and slid down. Her body jerked convulsively, and she went abruptly still, half-sitting, half-lying, hotel uniform twisted about her hips.

As Jessi stared in shock, blood suddenly bubbled between the woman's lips, and her eyes went eerily empty.

Oh, God, she was dead; the woman was *dead!*

Cian pounded on the inside of the mirror with his fists. "Stop screaming, Jessica! Bloody hell, listen to me, if you draw people to us, they'll think *you* killed her. No one will believe your story of a man in a mirror and I will not show myself. I'll *let* you go to prison, Jessica!"

Jessi jerked, his harsh words a bracing slap in her face. She stopped screaming so abruptly it turned into a screeching hiccuping noise, then silence.

He was right.

If her screams drew neighboring guests to her room, she would be found covered with blood, in possession of a stolen artifact, with a dead woman on her floor — said woman having been killed by yet another artifact Jessi wouldn't be able to explain having in her possession.

She'd be arrested in a heartbeat.

And not just for theft, as she'd worried about earlier when leaving campus, but for murder.

And she couldn't see a thing he might have to gain by showing himself and taking the blame.

In fact, considering that all he wanted to do was to hide for another twenty days so he could have his millennium-old vengeance, he'd probably be *happy* to end up in the Chicago Police Department's stolen-goods/evidence lockup. He could hide really well there, under police protection. No, he certainly had no incentive to save her ass.

Shit, shit, shit.

She clamped her lips shut, unwilling to risk so much as another peep.

"Shut the door and bolt it, Jessica."

She scrambled over the bed so fast that she fell off the other side. She'd left the entry door cracked, with the security bolt flipped between door and frame when she'd let the woman in. Leaping up from the floor, she hurried to the door, eased it open only as far as necessary to flip the metal latch back in, ducking well back from the line of vision of anyone who might be beyond it, closed it, and secured the lock. She could hear voices murmuring down the hall and footfalls approaching.

She didn't bother stepping away from the door. Though she'd been screaming for only a few seconds, she had good lungs and knew how loud she'd been.

A few moments later there was a firm knock.

"Is everything all right in there, ma'am?" came a man's worried voice. "We're in the room a few doors down and heard you screaming."

Her heart hammering against the wall of her chest, she took two slow, careful breaths. "Uh, yeah," she managed, "I'm fine. I'm sorry I disturbed you." She forced a shaky, self-deprecating laugh. "There was a spider in the shower and I have a touch of arachnophobia. I guess I kind of freaked out." She injected what she hoped was a convincing note of embarrassment into her voice.

There was a silence, then the sound of soft male laughter. "My friends and I would be happy to take care of it for you, ma'am."

Men. They could be so condescending sometimes, even when they thought they were only trying to be helpful. She'd never been afraid of spiders in her life. And if she was, that was still no reason to laugh at her. Dead bodies — *they* threw her. But she was no sissy about bugs. People couldn't help what they were afraid of. One of her good friends, Cheryl Carroll, was afraid of flowers, and there was nothing funny about it.

"No, no," she said hastily, "it's all right, my husband took care of it." *Say something,* she mouthed over her shoulder at Cian.

"All is well now," Cian boomed. " 'Twas good of you to inquire."

She scowled at him. *All is well. 'Twas?* she echoed silently, wrinkling her nose. Could he have sounded more archaic?

At the sound of another man's voice, a note of cordial reserve entered her would-be-savior's tones. "You might want to call the front desk and let them know. There shouldn't be any bugs in the rooms. My girlfriend hates spiders too."

"I'll do that. Thanks." *Go. Away.*

As the footfalls faded down the hall, she sagged limply against the door. She made the mistake of rubbing her eyes and compounded it by looking at her hands.

Her lips parted. Breath rushed into her lungs, prelude to a scream.

"Doona *do* it, lass," Cian hissed. "He won't believe you twice."

Pursing her lips, she forced the air back out in small, silent explosions. She puffed short, shallow bursts, as if breathing in a paper bag. *I am not going to scream. I am not going to scream.*

"Why did you kill her?" she asked a few minutes later, when she trusted herself to speak.

"Look in the woman's hand. I cannot make out what it is, but she meant to harm you with it."

Steeling herself, Jessi moved reluctantly back into the room and gazed down at the dead woman. Her left hand was closed around something. Jessi nudged it with her foot. A syringe spilled from her fingers and rolled across the blood-spattered carpet. Jessi shivered.

"Jessica, try to summon me out."

Neither of them expected it to work. It didn't.

"Remove the comforter from the bed and cover the body with it."

Gingerly, she did so.

It didn't help much. Instead of a dead body in the same room with her that she could see, now there was a dead body in the same room with her she *couldn't* see, and that creeped her out even more. Everybody knew villains never really died. Just when you thought you were safe, they got up again, eyes terrifying abysses, arms sickly groping for you like in *Night of the Living Dead.*

"You will go bathe now, Jessica."

She didn't move. She wasn't about to go off and get in the shower, only to end up having a *Psycho* moment.

"She's dead, lass. I swear. She was human, nothing out of the ordinary. Now go bathe," he said in a voice that brooked no resistance. "I will protect you. *Go.*"

After searching his burnt-scotch gaze a moment, Jessi went.

Near dawn on Friday, October thirteenth, Jessi stared into the mirror, blew out an exasperated breath, and muttered the spell to release Cian for the gazillionth time.

It *finally* worked.

Hours had passed since the long, scalding shower she'd taken, using up two entire bars of those little pink soaps.

Cian had kept her occupied with tales of life in the ninth century. He'd told her of his seven doting sisters, his mother who tried to manage them all, of his eventual attempts to secure them worthy husbands.

He'd spoken in great, loving detail of his castle in the mountains, and of the rugged bens and sparkling burns surrounding it. It was obvious he'd adored his home, his family, and his clan.

He'd told her of the heather that grew wild along the hillsides and so fragrantly scented a fire; he spoke at length of the savory Scots meals that he'd been missing for centuries.

His words had brought the Highlands brilliantly to life in her mind's eye, and the constant purr of his deep rich burr had soothed. She knew he'd been trying to keep her from going nuts while killing time in a room with a dead body, and it had worked.

As the shock of yet another attempt on her life and Cian's swift dispatch of the would-be assassin faded, Jessi faced the cold, hard facts.

Fact: The woman had intended to kill her. Fact: One of them had to go. Fact: Jessi was glad it hadn't been her.

Problem: In a short time, she'd be slinking out of a room that had blood splattered all over it, leaving a dead body in it. Even if they somehow managed to get the body out of the room — and she couldn't see how they could possibly sneak it from the hotel without being seen — there was no way they could get rid of all the blood.

Fact: She was now a fugitive.

That was the fact that could make her nuts. PhD, life, future — all of it gone to hell.

What was she going to do now?

She had a sudden, horrible vision of herself at some point in the not-so-distant future, calling her mom from a strange, frightening foreign country where the beetles and roaches were the size of small rats, trying to assure Lilly St. James that she really hadn't done whatever the police were saying she'd done.

On top of it all, she didn't even have clothes to sneak out of the hotel in. Though she'd been able to get some of the blood out of her jeans, her sweater was a lost cause. Though her panties had been salvageable, her bra was not.

She could hardly walk out into downtown Chicago in the blanket she was wearing. One might be able to pull that kind of thing off in New York City, but not in Shy-town.

As brilliant golden light blazed from those mysterious runes on the frame, and the sensation of spatial distortion grated across her already frayed nerve endings, she tugged the blanket more securely around her.

She began to push herself up from where she'd been sitting, cross-legged, on the bed, as far back against the wall as possible, so she could pretend the lump on the floor wasn't there. Suddenly, he was standing beside her.

Before she could so much as squeak a protest, he cupped her shoulders, dragged her against his body, and kissed her hard, fast, and deep, before dropping her back onto the bed.

He looked at her a moment, then he plucked her back up and did it again.

This time he drew her into his arms, one arm around her waist, the other hand palming the back of her head, and kissed her so deeply and passionately that she could have sworn she was throwing off steam, sizzling like an iron on the High Mist/Steam setting.

She clung to him, taking all he was giving. Sinking into his body, absorbing the steel and heat of the man.

When he released her this time, she plopped back down on the bed, kissed breathless.

She felt infinitely better than she had moments ago, as if some of his formidable strength had seeped into her through their kiss. God knew the man had strength enough to spare.

He stared down at her, his whisky gaze narrowed with desire and something else, something she simply couldn't quite define; an emotion that eluded her. It almost seemed like regret, but that made no sense to her. What could he possibly be regretting?

When he lifted his hand and traced the backs of his knuckles up her cheek, slipping his fingers into the short dark curls at her temple, she dismissed the odd thought from her mind. He threaded his fingers through her hair slowly, as if savoring the silky texture of each curl.

It gave her a tiny chill, the lightness of his touch.

The man was a walking dichotomy. Those powerful neck-snapping, knife-throwing hands that did murder without pause were equally capable of tenderness and delicacy.

"Lock the door behind me when I leave, lass. I will be but a short time. Doona open it for anyone but me. Will you obey me?"

She opened her mouth to ask why, and what he was going to do, and just how he thought they were going to get out of the mess they were in, but he pressed the tip of his finger to her lips.

"Time is truly of the essence," he said softly. "I never ken how long I'll have. 'Tis action that will serve us best here, not words. Will you obey me for the now, Jessica?"

She blew out a pent breath and nodded.

"Good lass."

She stuck her tongue out and mimed panting like a dog, grasping for any shred of levity she could find.

He gave her a faint, approving smile. "Keep your laughter, Jessica. 'Tis a saving grace."

Her thoughts exactly.

He turned, scooped up the comforter with its bloody burden, and stalked from the room, closing the door behind him.

"Lock it," came the soft, low command from the other side.

Jessi slid the bolt and flipped the latch. Only then did his footfalls fade down the hall.

Forty minutes later, Jessi and Cian stepped in tandem from the elevator.

He was holding her hand, and although she'd never considered herself much of a hand-holder, she thoroughly liked the feel of her small hand in Cian's big, strong one, and the snug interlacing of their fingers. She felt dainty, girly — actually, more like consummately womanly — beside this man.

She glanced up at him and inhaled a swift, shallow breath. He was devastatingly attractive. He was wearing faded jeans and a much-washed black *Ironman* T-shirt. His kilt was tossed over a shoulder, and his knife sheath was strapped blatantly around his thigh, the lethal blade now cleaned and returned to its protective casing. She'd tried telling him he couldn't wear it that way, that he'd get them arrested. He'd replied that she could save her breath because Cian MacKeltar obeyed no laws but his own.

She'd not found that particularly surprising.

His muscular body rippled beneath the thin cotton fabric. With those crimson-and-black tattoos licking up his neck and encircling both powerful biceps, those wicked-looking wrist cuffs, his long braids, and his imposing height and brawn, he looked downright dangerous.

Considering that the clothing fit him, she wondered how he'd gotten it off of whomever he'd gotten it off of. It must have been one heck of a fight.

Then there was the matter of the clothing he'd brought *her* . . . smelling of another woman's perfume. She had on hip-hugging *Lucky* jeans (with the cheeky words *Lucky You* stamped on the inside of her fly) that were X-treme Low Ride — as in, she sure wouldn't be sitting down with her backside facing a roomful of people anytime soon — and a white, V-necked sweater so snug that it would have revealed every line of her bra.

If only he'd brought her one.

Oh, well. Beggars couldn't be choosers. All she needed to do was get to her car and she could toss a jacket over it.

When he'd returned to the room and thrust the bundle of clothing into her hands, she'd exclaimed, *Where did you get —*

Hush, he'd said instantly. *Dress and move. We must accomplish as much as possible as quickly as possible. When the glass reclaims me, we will have time to talk then.*

Okay. She'd shrugged. She knew she couldn't extricate herself from her current problems. Maybe he could. He'd already managed to accomplish two things she'd not thought she'd had a snowball's chance in hell of accomplishing: body disposal and clothing procuring. Though she really would have liked a bra. Enthusiastic was hardly an adjective she would have applied to herself at the moment, but parts of her were acting downright perky with every step. She hoped she wouldn't need to run for any reason.

The lobby was nearly deserted at this early hour. As they stepped into the long, gleaming foyer, her attention was drawn by a ripped, steroid-bulked man standing at the front desk with his arm around a sultry blonde who didn't look nearly as distraught as he. Coincidentally, he looked like exactly the kind of guy who might wear an *Ironman* T-shirt.

The man was shouting furiously at two desk clerks. Good, Jessi thought. She couldn't shake the paranoid feeling that any moment now a police officer was going to appear out of thin air and arrest them. Any distraction was a welcome one. Hopefully the clerks would be so busy dealing with the irate brute that they wouldn't notice her and Cian skulking out. Although, with a six-and-a-half-foot-tall mirror tucked beneath his arm, nothing the six-and-a-half-foot Cian MacKeltar did remotely resembled skulking.

Cian's hand tightened on hers. "Hurry, lass."

She picked up the pace, jouncing jauntily along.

"I'm telling you, the man is one of your guests. I watched him go back up on the elevator. The son of a bitch took our clothes!" the man shouted.

Jessi blinked. Eyed the man and his wife. Glanced down at herself.

Glanced up at Cian.

He shrugged. "Not all of them. I left them their undergarments." When her brows rose, he added, "They were our size. We needed clothing. I suspected they had more, and look, they do. I ran into them in the elevator. Keep walking, lass. Move."

They were halfway across the lobby when the man abruptly threw his hands up in exasperation and whirled around.

Oh no, here it comes, Jessi thought, stiffening. *We're screwed. Now he'll call the cops. We're going to jail.*

"There he is!" the man roared furiously. "That's the prick who made my wife take off her clothes!"

Jessi noticed the sultry blonde wasn't looking too terribly upset by it, not nearly as upset as her husband seemed to be. She had a sudden vision of the pretty woman stripping down to her panties and bra in front of Cian and had the weirdest urge to go punch her. As if anything was the blond woman's fault.

"You will be silent and cease looking at us. The four of you will turn and face the wall. Now," Cian said coolly.

Jessi rolled her eyes. Obviously Cian MacKeltar had been some kind of aristocrat or member of the ruling class in his time. A feudal lord, maybe, perhaps even a relation to one of the ancient Pict kings, or Kenneth MacAlpin himself. He behaved like a tyrannical dictator, expecting the world to obey his slightest whims. *Cease looking at us,* indeed!

"Oh, please, you don't really think they're going to —" Jessi scoffed, only to break off in stunned disbelief.

Four people had just turned, as one, to face the wall behind the Check-In desk, without uttering so much as another peep. Not a curse, not a protest, not even an ill-concealed, disgruntled sigh.

She blinked at the bizarre sight. Then gaped up at Cian. Then back at the obedient little sheep.

"You will not attempt to follow us when we leave," Cian added. *"You will remain silent and unmoving until well after we're gone."*

His words reminded her of the way he'd dispatched Mark in the hallway, how he'd ordered the valets about and dominated the desk clerk when they'd checked in.

How was he doing it? What *was* Cian MacKeltar?

"Come, lass," he said.

She stood rooted to the ground for a moment, assessing herself suspiciously, trying to decide whether she was feeling, in the least little way, compelled in some strange way to obey him.

Nope.

She inched away from him, just to be sure. Tipped up her nose defiantly. Made a face at him.

Ducky. She felt just like her usual self, chock-full of free will.

But apparently *they* weren't, she thought, looking at people at the desk again.

"What did you do to them?" she demanded.

" 'Twould require a lengthy explana—"

"I know, I know," she interrupted peevishly, "and we don't have time, right? Fine. Just tell me this: Could you make them erase all record of my having been here from their computers?"

He looked perplexed a moment, then slow understanding dawned in his whisky eyes. "Ah, you mean so you cannot be linked to the blood-stained room! Aye, I can do that. You must direct me, though. There is much about your century that eludes me."

They hastened to the desk, where Jessi told him what to do.

He issued a series of terse commands to the clerks, and Jessi watched in abject fascination as they complied without hesitation, pulling up their files for Room 2112. They rescinded all credit transactions, deleted all records, and wiped her clean from the hotel's memory banks. Whatever he was doing and however he was doing it, the man packed a serious punch in the charismatic persuasion department.

There was one great big problem solved. Gone were her visions of oversized beetles and roaches, and calling her mother from some Third-World country.

As they were finishing up, Jessi stepped away from Cian and circled around him to stare at the bodybuilder and his wife. They were motionless, silent, staring at the wall. Their eyes had the same glazed, eerily vacant expression as the clerk's. Somehow she'd overlooked that before, too, probably because she'd always been too busy looking at the sexy Highlander to really notice much about the people around him.

"What did you do to them? How?"

Tucking the mirror back beneath his arm, he took her hand. "Not now, lass. We must make haste."

" 'Not now,' " she grumbled. "How come whenever I have questions, it's always 'not now'? Will it *ever* be now?"

12

"Can you not make greater haste?" Cian glanced at Jessica over the top of the mirror that was once again propped on its side between the auto's bucket seats.

He hated not knowing how long he had. It imbued everything with a heightened sense of urgency.

"Only if you can somehow order rush-hour traffic in Chicago on a rainy Friday morning to go somewhere else," she said with a roll of her eyes, waving a hand at the wall-to-wall cars packing the streets. Then she frowned at him over the mirror. "You can't, right?"

"Nay. Lass, you must go as fast as 'tis possible. Seize any opportunity to escape this pandemonium."

Returning to full immersion in his thoughts, he barely heard her sardonic "Aye, aye, sir."

The second attack had come long before he'd expected it. Truth be told, he'd not expected it at all. Not once they'd checked into her immense "hotel."

It had made him realize that he was at a tremendous disadvantage in her century, one for which he couldn't compensate. For, though he'd devoured tomes and papers and incessantly studied the world beyond Lucan's window — preparing, always preparing for any opportunity to take his chance at vengeance — though he knew of such things as computers and cars and airplanes and televisions, he knew also the world's current population. And the ninth-century Highlander in him had believed — as far as they'd traveled from her university into the heart of a city of such proportions — that they'd be as difficult to locate as a dust mote in a haystack the size of all of Scotland.

He'd been wrong. Dead wrong.

He simply couldn't fathom the bird's-eye view of her world. He might be familiar with the statistics, he might be cognizant of modern inventions, but he couldn't *feel* the way things were put together. All the book learning in the world wouldn't keep a man alive in battle. A warrior had to know and understand his terrain.

And he didn't.

He needed to get her somewhere he did.

Lucan would not take this woman. He would not let the bastard harm so much as a hair on her lovely head. "I doona ken how he found us," he muttered darkly.

There was a gusty sigh beside him. "I do. I'm a dick," Jessi informed him glumly.

He glanced over at her, lips twitching. Modern idioms were confounding, but at least he recognized them for what they were. "Nay, lass, I doona see that. Naught about you resembles any portion of my anatomy," he said playfully, seeking to lighten her mood and prevent her from dwelling on the horrifying scene that had played out so recently in front of her.

He'd never been so frustrated in his life as he'd felt, trapped inside the glass, having to push her, goad her by threatening to let her go to jail to get her to stop screaming, when all he'd really wanted to do was pull her into his arms and gentle her with his body. Take her cries with his kisses, comfort her. Remove the damned offending corpse from her environ.

Instead, he'd told her stories from his childhood to try to take her mind away and help her pass the time. Speaking soft and low, he's woven what Highland magic for her he could. He'd left out the grimmer memories, those of a lad at a tender ten years of age who'd been responsible for choosing battles and sides and sending men who'd been his father's closest companions, men who'd been as fathers to *him,* off to die.

A lad made laird in the Highlands at birth grew up fast. Or lost his clan. Or died. He accepted neither loss nor death easily.

He'd told her instead of summer days of sunshine and heather, of the icy pleasure of a cool loch on a hot day, of tales of his seven bonny sisters and their endless quests for husbands of whom he would approve.

At last, the panicked expression had receded from her eyes. She was no willy-nilly peahen. In fact, by the hour, his estimation of her continued to rise.

She was a fascinating woman.

And not for you, the tatters of his humanity warned.

Nay, not for him, he agreed with those tatters, glad they were tatters and not capable of mounting a compelling argument.

For he *would* have her. Despite the feeble protests of his honor, he was going to seduce her the moment he got her somewhere safe. He'd known since the night she'd licked him that he was going to make her his woman. Consequences be damned.

Why not? He already was.

Before disposing of the assassin's body, he'd searched the dead woman thoroughly. She'd carried nothing but weapons. He'd relieved her of a knife and two guns, which were now concealed in his boots.

The woman had not meant to kill his Jessica.

Had she, she would have used one of the guns. He knew a great deal about modern weapons; they fascinated him. He'd long itched to get his hands on a gun and test its capabilities. There was a ninth-century warrior in him that would never lose his love of a good battle and fine armament.

No, the assassin had intended to subdue his woman, not kill her. 'Twas the why of the needle, not the blade or the bullet.

The realization had given birth to a whole new wellspring of hatred for his long-time gaoler. Somehow Lucan had learned of Jessica St. James and wanted her alive. From time to time, Lucan had entertained himself with a woman before the Dark Glass, uncaring if she saw or heard Cian, because the woman didn't survive to tell of it anyway. Lucan liked to break things. He always had. The harder it was to break, the more he enjoyed it.

But those were dark thoughts. Thoughts from a time that would never be again, for he would never again be owned by Lucan Trevayne. Never again be forced to hang on that bastard's wall and watch an innocent woman sexually brutalized and murdered.

No matter the price of vengeance. Of freedom.

He'd come to terms with that price long ago.

"Don't you want to know what I did?" she was saying.

"Aye, I do." His gaze fixed on her profile. She nibbled her lower lip a moment and it made him abruptly rock-hard at the mere thought of her luscious mouth nibbling on *him*.

"I used a credit card." She sounded disgusted with herself. "I know in books and movies the bad guys always track you by credit or ATM transactions, but I thought that was just an exaggeration cultivated by the media to facilitate plot momentum. That if it could really be done, it would take time — like days or a week." She frowned up at him. "I mean, come on, how powerful is this Lucan-guy that he can find out where I've used my credit card within hours of my using it?"

He firmly corralled his lustful thoughts. He needed to understand such matters. They were imperative to his ability to keep her alive and safe from harm. "Explain to me about 'credit cards,' lass." He'd once seen an advertisement on television for such a thing, where club-wielding, painted warriors had poured down in a blood-thirsty horde on someone who'd chosen the wrong card, but he couldn't begin to see how using such a thing had betrayed them.

When she'd clarified its purpose, and ex-plained the records generated by the use of it, he snorted. Now he understood how Lucan had found them so quickly. Bloody hell — was there no such thing as privacy left in her world? Everything was con-nected to everything else by those com-puters of hers. All a man did and said was a matter of public or semipublic record, which was appalling to a mountain man who liked to keep his matters his own. "He's that powerful, lass. You may not use such things again. Have you no other form of coin?"

"Not enough to get us out of the country, which is what I'm beginning to think we need to do," she said gloomily.

Aye, she had the right of that.

The fact that he'd not even *known* she'd done something that could be traced — revealing them as clearly as an X on a map — because he'd not understood what a credit card was, meant he couldn't possibly hope to contain their exposure.

Not here, anyway.

Her twenty-first-century world had too many variables beyond his comprehension for him to control.

Which meant he had to take her back in time.

Och, nay, not literally — not through the *Ban Drochaid*, the stones of the White Bridge that the Keltar guarded; even *he* gave credence to the legend of the Draghar, having no wish to be possessed by the thirteen evil ancients — but figuratively.

That he could do.

If he could get her deep enough into the Highlands, then he could live with her for the next nineteen days by ninth-century means. Means untraceable by modern methods. He could shelter her in caves, warm her with his body, hunt for food, and feed her with his hands. In the Old Ways, time-honored ways in which a man had once seen to the needs of his woman.

All they had to do was somehow get across an ocean. Quickly and without leaving a trace.

Would Lucan look for him there?

Certainly, once he realized he was no longer in Chicago. Lucan knew him, nigh as well as he knew Lucan.

But there, in the wilderness, Cian would have more of an advantage. Even in the ninth century, Lucan had never been an outdoorsman, eschewing physical exertion in lieu of creature comforts. Och, aye, Cian would have the edge in his hills.

"Tell me everything you know about modern travel," he commanded. "Tell me about your airplanes, where they go, how often they go, where one may procure one, and how. Tell me in the greatest detail you can. Give me a bird's-eye view, lass. I need ken it all, even the most minuscule facts you might deem unimportant. I'm a ninth-century man, lass. Teach me as one."

Near noon, Jessi demanded they stop for food. She was starving. He might not need to eat, being immortal or whatever he was, but she sure did. The first time she'd ordered room service it hadn't come. The second time, the dishes had gotten splattered by blood. Aside from a PowerBar and a bag of peanuts she'd found in her back-pack, she'd had nothing else to eat in the past thirty-six hours.

Since leaving Chicago, Cian had grilled her intensively about everything from transportation to computers to accommodations to monetary transactions.

After listening for a short time, he'd told her that they dare not leave the country from O'Hare or Midway; that if Lucan had men watching for them anywhere, it would be at the two local airports.

Jessi still couldn't quite believe that they were actually going to try to leave the country, and had no idea how he thought they were going to pull it off.

He'd told her to drive them to the next nearest airport. She didn't know if Indianapolis really was the next nearest, but it was the only other airport she'd been able to figure out how to get to from a map.

They stopped to eat just east of Lafayette, Indiana, about forty-five minutes up I-65 from the airport.

The smell of deep-fried chicken and fries made her mouth water the moment they stepped inside Chick-fil-A. She always felt like she was doing cows a favor when she ate there; she loved those silly billboards along the highways with their EAT MOR CHIKIN cow campaign. From NEW DIET CRAZE: LOW-COW to EAT CHIKIN CUDDLE COWZ, the ads sporting black-and-white spotted cows clutching poorly penned placards promoting chicken consumption made her laugh out loud every time she drove past one.

I will procure food and we'll dine in the car, he'd insisted. *We must continue moving.*

She could just imagine how he planned to "procure" food. He'd probably leave the entire restaurant standing frozen until "well after we are away from here."

If I eat while driving, she'd disagreed, *I'll wreck. If I wreck, the mirror will probably break.* Her legs were stiff, she had to pee, and she was getting grumpy. *What would happen to you then?*

He'd looked stricken. *We'll dine within.*

She'd ordered six baskets of chicken fingers and wedges of crinkly fries, and now, perched at a brightly colored yellow-and-white table, was contently making headway into her second basket. He was halfway through his third.

"These resemble no chicken fingers I've ever seen, lass. And I saw a fair amount of chickens in my day. There was this wench

230

in the stables with the most remarkable . . . well, never mind that. You must grow fowl considerably larger now. I shudder to ponder the size of their beaks,"

"They're not really chicken *fingers,*" she hastened to explain, not caring for the imagery at all, as she dipped one into a tub of spicy barbecue sauce and snapped off a bite. She was going to stop there, she really was, but her treacherous lips had other ideas. " 'Most remarkable' what?"

" 'Tis of no import, lass." He devoured another chicken finger in two bites.

"Then why did you bring it up?" she said stiffly.

"I put it to rest, too, lass." There went two more fingers.

"No, you didn't. You left it hanging. Now it's hanging out there. I hate things hanging out there. Fix it. 'Remarkable' what?"

He dipped a potato wedge into ketchup and made short work of it. "Chickens, lass, she had remarkable chickens. What did you think I meant?"

Jessi's nostrils flared. She glared at him a moment, then looked away. Why did she even care? So, maybe the ninth-century bimbo had had remarkable eyes or legs or something. No way her breasts were better.

At that thought, she shrugged her jean-jacket off her shoulders and sat up straighter. And so what, anyway? The bimbo had been dead for eleven centuries. The only thing remarkable about her now was that anyone even remembered her at all.

"Back to the chickens, lass, if they're not fingers, why are they named thusly?"

"It's just a catchphrase," she said irritably, snapping off another bite. "Something some marketing guy came up with to make them more appealing."

"Your century finds the notion of eating fingers of chickens appealing? What of their toes?"

She took a sip of Coke. The chicken was suddenly dry as sawdust on her tongue. "I don't think anybody who orders them thinks, for even a minute, about fingers, or toes, any more than they think about little pink chicken nipples when they're eating chicken breasts —"

She broke off, eyes narrowing. His head was canted down, his hair shielding his face, but she could plainly see his shoulders shaking with silent laughter.

The Neanderthal was yanking her chain.

And she'd fallen for every bit of it.

After a moment, she shook her head and

snorted. He'd been poking fun not only at her century but himself, in a dry, subtle way. And she'd bought right into the stereotype he'd been feeding her: me-big-and-stupid-archaic-he-man. Her snort became a snicker, her snicker a laugh.

He glanced up sharply, his dark amber gaze fixing on her face. "I hoped to make you laugh," he said softly. "I've not seen much in the way of happiness in your eyes since we've crossed paths."

"No, I don't suppose you have," she agreed. "It's been a bit grim." They shared a companionable silence for a moment, across the table in Chick-fil-A.

"So was it really her chickens that were remarkable?"

Cian shook his head. "Nay, lass."

She scowled. "What, then? Come on, you're the one who brought her up."

He flashed her a devilish grin. "There was no wench in the stables, Jessica. I but wondered if you'd care."

Two could push for information, she thought mulishly a short time later as they hastened over soggy, slippery autumn leaves on their brisk walk across the parking lot toward her car. The October breeze ruffling her short dark hair held the promise of the long, cold midwestern winter to come. The chilly drizzle that had been falling steadily since they'd left Chicago had eased to a mist, but the sky was still leaden with thunderheads, threatening worse rain ahead. She fluffed her short curls back from her face and tugged her jean-jacket closer. In contrast to the cool clime, her temper was hot; she was steamed and humiliated that he'd gotten a rise out of her. She hardly knew the man, and she'd felt a vicious stab of jealousy over him. Twice. In a matter of hours. That wasn't like her at all. And the fact that she hardly knew the man was really beginning to bother her. She'd accepted that she was going to have to entrust herself to him to survive, but, by God, she wanted to know more about the man that she was entrusting herself to.

Who and what was Cian MacKeltar? And who and what was this Lucan Trevayne person who wanted her dead just because she'd seen his blasted artifact? They were both clearly more than mere men.

As they approached the car, Jessi stopped at the driver's-side door and scowled across the roof at him.

He arched an inquiring brow.

"I'm not going any farther until you answer a few of my questions."

"Jessica —"

"Don't 'Jessica' me," she said peevishly. "Five minutes is all I'm asking for. Surely five minutes won't get us killed. What are you, Cian?"

He assessed her a long moment, then shrugged one powerful shoulder. "I'm a Druid, lass."

" 'A Druid'?" She blinked. "You mean, as in one of those white-robe-wearing, mistletoe-loving guys that thought they could communicate with the otherworld by performing human sacrifices?" In her area of specialization, she was constantly encountering references to the mysterious, much-maligned priesthood. The famous Lindow Man, a late–Iron Age body found preserved in a Cheshire bog by peat cutters in 1984, evidenced signs of ritual murder and, with mistletoe pollen in his stomach, there'd been much speculation about his possible link with Druids.

He winced. "Ouch, is that how the world thinks of us now?"

"Pretty much. Are you telling me Druids were actually magicians of some kind? Like Merlin or something?"

He glanced guardedly around the parking

lot. "Jessica, there's magic all around you. People doona ken it because those who possess it take every precaution to conceal it. Magic has always been, and will always be."

Her eyes narrowed. "So this Lucan guy is also a Druid?"

"He was once a Druid. He became a dark sorcerer."

A week ago, she would have laughed herself silly at anyone who'd claimed such things existed. She would have asked them about lions and tigers and bears and ruby slippers with built-in teleportation devices. Now, resting her elbows on the wet roof of her car, propping her chin on her hands, she only sighed and said, "Okay, so what's the difference?"

"A Druid is born with magic in his blood. A dark sorcerer's magic is acquired via rigorous study and apprenticeship to black magycks, enhanced by rituals and spells. A Druid respects the innate nature of things and permits the universe its pattern. A dark sorcerer perverts the nature of things to his own aims, changing the universe's pattern without thought to ramifications. A Druid seeks knowledge to heal and nurture. A sorcerer seeks dangerous alchemy to transform and control. A

Druid-turned-dark-sorcerer is far more powerful than either a mere sorcerer or a mere Druid."

"Well, if he's a Druid-turned-dark-sorcerer and you're just a Druid, and a Druid-turned-dark-sorcerer is so much more powerful, then just how do you plan to defeat — oh! Crimeny! Shit!"

Understanding belatedly dawning, she backpedaled away from him, butting up against the rain-slicked side of the car parked parallel to hers. "I can be so dense sometimes," she breathed. "Because *you're* one of the bad guys, too, aren't you? *You* turned dark sorcerer, too, didn't you? It's the only way it makes sense."

His whisky eyes narrowed. "Get in the car, Jessica," he said softly.

She shook her head. "Uh-uh. No way. I'm not done yet. You still haven't told me about that commanding thing you do. When you tell people to do things, and they just do it — what is that, anyway?"

A muscle in his jaw worked and he regarded her a long, silent moment. Then, " 'Tis the Druid art of Voice. Some call it the Voice of Power." He saw no need to tell her that others called it the Voice of Death, if the Druid was powerful enough. And he was. Though he'd not known he could kill with his tongue until it had been too late and he'd already killed with his tongue. " 'Tis a spell of compulsion, lass. Now get in the car. The storm worsens."

As if to support his words, the rain chose that moment to turn into a steady, soaking drizzle and a boom of thunder crashed overhead.

But Jessi wasn't going to let an inconvenient storm interrupt her now. She had a small storm of her own brewing. This compelling thing bothered her. A lot. "Can you make people do things they don't want to do? Like bad things that would seriously go against their will? Are they even aware of it when you're doing it to them? Do they remember when it's over?" she demanded.

The muscle leapt in his jaw again. "Get in the car, Jessica. I'm trying to keep you alive," he said coolly.

"What if I refuse?" she said just as coolly. "Will you *force* me into the car? *Compel* me into it? Now that I think about it, I'm surprised you haven't already tried to use this Voice of yours on me. Why bother being nice to anyone when you could just command anything you want? Geez, you wouldn't even have to seduce a woman, you could just order her to —" She broke off abruptly, eyes widening.

"Get. In. The. Car. Jessica."

"Oh, God, you *did* try it on me," she exclaimed. "You tried it the second I set you free. You tried to make me kiss you and show you my breasts. Didn't you?"

His dark, chiseled face was a fortress. If he felt any emotion at all, it was completely concealed. Gaze remote, he inclined his head, a single time.

Behind him, lightning flashed, brilliant and jagged, against the grim, steely Indiana sky.

A short, caustic laugh escaped her. "And it didn't work, did it? For some reason, it doesn't work on me at all, does it?"

He gave a single shake of his head. "None of my magyck does."

Jessi stared at him, struggling to take in this new information that put such a different slant on the way she'd so naively believed things to be. She'd been walking around thinking that the good guy was keeping her safe from the bad guy.

Only to find out that there were no good guys in Jessi St. James's world.

Just bad and badder.

She wanted to know exactly how bad. "So how far would you have taken it, Mister Poor-me-I'm-trapped-in-a-mirror-dark-sorcerer? If it had worked, if I'd 'removed my woolen and shown you my breasts,' how far would you have pushed?"

"How the bloody hell far do you think?"

"I'm asking *you.* How far?" she demanded.

"I haven't fucked in eleven hundred and thirty-three years, Jessica," he said flatly. "I am a man."

"How far?" she repeated frostily.

"All the way, woman. All the frigging way. *Now get in the damned car.*" A flash of lightning, followed by a booming thunderclap, punctuated his final words, as if Nature herself conspired with him.

Jessi stared at him in silence, rain dripping down her face, splattering on her chest, pondering her options. Being brutally honest with herself.

She could walk away now. Try it on her own. See if she could manage to disappear for the next nineteen days.

She was being hunted by a bona fide, ninth-century sorcerer who wanted her dead.

She was being kept alive by another bona fide ninth-century sorcerer who wanted to have sex with her and was willing to use magic to score.

Her life or her "virtue."

It bore considering that it was a virtue

she'd very nearly given him of her own accord.

Granted, she'd hardly been in her right mind at the time, but still.

She got in the damned car.

13

They were flying at a cruising altitude of 36,000 feet above the Atlantic Ocean when the Dark Glass reclaimed him.

At least they hadn't been about to have sex this time, so Jessi wasn't left with a bad case of hostile hormones, and aghast at herself for yet another appalling lapse in moral fiber.

She glanced hastily around when he vanished, and caught several other passengers doing double takes. It didn't surprise her to discover other people were looking straight at him when he disappeared. He was just that kind of man, the kind people watched. Some because they wondered what it would be like to have sex with such a gorgeous, dangerous-looking hunk of testosterone (the category she was in), others because they were concerned about their purses, wallets, or lives (the category she was in).

None of the onlookers said a word. Assuming any of them believed it had genuinely happened, not one of them appeared in any hurry to talk about it.

She smothered a dry laugh. *Been there, done that, thought I was going nuts, too, the first few times I saw him.*

Tugging the worn blue airline blanket up to her chin, she pretended nothing was amiss, that she'd boarded alone, and been alone all this time. She'd been braced for him to disappear. He'd told her before they'd embarked that the Dark Glass would no doubt reclaim him long before they got to Scotland.

Scotland. Crimeny. She was on her way out of the country! Life as she'd known it — work, school, and all her tidily scheduled plans — were slipping away from her at the astonishing rate of 565 miles per hour.

She'd not believed they were going to be able to pull it off until they'd arrived at the Indianapolis airport and he'd proceeded to give her a mind-boggling display of his formidable "talents."

He'd used his "Voice" to coerce airport employees to crate and ship the mirror to Edinburgh. Unwilling to generate any records of their passage, he'd bypassed procuring tickets, and instead "persuaded" their way through security, past armed officers. There'd not been a direct flight available to Scotland, and he'd refused to go through London, as it would take them too close to Lucan for his comfort, so he'd "Voiced" them onto a Boeing 747 bound first for Paris, showing only his palm as necessary documentation, accompanied by terse commands.

She'd watched in abject amazement. Quite simply *anything* the man said, people believed and obeyed. Mutely, docilely, blankly. He'd used a few "forgetting" commands as well, though he'd told her they were tricky things and he was employing mild ones only to buy them all the time possible. He'd told her that a true forgetting spell took much time and was risky, as the mind endeavored to retain the imprints it bore, and stripping away one memory frequently damaged many others. It was a damage he was clearly reluctant to be the cause of, which she found interesting for a Druid-turned-dark-sorcerer.

By the time they'd boarded, and dropped into emergency-exit seats (two cooing female flight attendants had much-too-sweetly for her taste volunteered to rearrange things so the six-and-a-half-foot sexy Scotsman could "stretch out his legs a bit," *Grrr . . .*),

Jessi'd had a pretty darn good idea why his "talents" didn't work on her.

She'd actually felt it *trying* to work on her.

Each time he'd laid the compulsion on thick, her head had itched inside, just above the metal plate splicing her skull together, the same way it had when she'd first freed him and he'd been attempting to compel her.

It felt as if his commands were buzzing up against her metal plate, making it vibrate beneath her skin. She couldn't begin to comprehend the mechanics of it, she just knew it somehow shielded her from his magic.

Thank heavens! For the first time in her life, she was grateful she'd taken that horrendous, skull-splitting fall.

All the way, woman, he'd said back in the rainy parking lot of Chick-fil-A. Meaning he would have used Voice on her to have sex with her.

It had perturbed her. Deeply.

Until she'd realized he was lying.

Maybe he believed he would have pushed her all the way, but she didn't.

She judged people by their actions, not their words. And his actions just didn't support his words. Big bark — little bite.

Even his commands to get them on board the plane had been tempered. He'd wielded the least coercion necessary to accomplish their goals.

Bottom line was: Any man who would have used magic to have sex with her against her will would simply have changed tactics when magic had failed, and raped her with his brutally superior strength.

Especially after eleven centuries of enforced celibacy.

Cian was nearly six feet six inches of pure muscle. He'd had multiple opportunities to do anything he wanted to her.

And he'd not harmed her in any way.

Tucking her legs up, she snuggled deeper into the blanket. The lights were low, it had been yet another long day, and the steady hum of the engines was lulling her to sleep.

She closed her eyes, pondering the power he had — the Druid art of Voice, he'd called it — trying to imagine what it would be like to have the ability to make anyone do anything you wanted them to do, merely by telling them to do it.

She was blown away by the possibilities.

And by the awesome responsibility.

Druid-turned-dark-sorcerer? She wasn't so sure she believed that. Oh, maybe a little bad, but the man wasn't evil. In fact, he seemed a near paragon of restraint, in light of all he was probably capable of doing.

She yawned, wondering how young he'd been when he'd realized such a thing was within his means. "Voice" meant consummate power, consummate freedom. It meant being able to live with absolute impunity.

No excuses, no apologies necessary.

If it were her gift, she thought drowsily, she could hop on a plane anytime she wanted, fly to England, and make them let her pet Stonehenge. Or she could go to Ireland and visit the museums and touch things. Take things home with her, for heaven's sake!

Or, she mused dreamily, she could go to a bank, make them give her millions of dollars, buy herself houses in ten different countries, and spend her life playing on pristine white beaches in the sun. Or, the heck with money, she could just go to those countries and make people *give* their houses to her. She wondered how many people Voice could control at any one time, and for how long. Surely there were limits.

Still, "What a ridiculous amount of power," she murmured on a sleepy sigh.

The world would, quite literally, be one's playground.

Still, even with it, he'd somehow gotten trapped in a mirror for centuries on end.

Strong warrior's body, yet gentle hands. Formidably endowed with magic, yet trapped.

What an enigma he was!

It occurred to her, as she drifted off to sleep, that it should probably worry her a lot that — even in the middle of the utter chaos her life had become — he was an enigma she was greatly looking forward to deciphering.

An áit a bhfuil do chroi is ann a thabharfas do chosa thú. (Your feet will bring you to where your heart is.)

— OLD SCOTS SAYING

PART 2

SCOTLAND

14

THE GOD-AWFUL HOUR OF 3:00 A.M.
EDINBURGH AIRPORT
SUNDAY, OCTOBER 15

"No, I don't have a claim ticket," Jessi told the woman behind the desk, for the fifth time, beyond exasperated. "I keep telling you that. But I can describe it. Exactly. Every tiny little detail. Both crate and contents. Now how could I possibly know that such a crate even existed, not to mention what was inside it, unless it was mine?"

"And I keep telling *you,*" the woman huffed, "that nothing gets claimed without a claim ticket, young lady."

"You don't understand, I need that crate," Jessi said urgently.

"I understand perfectly," the fifty-something, ash-blonde replied, without a flicker of emotion on her Botox-smoothed face, but with an unmistakable sneer in her voice. "You want to collect something for

253

which you have no claim ticket. How would you feel if I permitted someone else to claim *your* package with no claim ticket? How could we hope to control our packages at *all* if we permitted such unauthorized claimings to occur? That's why, young lady, we give claim tickets in the first place. One ticket retrieves one corresponding package. You may file a missing claim ticket claim, if you wish."

"How long will it take me to get my package if I file a missing claim ticket claim?"

"Processing a missing claim ticket claim can take several weeks to several months."

Jessi was not pessimistic by nature, but she could have sworn a note of smug satisfaction had just entered the woman's voice, and she suddenly had no doubt any claim *she* filed would lean toward the several months mark. For whatever reason, the woman didn't like her and didn't want to help her.

And without the mirror, Jessi was doomed. She had a whopping forty-two dollars and seventeen cents in her purse. Oh, sure, she had a credit card, but the moment she used it Lucan would know exactly where she was. She needed the bottomless bank account of Cian MacKeltar's deep, sexy, magical voice.

One way or another, she had to get the mirror back. And it was pretty clear that this woman had no intention of facilitating things. Some people were problem-solvers and some people were problem-compounders. This woman was a Compounder with a capital C.

Jessi muttered a nearly inaudible thank you and turned hurriedly away before she said something she'd regret.

Sighing, she shifted her backpack to her *other* sore shoulder, trudged back down the long hallway, out into the main part of the airport, and slumped wearily into a hard plastic chair.

She glanced at her watch, slipped it from her wrist, and moved the hour hand forward six hours. It was a little after nine in the morning, Edinburgh time.

Well, she consoled herself, *the bright side of things is that he'll definitely be able to come out now, if I can just get to him.* It had been over twenty-four hours in both time zones since he'd last been free and, drat it all, she actually *missed* the domineering barbarian. Missed his annoying testosterone overload, missed knowing that any minute now he might give her one of

255

those kisses that vacuumed her brain out through her ear and turned her into a vapid little sex-kitten.

Leaning back in the torture-chamber of a chair, she rubbed her eyes and took a deep breath.

"Flight 412 leaving Edinburgh for London will depart . . ." a woman's lilting voice spoke brightly from the speaker above her.

Leaving Edinburgh. She was in Scotland! The fabulous, five-thousand-year-old stone furniture of Skara Brae was near. The incredible Rosslyn Chapel was a mere eight miles from Edinburgh. The ruins of Dunnottar and countless other ancient treasures loomed just beyond the airport doors.

And she was beginning to think she might never make it that far. Her connecting flight from Paris had landed five hours ago.

And she'd been trying to get her hands on the mirror ever since.

It had taken her nearly an hour just to find the idiotic Special Items Claim Pickup Office.

It hadn't been anywhere near baggage, as she'd expected, but down a long hallway, tucked back in the rear of the airport, accessible only through a window that opened onto a long counter built into the wall. It had been so deserted that she'd not believed she was in the right place until she'd glimpsed the tiny handwritten sign perched on the corner of the desk. It seemed almost as if they *wanted* to keep the unclaimed items. Maybe, she thought cynically, they auctioned them off to employees or something when their time was up.

There wasn't even an exterior door into the office; apparently staff gained access some other way.

If there's no name on the crate, where will it go when it arrives in Edinburgh? Cian had asked, prior to compelling the airline employees to crate and ship it.

It would have to go to unclaimed baggage. She couldn't imagine it going anywhere else. Without a name or a return shipping address, they certainly couldn't send it back. She'd learned that lesson herself, trying to get rid of the crate. She also knew that airports were required to hold items, even unmarked ones, for a certain number of days. She'd lost her luggage once, between home in Maine and school in Chicago, and by the time it had resurfaced, there'd not been a single identifying tag on it.

If you go to this "unclaimed baggage" place and can identify it, will they give it to you? Cian had pressed.

I don't know, she'd replied.

We'll have to take the chance. I'll not leave any records of our travel. If you can but get into the same room with my crate, and say the spell, I can break free and use Voice to get us out of there. Jessica, lass, I'm sorry 'tis not a foolproof plan. You'll have to improvise.

Improvisation hadn't seemed such a daunting task back in Indianapolis. But then she'd been feeling weirdly invincible walking along beside him, and they'd both mistakenly thought the crate would be somewhere that she could *see* it, if not actually collect it.

She groaned, wishing she had a single ounce of Cian's incredible powers of Voice to use on Ms. Erase-My-Face at the Special Items Claim Desk.

Then again, she mused, she wasn't entirely certain she would want that kind of power, if given the opportunity. It would certainly be a test of just how good a person really was deep down.

Shaking her head, she pushed to her feet. She would kill a bit of time grabbing a cup of coffee and a croissant, then she would trudge back down the long silent corridor and try again.

Maybe by then the woman would be on break and somebody else would be working.

The woman was not only *not* on break by the time Jessi got back to the Special Items pickup window; she got an expression when she saw Jessi walking toward the desk again.

It was hard to pick up on it, unnoticeable as it was from more than a few feet away, but if Jessi peered really hard, she could see the faintest pucker of a muscle trying to contract between the woman's brows.

Not good.

"Could you just bring it out here and let me see it?" Jessi asked the woman. "Just let me make sure it's okay and it's really here, then I swear I'll go away and leave you alone. I'll fill out your forms and go through the red tape. Just let me make sure it actually got here. I'm worried about it. Please? Could I please just see it?"

"There are *no* exceptions," the woman said with a sniff.

"But I —"

"Which word didn't you understand? It must have been the 'no.' You are *so* typical. People like you *always* think they should be exceptions."

Jessi blinked. "People like me?" she echoed, stymied as to just what kind of "people" this woman thought she was.

"Yes. People like *you*." The woman's gaze dropped to her breasts. "I'm sure you've gotten used to manipulating men to get them to do whatever you want, but you can't manipulate me. And no men work this desk, young lady, so don't even *think* about trying to come back at another time. I've already warned my coworkers about you. No one is going to fall for your shenanigans. You're going to have to follow the rules for a change, little missy, just like everyone else."

Jessi blinked, rendered speechless by the unfair attack. She'd never used her looks to get anywhere in life, and if they'd ever helped her, she'd certainly not been aware of it.

Without another word, Stone-face inclined her pinched nose, moved away from the window, and made a big show of dismissing her. After a moment, she began typing busily away at a computer terminal with lethal-looking orange nails.

Jessi swallowed a little growl. *Focus,* she told herself, *and not on Stone-face's un-*

warranted nastiness. She is not your problem. Getting the mirror back is.

Backing up a few steps, she scanned the counter.

The mirror *had* to be nearby. It just had to. If one came to this window to claim special items, logic dictated the items would be stored close at hand for the purpose of expediency. One would present their ticket and the item would be brought to the counter. Which seemed to imply that the items had to be somewhere behind the counter.

She pushed up on tiptoes and glanced over the desk. Stone-face was still making a big show of ignoring her, which was just fine with Jessi. There were no crates stacked back there that she could see, and the little room, which was about twenty feet wide and maybe ten feet deep, didn't look as if it was large enough for more than three or four employees to stand lined up at the desk.

On the left wall hung a gaudily framed, turbulent seascape, adjacent to a phone marked SECURITY. The rear wall was dotted by small paintings of ships at sea, interspersed with various official-looking certificates in utilitarian black frames.

Aha — there! On the right wall, a half-

261

opened door revealed a long, brightly lit corridor stretching off into the distance.

"My crate is down that hallway, isn't it?" Jessi exclaimed. She didn't expect an answer from the woman. She knew she'd have to get it from her face.

The woman glanced up, the hint of a muscle contracting between her brows.

Yes — Cian was close! *Improvisably* close.

I can do this, I can do this, I know I can, she told herself. She stared down at the floor for a few seconds, steeling her nerve. Then she turned and began walking away from the counter.

Behind her, the woman muttered snidely, "About time. And good riddance to you, you spoiled little —"

The rest of it was muttered too low for Jessi to hear, but she didn't need to, she'd already picked up on the general gist of it. *Oh, you are going to be sooo surprised,* she thought just as snidely. She didn't mind people getting upset with her when she'd done something to deserve it, but she'd not done a thing to earn this woman's animosity, other than being young and curvy. And she couldn't help being either of those things. It wasn't as if either of those things had ever gotten her anywhere in her life. Hard work had. Boobs certainly hadn't. In fact, were she pushed to divvy up percentages, she'd attribute 90 percent to aggravation and 10 percent to pleasure.

Wiggling her shoulders to make sure her backpack was snug enough, she glanced behind her, assessed the distance to and height of the counter, and took a deep, fortifying breath.

Then she whirled around, took a running leap, and catapulted herself into the air.

She managed to pump up more speed with her short dash than she actually needed, and upon clearing the exterior wall of the counter, she couldn't check her forward momentum. Skidding pell-mell over the veneered surface on her hands and knees, she crashed to the floor, taking down two mainframes and a stack of manuals with her. She hit the floor so hard it made her teeth *clack* together.

"Oh!" the woman shrieked. "Out! Out! *Out!* You are not allowed back here! Only airport employees are permitted behind the desk!"

Jessi didn't waste breath replying. Scrambling to her feet, she clambered over monitors and manuals, and pushed through the half-opened door. Her heart was pounding and adrenaline was rushing through her veins, making her feel shaky, yet intensely, aggressively focused. It was no wonder some people got addicted to adrenaline rushes.

"I'm calling security!" the woman screeched after her, snatching the phone from the wall.

"You just do that . . ." Jessi dropped her voice, but despite her best efforts, "bitch" didn't come out quite as *sotto voce* as she'd intended. Oops. Darn it, now she was going to have to outrun security too!

But the woman's nastiness worked to her advantage this time. Apparently, Stone-face had been secretly itching to take matters into her own hands and Jessi's expletive was just enough to push her over the edge.

Slapping the phone back on the wall, Stone-face shot through the door after her. "I don't need security, I can deal with you myself, you brazen little hussy!" Sharp orange talons closed on the fabric of Jessi's backpack, yanking her to a halt. "You are *not* going back there!"

Jessi dug in her heels, scanning the corridor. It was roughly a hundred yards long, with a maze of hallways branching off it, and doors dotting both the left and right sides.

At the far end of the corridor, two tall steel doors gleamed, the kind that looked like they might open onto a warehouse. Near those doors, several carts and a small front-loader waited.

That would be where the mirror was, then, through those double doors.

She needed it. It was nonnegotiable.

And this red-tape-wielding, small-mean-souled twit clutching a fistful of her backpack was all that was standing between her and the small matter of her continued survival.

Her life depended on that crate.

And there was no other way she could get to it.

She twisted her shoulders, yanking her backpack from the woman's grasp. When it tumbled down her arm, she caught the straps of it in her hand.

Bracing herself, she gulped yet another fortifying breath. She was going to need this one.

Muttering a silent prayer that it would work and not actually injure the woman beyond a temporary black eye, she swung around and coshed the woman in the side of the head with her thirty-eight-pound-Krispy-Kremes-earning backpack.

Much to her relief — she wasn't entirely certain about doing it twice, no matter how nasty the witch was — Stone-face's eyes glazed, she swayed woozily, and sank limply to the floor.

Glancing hastily around, Jessi spied a door labeled "Supplies" down the hall. Grabbing the woman's feet, she hooked her ankles beneath her armpits and hurriedly slid her down the polished tile floor.

It took her a few moments to wedge her in with all the brooms and mops and cleaning supplies, but she managed it. Closing the door, she examined the handle. There was no way to lock it. That sucked.

And meant she had to hurry. She couldn't imagine the woman would stay out for very long.

Heart pounding, Jessi dashed off for the double doors and Cian.

Lucan slammed his fist through the silk-papered plaster wall of his study.

Again.

And a third time.

Blood beaded swiftly across his shredded knuckles and just as swiftly disappeared. The skin healed, not shiny and pink, but it healed.

He turned back toward his desk, glanced up at the offending darker rectangular spot on the wall, and snarled at the speaker-phone, "Tell me again exactly what they said. In detail."

"None of them recalled many details, Mr. Trevayne, sir," Hans replied from the receiver. "Just that they saw a tall, tattooed man with dark braids carrying a large, gold-framed mirror, accompanied by a young, attractive woman, walking through the Sheraton's lobby on Friday morning. If the two of them stayed at the hotel, all records have been erased. One of the guest rooms was found with fresh human blood on the carpet, drapes, and furniture, but the hotel has no record of having assigned that room to anyone for several nights, and no body has been found."

Son of a bitch, the worst was true. Eve was most certainly dead and the High-lander was being aided and abetted by the St. James woman. They'd united efforts against him.

And he had less than seventeen days to find them.

"Were you able to learn where they went from there?"

"No, Mr. Trevayne, sir, we've not been able to ascertain that. We're working on

267

it. Do you have any ideas, sir?"

Lucan rubbed his jaw. Where would Cian MacKeltar go, now that he had someone beyond the glass who was willing to help him get there? That was the determining factor, after all. The rules of their little game had changed dramatically. Not once in a thousand years had Lucan ever imagined that such an improbable sequence of events might ever come to pass — that something might shatter his unbreakable wards; that he might be out of the country at the time; that a thief might break into his home and steal the glass; that the glass might end up in the hands of someone willing to help the Keltar.

It reeked of preposterous synchronicity.

Nevertheless, it had happened.

Where would the Keltar go? There was no doubt in Lucan's mind: home to his Highlands, of course. The mountain-man would move heaven and earth to walk on Scots soil again, especially now.

It had been a long time since Lucan had visited the hills above Inverness. For countless generations, after he'd imprisoned Cian in the Dark Glass, he'd kept close tabs on the Keltar bloodline.

He'd wanted to be certain Cian's mother had done as she'd sworn in exchange for the continued health and well-being of her seven precious daughters: sealed away all Keltar lore from future generations and stricken her son's name from all Keltar annals — thereby preventing any future Keltar from nursing a blood-grudge and trying to free their ancestor.

But by the early fourteen hundreds, when his sources had confirmed that the MacKeltar — to the last man, woman, and child — believed the legendary Cian nothing more than a myth, Lucan had quit watching and quit caring.

He'd turned his attentions elsewhere, immersed himself in the building of his empire and his search for the remaining Dark Hallows.

Time and success had made him careless. He'd not been challenged in so long that complacency had dulled his edge.

Christ, seventeen days! It was unthinkable! He was so near to achieving his goals. He couldn't afford these idiotic distractions!

"Scotland, Hans," Lucan clipped at the phone. "Search Inverness. I suspect he'll bypass civilization and head for the hills. Find out if any MacKeltar still live in the area and let it be known I'm offering five million to whoever gets me that mirror, ten for the mirror *and* the woman. However, I must be informed the instant the mirror is located, and kept constantly apprised of its whereabouts. There's another ten million in it for you, Hans, if you bring this to successful completion within a week."

"Yes, sir, Mr. Trevayne, sir! I'll let the others know, sir. I'll get every man on it. I'll take care of this for you. You have my personal guarantee, sir!"

Lucan stared into space for a long time after he terminated the call. What was twenty-five million to him? Nothing. He'd wearied of wealth centuries ago. He wanted what he'd always wanted: more power.

He was so close to the culmination of all his dreams, a hairsbreadth away from finally possessing the Unseelie Dark Book. From finally being the greatest sorcerer the world had ever known, both mortal and Fae.

He should have seen these complications coming. He knew that when a man poised on the brink of achieving true greatness, the world tested him. It had happened to him before. It would happen again. He should have been better prepared this time. He would be in the future.

He, Lucan Myrddin Trevayne, fathered by an unknown Druid on a whore of a mother who'd lain with dozens of Druids from all over Great Britain during the course of a three-day council held in the tiny Welsh village of Cochlease, eleven hundred and seventy-eight years ago, had risen high above the ignominy of his birth and was *this close* to becoming powerful beyond his wildest dreams, able to command even the legendary Tuatha Dé Danaan themselves.

His earliest years had not been easy. He'd struggled, he'd worked, he'd studied, he'd traveled the world seeking knowledge and power. He'd transformed himself from the bastard son of a whore other Druids had refused to recognize, to a man respected and deeply feared by the mightiest among Druids and sorcerers alike.

It had been during those early years of travel that he'd learned of the Dark Hallows. He'd managed to secure rubbings from three sacred pages of the incredible Dark Book at the tender age of twenty-eight. He'd devoted the next eight years of his life to deciphering the encrypted rubbings.

Upon succeeding, he'd learned much from those rubbings, including the location of the Dark Glass of the Unseelie Fae, as well as the necessary tithing and the binding spells to use it. In exchange for the

271

triple boon of the sacrifice of innocent blood, the ensorcellment of a captive, and a recurring tithe of pure gold, it bestowed eternal life.

It was rumored that Merlin himself had once possessed the Dark Glass, until it had been seized from him by an army a thousand strong and a mysterious group of Irish holy men.

Unfortunately, knowing where it was and how to use it hadn't been enough.

Lucan had tried four times to get to the Dark Glass. And four times he'd failed. The final time, he'd barely escaped with his life, and he'd been forced to concede that he simply didn't possess the power necessary to get past the guardians.

He'd spent the next seven years of his life looking for someone who did. He'd found him in Cian MacKeltar.

He'd hated the Highlander on first sight.

15

Jessica lay facedown in a pool of blood, her glossy black curls wetly matted to her head.

She was bled white, stiff and icy in death. Her spine was drawn in a painful bow, her right leg splayed at an impossible angle. Her left arm was bent awkwardly over her head, the underside of the wrist down, the palm twisted gruesomely up. Her other hand was clenched in a bloody fist.

It was obvious she'd suffered as she'd died. Not just pain. Horrific pain.

She'd cried out for him.

She'd never stopped believing he would save her.

He'd told *her that he would; that he would be her shield — he'd vowed to stand between her and all others.*

He'd failed.

Pounding the wall with his fists, Cian tossed back his head and howled like an animal. The sound echoed from walls of stone, ricocheted off a stone ceiling, bounced back at him from a stone floor.

One thousand one hundred and thirty-three years had not driven him insane.

But the past two days had managed to accomplish what eleven centuries had not.

She was out there, his Jessica, with only her wits and will to rely upon. And he was trapped in the mirror, unable to protect her.

From the moment the Dark Glass had reclaimed him, the terrible possibilities had begun playing themselves, with chilling detail, in never-ending repetition through his mind.

An assassin had slipped onto the plane and into the seat behind them, then taken her captive the moment she'd disembarked. She was, even now, drugged and on her way to London.

Nay — the bloody frigging plane had simply plummeted from the air, crashing thousands of miles to the ocean below, sinking like a stone. He didn't understand how the hell it stayed up there, anyway. It might have wings, but they didn't flap. (This was the kindest of his hells; she suffered no indignities and death came more swiftly in this than any others.)

Nay — when his mirror was next un-covered, it would be to discover himself once again hung upon Lucan's study wall, staring down at his beautiful Jessica, tied and gagged, being raped and tortured by his ancient enemy.

Nay — when his mirror was next un-covered, he would see only Lucan's hated face and the bastard would do the same thing he'd done to him with word of Cian's mother and sisters — never utter a word about Jessica again, no matter how Cian pleaded, leaving him to imagine the worst of all possibles *every single day* for the rest of his eternal existence.

Each hellish possibility was worse than the last, slicing like a sword into his gut.

Cian slumped down against the wall, hands fisted, jaw clenched.

Waiting. Waiting.

"Aha — *there* you are!" Jessi exclaimed brightly, as she rounded the corner. "Finally!" A dozen yards away, at the end of the very last row (did it ever work any other way?) with the words **UNAUTHORIZED ENTRY** emblazoned in red across it, be-tween a few dozen smaller stampings of the word *FRAGILE,* the tall plywood crate perched on end.

She glanced anxiously at her watch. It had taken her forever to find him. She was afraid that any minute now Stone-face was going to come crashing through the doors behind her, with half of Edinburgh's Airport Security in tow.

When she'd first pushed through those double doors, she'd expected to find a small storehouse, not an industrial warehouse that stretched the length of a football field, with tiers that climbed all the way to a forty-foot ceiling, and row after row of numbered boxes, crates, and assorted packages.

She'd wasted precious time searching aisles of numbered items, before deducing that the unnumbered items lacking tickets were probably stored at the far end of the humongous building because the staff knew no one would be collecting them anytime soon.

The crate must have been the most recent arrival, as it was all the way down in the final spot at the end of the row. Sprinting toward it, she called out the summoning spell. *"Lialth bree che bree, Cian MacKeltar, drachme se-sidh!"*

Nothing happened.

She repeated the chant, expecting light to blaze from the cracks, and the crate to begin rocking or something.

Again nothing.

Drawing to a breathless halt in front of it, she pressed her ear to the wood panel. "Cian?" she called. She glanced warily over her shoulder. Despite the vastness of the warehouse and her apparent solitude within it, she was nonetheless reluctant to make a commotion. Squaring her shoulders, she opted for something more than an exclamation but less than a shout: *"Cian!"*

She pressed her ear to the plywood again. Was that a muffled roar? She listened a moment. Sure sounded like it. Yup, there was another.

She drew back and pounded on the crate with her fists. "Cian, I'm here! Can you hear me? Come on! Get your butt out here *now!* We have to hurry. I don't know how long we have before they find us. *Lialth bree che bree, Cian MacKeltar, drachme se-sidh!*"

Total silence.

Just when she'd begun to think something must have gone seriously wrong en route, or she had the wrong crate or something, brilliant light blazed from the cracks, the warehouse felt even larger than it was, and she heard the rustle of inner packing.

A powerful fist splintered through the wood half an inch from her left ear.

Blinking, Jessi scrambled back.

He heard her, calling him.

At first Cian thought her voice was but another figment of his tortured imaginings, then it snapped impatiently, "Get your butt out here *now!*" and he laughed aloud. She was his prickly Jessica; they'd made it to Scotland, and she was freeing him again.

Pushing against masses of packing and cushion-wrap, he shoved from the mirror and turned his body into a battering ram.

He crashed a fist through the wood, then another, kicked and pounded at the crating with all the caged fury and impotent rage that had been riding him for two endless days.

He demolished the front of the crate, ripping it to shreds with his bare hands.

When he glanced up from the splinters, it was to find Jessica backed up flush to a shelving unit, staring at him, her face pale.

"Och, Christ, woman," he hissed. Devouring the space between them in two strides, he cupped her jaw with one big hand, tipped her face up, and claimed her mouth in a kiss. Once, twice, three times. Then he drew back and glared down at her. "I thought you were dead. I couldn't *fucking* get out of there and I thought of a thousand things I'd done wrong and imagined a million deaths for you. Kiss me, Jessica. Show me you're alive."

Jessi blinked up at Cian, stunned.

Kiss me, Jessica, his words hung in the air. *Show me you're alive.*

When he'd come crashing out of the crate, for a moment she'd genuinely thought he'd gone crazy, so stark and inhuman was the expression in his eyes. Then he'd turned a look on her that had scorched right through her clothing, her skin, seared all the way to her bones, and before he'd even spoken, she'd known it had been fear for *her* that had put that wildness in him.

She'd been stunned. She'd been secretly thrilled. Because, although she'd been refusing to admit it even to herself, the whole time she'd been sitting in the airport, trying to figure out a way to get to him, she'd been suppressing an ever-growing panic, and not just because he was her best chance of staying alive. Somehow, it had gotten personal. A thousand worries had been plaguing her. Worries about *him:* Where was he? Was he okay? What if the mirror had inadvertently gotten broken? Would he die? Would he be stuck in there forever?

What if Lucan had somehow gotten his hands on him? How would she find him? Would she have to hunt down this scary Lucan guy and steal Cian back?

What if she never saw the towering, dark, infuriatingly barbaric, sexy Highlander again?

It's just hormones. Combustive chemistry compounded by danger, nothing more.

Whatever it was, his reaction was playing right into a fantasy she'd not even known she'd been having: that when she found him he would not merely stalk out of that mirror to save her, he would stalk out of it to *claim* her. Crush her against the steely, hard strength of his body, and take slick velvety possession of her with his tongue. Give her the most base, elemental affirmation that he was alive, and she was alive, and they lived to fight another day.

It was, she realized, how women throughout all of history must have felt each time their men returned from battle on their own two feet, not bound over the back of a horse, or piled, dozens deep, atop a wagon.

Desperate for every morsel of passion life had to offer.

Or, at least, for a few steamy kisses,

anyway. Surely there was no harm in a few kisses . . .

Famous final words, she would think later.

She tipped her head back and wet her lips. He needed no further encouragement. Whisky eyes glittering with lust, he cupped the back of her head with a big palm and slanted his mouth over hers.

The moment their lips met this time, heat lightning crackled between them and they both went wild.

She'd seen crazy passion in movies, but had never experienced it herself. She did now.

Wriggling her backpack off her shoulders, she molded herself against him, trying to get closer. He thrust back in kind, pressing his thick, hard erection against her stomach. She tried to scramble up his body, but her impromptu climbing attempt threw him off balance. He overcorrected and they banged against the metal shelving, then bounced off it.

Careening across the aisle, they stumbled and staggered over crate debris and crashed to the concrete floor.

Yet never broke the kiss.

Clamping her face between his big hands, he claimed her with hot, deep glides of his tongue. Closing his teeth over her lower lip, he gave it a gentle tug followed by a not-so-gentle suck, before resuming his sleek, erotic slides into the slick interior of her mouth.

He teased her with slow rhythmic thrusts, plunging in and out, and she sucked frantically at his tongue, as if it were some other part of him she was trying to capture and take deep inside her. He let her suckle him for a moment, growling soft and low in his throat, then he dragged his mouth away, lightly chafing his shadow-beard across her jaw, nipping the edge of it. He trailed scorching kisses down her throat, then bit her in the hollow where her shoulder met her neck, catching the tendon with his teeth.

She sucked in a hissing breath, her back arching, straining up against him. She tipped back her head, yielding greater access.

Pushing impatiently at the collar of her jean jacket, he bared her skin and scattered tiny love-bites over her shoulder, riding the fine edge between not-enough and almost-too-much.

She had a sneaking suspicion Cian MacKeltar rode that edge a lot.

God, what was happening to her? she wondered dimly. She was going to tell him they needed to hurry and get out of there. That Stone-face was coming. That Security was no doubt on its way. Just a few more kisses and she was going to tell him all of that. Any minute now . . .

She tugged at his shirt, worked her hands beneath it, gliding them up his sexy, sculpted abdomen, slipping them around to his magnificently muscled back.

He shoved his hands beneath her sweater, subtly shifting so the hot, hard ridge of his erection was cradled snugly between her thighs.

We have to go now, she was going to tell him. "I can't breathe," she told him. "You're too big. I want to be on top."

He made a half-choking, half-laughing sound and rolled her over on top of him. She slipped into a straddling position and glanced down, eyes widening. His bulge was straining the fabric of his faded jeans and he was worrisomely large.

"Take off that damn jacket."

But we need to go, she opened her mouth to say. Except just as she was about to form the words, he pressed the pad of his finger to her parted lips, and she ended up nipping the tip of his finger then sucking it into her mouth.

He groaned, eyes narrowing, gaze fixed heatedly on her mouth.

She shrugged the jacket from her shoulders. When he tugged at her sweater, she raised her arms above her head and yielded that too. Her breasts sprang free, jiggling, her nipples hardening into tight puckers.

Beneath her, Cian stared up, lust stringing his gut tighter than a corded bow about to shoot wildly into anything that moved.

Bloody hell, she was magnificent!

She sat astride him, her lush, heavy breasts bobbing and swaying, and she was so ripely curved that a man could come just looking at her. Her skin was silk and cream, and he knew she was going to feel that way all over, inside and out. More creamy in some places than others, and he couldn't wait to taste all of them. Her breasts were full, high, and sexy as hell. Her nipples were hard pink peaks swaying above his face. Abs contracting, he reared up from the concrete floor, caught those pretty boobs with his hands, and drew a nipple deep into his hot, wet mouth. He tugged lightly, gave it a delicate scrape with his teeth, savoring the pearly hardness of it with a lingering swirl of his tongue.

Back arching, Jessi buried her hands in

Cian's braids, moaning as he used his un-shaven jaw to gently abrade the sensitive skin of her damp, kiss-puckered peaks. Then he started licking with slow, lazily erotic strokes of his tongue until she was squirming and wiggling impatiently on top of him. Turning his head from side to side between her breasts, he teased her nipples mercilessly with light flicks, intermittently taking tiny nips beneath the hard pink points.

Her breasts ached from his slow, teasing strokes. She needed more friction. She wanted his mouth closed firmly on them, his fingers pinching and rolling, the rake of his teeth. She wanted hot and hard and de-manding. She wanted claiming.

She was so turned-on that she was achy, needy with it. His tongue flicked across one nipple, then the next as he doled out more of those torturously light caresses. "Please, Cian, *more,*" she whimpered.

She lost her breath in a *whoosh* of air when he pushed her off him and flipped her onto her back.

A hot purr rumbled deep in his throat.

The concrete felt cool in contrast to the burning heat of her skin. Lowering himself over her, he propped his formidable weight with his palms splayed at each side of her body. Burying his face in her breasts, he — *oh, thank you, finally* — drew one nipple after the next deep into his mouth. He suckled. He nipped. He rolled the taut buds between his tongue and his upper palate, scraping gently with the edges of his teeth. Shifting his weight to one forearm, he slipped his hand down to work at her jeans.

"Cian," she gasped.

"Aye, lass?" His mouth moved lower, trailing hot, wet kisses over her tummy, pausing at her navel to dip in and lave it.

"Oh, God, Cian!" She twisted her hips to give him slack in the waistband of her denim second-skin.

A few moments later, a soft, wicked laugh escaped him and she knew he'd just unbuttoned her jeans and seen the words **LUCKY YOU** emblazoned in gold down the inner fabric of the fly.

"So that's why they're called *Lucky* jeans," he murmured.

"Uh-hmmm," she managed.

"You'll get no argument from me, lass. I ken I'm a lucky man." He paused. "Woman," he said then, "I'm going to make you forget every other man you've ever known."

"But —"

286

"Hush." Then his demanding mouth was hot on her body again, scattering tiny love-bites over the delicate skin of her hips as he peeled her jeans down inch by inch.

She didn't hear them — the people approaching.

She was too lost in an erotic haze for anything to penetrate.

Fortunately, Cian heard the furious voice snapping, "Did you hear that? I'm telling you, she's back there!"

Jerking back from her, he cocked his head, listening. Abruptly, he tugged her into a sitting position and began yanking her jeans back up over her hips.

Befuddled, dazed by desire, Jessi sat up on the cool concrete, gaping at him.

Someone comes, he mouthed, miming a gesture to be silent. He stood, hoisted her into midair by the waistband of her jeans, and jiggled her back into them, the muscles in his arms bunching and rippling.

His eyes glazed over a little when he shook her, and he got a wild look in them. He turned sharply away, leaving her to fasten them. After a long moment, he turned back with her sweater and helped her tug it over her head.

It was so snug it got stuck above her breasts.

His eyes took on a stark, defeated expression. He backed away, unbuttoning his jeans. Jamming a hand down the front, he sucked in a slow hissing breath and repositioned himself.

She finished squeezing herself back into the sweater and slipped on her jean-jacket. Scooping up her backpack, she slung it over her shoulders.

The *rat-a-tat-tat* of high heels tapped a brisk staccato across the concrete floor, drawing ever nearer, accompanied by softer-soled shoes — many of them.

God, she'd *completely* forgotten about Stone-face! In a matter of minutes. Kissed brainless once again. What in the world was wrong with her? How could a man's touch so utterly obliterate the calm, cool intellect and impressive powers of reason on which she'd once prided herself?

She frowned at him, eyes narrowed, trying to figure out what it was that Cian MacKeltar had that no other man had.

She was familiar with the theory that women were instinctively sexually attracted to men who were their most favorable genetic complement; men who possessed the DNA that would strengthen hers, and vice versa, thereby guaranteeing stronger children and ensuring the human race's greatest odds of survival.

Was Cian MacKeltar biologically her most favorable match? Was she doomed to be hopelessly and helplessly attracted to him? Was Nature herself conspiring against her in some diabolical evolutionary plan to get her pregnant?

If so, a devilish little inner voice proposed, *then we should probably just sleep with him and get it over with, huh? Don't you think?*

"Nice try," Jessi muttered.

Though the anthropologist in her appreciated the logic of the theory, she greatly preferred to believe that love and sex were matters of level-headed choice and free will.

There wasn't a single thing levelheaded or remotely free-willish about her response to Cian MacKeltar.

"I can't imagine *what* she's doing back there!" Stone-face was saying. "Can you? Did you hear that *noise?* She's like a wild little animal. She didn't just hit me. She brutally assaulted me. I hope she has an attorney, because she's going to need one. I'm suing. My face might never be the same. I'm probably going to need plastic surgery."

Oh puh-leeze. Jessi snorted.

Cian glanced at her, the raw sexual frustration in his dark amber gaze tempered by amusement.

You hit her? he mouthed.

I had to get to you somehow, she mouthed back, wrinkling her nose. Smoothing her sweater. Trying not to blush, remembering what they'd just done and, worse still, what they'd been about to do. Good grief, she thought crossly, maybe she should just *throw* her virginity at him the next time.

Oh, gee, wait a minute, she'd just tried to do that.

His shoulders shook with silent laughter. He stepped closer, ducked his head, and pressed his mouth to her ear. He kissed the dainty ridges, tasting it lightly with his tongue. "You'd do a Highland husband proud, lass," he whispered.

She shivered from the hot eroticism of his tongue against her ear. "Thanks," she whispered back. Coming from a ninth-century warrior-Druid, that was quite a compliment. "I knocked her out with a single blow too." She couldn't help but brag on herself a little bit.

His shoulders shook harder.

"So, Mr. Druid-turned-dark-sorcerer, we're in a bit of a fix. Think you can get us out of here?"

He tossed back his head and laughed out loud. The deep sound rumbled from his chest, echoing in the warehouse.

"Did you *hear* that?" From a few aisles away, Stone-face sounded scandalized. "There's a man in here with her! How in the world did that creature get a man in here with her?"

Cian flashed Jessi a cocky, sexy smile that couldn't have been more full of himself. It was the smile of a man who knew his power and thoroughly enjoyed having it.

"Aye, I can. Just you sit back, woman, and relax. I'll take care of everything."

Jessi had no doubt that he could. And, damn, but she liked that in a man.

16

Scotland: bounded by the Atlantic, the North Sea, and England; approximately half the size of its neighbor; comprised primarily of moors, mountains, and seven hundred and eighty-seven major islands, including the Shetlands, Orkneys, and the Inner and Outer Hebrides.

Jessi's sticky memory made her a lint brush for facts.

She knew that if one were to draw a straight line from the far south of the rugged country to the far north of it, it was a mere 275 miles, although its coastline covered a scenic 6,200 miles.

She also knew that the true collision of England and Scotland had predated the clash of politics and hot tempers by some 425 million years, when continental drift had caused Scotland — previously part of a landmass that had included North America — and England — previously part of Gondwana — to collide into each other, not far from the current political boundary.

A historical treasure trove, Scotland was close to the top of a lengthy list of places Jessi had long wanted to see, along with Ireland, Germany, Belgium, France, Switzerland, and all of what had once been part of ancient Gaul where the P-Celts had so passionately lived and loved and warred.

Still, she reflected, swerving to avoid a pothole in the meandering, single-lane dirt road, she'd never imagined she'd make it to Great Britain so soon.

And certainly not as a hunted fugitive, in the company of a ninth-century Highlander, driving a big black stolen SUV into the Highlands.

Cian was back in the mirror now, and being downright pissy about it.

She wasn't. She was relieved that it had sucked him back in so soon after he'd used Voice to escape the airport and commandeered their "rental" vehicle.

Twice now, she'd nearly given him her virginity. In fact, had they not been interrupted, she would have either time.

She didn't understand it. She was a woman who did nothing without a solid, well-thought-out reason. She knew the largest part of why she hadn't slept with a man yet was because she'd watched her mother go through four husbands. She had three sisters, fourteen stepsiblings (some of them step-steps from the man's earlier marriage), a bad case of cynicism, and an intense need for commitment as a result.

She adored her mother, and if anyone dared criticize Lilly St. James, Jessi would slice and dice 'em. Nobody put down her mom.

She even liked all of her stepsiblings.

But she hated having such a complicated family; it was one of the reasons she'd left Maine for Chicago and stayed there, preferring long talks on the phone every Sunday with Lilly to being fully consumed by the chaos that was the St. James household. Though not currently married, her mom was dating again, and sometimes that was worse than suddenly getting a few extra brothers and sisters who borrowed clothing and car keys with teenage impunity.

Birthday dinners and graduations inevitably turned into scheduling disasters. Holidays were a nightmare. Jessi would never be able to fathom her mom's idea of marital commitment. A commercial realtor, Lilly treated the sacred vows of matrimony like any of her other "deals": a short-term contract with an option to renew — that she rarely exercised.

Jessi was getting married once. Having babies with one man. Three or four kids would be just fine; maybe a boy and two girls who would never suffer any confusion about who they were related to, and how, not to mention the often-baffling whys. Her mom had picked a few strange ones from the parade of boyfriends.

Jessi wanted a small, insular, well-tended world. The fewer people one tried to love, Jessi believed, the better one could love them. She was a quality girl, not a quantity one.

Yet, with Cian MacKeltar, all her well-thought-out prequalifiers for relationships went sailing right out the window.

He looked at her — she got wet.

He touched her — she melted.

He kissed her — her clothing started coming off.

She couldn't come up with a single reason for it. Yes, he was sexy. Yes, he was pure male and — so what if it wasn't in keeping with the current feminist movement that seemed to prefer emasculated men — she *liked* manliness in a man. Liked them a little rough around the edges, a little untamed. Yes, he was fascinating, and she really couldn't wait to get him somewhere that she could pick his brain about the ninth century, and find out just what had happened to him eleven centuries ago.

But he was also a logistic impossibility.

He was currently living in a mirror. He was a sorcerer with a blood-grudge against another sorcerer. And he was *way* older than she was.

He wasn't the marrying kind. Not even the keeping kind. And she knew it.

But despite all that, whenever he touched her, she instantly began de-evolving into one of her primitive ancestors, driven by the three basic prime directives: eat, sleep, have sex. Though if she were going to line those directives up in the order *she* would enjoy them, it would be sex first, while she felt skinny and her tummy was at its flattest, then food with lots of decadently sedating carbs, then sleep. Then wake up and have sex again, with the added benefit of working off some carbs. So she could eat again.

But that was neither here nor there.

Here was a man she couldn't seem to keep her hands off of.

And no doubt when he came out of that mirror, they were going to fall on each other again. And she wasn't going to be able to count on an interruption way up in the desolate hills where he was taking her, unless a meteor were to serendipitously plummet from the sky, or they were overrun by marauding sheep.

"I'm sliding again, lass," came the disgruntled growl from the seat beside her. "Naught but a view of the ceiling over here."

Jessi slowed and pulled over to the side of the road. When they'd gotten into the SUV, Cian had originally positioned the mirror across the two back rows of seats, then slid into the front passenger's seat. But when the Dark Glass had reclaimed him less than an hour outside of Edinburgh, en route to Inverness, he'd instructed her to push the front seat back as far as it would go — which was pretty far in the roomy SUV — tug the looking glass forward, prop it at an angle, and strap it in with the seat belt so he could see where they were going. *I'm uncertain of the terrain, lass,* he'd told her. *I know where I want to go, but I doona ken how it will look after the passage of so much time. There will be roads and buildings and such that weren't there before; however, I should be able to identify the mountains if I can get a good-enough view.*

Unfortunately, the seat belt was designed to hold a person with assorted person-sized bumps and lumps, not a flat mirror, and the glass kept slipping down into a more horizontal position. If she'd had a single piece of luggage, she might have crammed it at the base of the frame, on the floor, but as it was, they were traveling outlaw-light. The only things in the SUV were three empty fast-food bags from the lunch they'd grabbed at the airport and a handful of maps and pamphlets he'd snatched from a newsstand while leaving.

As she leaned over to adjust it yet again, he muttered something in that mysterious language of his, and suddenly a book tumbled out of the mirror, narrowly missing her nose, followed by several more. She ducked out of the way. She'd broken her nose once already, that day at the climbing gym, and it was crooked enough, tipping slightly to the left.

"Wedge them at the base," he commanded.

She blinked. "You have books in there?"

"I've accumulated a few items over the centuries. Things I believed Lucan wouldn't miss. Once stolen and in transit, when the opportunity presented itself, I picked up still more."

She arranged the books at the foot of the

mirror, laying them end to end, gawking at the titles: Stephen Hawking's *A Brief History of Time*; *Webster's Unabridged Dictionary of the English Language*; Pliny's *Natural History*; *The Illustrated Encyclopedia of the Universe*; and *Geographica*, a massive book of maps and charts.

"Like a little light reading, huh?" she muttered. Personally, she went for Janet Evanovich's Stephanie Plum series (she was a Ranger-girl herself) or any Linda Howard book, on those rare occasions she got to read for pleasure. Which was like once a year.

"I have endeavored to keep up with the passage of the centuries."

She glanced into the mirror. After seeing him in the flesh only a short time ago, it was weird to be seeing him as a one-dimensional, flat figure in the glass. She didn't like it at all. She was beginning to resent that mirror. Resent that it could take him back anytime it wanted to. She shook her head. A few minutes ago she'd been *glad* it had reclaimed him. Now she was irritated that it had. Would she ever be of a single mind around him? "For the day you'd finally be free? That's why you kept up?"

He stared down at her, burnt-whisky gaze unfathomable. "Aye."

Free. After eleven centuries, the ninth-century Highlander was going to be free in a little over two weeks. "Seventeen more days," Jessi breathed wonderingly. "God, you must be climbing the . . . er, walls . . . or whatever's in there, huh?"

"Aye."

"So, just what *is* in there, anyway?" She tested the glass by shaking it gently, and deemed it secure enough. It shouldn't slide now.

"Stone," he said flatly.

"And what else?"

"Stone. Gray. Of varying sizes." His voice dropped to a colorless monotone. "Fifty-two thousand nine hundred and eighty-seven stones. Twenty-seven thousand two hundred and sixteen of them are a slightly paler gray than the rest. Thirty-six thousand and four are more rectangular than square. There are nine hundred and eighteen that have a vaguely hexagonal shape. Ninety-two of them have a vein of bronze running through the face. Three are cracked. Two paces from the center is a stone that protrudes slightly above the rest, over which I tripped for the first few centuries. Any other questions?"

Jessi flinched as his words impacted her, taking her breath away. Her chest and throat felt suddenly tight. *Uh, yeah, like, how did you stay sane in there? What kept you from going stark raving mad? How did you survive over a thousand years in such a hell?*

She didn't ask because it would have been like asking a mountain why it was still standing, as it had been since the dawn of time, perhaps reshaped in subtle ways, but there, always there. Barring cataclysmic planetary upheaval, forever there.

The man was strong — not just physically, but mentally and emotionally. A rock of a man, the kind a woman could lean on through the worst of times and never have to worry that things might fall apart, because a man like him simply wouldn't let them. She never met anyone like Cian before. Twenty-first-century society wasn't conducive to churning out alpha males. What did a man have to hone himself on nowadays, test himself against, build character on? Conquering the latest video game? Buying the right suit and tie? Smacking little white balls around a manicured garden with ridiculously expensive sticks? Doing battle over the parking space nearest the store?

"Nope," she managed. "No other questions."

Eleven centuries of captivity. Hung on his hated enemy's study wall. Eleven centuries of not touching. Not eating. Not loving. Had he had anyone to talk to?

Her face must have betrayed her thoughts, for he startled her by saying softly, " 'Tis no longer of consequence, lass, but thank you for the compassion. 'Tis nigh over. Seventeen more days, Jessica. That's all."

For some reason his words brought a sudden hot burn of tears to the backs of her eyes. Not only hadn't eleven centuries turned him into a monster, he was trying to soothe *her,* to make her feel better about his imprisonment.

"You weep for me, woman?"

She turned away. "It's been a long day. Hell, it's been a long week."

"Jessica." Her name was a soft command.

She disobeyed it, staring out the window at the rolling hills.

"Jessica, look at me."

Eyes bright with unshed tears, she whipped her head around and glared at him. "I weep for you, okay?" she snapped. "For eleven centuries stuck in there. Can I start driving again or do you need something else?"

He smiled faintly, raised his hand, and splayed his palm against the inside of the silvery glass.

Without an ounce of conscious thought, her hand rose to meet his, aligning on the cool silver, palm to palm, finger to finger, thumb to thumb. And though she felt only a cold hardness beneath her palm, the gesture made something go all warm and soft in her heart.

Neither of them spoke or moved for a moment.

Then she glanced hastily away, fished a napkin from the fast-food bags, blew her nose, shifted into drive, and resumed their winding ascent into the rugged Scottish Highlands.

Gloaming in the Highlands.

It had taken him most of the day to find the caves he'd played in as a lad.

The terrain had changed greatly over the past thousand years, and new roads and homes had made it difficult to recognize landmarks he'd once thought immutable and uniquely unmistakable. Even mountains looked different when one was gazing up at them from the busy streets of a city, as opposed to regarding them across a wide-open expanse of sheep-dotted field.

Unwilling to permit her to enter the caves until he had a chance to explore them for potential animal or erosive threats, he'd bade her prop the mirror securely next to the entrance to the stone lair so he could keep close watch on the vista around her. Armed with knives and guns, he was prepared for any threat, though he truly doubted one would come this evening, or even the next.

Now, from high atop a rugged mountain, Cian stared out of the Dark Glass at two of the loveliest sights that had ever graced his existence: Scotland at a fiery dusk and Jessica St. James.

His beloved country made a worthy backdrop for the woman.

Sitting cross-legged, facing him, scarce a foot beyond his glass, her short, glossy black curls were backlit by flaming crimson and gold, her forehead and cheekbones dusted burnt rose, her lips plush red velvet. Pretty white teeth flashed when she smiled, her eyes lit with an inner fire that nigh matched the sky behind her when she laughed.

She'd been laughing often as they'd talked. She was a woman who seemed able to find something humorous in nearly all things, even her own grim lot right now, which was a warrior's strength in Cian's estimation. Fear accomplished nothing. Nor did regret — sweet Christ, he knew that. All the regret in the world wouldn't change a damn thing now. Not what had been. Nor what would be.

Still, humor and tenacity could frequently see one through the most difficult of times, and she possessed both in spades.

At his urging, she'd been telling him about her trials and tribulations while trying to reclaim his mirror at the airport.

When she grew excited about one part or another, she spoke with her hands, accompanying her words with gestures, and her fingertips would brush his glass. He was so physically attuned to her that it gave him the kiss of a shiver each time, as if she were brushing her fingers against *him,* not a cool mirror.

For the first time in over a millennium, he got to watch the night take his Highlands — a thing he'd missed fiercely — yet he found himself savoring even more listening to Jessica's tale, laughing at the images she painted for him. He could see this wee hellion vaulting over the counter, bashing the contrary woman, and stuffing her in a closet. There was a bit of a heathen inside Jessica St. James.

It was just one more thing he liked about the lass, he thought, smiling faintly.

He stared, drinking her in, his smile fading. She had his plaid draped around her shoulders, and was snuggled into its warmth as the sun worked its way slowly down to kiss the dark ridge of mountains filling the horizon. It did something to him, seeing her in his tartan. Though it wasn't the Keltar weave or colors, only a bit of Scots-woven cloth he'd swiped centuries ago, heartsick for his home, he still thought of it as his. 'Twas as if she belonged in it. Crimson and black suited her well. She was a vibrant woman, fashioned by a generous creator of bold jewel tones: jade and raven and rose and skin of sun-kissed gold.

They'd been talking for some time now. For the first time since they'd cast their lots together, all manner of calamity was not erupting around them. He could do nothing further to ensure her safety at this time from inside the mirror, so he'd seized the opportunity to learn more about Jessica St. James.

Where had she grown up? Did she have clan? How many, who, and where were they? What was she learning at her university? What kind of things did she one day dream of doing?

I'm learning about digging in the dirt, she'd told him with a cheeky smile, *and that's what I one day dream of doing.* Once she'd explained what she really meant, he realized 'twas but another thing that drew him to her. She was curious as a Druid about things. In his mind's eye he could see her toiling in the soil for treasures of the past, delightedly unearthing pottery shards and bits of armor and weapons. Och, Christ, how he'd like to be there beside her while she did it! To tell her stories of those things she found and, later, take her beneath him and show her another real, live artifact.

If she could have anything in the world, he'd asked her, what would it be?

She'd answered that one without hesitation: a best friend. She'd hastily added, *a truly, seriously best friend; one that I couldn't wait to talk to first thing in the morning as soon as I woke up, and one that I still wanted to be talking to, right up to the last minute before I went to sleep.*

He'd smiled faintly. *You mean a soul mate,* he'd thought but not said. She'd meant a man, a lifetime lover. He could see it in her eyes.

Now she was telling him how she'd decided to be an archaeologist; that she'd read a book when she was young that had inspired her and set her on her path.

He listened intently, watched intently. He fancied he could sit like this for two eternities, mayhap more, drinking her in. He wanted to hear the minute details of her life, to know as much of this woman as he possibly could.

"So there I was, in college, second year into my major, realizing that it wasn't going to be like Anne Rice's book *The Mummy* at all. That it wasn't glamour and travel and the thrill of discovery. That it was really a lot of grunt work and paperwork. Most archaeologists *never* get to dig in the dirt.

"But by then it was too late," she told him with a sheepish smile, "I'd fallen in love with it for totally different reasons. I'd gotten addicted to the history. I'd been sucked in by the mysteries of our origins, of the world's origins, of trying to piece together the big picture."

She spoke of Druid things now, the things that had always fascinated him. Life was full of tiny slices of truth and knowledge, here and there, and a wise man or woman endeavored to collect them.

An unwise man endeavored to collect other things. Like Unseelie Hallows.

And paid the price. Och, Christ, and paid the price!

"My mother hates my choice of major," she confided. "She can't understand why I'm not married and popping out babies left and right. She can't imagine how I could prefer to spend time with artifacts when I could be out trying to find a husband."

His gut twisted. *Out trying to find a husband.* He hated those words. They pissed him off to the last sorcerous, fiery drop of blood in his veins. "Why have you no man?" he said tightly.

Her smile faded. She was quiet a moment. Then she smiled again, but this one was softer, older than her years, and achingly bittersweet. "I think I'm misplaced in time, Cian. I think that's part of the reason I'm drawn to the past. I'm an old-fashioned girl. My mother has had four husbands and she's already looking for the next."

"Do they die, lass?" he asked. He wondered if she had any idea what she did to him, sitting there like that. Plaid soft and rumpled around her shoulders, her dainty hands relaxed in her lap, her palms upward, fingers half-curled. She was utterly unself-conscious, reflective, her shimmering jade gaze turned inward.

"Nope," she said, shaking her head slowly. "They just seem to decide they don't love each other anymore. If they ever did. Usually she leaves them."

"And they *let* her?" Were mother aught like her daughter, 'twas unfathomable that a man would let her go, inconceivable that a husband wouldn't do all in his power to make her happy, to breathe life into every last one of his woman's dreams.

He would never understand modern marriages. Divorce was beyond his comprehension. Though at times he made light of it, the truth was, a Keltar Druid lived for his binding vows and the day he could give them.

For him, that day would never come. But for him, many days would never come. Canceled out by too many days gone wrong.

"I doona ken it, Jessica. Love, once given, is forever. It canna simply go away. Do they not love her, these men she marries?"

She shrugged, looking as baffled by it as he felt. "I don't know. I wonder sometimes if people even know what love is anymore. Some days, when I'm watching my friends at school change lovers as unperturbedly as they change shoes, I think the world just got filled with too many people, and all our technological advances made things so easy that it cheapened our most basic, essential values somehow," she told him. "It's like spouses are commodities nowadays: disposable, constantly getting tossed back out for trade on the market, and everyone's trying to trade up, up — like there is a 'trading up' in love." She rolled her eyes. "No way. That's not for me. I'm having one husband. I'm getting married once. When you know going in that you're staying for life, it makes you think harder about it, go slower, choose really well."

When she fell pensively silent, Cian smiled bitterly, brooding over the vagaries of fate. Jessica St. James was strong, impassioned, true of heart, funny, fierce, and sexy as hell.

She was perfect for him. Right down to his frustrating inability to deep-read her or compel her. She, alone, was forever beyond his magic, that wild talent that had always made his life so easy. Too damnably easy. Dangerously easy.

This woman had been custom-crafted for a man of his ilk.

"What about you?" she said finally. "Were you married in your century?"

He didn't miss the shadow that flickered in her lovely sparkling eyes. She didn't like the thought that he might have been wed. She didn't like the thought of him loving another woman. That knowledge eased some of the pain in that twisted place in his gut. A twisted place that he knew would only grow worse again, and continue to worsen, day by day. "Nay, lass. I'd not found the woman for me before I was imprisoned in the Dark Glass."

Her brow furrowed and she looked as if she would pursue that thought further, but then she seemed to change her mind. "God, there are so many questions I keep wanting to ask you but I never seem to get around to them! How old are you, anyway? I mean, excluding the time you've been in the mirror."

"A score and ten. I'd gained a new year shortly before I was imprisoned. And you?"

"Twenty-four."

"In my time, you would have —"

"I know, I know, I would have been an old maid, right?" She laughed. "You and my mother."

"Nay," he told her, "you'd not have been unwed. Like as not, you'd have been on your third or fourth husband. Beauty such as yours would have been highly sought by the richest men in the land. Unfortunately, they were often the oldest."

Her eyes widened ever so slightly and her lips moved. " 'Beauty such as —' " She broke off with a blush. "Thank you," she said softly. Then she flashed him a cheeky smile. "Ugh. Great. I get married; he dies. I get married; he dies. And it's not like I would have been left a wealthy widow to do what I wanted, either. Some male relative would have just married me off again, wouldn't he? Keeping me in the family so they could hold the dowry and lands?"

Cian nodded. "Though my clan was not so barbaric. Having seven sisters who could all talk at once — and *very* loudly when fashed — taught me a thing or two."

Jessica laughed. They both fell silent.

Then she opened her mouth, shut it. Hesitated, then opened it again. Leaning forward, she said in a hushed voice, "How did it happen, Cian? How did you end up in the mirror?"

He drew ripples of silver around him, sliding deeper into his prison.

"Another time," he said. Though, on

occasion, some perverse part of him seemed determined to make her think the worst of him, he relished the intimacy taking root between them. He had no desire to besmirch it with tales of ancient sins. "For now sleep, sweet Jessica. We have much to do on the morrow."

Later that night, Cian stood naked behind the silvery Unseelie veil, armed with knives and guns, watching over Jessica as she slept.

Clad in an assortment of oversized garments, she was curled on a pallet of his clothing at the foot of the mirror. Over the centuries, he'd accumulated various items of attire. As full night had fallen and the temperature dropped still more, he'd tossed out every last piece of it to her, right down to the jeans and T-shirt he'd been wearing, in an effort to warm her against the chilly October night.

Sleep was obsolete within his mirror, as were all physical needs. He would stand guard until she awoke. He'd made her as safe as he could for now. It was not nearly as safe as he could and would make her, using any and all means at his disposal, no matter the cost.

It was the truth that they had much to

do on the coming day. On the morrow, they would return to Inverness and gather supplies. On the morrow he would walk the perimeter of their retreat and bury wardstones at eight points and chant spells at sixty-four.

On the morrow he would find something to tattoo himself with, for he would need more protection runes on his body to keep him safe from the backlash of the black arts he must call upon to lay the traps necessary to ensure her safety from Lucan and any of Lucan's minions. On the morrow he would transmute the soil, in the fashion those most ancient of burial grounds had once been alchemized, brutally forcing the earth to change, calling it alive, making it answerable to him and only him.

If there were anything dead in the soil he'd chosen, things could get . . . unpleasant, but he would shield her. If he had to tattoo himself from head to toe, shave his hair, and dye-brand his scalp, the palms of his hands, the soles of his feet, and his tongue, he would shield her.

One day you'll have tattooed your entire body. Tears had shimmered in his mother's eyes when she'd spotted the fresh crimson tattoos on his neck, so fresh his own blood was still beading, mingled inseparably with the dye. *Then how will you safeguard your soul? Cian, you must stop. Send him away.*

He'd laughed at her. *I've scarce yielded a tenth of my body, Mother. And Lucan may be a learned man, but he hasn't enough power to be dangerous.*

You're wrong. And he's making you *dangerous.*

You know naught of what you speak.

But she'd known. From that first blustery winter's eve the dark Welsh stranger had appeared at their gates petitioning shelter, claiming to have lost his way in the storm, she'd known.

Turn him away, Cian, she'd begged. *He comes to our step with darkness at his back in more ways than one.* His mother had often been sought for her touch of prescience.

We'll but feed and shelter him for an eve, he'd said to please her. There'd been a time when pleasing those he loved had pleased him most. His sisters and mother especially. The eight of them had been a cluster of bright, feminine butterflies, swooping through his days, brilliantly coloring his existence, making him impatient for a mate of his own.

But then he'd discovered a fellow Druid in the man across his table that eve; a thing he'd not encountered before, and he'd been too curious to turn him away. His da had died before his birth, he'd had no brothers, and he'd never heard of another like himself in all of Albania.

One thing had led to another. Ego and arrogance had played no small part.

I can work this spell, can you?

Aye, can you work this one?

Aye. Ken you how to summon the elements?

Aye, ken you Voice? Have you heard of the Unseelie Hallows?

Nay, though I know of the Seelie Hallows: the spear, stone, sword, and cauldron.

Ah, so you've heard not of the Scrying Glass. . . .

It was what Lucan had called it then, the Dark Glass. The Welsh Druid had begun laying his trap that very eve, baiting it brilliantly. *Can you imagine foretelling the winds of political change? Or knowing which contender for king with which to ally your clan? Or when a loved one might suffer a tragedy? 'Tis said the glass reveals the future in exacting detail, unlike anything our spells could ever hope to achieve.*

Mayhap, Cian's blood had quickened at the thought, it could even show the coming of a Keltar's life mate.

The mere opening of a door that night, of not heeding a mother's words — how life drew its complex design from the simplest of choices, the smallest of moments!

All those he once loved had been dead for more than a thousand years.

Was Lucan out there, counting the hours to Samhain — or the Welshman's counterpart known as Hollantide, a night of ghostly visitation, divination games, and bonfire burning — as was he? Though he spoke aloud of days, Cian knew to the minute how long he had.

"A little over sixteen days, Trevayne," he growled into the chill Highland night, "and you will answer for all you took from me."

In three hundred eighty-four hours and forty-three minutes, to be precise, vengeance would finally be his.

His gaze dark, he glanced down at Jessica.

He'd never thought it would be such a double-edged sword.

17

Cian MacKeltar was a machine.

And Jessi didn't like it one bit.

After their intimacy at the airport and the warm camaraderie of their conversation last night, after sleeping drenched in the sinfully sexy man-scent of him, dressed in his clothing, sprawled on top of more of it, after having wickedly erotic dreams about him in which they'd had sex that would have made the author of the Kama Sutra sit up and start taking notes, after waking to find him standing naked over her, staring down at her from his mirror with that incredible rock-hard erection that had made her mouth dry and other parts of her oh-so-not-dry-at-all, she'd expected . . . well, at least a few hot, slippery kisses.

She'd not gotten a single, quick brush of his lips.

Not even a horny comment.

Just a *Are you awake?*

She'd blinked, unable to tear her gaze

away from him. The man had, quite simply, the most amazing package she'd ever seen, and although most of the ones she'd seen had been in pictures, she still considered herself a fair judge. *Uh-huh, I'm awake,* she'd managed breathlessly. Some parts of her more than others.

Call me out.

She'd obeyed, wetting her lips.

Six and a half feet of muscle-ripped, naked Highlander had separated from the glass and reached toward her . . .

And *past* her, retrieving his clothing.

He'd *dressed,* for heaven's sake — covering up all that magnificent masculine nudity with swift efficiency. Then he scooped up the mirror and loaded it into the back of the SUV. He'd returned, scooped her up as well, and dumped her into the driver's seat.

As he'd deposited her behind the wheel, he'd *pecked* her freaking *forehead.*

When he'd lowered his head, like an idiot, she'd actually puckered, thinking he was finally going to kiss her. She'd smooched air, putting her in a positively foul mood — no matter that the sun was shining and it looked like it was going to be a glorious, unseasonably warm autumn day in the Highlands, *and* she was alive to see it.

Behaving with all the automated efficiency of a cool, detached Terminator, with steely insides and computer chips dictating his every move, Cian had referenced one of the pamphlets he'd swiped from the airport along with the stack of maps, and directed her to a store called Tiedemann's, an outdoorsman's store, specializing in camping equipment and survival gear.

For the past thirty minutes — ever since he'd so unceremoniously "parked" her at the front counter — he'd been oblivious to her, examining everything, asking the salesman he'd ensorcelled dozens of questions, selecting and sending to the counter insulated clothing, sleeping bags, a small gas stove, cooking implements, along with dozens of other things she had no idea what he planned to do with.

We will gather foodstuffs next, he'd informed her brusquely on one of his circuits through the store.

That had cheered her a bit. Her stomach was growling. She was starved. Food would be heaven. A cup of steaming cocoa or coffee with it would be even more heavenly. The skintight *Lucky* jeans he'd swiped for her days ago weren't nearly so snug on her waist as they'd been when he'd procured them, and they were in serious need of a washing. She'd slept on the plane in them, she'd slept on the ground in them. She'd been living in them twenty-four/ seven for four days now. Same panties too. It had been four days since she'd last had a shower, and if she didn't get one soon, she might hurt somebody.

Pushing up on her tiptoes, she spied a collection of women's athletic gear and outdoor clothing just beyond the tent department. The least he could do, she decided peevishly, was Voice her some new clothes. And she wanted a bra, damn it. Even a sports bra would do, and it looked like there were several racks of them. She doubted she'd find panties in this store, but she'd settle for a few bottles of water and some soap to wash them out by hand.

Shoving away from the counter where she'd been dutifully obeying his "wait right here" command, she wended her way through the camping gear to the women's department. As she approached the sports-bra racks, she saw the sign for the ladies' rest room and veered off toward it.

Just in case she didn't get a shower today — and there was no telling how any of her days were going to go in the care, custody, and control of one Cian MacKeltar — she was opting for yet another paper-towel bath to be on the safe, not-quite-so aromatic side.

"You will tell me how many of these gas refills I will require to use such a stove for sixteen days in the wilds. Assume it will be in constant use." Cian needed to keep Jessica warm and prepare meals for her, but dare not risk the smoke of a wood fire, inside the cave or out. Colorless, odorless, virtually smokeless gas was a welcome discovery.

The salesman performed a series of calculations and gave him a number, his hazel eyes glazed by the spell of compulsion, his gestures jerky, as if automated.

Cian had been using Voice since the moment he'd walked in the door. He wanted in and out fast. He had too much to accomplish today to permit the indulgence of the slightest of his personal desires, to waste even a moment of time. If he was lucky enough to have eight hours free of the glass today, he could accomplish all of his goals. He'd only had three hours and forty-two minutes free yesterday, so he felt it reasonable to expect a longer reprieve today — if aught about the Unseelie Hallow could be expected to function in accordance with even a loose definition of "reasonable."

Jessica was feeling slighted, he knew. He hated that, but it had to be for now.

She seemed not to ken that he had an inferno of need for her raging inside him and that if he fed it the least bit of oxygen, the blaze would burn out of control and consume him, along with the entire day, leaving it in a waste of ashes around them.

Then nightfall would come and she would not be safe enough. And it would be his fault. He refused to bear such blame or take such risks with her life. By eventide she would be as safe as he could possibly make her. Until that time, he dare not begin touching her, or he'd not be able to stop. He'd watched her sleep all night, studying the planes and angles of her face in the changing light, from moonlit night through a rosy dawn and finally in the brilliant blaze of full sunrise, committing them to memory. Were he a sculptor, he could now carve her face in stone, even were he blind.

It had been agony to stand watching her, caressing with his gaze what his hands could not. It had been a joy. He'd learned centuries ago to suck from life what pleasure his hellish circumstances would permit.

When she'd awakened, she'd rolled over and stared up at him with sleepy-sexy eyes. She had three cowlicks, unruly thatches of hair that curled wildly. Now he possessed an image of her that only a lover might know — how she looked in the morning with her face sleep-flushed, her lips sleep-swollen, and her curls askew in a short, dark tangle. She woke up looking soft and warm, more than a little be-mused, and utterly sensual. Made a man want to scoop her into his arms and de-vour her.

He'd briefly envisioned himself stepping from the mirror, yanking her jeans down, taking her hard and fast, then throwing her in the SUV.

But he'd known better than to delude himself with the notion that he could be "hard and fast" with Jessica. Hard? Aye. Fast. Not a holy chance in hell. If he got started, he'd not be able to stop, and her life, and his vengeance, was of far more im-port than his lust.

Today was for the procuring of shel-tering goods, foodstuffs, dyes and needles and wardstones.

Tomorrow was for the claiming of his woman. And the next day and the next and the next. Once she was safe, he would devote every moment of his freedom from the glass to the thorough claiming of Jessica St. James.

"Shall I package these items up for you as well, sir?" the salesman asked.

Cian nodded, glancing over to where Jessica was standing. Last he'd looked, her arms had been crossed over her bountiful breasts, shoving them together and even higher, her lower lip had been sulkily and delectably pushed out, and she'd been tapping one foot impatiently.

She wasn't there.

Where the bloody hell was she? He'd told her not to move. In English. And there was naught wrong with her hearing of which he was aware.

"Sir, did you wish the tent, as well?"

"Nay," Cian growled, eyeing a man who now stood, with his back to him, at the same counter where moments ago his woman had been.

Was that why Jessica had moved away? Had the man behaved toward her in some unseemly fashion? He'd kill the son of a bitch.

Cian assessed the interloper. The man was tall and powerfully built, wearing black trousers, black boots, and a black leather jacket. His long black hair was braided and folded under, wrapped and bound by a leather thong.

It was a manner in which Highlanders had once worn their hair, before even Cian's time. When they hadn't been liming it for battle to make themselves look more terrifying to the effeminately tidy Romans.

The man thought much of himself; 'twas obvious in the way he stood, the way he held himself. He reeked of arrogance. Cian didn't like him. Didn't like him at all. If the bastard had breathed so much as a single improper word to Jessica, he was dead.

"Jessica!" he barked. "Where are you, lass? Answer me!"

There was no reply.

He scanned the store, seeking the top of her head, her glossy black curls. There was no sign of her. Where had she gone?

He couldn't deep-listen to her, he couldn't compel her, but he suspected a deep-scan of the store would detect her presence. Hers was a unique imprint, a space of serenity and silence in an otherwise clamorous world.

He stretched his senses, casting a wide net, probing.

Something probed back so unexpectedly and with such ferocity that he flinched.

He immediately slammed up mental walls, one after the next, sealing himself off. Sealing out whatever the frigging hell *that* had been.

They were walls he'd never needed before.

No one had ever been able to probe him, not even Lucan with all his dark arts. It had been one of the things that had so infuriated his captor. Lucan still couldn't probe him, even after a thousand years of continually gaining more power and knowledge, though he'd never stopped trying, convinced that Cian knew spells he was hiding (he did and was), determined to get them one way or another (never going to happen).

During none of Lucan's attempted probings had Cian ever felt anything touch his mind. Trevayne hadn't been able to get even that far inside his skull.

But just now he'd felt a distinct *push* against his mind. A distinct presence, though he hesitated to say a single presence, for what had pushed at him possessed such complexity of character, such ancientness — older even than he — that he was unable to call it . . . well . . . exactly human. Or if it was, 'twas unlike any human he'd ever encountered.

Focusing his mind, he pushed back in the general direction from which it had come, trying to isolate it.

The man at the counter suddenly whipped around, gaze seeking restlessly, scanning the store.

Unusual golden eyes met Cian's and locked over racks of clothing and aisles of camping equipment. They were old eyes, aware eyes, eyes full of fierce intelligence.

They were the eyes of more than a mere Druid.

Cian shoved past the glassy-eyed salesman and stalked toward him, pushing racks of clothing out of his way. "Who the hell are you?"

"Who the hell are *you?*" the man flung back coolly. Softly. Arrogantly. The man moved toward him as swiftly and surely as Cian stalked the man; there wasn't an ounce of hesitation in him.

They met in an aisle, stopped half a dozen paces apart, and began circling each other, sizing each other up, like two dark, wild beasts, preparing to battle over territory and mating rights.

Cian felt a rapid battery of hammer blows against the mental walls he'd erected. He permitted them, analyzing them, assessing his foe's strength.

Then he lashed back savagely. Just once.

It should have nigh split the prick's head.

If his opponent felt anything, he betrayed naught. Who *was* this man? "Where is my woman?" Cian snarled.

"I haven't seen your woman."

"If you've so much as touched a hair —"

"I have my own woman. Yours couldn't hold a candle to her."

"You have a death wish, Highlander."

"Nay." The man laughed. "Laid that to rest some time ago. On an icy ledge outside a Manhattan penthouse."

The man spoke nonsense. "Leave now and I won't kill you."

"Can't. I'm picking up hiking boots for my wife. She wants them today and 'tis her good graces that signify." His tone was lightly mocking, his smile a hundred-proof testosterone, spiked with dark irreverence.

Just the kind of smile Cian usually wore.

Och, aye, the man had a death wish.

There was no telling what Cian might have done next had a hand not closed over his forearm at that moment. He glanced down, his muscles instantly sliding smoother beneath his skin. Jessica was gazing up at him, lovely as ever, and unharmed.

"Woman, where have you been? I in-

330

structed you not to move from that counter."

"I stood there for half an hour," she replied crossly. "I went to the bathroom. I'm starving. Can we eat soon? I need coffee. And I want a shower. I took a little towel bath in the ladies' room, but I'm starting to feel like the wild animal that woman at the airport accused me of being. Cian, why is that man staring at you like that? Do you know him?"

" 'Cian'?" the man demanded. "Your name is 'Cian'?"

"Aye. What of it?"

The man stared at him a long moment. Then he laughed, a darkly amused sound, and shook his head as if he'd been pondering an absurdity. "Nay. 'Tis not possible," he murmured.

"What?" Cian snapped.

"Nothing. 'Tis nothing."

"What's with all these 'tis's? I didn't think Scottish people still talked like that," Jessica said, sounding puzzled, as she stood looking from one to the other. Suddenly, she sucked in a breath and cocked her head, staring back and forth again.

"You have my name. Give me yours," Cian said sharply.

"Dageus."

Cian looked down at Jessica. "Did this 'Dageus' say aught untoward to you, lass?"

She shook herself, as if jarred from thought. "How could he? This is the first I've seen of him. Do you know —"

"He was standing at the counter where I left you. You were gone when next I looked for you, and he was there."

She shrugged. "He must have gotten there after I'd already left. Cian, do you know that the two of you —"

Cian turned his attention back to Dageus. "You may go. But doona cross paths with me again, Highlander. 'Twill result in bloodshed. I doona care for you."

"I doona care for you, either," the man replied coolly. "But I'm not going anywhere until you release that salesman from your spell." He nodded past Cian, where the salesman waited. Where he would wait dazedly until Cian was through with him.

"What ken you of spells?" Cian asked softly.

"More than you, I'd wager."

"Not a chance. Stay out of my affairs."

Jessica tried to interject, "Do either of you see the slightest re—"

"This village and all in it *is* my affair. This is my world, stranger," Dageus retorted flatly.

" 'Twas my world long before it was yours, Highlander." Cian's smile showed teeth, but no amusement.

Dageus went motionless but for that intense golden gaze, scrutinizing Cian thoroughly. Again Cian felt a push at his mind, more subtle than the last, yet much more forceful.

He shoved back, much more forcefully, as well, and this time the man's unusual eyes flickered the tiniest bit.

"You doona mean what I think you mean by that," said Dageus.

"Thinking implies sentience. I see little of that in you."

"Look in a mirror, you'll see even less. I'll have your clan name, Highlander. What is it?"

Jessica piped up, "Speaking of looking in a mirror —"

"You'll have my clan name and a battle. 'Tis Keltar," Cian spat. "And yours?"

"Keltar," Dageus spat back.

Cian stared at him, stunned.

Beside him, Jessica exclaimed, "I knew it, I knew it! That's what I was trying to tell you, Cian. That the two of you *look* alike!"

18

"Get *back* here. You can't be finding out that you're my kinsman and then just go stomping off," Dageus snapped at Cian's broad retreating back.

"Watch me," the towering barbarian flung over his shoulder. To the dazed salesman, he ordered, *"Pack it all up and load in the black SUV outside the door. Here are the keys. Lock it when you've finished. I'll return for it anon. You will not speak of me or my woman to anyone."* Banding an arm around the curvaceous, raven-haired woman's shoulder, he steered her toward the door. "We have much yet to do. Come, lass."

Dageus watched in disbelief as his ancestor, Cian MacKeltar — he was assuming it *had* to be the ninth-century Cian MacKeltar standing before him, for he'd ne'er heard of any other Keltar with that name — prepared to stalk off into the Highland morn without so much as a "fare-thee-well." Without even having offered a "good-morrow, kinsman," for that matter.

Without so much as a blethering word of clanly tidings.

Without a single explanation for this incomprehensible happenstance!

Furthermore, the man was indiscriminately using Voice, left and right, as if no rules applied to him whatsoever.

"I assume you'll be *paying* for those goods," Dageus said pointedly.

"You assume wrong."

With that, the massive, wild-looking, tattooed Highlander guided the woman out the door, the salesman close on their heels.

Dageus glowered at the closing door. Christ, his ancestor was a savage! No wonder he'd gotten such a bad name. He looked uncontrollable, and he behaved like a barbarian. And by Danu, the power he sensed in him! Raw, rich, potent magic flowed through the man's veins, not blood. If the Draghar had gotten their claws into Cian rather than him . . .

He blew out a long, deep breath. 'Twas a damn good thing they hadn't. Though he couldn't fathom for a moment what might have prevented such a primitive, egotistical beast from breaking any rule he damn well pleased, including using the standing stones of *Ban Drochaid* for his own purposes.

What was he doing here? How had he gotten here? Where had he *been* for the past eleven centuries? Who was the woman with him?

He'd tried probing her while she'd stood at Cian's side, but had encountered some kind of sleek, smooth barrier. Was she a practitioner of magycks, too? His deep-listening talents had been growing by leaps and bounds over the past few months and he should have been able to pick up something. But he'd not gotten a flicker of a thought or emotion from her.

"Drustan's not going to like this," he muttered darkly. "Nay, he's not going to like it at all."

If a willingness to sacrifice everything for those he loved characterized Dageus, an abiding, unrelenting honor and a desire for a simple life uncomplicated by matters of Druidry and the Fae characterized his elder twin Drustan.

When he heard tell of this latest news, Drustan would undoubtedly say, "Why the blethering hell can't people stay where they belong, in their own century and out of mine?"

At which point his wife, Gwen, would remind him that it *wasn't* his century. That, in fact, it was *he* who'd begun it all by refusing to stay in the sixteenth century where he belonged. That if Drustan hadn't opted to slumber for five hundred years in a Rom enchantment so he could be reunited with Gwen in the twenty-first century, he never would have died in the fire that night so long ago. And if he'd not died in the fire, Dageus wouldn't have had to breach Keltar oaths and use the standing stones of the *Ban Drochaid* in violation of the sacred Compact between Man and the Tuatha Dé Danaan for personal gain, to go back in time and save Drustan's life. And if Dageus hadn't breached those oaths, he never would have been possessed by the souls of the thirteen evil Draghar, and forced to come forward himself to the twenty-first century, seeking a way to escape them.

And by the time his brainy physicist sister-in-law was done, Dageus had no doubt she'd have found some way to postulate an obscure yet peculiarly synchronistic link between Dageus and Cian himself, and Drustan would heap the blame for this new visitor soundly at Dageus's feet.

Which was *beyond* far-fetched. There was no way he was taking the blame for the sudden appearance of their controversial ninth-century ancestor. He'd only been reading up on him, not trying to summon him.

He rubbed his jaw, frowning, wishing he could be entirely certain of that last fact.

The problem was, months ago in London, when Aoibheal, Queen of the Tuatha Dé Danaan, had personally appeared and wielded her immense power to strip away the souls of the thirteen evil Druids possessing him, freeing him from their dark control, she'd left their memories inside him, and he wasn't always certain of precisely what he was capable or not.

Initially, when the Queen had removed the thirteen souls of the Draghar from him, he'd believed himself entirely free. After suffering the din of thirteen rapacious, twisted, demanding entities inside him, the silence inside his skull had made him think them completely eradicated.

It had been some time before he'd realized that, although their consciousnesses were gone, every last memory of thirteen entire lives had been left in him, buried deep in his subconscious. He'd not wanted to believe that he still contained the terrible and forbidden lore the Draghar had so long ago amassed and, at first, when inexplicable knowledge had begun popping into his head, he'd denied it.

But he no longer could. Each day he discovered something new about himself. And on occasion, of late, he'd caught himself muttering bits of a spell beneath his breath that he'd never read or practiced, and he knew he'd somehow plucked it from the endless vaults of the Draghar within him, as if his subconscious was sorting through the banks of memories, filing them away according to some mysterious design.

Had he inadvertently used a spell?

He sighed.

If he had, this was his fault and he had to fix it.

If he hadn't, he still had to do *something*. He couldn't just let the oversized heathen stalk and stomp about their Highlands, using Voice on all and sundry, stealing goods from simple merchants honestly endeavoring to support their clansmen.

As if you've ne'er stolen anything, his conscience jabbed.

"Aye, but I always gave it back, eventually." And he had. He didn't think Cian MacKeltar had any intention of making eventual amends. He didn't look like an eventual-amends kind of man.

Sighing, he tucked the box containing Chloe's hiking boots beneath his arm and walked out the door after his ninth-century ancestor.

As he stepped into the sunny Highland morn, he looked left, then right. He spied neither hide nor hair of Cian MacKeltar.

Back at the castle, his four-and-a-half-months-pregnant wife awaited him. Pregnancy suited his lovely Chloe like a Highlander's wet dream; she was even more amorous of late, and she was quite the sensual vixen under the usual circumstances. He was of no mind to be separated from her for long. They'd planned a hike in the hills today and a leisurely picnic. It was warm enough to toop outside on a plaid beneath an endless blue sky, and he'd been greatly anticipating hours and hours of hedonistic love play. Her breasts were getting fuller, her hips widening, and her skin glowed with the inner radiance of impending motherhood. He was impatient to taste and touch and explore every last changing inch of her. He was of no mind to alter his plans to accommodate this recent unexpected development. *Highly* unexpected development, at that.

Drustan, remember our ancestor, Cian, who I was talking about recently? Well, uh, he's here.

He shook his head, muttering a string of curses.

He thought for a moment, absently watching the still-fully-compelled salesman — that was a serious wallop his ancestor's Voice packed — load the stolen goods into Cian's SUV, wondering how he might spend the most time with Chloe yet still manage this new wrinkle.

His eyes narrowed. Camping gear. His kinsman was purloining camping gear. Was he squatting somewhere on Keltar land? The gall! How long had he been there?

He angled around the store employee and peered deeper into the SUV.

He blinked. Then he blinked again, very slowly, keeping his eyes closed for a moment before opening them.

It was still there.

It couldn't be! By Amergin — 'twasn't possible!

Was it?

"Move," he growled at the salesman, employing Voice without even thinking about it.

The salesman stepped obediently aside.

Dageus reached into the SUV, pushed

aside the blanket half-concealing the object, and another string of curses spilled from his lips.

"Impossible." But the proof of it was right there before his very eyes.

He'd never seen it before — verily, he never thought to see it — but the Draghar had.

The Dark Glass.

One of four unholy Unseelie Hallows.

At one point, the glass had actually been in their possession. They'd never been able to translate the spells necessary to use it, though not for lack of trying. Nor had they ever discerned its purpose.

It was a mystery to him as well, but he knew all he needed to know: His legendary ancestor of allegedly epic moral turpitude had one of the forbidden Unseelie Hallows in his possession.

And he was alive. And here in present day.

What the blethering hell was a Keltar Druid doing with the blackest of black magycks? They were Seelie guardians, not Unseelie!

The situation was far grimmer than he'd thought.

Rubbing his jaw, he pondered his options. They were few. He'd felt the power in his ancestor. He didn't delude himself for a moment that he'd be able to subdue him with magyck, unless he called on some of the Draghar's tricks, a thing he was highly reluctant to do.

Nor could he hope to use brute force without the possibility of innocent bystanders getting caught in the fray. Especially not if the formidable Druid simply lashed out with a spell to stop him.

Yet he needed to get the man to Castle Keltar.

Once there, mayhap together he and Drustan could bind him, question him, discover what was going on, and what to do about it.

His gaze slid back to the Dark Glass.

It exerted an unpleasant pull on him. Made him hunger to touch it. He'd heard tell that the Dark Hallows tended to have such a dangerous effect on men with power in their veins. He'd never experienced it before and hoped not to again. He felt both a constant, irresistible urge to reach for it, and also a bone-deep chill warning him away.

Eyeing it warily, the simplest solution occurred to him. One that would keep his need to touch it to a minimum.

His ancestor wasn't the only one who

could use Voice. Dageus excelled at it too. Though he doubted he could outright contradict anything his ancestor had commanded, he was fair certain he could work around it.

Placing a hand on the salesman's shoulder, he instructed him quietly but forcefully, *"You will give me the keys to that SUV. And when he returns for his vehicle you will tell him he will find it here."* Plucking a pen and one of the young salesman's business cards from the pocket of the glassy-eyed man's crisp white shirt, he scribbled the address of Castle Keltar. *"You will give him these keys, and direct him to that vehicle."* Handing the salesman his own set of keys, he pointed down the street to the vehicle he'd recently purchased, a Hummer it was called, though in his estimation it leaned more toward a roar than a hum.

The salesman nodded blankly.

Dageus had no doubt his ancestor would come, sword swinging, to reclaim the Dark Glass. The man was fiercely aggressive by nature and, given that he was freely dabbling with black arts, he would be even more so.

Like as not, he'd be dangerously violent. He and Drustan would be wise to sequester Chloe, Gwen, and the young twins away.

Carefully, without making contact with the glass, he rearranged the blanket over the mirror.

Then, circling round to the driver's side of the SUV, Dageus tossed Chloe's boots onto the passenger's seat, climbed in, fired up the engine, and headed for home.

"But he's your descendant, for heaven's sake!" Jessi exclaimed. "How can you just walk away from him?"

The moment she'd seen the man "Dageus" scowling at Cian, she'd been struck by their sameness. The more she'd stared back and forth between them, the more convinced she'd become that they *had* to be related somehow.

Though Cian's descendant had been dressed in expensive, tailored black trousers, a black turtleneck, and a buttery-soft leather jacket, though he'd been well groomed and polished, his civilized appearance had failed to conceal an innate primitiveness that was just like Cian's.

She'd tried to point it out, but they were kindred even in their edgy tempers and excess testosterone. She'd not been able to spit the whole sentence out because they'd kept talking over her.

She'd continued her assessment, periodically attempting to interject her thoughts, to no avail.

Both had long dark hair, both had strong, chiseled Celtic features, both had arrogance shaping the very curve of their spine, conquest in the cant of their heads upon their shoulders, and an extra *something* running in their veins besides very blue, very pure blood.

Both had a base, seething sexuality. Both had powerful, highly developed physiques. And there was no denying it, Dageus was incredible looking.

But Cian was more *man* than his descendant. Rawer, more elemental. Dageus was leaner and prettier. Cian was larger, rough, tough, down-and-dirty — and hands-down sexier.

"Hey, wait for me!" she called, sprinting to catch up with him. While she'd been mulling over her thoughts, he'd stalked off again. He was disappearing from her view down the Sugar/Spice/Dry Goods aisle.

For a man from the ninth century, he was a quick study. Upon entering the grocery store, he'd eyed a cart consideringly, glanced around at other customers, snatched it, and begun pushing up and down aisles, examining items, selecting various cans and tins, tossing them in.

Instant Suisse Mocha — woohooo! Jessi took two tins of it from the shelf as she sped by, caught up with him, and dumped them in the cart. She'd not missed the gas stove and pots he'd heisted, and was greatly looking forward to a cup of chocolaty coffee once they got back to their "camp."

"Aren't you the least little bit curious about him?" she pressed.

He grunted. "Now is not the time for new beginnings, lass." He cast the words over his shoulder at her with a scowl. "I'll make none."

Though she tried to hide it, a flicker of hurt flashed across her face. No new beginnings. She knew that.

And it shouldn't bother her. It wasn't as if *they* were making a new beginning or anything like that.

They were just stuck with each other for a while.

He wanted sex from her, nothing more. And this morning, he'd not even wanted sex. She was merely his means of remaining free from Lucan until he could have his vengeance. And he was merely her means of staying alive.

He couldn't have made his feelings any

plainer, really. Since the airport, all she'd gotten in the way of a kiss had been a stupid peck on the forehead that a chicken could have done better.

But like an idiot, she'd begun reading more into things than was actually there. They were forced to share close quarters, there was danger, and it was just making everything feel more intense than it was. On top of it, the man was devastatingly sexy, powerful, smart, and magic, to boot. Who could blame a girl?

No new beginnings.

Damn it, it shouldn't bother her!

But it did. She tried to turn away, but his hand flashed out and caught her by the chin.

"Let me go," she snapped.

"Nay." His grip was implacable on her jaw.

There was little point in fighting for control of her face; he could have hoisted her into the air with that one big hand on her jaw, if he'd wished.

He searched her gaze a long silent moment. "You truly doona ken it, do you? Excepting with you, Jessica. You, lass, are the exception to everything," he said softly.

As if he'd not just knocked the breath out of her with those words and left her feeling weak-kneed, he released her chin, turned away, and began pushing the cart again.

Jessi stood in the aisle, gaping after him. Then she broke into a sprint and caught him again. Closing a hand on his forearm, she tugged him to a stop. "You mean, you're not just stuck with me? You like me?" She wanted to kick herself the moment she blurted the stupid question. *Puh-thetic, Jessi,* she winced inwardly. *That was worse than the "I carried a water-melon" line from* Dirty Dancing.

His gaze was dark with some unfathomable emotion as he stared down at her. She stared, trying to determine what it was. It was an emotion she'd seen several times before, and at the oddest moments.

It was regret, she realized abruptly.

A subtle yet bottomless sorrow in those beautiful, darkly lashed eyes.

But what was he regretting, and why at this moment, as opposed to any other? It made no sense to her!

Suddenly he smiled, and the sadness was vanquished by whisky heat. "Aye, Jessica, I like you. And I'm not just stuck with you. You fit me here, woman." He *thump*ed his chest with his fist.

Then he shook her hand from his

forearm and pushed off with the cart again. Jessi watched him move down the aisle, all sleek animal muscle and dark grace.

Wow. He wasn't a man of many words, but when he used them, he certainly used the right ones. *You fit me here. You are the exception to everything.*

Crimeny.

It was how she'd always thought a relationship should be. People should fit each other: some days like sexy, strappy high-heeled shoes, other days like comfortable loafers — but always a good fit. And if you cared about someone, they *should* be the exception to everything; the number-one priority, the one who came before all others.

He was halfway down the aisle from her now, plucking a can from the shelf — her primal hunter/gatherer procuring food by modern means, she thought, with a soft snort of amusement. As she watched, he examined the can intently, read the ingredients, then returned it to the shelf and chose another, repeating his thorough study of it.

The contrast between his rough, tough-guy appearance and the domestic act he was performing did funny things to her head.

She had a sudden, breathtaking vision of a dark-haired little boy sitting in the seat of the cart, laughing up at Cian, grabbing at his swinging braids with chubby little fists, while his daddy inspected the ingredients on a jar of baby food. Her mind's-eye picture of sexy, strong man with beautiful, helpless child made something soft and warm blossom behind her chest.

Just then, two women sashayed around the corner, toting baskets on their arms. They were about her age, model-slim and very pretty.

When they saw Cian, their eyes widened and they did double takes.

Her soft and warm feeling popped with the abruptness of a balloon bursting.

As they made their way down the aisle toward her — the nerve of them! — they turned around *three* more times to check out his butt.

His butt. Like it was public property or something.

Her hands fisted. A thundery little storm began to brew.

Unfortunately the women ruined the beginnings of a perfectly good brood by smiling at her and whispering in a sisterly, conspiratorial manner as they passed,

"Heads-up, sweetie, *major* eye-candy ahead. Check it out."

As they moved into the next aisle, Jessi blew out a gusty sigh. They'd just had to be nice.

Crossing her arms, she glared at Cian's butt. Did it have to be so perfect? Couldn't he have been a little shorter? Maybe he should cut his hair. No, she amended hastily, she loved his hair. It was sexy and silky, and she really wanted to see it without all those braids in once. Not to mention, feel it sweeping her bare skin.

Something in her tummy did a flip-flop. It wasn't a comfortable feeling. It was a scary feeling. The dratted green-eyed monster had gotten her again. She felt downright possessive of him. Like he was *hers* or something. What was happening to her?

Cian turned just then and glanced back at her. His eyes narrowed. His hot gaze swept her from head to toe. He wet his lower lip, caught the tip of his tongue between his teeth, and flashed her a wicked smile.

His expression could not have more clearly said, *The moment I get through doing what must be done, I'm going to be all over you, woman.*

She brightened. "Okay," she said, nodding agreeably. It was looking like it might just turn out to be a banner day in Jessi St. James's world, after all.

He tossed his dark head back and laughed, his gilded-scotch gaze glittering with lust and unconcealed masculine triumph.

He was still laughing when he disappeared.

19

Banner day, her ass.

No bones about it — she *hated* that mirror.

It took Jessi nearly an hour to find her way back to the SUV.

Or rather, back to where the SUV had been in her other life — the one in which her possibilities for survival hadn't looked quite so grim.

When they'd stormed from Tiedemann's earlier, Cian had swiftly rearranged the mirror to his satisfaction, so their new "purchases" might not slip and slide in transit and damage it, then he'd turned and loped down the streets of Inverness at such a furious pace that it had been all she could do to keep up with him. She'd hardly glanced left or right, and hadn't paid any attention to where they were going, nor had she even bothered trying to gather the breath to talk to him, until they'd finally stopped at the grocery store. Ergo, she'd not realized how far he'd taken her, evading his descendant, until she'd attempted to retrace her steps through the unfamiliar Scottish streets.

Then — because she'd been watching for the SUV, not the store — she'd actually sprinted past Tiedemann's twice before realizing their stolen rental vehicle was no longer there.

"Shit, shit, *shit!*" she cried, staring at the empty space in front of the store.

She glanced farther down the street, thinking perhaps the SUV had inexplicably sprouted feet and moved itself while they'd been gone — stranger things had happened of late. Or maybe she'd just forgotten exactly where she'd parked it on the cobbled avenue.

Nope, not a single big, black, stolen SUV. On either side of the street.

How bad could one person's luck get?

"Don't answer that," she snapped hastily, in a general upward direction. "That was a purely rhetorical question, not a show-me-proof one." She was beginning to suffer the paranoid suspicion that the Universe was using her as the butt of a series of perverse jokes.

The whole time she'd been winding down street after street, she'd been damming a rising tidal wave of panic, assuring herself that everything was going to be just fine, that this was only a minor setback, that Cian had just been sucked back into the mirror earlier than either of them had expected, and once she got back to the SUV, she'd drive them back to their camp and they'd try again tomorrow, with greater success.

Which wasn't to say that she hadn't been pissed when he'd vanished. She had. She'd left her purse inside her backpack in the SUV, figuring she wouldn't need it because Cian could Voice her whatever she wanted, and her forty-two dollars and seventeen cents certainly wasn't going to go very far.

Then, when he'd so abruptly disappeared, she'd stood in the grocery with a cart full of lovely snacks, her stomach growling hungrily, and realized that she was going to have to *leave* all that scrumptious food, because she didn't have even a few dollars stuffed in a pocket somewhere, and couldn't buy so much as a measly candy bar to get her through for a while.

She'd been so hungry that she'd actually considered shoplifting. It had not been a stab of conscience that had prevented her from embarking on a larcenous spree — hunger was a brutally compelling motive

— but fear of being caught, because *then* what would happen to Cian?

With that worry foremost in her mind, stomach protesting her every retreating step, she'd left the grocery and dashed off to find him.

Only to find this — a great big, empty parking space.

Where was he?

She slumped down onto the curb and perched on the edge of it, propping her elbows on her knees, her chin on her fists.

She couldn't believe that Lucan could have found them so quickly.

If he had, wouldn't she be dead? Or at least under attack right now? She glanced hastily, warily around.

No one was staring at her or moving toward her in a menacing manner.

Which left only two other possibilities that she could think of: 1) a thief had stolen their stolen auto, which — in addition to pushing the limits of the absurd — sucked because, for the life of her, she couldn't see a way she was going to be able to track down a thief by herself, nor could she report a stolen vehicle stolen to the police, because the police *were* dread possibility number two; 2) the police had spotted it and impounded it and Jessi St.

James was now wanted for Grand Theft Auto (thanks to half a dozen pieces of identification in her purse) in addition to being wanted for theft of the mirror and probably all the stuff Cian had Voiced from Tiedemann's, and possibly Murder One (though she was really hoping deletion of the hotel records had gotten her out of that), as well as Just Plain Dead by one evil sorcerer.

She'd never been wanted for so many things in her life.

And not a single one of them any good.

Dageus grimaced as he tugged the Dark Glass from the back of the SUV.

Though he had no desire to make contact with it (mostly because he had *every* desire to make contact with it), he wanted it in the castle proper, the most heavily warded portion of the estate. 'Twould be safest there, and he hoped mayhap those wards would diminish the pull it was exerting on him.

There were no protection spells laid around the vast, detached garage behind the castle, where he'd parked the purloined SUV. 'Twas too new of a building, and one of which he'd not overseen the construction. He intended to properly ward it soon, for he hoped to make much use of it. He was developing quite a liking for modern modes of transportation. They were far easier on a man's privates than a horse betwixt the thighs.

He was already sorry he'd left his Hummer down in Inverness. The muscle-packed *H1 Alpha* was the first vehicle he'd purchased since he'd been living in the twenty-first century, and 'twas a truly magnificent machine. A man could go virtually anywhere in the rugged Highlands in it. He'd gotten attached to it in the manner a lad did his first fine stallion. He hoped his barbaric ancestor was a responsible driver.

"Arrogant Neanderthal," Dageus muttered, standing the mirror up on end, at arm's length, and taking a good look at it.

He inhaled a sharp, fascinated breath.

The legendary Dark Glass. In *his* hands.

Astonishing. He traced his fingers lightly over the cool silvery surface, then across the runes chiseled deep into the golden frame.

Not even the thirteen within him, who'd lived side by side with the Tuatha Dé many millennia ago, knew the language with which the frame was adorned.

It was said that the Seelie and Unseelie Hallows had been *spoken* into existence by the sheer magic of the Tuatha Dé tongue. The sacred relics had been spelled into being by words and song — and not in the tongue of Adam Black and his contemporaries but in a far more ancient language that had been spoken eons past, long before the Tuatha Dé had come to this world. A language allegedly forgotten by all but the most ancient among them.

A chill was inching up his arms.

'Twas not an entirely unpleasant sensation.

In fact, 'twas strangely invigorating. Made him feel positively powerful. Not good. Not good at all.

Scowling, he turned, hurrying with it from the garage. The moment he stepped from the cool, windowless interior into the brilliant sunshine, he felt better, stronger.

Still, he wasn't about to dally with the infernal thing in his hands.

Tucking the glass beneath his arm with the silvery side facing him so as not to blind anyone who might be looking his way, he walked around the castle and began heading across the front lawn.

"YOU BLOODY FUCKING IDIOT!" the mirror roared. "HAVE YOU ANY IDEA WHAT YOU'VE GONE AND DONE?"

Dageus was so startled by the bizarreness of the Dark Glass roaring at him that he did what most men would have done.

He dropped it.

Drustan lay flat on his back, his arm around his wife, breathing hard. 'Twas high noon and he was still in bed. Which wasn't to say he was a lazy man and hadn't yet been up that morn. He'd been up. And up. With his lovely wee Gwendolyn in his arms, he was nigh always up.

"God, that was amazing," his wife said fervently just then, curling closer into his side, one of her small, dainty hands caressing his lightly stubbled jaw.

He had a sudden urge to leap from the bed and proudly pound his chest with his fists. He settled instead for turning his head, kissing her palm, and saying with studied casualness, "Mean you the third or the fourth time, lass?"

She laughed. "*All* times. As it has been since our first time, Drustan. You're always amazing."

"I love you, woman," he said fiercely, recalling their first time. 'Twas a night he'd never forget, not a detail of it: not the crimson kitten thong he'd believed a fancy hair ribbon when he'd glimpsed it in her pack — until she'd slipped her shorts down that night, showing him what it was really meant for. Not the intense way they'd made love right there in God's great wide-open, beneath a star-drenched sky, in the center of the standing stones of *Ban Drochaid*. Nor the way she'd later stood, so true of heart and trusting, as he'd cast her back in time.

Gwen Cassidy was his soul mate, they were bound in the ancient Druid way, forever and beyond, and every moment of life with her was priceless. She'd enriched his world in so many ways, not the least of which had been the recent gift of two beautiful dark-haired twin daughters who, at scarce five months of age, were already showing rather startling signs of intelligence. And why shouldn't they, he thought proudly, betwixt his Druid gifts and his wee Gwendolyn's brilliant physicist's mind?

On the topic of their babes . . .

"Think you we should —"

"Yes," she agreed instantly. "I'm missing them too."

He smiled. Though they'd been wed for little over a year, they knew each other's mind and heart as well as their own. And although they had the best of care for their

362

daughters with two live-in nannies, they were reluctant to be parted from their bairn for long. Unless they were tooping, of course. *Then* they tended to forget the whole world.

When she peeled herself from his side and moved toward the shower, he rose to join her.

But as he passed the tall windows of their bedchamber, a flicker of motion beyond them caught his eye. He paused, glancing out.

His brother was standing out on the lawn, gazing down at the grass.

Drustan's smile deepened.

They'd been through a time of it when Dageus had turned dark. It had been hellish there for a while, but his brother was once again free and, by Amergin, life was rich and sweet and full! His da Silvan and their next-mother Nell would be delighted to know how well their sons fared in the modern day.

He had all he'd ever wanted: a cherished wife, a burgeoning clan, his brother wed and blissfully happy, and the prospect of a long, simple, good life in his beloved Highlands.

Och, there'd been a bit of a ruckus last month when one of the Tuatha Dé, Adam

Black, had appeared, but things had swiftly settled back into an easy cadence, and he was looking forward to a long time of —

He blinked.

Dageus was conversing with a mirror.

Standing in the middle of the front lawn, holding it gingerly by the sides, and speaking heatedly to it.

Drustan rubbed his jaw, perplexed.

Why was his brother talking to a mirror? Was it some strange twenty-first-century way of mulling things over, of — literally — consulting with oneself?

Come to think of it, he mused, where had the mirror come from?

It hadn't been there moments ago. It was taller than his brother. Wider too. 'Twas hardly as if Dageus might have been concealing it in a pocket or beneath a fold in his kilt, not that he was wearing a kilt. They'd both adopted modern modes of dress and were slowly adapting to new ways.

Drustan leaned against the windowpane. Nay, not only was the looking glass quite awkwardly large, it flashed brilliant gold and silver in the sun. How could he have overlooked it earlier?

Mayhap, he decided, it had been lying on the ground, and Dageus had picked it up. And mayhap he was merely saying something along the lines of "Oh, my, how peculiar, where did you come from?"

Drustan's silvery eyes narrowed. But why would a mirror be lying about on the front lawn? They had gardeners. Surely one of them would have noticed such a thing and relegated it elsewhere. How had it gotten there? Perchance dropped from the sky?

He was getting a bad feeling about this.

"Are you coming, love?" Gwendolyn called.

He heard the sound of the shower spray change as she stepped beneath it. In his mind's eye, he could see her; water sluicing down her beautiful body, glistening wetly on her smooth, pale skin. He adored modern plumbing, couldn't get enough of his wife when she was soapy and slippery and feeling frisky.

Below him, Dageus was now shaking a fist and shouting at the mirror.

Drustan closed his eyes.

After a long moment, he opened them again and cast a longing glance in the direction of the running shower and his gloriously naked, wet wife.

Then a glare out the window.

He exhaled gustily. "I doona think so, love. I'm sorry," he called, "but 'twould seem Dageus is, for some unfathomable reason, having a heated discourse with a looking glass out on our front lawn."

"Dageus is doing *what* with a heated horse and a looking glass?" Gwen exclaimed from the shower.

"Discourse, sweet, discourse," he called back.

"Huh?"

He sighed again. Then, "He's talking to a mirror," he called much more loudly. "I must go discover why."

"Talking to a — oh! On the front lawn? Dageus? Really? Wait for me, Drustan! I'll just be a minute," she yelled back. "This sounds positively *fascinating!*"

Drustan shook his head. *Fascinating,* his woman said. She had the oddest perspective on things sometimes.

He smiled faintly then, suddenly far less chafed by the prospect of yet another ruckus in his life. After all, wasn't that what life was about?

Ruckuses.

And if a man was truly blessed, he got a woman like his Gwendolyn with whom to share them.

"Pick me *up,* you ham-fisted oaf. The bloody frigging sun is bloody frigging *blinding* me," the mirror snarled.

Dageus blinked down at the glass. 'Twas lying faceup on the lawn and stuffed nigh to bursting with an enraged Cian MacKeltar.

One of his ancestor's hands was braced at the side of the mirror on the *inside* of the glass, the blade of his other hand to his forehead as if shielding his narrowed eyes from a glare.

For a long moment, Dageus simply couldn't find any words with which to form a sentence. Then, "What the hell are you doing in there, kinsman?" he managed blankly.

There was a man inside a mirror. His relative. His *ancient* relative. He thought he'd seen it all, but he'd ne'er seen aught like this. Dozens of questions collided in his mind.

"Sun. Blinding. Pick me up," his ancestor snapped.

Dageus glanced up. The sun *was* directly above him.

He glanced back down. Mystified, he bent and stood the glass up on end, facing him. He handled it gingerly, trying not to touch much of it. Because his grip was not firm, it slipped from his fingers and nearly went right back down again. He scarce managed to catch it in time.

"For Christ's sake, be careful with the

damn thing!" his ancestor hissed. " 'Tis made of glass. Sort of. In an odd sense of the word. Are you always so clumsy?"

Dageus stiffened. "Are you always such a foul-tempered arse? You've the manners of a blethering Lowlander. 'Tis no wonder you've such a bad reputation."

"I've a bad —" His ancestor broke off, raising his hands as if to ward off further talk on that topic. "Forget it. I doona wish to ken what they say about me." He glanced around the lawn. "Where the hell have you taken me?"

"Castle Keltar." Dageus thought a moment, then added, "A second Castle Keltar, not the one you likely knew."

A muscle worked in his kinsman's jaw. "And how far would this second Castle Keltar be from Inverness?"

Dageus shrugged. "Half an hour or so."

"Let me guess, you interfering barbarian. For some reason, you took my vehicle?" the mirror snapped.

"*I'm* a barbarian? Look who's talking," Dageus said indignantly.

"You bloody fool, you will go back down there and get my woman. *Now.*"

"Your woman? The lass 'twas with you in the store?"

"Aye."

368

Dageus shook his head slowly. This was leverage. "Nay. Not until you tell me what's going on, and explain yourself to my brother. What are you doing in the mirror? I ken full well what it is. 'Tis the Dark Glass, an Unseelie Hallow, and the Keltar have no business with Unseelie relics. How are you using it? Are you practicing black magycks? My brother will not permit such doings in his keep. Drustan suffers no —"

His kinsman pounded his fists on the inside of the mirror, actually rattling it in the ornate frame. "Go *get* my woman! You left her unprotected, you son of a bitch!"

"Nay. Answers first," Dageus said flatly.

"Not a word until she's here," Cian said just as flatly.

They glared at each other, at an impasse.

A sudden thought occurred to Dageus. Why wasn't his temperamental, formidably gifted ancestor bursting forth from the glass and going after his woman himself? What could stop a Druid as mighty as Cian MacKeltar. "You're *stuck* in there, aren't you?" he exclaimed.

"What the bloody hell do you think? You think I'd be sitting in here twiddling my thumbs if I could do something? Go. Get. My. Woman."

"But you were out earlier. How? Why —"

"You said you had a woman of your own," his ancestor cut him off roughly. "How would you feel if she'd been left by herself in the middle of a city she'd never been in before, and there were trained assassins hunting her? My woman is in danger, damn you! You *must* go after her, man! Then I'll tell you aught you wish to ken!"

A fist closed around Dageus's heart at the thought of Chloe in such a situation. He'd seen her in danger before and it had damn near killed him. A man's woman took priority over everything else. Questions could wait. The care and well-being of loved ones could never be deferred.

Never.

"Och, blethering hell, I didn't know. I'll go get your woman," he said instantly. Tucking the mirror beneath his arm again, he hastened with it toward the castle.

"We're going the *wrong* way!" the mirror shouted for the third time, as Dageus walked up the front steps and entered the castle.

"Nay, we're not. I told you, I'm not taking you with me," Dageus said flatly. "I will find your woman far more quickly if I doona have to be worrying about breaking you. I know what she looks like. I'll find her, I vow it."

'Twas truth that he didn't wish to have to be concerned about damaging the mirror, but even more truth that he didn't want to be in such close proximity to the Dark Hallow any longer. He suspected its strange pull had been working subtly on him the entire time he'd been driving home, peaking when he'd opened up the back of the SUV. He had no desire to spend what could be hours driving around, with the Hallow no more than a few feet away from him, in an enclosed space.

Tossing his head back, he bellowed, *"Drustan!"* with enough volume to rattle the eaves.

"Christ, Dageus, I'm right above you," his brother replied, wincing. "There's no need to go shouting the walls down."

Dageus glanced up. His twin was standing at the balustrade that overlooked the great hall entrance, gazing down. "How was I to know that? Why are you standing there, Drustan?"

"Why are you talking to a mirror, Dageus?" Drustan said very, very quietly.

"I said 'wait for me!' " Gwen cried at that moment, from somewhere down the corridor behind his brother.

371

Dageus shook his head. He had no time for explanations. The woman's name, Cian had told him as they'd crossed the lawn, interspersed with his increasingly pissed-off demands to accompany him back down to Inverness, was Jessica St. James. She was an innocent in this — whatever "this" was — and she was in mortal danger.

He had to go. *Now.*

Propping the mirror against the wall near the door, he waved a hand at it and clipped, "Drustan: Cian MacKeltar. Cian: Drustan MacKeltar."

"Dageus," Drustan's voice was soft as velvet, never a good sign, "why are you introducing me to a mirror?"

"Look *in* the mirror, Drustan," Dageus said impatiently, angling it a bit so he could see into it from above.

His brother's jaw dropped.

Dageus smiled faintly. 'Twas nice to know he wasn't the only one utterly discombobulated by the sight of a man inside a mirror. "I doona believe he can get out, Drustan, so he shouldn't present a danger. However, you may wish to store him away from women and children until we know more."

Drustan was still gaping, speechless.

The mirror growled, "Away from women

372

and children? I've *never* been a threat to women and children, you lummox!"

"Verily, kinsman, we know naught about you," Dageus retorted. "So why doona you try explaining things to my brother while I'm gone? Then mayhap somebody can explain them to *me* when I return."

"Doona leave me here," Cian hissed. "Take me with you."

"I said I'll find your woman, and I will."

Above him, Drustan finally found his tongue. "Cian MacKeltar!" he exploded. "Mean you our *ancestor* Cian? The one from the *ninth* century?"

"Aye. And 'tis the Dark Glass, Drustan, one of the Unseelie Hallows," he imparted tersely. His brother didn't contain the vast knowledge of the Draghar within him, and Dageus doubted his ability to recognize it for what it was. "You may wish to keep your contact with it to a minimum. It works on the magic in our blood, enticing us." He added a final aside: "I inadvertently left his woman unprotected. I must go get her. I'll return as soon as I can."

Without further ado, Dageus turned and raced from the castle.

20

Jessi polished off her third hamburger, balled up the paper wrapping, and tucked it back in the bag.

"Better, lass?" Dageus asked.

"Oh, yes," she said with a contented sigh. She'd never tasted such scrumptious, decadently juicy, perfect hamburgers in her entire life, though she suspected not having eaten in over twenty-four hours might be biasing her the teeniest bit. She gulped thirstily at her super-sized water; all the walking and worrying she'd done today had left her feeling dehydrated.

Leaning back against the seat of the SUV, she stretched out her legs. She was feeling tremendously better, buoyed by food, heartened by the discovery that Cian was somewhere safe, and quite frankly delighted that she wasn't going to have to sleep beneath a bridge somewhere tonight using newspaper for blankets.

"Och, Christ, have I told you how sorry I am?"

"Only about a hundred times now," she told Dageus dryly.

" 'Tis but that I feel like such an ass, lass. I'd ne'er have taken the mirror if I'd thought 'twould leave you in any danger. Please believe that."

"I do," she assured him. "And it's all right. Everything turned out okay. I'm here, Cian's safe, and no one's the worse for wear." Although, she appended silently, she wasn't going to feel a hundred percent okay until she saw Cian with her own eyes.

She glanced over at Dageus. It was full dark outside and the only light in the SUV came from the faint green glow of the dashboard's electronics. He looked a lot like Cian in the low light; same strong features, long hair, powerful body. His quiet respect and responsibility toward women reminded her of Cian as well.

He'd been searching for her for hours, he'd told her, when they'd finally crossed each other's path.

At a complete loss for what to do upon discovering the SUV missing, Jessi had commenced methodically searching every street, alley, and parking lot in Inverness, hoping against hope that she would somehow miraculously stumble upon it somewhere. It was a terrible plan, and she knew it, but she'd needed to take some action, *any* kind of action, to avoid having a mcltdown.

The truth was, she'd not really expected to find the stolen vehicle again and, near dusk, when she'd spotted it at the end of the next block, idling by the curb, she'd been flabbergasted.

She sprinted eagerly, stupidly toward it the moment she'd glimpsed it. Belatedly, she'd checked herself and stopped warily, a dozen feet away.

Then Cian's descendant had stepped from it.

Hey, she'd blurted to his back, without thinking, *I know you! What are you doing with our SUV?*

The sudden fear that he might be a bad guy, too, had spiked through her then. But he'd turned and looked at her and his expression had been one of such pure relief that her fears vanished. *Thank God! There you are, lass. I've been looking all over for you!* he'd exclaimed.

Exhausted and starving, she'd nearly burst into tears.

She wasn't all alone and lost in Scotland with nowhere to turn, after all. Someone had been looking for her. Someone was glad to see her.

He'd told her, with the first of his many apologies, that he'd only taken the SUV because he'd seen the Dark Glass in it and been worried about what was being done with the Hallow. He'd been home already when he'd discovered Cian in the mirror, and been sent back by his furious ancestor to find her.

His furious ancestor, he'd said. He *knew.* And he wasn't the least bit weirded out by it!

Although Dageus had referred to Cian as "kinsman" in Tiedemann's, Jessi had decided that Dageus must have believed they were somehow distantly related in *current* day, that Cian was an illegitimate, distant cousin or something.

Certainly not that he was an ancient ancestor who'd been trapped in a mirror for eleven centuries. Really, what sort of person would readily accept that kind of nonsense? She certainly hadn't. She'd resisted until the last possible moment, only when she'd been forced to concede that her life was at stake.

But Dageus wasn't having any problem with it at all. Which pointed to only one logical conclusion.

"So, I guess none of you MacKeltars are normal, huh?" she probed.

He smiled faintly. "Nay, not exactly. I'm fair certain my wife will tell the tale better than I, but I and my twin, whom you'll meet shortly, are from the sixteenth century."

Jessi blinked. "Did you turn too? Is that how you got here?"

"Turn?"

"Into a dark sorcerer," she clarified. "Is that how you and your brother ended up here? Did you guys get stuck in things, too?"

Dageus made a choking sound. "By the sweet saints, is Cian a dark sorcerer, then, lass?"

"Don't you know anything about your ancestor?"

"His name was stricken from all Keltar annals eleven centuries ago. Verily, until just recently when the underground chamber was reopened, we believed him a legend, naught more. Is he a dark sorcerer, then?"

"He seems to think so. I'm not so sure."

"How did he end up in the mirror?"

"I don't know. He won't talk about it. Yet," she added firmly. Jessi'd had several epiphanies today while hunting for Cian, terrified that she might never see him again. The day had stretched on and on, and, alone with her thoughts and fears, certain facts had attained a stark clarity in her mind.

One was that she wanted to know everything there was to know about Cian MacKeltar. All of it, good and bad. She knew from the parts of his stories that had penetrated her stupor the night he'd killed the assassin masquerading as Room Service, that he'd had a wonderful childhood in the Highlands. She knew also that, somewhere, something had gone terribly wrong. She wanted to know what it was; how he'd ended up in the mirror; how he could think he was a dark sorcerer when every time she looked at him, she saw light.

Oh, not pure sweet blinding light. Not even close. Cian MacKeltar wasn't that kind of man and would never be. Truth was, she didn't much like that kind of man anyway. Cian wasn't one of the bad guys — but he could be if necessary, at the drop of a hat and utterly without remorse.

But "bad guy" wasn't his primary persona. He was what psychologists and anthropologists would call an Alpha male, men who were defined by an inherent lawlessness. They obeyed only their own code, and if it happed to briefly converge with the laws of society-at-large, it was mere coincidence. One could never be completely certain what an Alpha male would do if he, or those he considered his, were threatened. One could only hope to stay within an Alpha male's protected circle — or as far out of his line of sight as possible.

Jessi knew where she wanted to be, smack at the center of Cian MacKeltar's protected circle. And not just because someone was after her, but because he wanted her there under any circumstances. That was the second epiphany she'd had today while frantically hunting for him.

"But you doona think he's dark, eh, lass?" Dageus jarred her from her thoughts. "You think he's a good man? Do you believe in him, lass? With your heart?"

She looked at him curiously. There was a note of urgency in his voice, as if the question was very important to him. "You don't even know me. Would it matter to you if I did?"

"Och, aye, Jessica. A woman's thoughts and feelings always matter to Keltar men."

Hmmm. With each passing moment, she was liking Keltar men more and more.

"So? Do you?" he pressed.

"Yes," Jessi said without reservation. "I do."

When they got to the castle — Crimeny, she was in a *castle!* — Dageus guided her through at such breakneck speed that her surroundings whizzed by and she hardly managed to see a thing.

She got a brief, astonished glimpse of a magnificent great hall with a fabulous fairy-tale staircase that descended from both sides of the upper stories, a rapid look at a stunning suit of armor in an alcove, and a much-too-hasty glance into a darkly paneled room adorned by ancient weaponry, with claymores, battle-axes, spears, and broadswords gracing the walls in intriguing geometric patterns. She'd positively itched to grab a chair, pull them down, and begin testing for authenticity. Though she suspected everything she was seeing was the genuine article.

Why wouldn't the contents of the castle be from centuries long past? The occupants were.

After steering her into a library, he deposited her there, then hurried off to "gather the rest of the clan and bring your man in. My brother and our wives will join you anon."

Now, waiting by herself, she proceeded to take a thorough, fascinated peek around.

The library was a beautiful, spacious, yet cozily inviting retreat, reminding Jessi much of the understated, impeccable elegance of Professor Keene's office.

Tall bay windows, draped in velvet, overlooked a manicured garden. Cherry bookcases were recessed into paneled walls. An enormous, dusky-rose stone and marble fireplace climbed one wall, the elaborate mantel climbing all the way to the ceiling. There were many richly brocaded, overstuffed chairs and ottomans arranged in various conversation areas, beside lavishly carved, leather-detailed occasional tables. The trey ceiling had ornate embossing and three tiers of elegant moldings. A stately bar was custom-crafted into a section of the bookshelves.

From what she'd seen on her rushed way through, the entire castle was a historian's dream, liberally scattered with antiques and relics, and the library was no different.

Centuries-old tapestries adorned the walls. The room was illumed by exquisite — and she was willing to bet real — Tiffany table lamps that cast a stained-glass amber and rosy glow about the room. The majority of the books on the shelves were leather-bound and some looked quite old, resting with care on their flats, not their spines. A massive desk with a top inlaid of three gleaming burled panels divided by intricate Celtic knot-work occupied one corner, with a tall leather chair behind it. Library tables perched beneath spotlighted portraits of Keltar ancestors. Muted antique rugs warmed the room, accented by an occasional plush lambskin. A pretty ladder with sides of carved scrollwork slid along the walls of bookcases on padded wheels, atop the gleaming perimeter of wood floor.

She was just moving toward the ladder, to push it to an especially interesting-looking pile of manuscripts, when two pretty blondes burst into the library, followed by a man she initially mistook for Dageus.

"Welcome to Castle Keltar," one of the blondes said breathlessly. "I'm Gwen and this is my husband, Drustan. This is Dageus's wife, Chloe."

"Hi," Jessi said tentatively. "I'm Jessi St. James."

"We know. Dageus told us," Gwen said. "We can't *wait* to hear your story. You can start now if you'd like," she said brightly. "We've been waiting all day."

Dageus walked in then, toting the

mirror, holding it by the sides.

She'd half expected to hear furious bellows heralding his approach, and was somewhat surprised that the glass was silent.

He crossed the room and propped the mirror up against the bookcase, near the conversation area where she and the MacKeltars had gathered.

She peered at it. It was flat silver and there was no sign of Cian.

Jessi hurried over to the looking glass, reaching instinctively for it.

At the same moment, Cian's hand rose within the silver as he stepped forward, making himself visible.

She heard feminine gasps behind her.

"So *there* he is," one of the women exclaimed. "Not only did he refuse to answer any of our questions, he wouldn't even *show* himself until you got here."

The world receded around her and narrowed down to nothing but Cian. The expression in his whisky gaze was stark.

"Och, Jessica," he said, his butter-rum voice rough and low. He was silent a moment, drinking her in. "I'm not much of a man when I can't even protect my woman. The bloody glass reclaimed me and I couldn't get to you!"

My woman, he'd called her. She could see in his eyes and hear in his voice that the day of worrying had been hell on him too. She was sorry it had been; and she was glad. Glad it hadn't been just her going crazy. Glad because it meant his feelings matched hers. "Yes, you *are,*" she told him fiercely. "You're more man than any I've ever known. You're more man than any other man could ever *hope* to be. You've saved my life twice! I'd be dead if it weren't for you. Besides, you couldn't possibly anticipate that your stupid descendant would *steal* you. Who could have seen that coming?"

Behind her, someone cleared his throat. She thought it might be Drustan, but he and Dageus were so alike that it was hard to be sure. Then she knew it was Dageus because, with a note of wry amusement in his voice, he said, "His stupid descendant wishes to know how you release him, lass."

She pressed her other palm to the glass. Cian aligned his to hers. They stared hungrily at each other. After being afraid she'd lost him, she needed to touch him, ached to feel his body against hers, to taste his kisses. To feel his hands claiming her. *His woman,* he'd called her, and she was pretty sure those weren't words a ninth-century Highlander ever used lightly.

"Is it okay if I tell him?" she asked Cian.

He shrugged. "Aye, I suppose so."

She said over her shoulder, "There's a summoning spell — *Lialth bree che bree, Cian MacKeltar, drachme se-sidh* — but it won't work right now because —"

Even as she was about to explain that not enough time had elapsed since that morning when he'd last been out, the runes carved into the ornate frame began to blaze with a brilliant inner light and the parameters of the library felt suddenly skewed. Her jaw dropped.

Cian looked just as startled as she. Then his dark eyes blazed with exultation. "Mayhap because the last two times were so short, lass," he exclaimed hoarsely. "Who cares the why of it?"

He pushed forward, reaching for her. One moment Jessi had her palms pressed to cool glass, the next it was full black and icy, and then the warm strength of his hands was closing around hers. He separated from the mirror, peeling away from the silvery rippling pool, walking her backwards, his gilt-whisky eyes glittering with passion and lust not-to-be-denied.

She shivered with anticipation.

Distantly, she heard Chloe and Gwen's startled exclamations, then heard nothing more when he ducked his head and slanted his mouth hungrily over hers. She melted into him, against the hot steel of his big body, threading her fingers into his braids, parting her lips, yielding utterly to him.

Abruptly, he dragged his mouth from hers. "Is this castle warded, kinsmen?" he grated over her shoulder.

One of the twins answered, "Well, aye —"

"Think you two puny Druids can hold this keep for a single night?" Cian cut him off.

"We two *puny* Druids," one of the twins spat, "could hold —"

"— this keep for a blethering eternity if we so wished," the other twin finished.

"Good. Go do it. Get the bloody hell out of here."

He slanted his mouth over Jessica's again.

Behind the passionately entwined couple, Drustan's eyes narrowed, his nostrils flared. "Of all the arrogant —"

"Remember the day I trapped you in the garderobe and you finally remembered who I was, my love?" Gwen interrupted softly.

Drustan swallowed the rest of his words. Did he ever! He'd been nigh crazed with desire for her. Naught in the world could have stopped him from making love to her then and there. In fact, they'd doffed every scrap of clothing the two of them had worn, right there in the great hall, and to this day, he was uncertain if they'd had an audience. And to this day, he still didn't care.

Which was exactly how it appeared Cian and Jessica were feeling. In fact, there went the man's shirt soaring over her head, to land on a lamp. The delicate stained-glass shade wobbled a precarious moment, then settled.

Drustan had no desire to see any more of his ancestor than he was currently seeing.

Except, he thought, scrutinizing the man's sculpted upper torso, *blethering hell, what are those tattoos?* Had another Keltar fallen from grace? If so, how far? He had wee bairn sleeping abovestairs, a wife and clan to protect, and he'd like to know what to expect. Who and what was this man and what was he doing here? And why did he have an Unseelie Hallow? He wanted explanations, by God, he *deserved* explanations. This was his castle, his world. He was the senior Keltar male, after all! Or . . . er, *och,* he *had* been the senior

Keltar male until a few moments ago!

His scowl deepened. If his ninth-century ancestor thought he was going to usurp lairdly duties of the clan based on birth order, he was sadly mistaken.

He regarded him irritably, but despite his displeasure, his expression softened.

Cian and Jessica were kissing like the world might come crashing to an end at any moment.

And Drustan knew exactly how that felt. Each time he kissed his wife, each time he held their precious twins in his arms, it seemed the world couldn't possibly grant him time enough to love, even if it spun out to eternity.

He didn't need to try deep-listening to his ancestor to know the woman Cian was kissing was his mate.

Some things required no explanations.

The matching of a Keltar with his woman was one of them.

He heard the metal groan of a zipper. His or hers, he didn't know. Nor was he about to stand about and find out.

His questions would have to wait.

Pivoting, he ushered the lot of them from the library.

21

The moment Jessi heard the *snick* of the library door as it closed behind the MacKeltars, her body tensed and her pulse began to race nervously.

They were alone, Cian was free of the mirror, and she was touching him. She couldn't have asked for more, yet all of a sudden she felt weirded out about it.

With the instincts of a natural-born predator, Cian sensed the change in her body. He broke the kiss and drew back, gazing down at her. His sexy mouth was kiss-slicked and half-opened on the hard, fast breathing of lust, and his dark, hooded eyes glinted dangerously.

She moved back a few steps and stood staring up at him, panting as raggedly as he.

He reached out and lightly brushed her jaw with the back of his knuckles. When he spoke his voice was rough, hot, and low. "Is aught amiss, woman?"

She shook her head.

"I doona think I would handle it well if you played games with me, Jessica."

Swallowing audibly, she shook her head again.

"What, then?" he demanded.

She shrugged helplessly. She had no words. She couldn't explain. She wanted him right now more than she'd ever wanted anything in her life and, at the same time, she felt as if she'd suddenly found herself perched on the edge of a precipice, and had no idea what she was doing there. Was goaded by some bone-deep, desperate imperative to back away, to seek safer ground.

She didn't understand it. She was no coward. She was certainly no cock-tease. She wanted him. And not just for sex, but much more, which was the way she'd always believed it should and would be when she finally slept with a man. Here he was, the man she desired, and he desired her too. Twice before she'd been ready to plunge right in and have sex with him. So what in the world was wrong with her now?

Cian scrutinized Jessica. Now would have been a fine time to be able to deep-read his woman, but he couldn't, so he turned his focus to her body instead of her mind.

Her jade eyes were stormy. Defiance shaped her stance. Her chin was uptilted, her delicate nostrils flared, her feet planted shoulder-width apart, like a little warrior.

Yet counterpoint to the blatantly telegraphed denial was — not merely invitation — but sheer feminine taunt. *Look at me.* Her spine was arched, her ass outthrust, her heavy breasts proudly raised and displayed to their finest.

Her nipples were hard, poking through her snug white sweater.

And she'd just wet her lips again. Tossed her head in a challenging come-hither.

Don't touch me/Come and get me, every ounce of her was saying.

Cian closed the distance between them, ducked his head, and inhaled sharply. She stepped back again, but not before he'd gotten what he'd been after. He smiled, pleased by her dichotomy. He fathomed it well.

She smelled of an exquisite combination of fear, defiance, and desperate sexual hunger. 'Twas a scent he'd waited all his life to smell, a desire that had intensified painfully in him over these past days.

He'd wager, even as learned as she was,

she didn't fully understand what she was feeling.

But he did. Perfectly.

It was all he'd dared hope for.

Jessica St. James had accepted him as her man, and for more than just this night. If she hadn't, she'd not have smelled of this unique combination. A woman seeking only a night's pleasure smelled of desire, little more. Certainly not fear and defiance, unless the man was doing something he shouldn't be, things the woman didn't want, and such a bastard should be put down. Women were precious, to be cared for, not despoiled and abused.

But a woman recognizing her mate smelled of those things because such recognition heralded significant life change. In his century, the woman would have recognized that babes were coming, that she was leaving her girlhood and her clan behind, bonding to a new clan, cleaving to her husband and his people, embarking upon the impassioned tear- and joy-filled route of her mother before her.

A strong, independent, modern woman like Jessica St. James would instinctively resist such change, in proportions equal to her desire for it. She was a woman accustomed to being in control. With him, her control would be threatened.

He intended to threaten the hell out of it.

It was time he made her his. Time he made it clear that, although she might one day lie with another man, none would ever be *him,* none would ever be good enough, none would *ever* make her feel the way he had this night. The way he would make her feel the next and the next and the next. He would sear his mark into her in ways she would never be able to forget. When one day she took another man to her bed, he would be on that mattress between them, a great, big, dark Highlander using up too much space, a barrier around her heart, forever alive in her memory.

When he reached for her and pulled her back into his arms, he got more of her womanly dichotomy, but 'twas a dichotomy a man could work with, verily, a wise man would savor.

For as she came into his arms, she turned her back to him as if to deny him, yet at the same time backed right up to him, thrusting her sweet ass against his hard, hot cock. She wanted what he wanted: claiming first, loving later.

With a soft moan, she quested back with

her bottom. The sound ripped into his groin, stringing his testicles tight. Dropping his head forward, he cupped her jaw, slanted her face around, and kissed her, deep and long, pumping his hard shaft against her lush behind.

He walked her forward, one hand at her waist keeping her pressed back to him, the other on her chin. He nipped at her kiss-glossed, lush lips, tasting her with slow, firm sucking pulls. He trailed more kisses over the delicate shape of her ear, down the edge of her jaw, over her neck. He continued walking her forward until he walked them into something, not caring what piece of furniture it might be, so long as he found one.

Something to lay her down on would be good.

Ah, his descendant's desk — better still! Groping blindly, he shoved everything off it, heedless of the crashing, tinkling sounds of objects hitting the floor. Filling his hands with her lush breasts, he bent her forward, over the ornately carved, cool wood. She gasped, bracing her palms on the high-glossed desk.

He needed to be inside her. Nothing less than final, incontrovertible proof that she'd chosen him for her man would sate him now. Reluctantly relinquishing those heavy breasts that jiggled so perfectly, so womanly, with his every thrust, he slipped his hands down to her jeans. "I'm going to take you now, lass."

She jerked and arched her delicate spine, glancing over her shoulder at him. Her eyes were as wild as he knew his must be. "Yes," she said raggedly. "Please, Cian."

Please, Cian. He could listen to her say those words for the rest of eternity! Die a happy man, hearing her beg carnal pleasure from him. Die trying to give it to her, any way she wanted it.

"Are you wet for me, Jessica?" He knew she was. He could smell her woman's heat. But he wanted her to say it. Wanted to hear her talk about how he made her feel, how she felt about him.

"I *always* am around you." She sounded both marveling and miffed by the admission.

"Does that fash you, lass?"

"I've never felt, *ooh!*" — she gasped when he ground himself in a slow circle against her as he slowly undid the top button of her jeans — "this way before. I'm always turned on, and I can't seem to turn it off."

"It makes you feel out of control."

"Yes." She sounded fully miffed and not at all marveling now.

"You're supposed to be out of control for your man, lass. That's the way of passion. Think you passion is tidy? Neat?" He laughed. "Hardly. Not in my bed."

"What about the man?" she demanded. "Is he out of control for the woman?"

He grunted. A man could never completely lose control with his woman. At least not a man his size with a woman her size. Still, that didn't mean he wasn't out of control in his thoughts, in his gut. He was. Just looking at her made something in him that had always been wild to begin with, even wilder. "I'm always hard for you. I got hard the moment I saw you that first night. And, nay, lass, I can't turn it off, either. But unlike you, I doona try to. I give into the heat. The need. The pain of the hunger. I savor wanting you, lusting for you, thinking about all the things I'm going to do to you." He cupped a cheek of her jean-clad ass in each big palm, squeezed. His voice deepened to a sexy, hot purr: "I relish every last thought of taking you, of knowing you as completely and intimately as a man can know his woman. And I'm going to know every inch of you, lass. You want that, doona you, Jessica?"

"Yes," she moaned.

"By the time I'm done with you, you'll never be able to forget me. I'm going to burn myself into you so deep that you'll bear the imprint of me beneath your skin for the rest of your life. Tell me you want me to, Jessica." *Forgive me now for sins you doona even know I'm committing.*

"I want you t— *oooh!*" Her reply turned into a gasp when he thrust strongly against her.

He smiled with dark satisfaction. There was too much clothing between them. He needed to feel her slick and wet and tight, closing on him. Popping the remaining two buttons of her jeans, he shoved them down over her hips, baring her luscious little ass.

He sucked in a ragged breath, pushed her jeans to her ankles, but no farther, leaving her feet caught in them.

"You want to feel me inside you, lass?"

"Yes!"

"Slow and easy, or hard and fast? What would you have of me, Jessica?"

"Yes," she wailed.

He laughed, a deep rumble of masculine triumph. A man dreamed of an unconditional "aye" from such an exquisite woman.

Lifting her hips, he repositioned her the

way he wanted her. Nudging her feet back, he pushed her thighs apart until her knees bent to accommodate the angle, and stepped between them. Catching her jeans behind his boots, he kicked back, drawing them taut at her ankles, pinning her helplessly in her jeans, trapping her between his big body and the desk.

With her legs spread on either side of his thighs, he could keep them wide apart, her ass up-thrust, her soft folds exposed. In her prone stance, she could only take what he was about to give her. Not control it a bit. And if she tried to, all he'd have to do was kick back with a boot to still her.

Later he might give her all the control she wanted — though it would chafe him to the very core of his manhood, he'd consider letting her tie him nine ways to Imbolc if it pleased her — but right now any control he yielded her would weaken his, and his was as threadbare as the original pair of trews he'd been wearing the day he'd been imprisoned.

They'd fallen to rags half an aeon ago.

Jessi gasped when Cian stepped between her legs. She was so wet and ready for him! She couldn't have moved her lower body if her life had depended on it, and she'd never been so painfully turned-on in her life as she was, helplessly spread for him like this.

He was behind her, her great, big, intensely sexual Highlander, and for a moment, she was reminded of the first time she'd seen him in the professor's office, a shadowy intimidating presence in the mirror. And the thought occurred to her then that from that very moment, *this* very moment had been somehow preordained. Inescapable. That no matter which way she'd tried to go, it all would have ended up with her bent over a desk, breathlessly waiting for him to take her, to make her feel this wildly alive. There was a word on the tip of her tongue, something about events lining up in improbable ways. It wasn't "synergy," it wasn't "coincidence" or "providence." It might begin with an S, she thought. . . .

Then his big hands were rucking up her sweater, lifting her shoulders, tugging it over her head, freeing her aching breasts, and she thought about words no more. He cupped and kneaded, pinching and tugging her nipples to hard peaks before stretching her hands above her head and pressing her firmly forward, flush to the desk, pillowing her breasts on it. Her nipples burned against the cool wood.

"Hold on to the edge of the desk, lass. Hands over your head like that."

Swallowing, she gripped the carved edge of the desk.

One of his big hands closed on the nape of her neck. He turned her head to the side, pressing her cheek to the desk. A band of intricate Celtic knot-work divided two inlaid panels a few inches from her eyes. His big palm cupped the back of her head, keeping her still.

He slid his other hand between her legs and began parting her slick, exposed feminine folds.

She mewled helplessly. His zipper was already open. She'd yanked it free herself the second time he'd kissed her, while the other MacKeltars had still been in the library. She waited, lower lip caught between her teeth, for that first burning hot thrust of him.

Her whole body convulsed when the hard, thick head of his cock prodded her with insistent, delicious friction. He rubbed back and forth in her creamy heat, spreading the erotic slickness on him, on her. She twitched, desperate for him to push inside her, to soothe her, to release the unbearable tension in her body. He kicked back against the jeans taut at her ankles, stilling her.

"Please," she gasped, trying to press back with her bottom, but she was unable to move even that much, the way he was holding her.

"Is this what you want?" he purred, his voice dark and rich, guiding himself between her sleek, swollen labia. Torturing her, stopping, poised at her entrance.

"Yes, *please,* Cian," she wailed.

He began to feed himself into her slowly. She clenched the edge of the desk, gripping it so hard she felt like she was gouging nail scores into the glossy wood. He was so big, so thick. Her body had never yielded for this before and her inner female muscles tensed, trying to resist the steely male intrusion, even as she was aching for it. She squirmed what little she could, desperate to accommodate him.

He hissed long and low between clenched teeth. "Bloody hell, Jessica, you're tight!"

"Probably because I've never . . . *ah!* . . . done this before!" she managed to force out, swamped by raw, intense sensation.

He went still behind her, barely in her. "Tell me you jest," he said tightly after a long moment.

"Cian," she cried, "don't you dare stop now!"

"You are maiden? At your age?"

"I'm not *that* old. Move, damn it!"

"By my time's standards, 'tis unfathomable!"

"By mine, too," she gritted. "So now that I've decided not to be a virgin anymore, is it too much to ask for a little h—*elp!*" He pushed forward, piercing her hymen in a smooth, even thrust.

He gave her but a moment of stillness to recover, to adjust. The brief stinging sensation passed quickly and once more she was burning with feverish need.

Gripping her hips with his big hands, he began to impale her slowly, inch by mind-blowingly delicious inch. Relentlessly he usurped every nook and cranny her body ceded.

"Can you take more, Jessica? I'm not yet half in, lass. Am I hurting you?"

"No! I mean, yes! I mean, yes and then no! Yes. More!"

He pushed yet more of himself in, stretching her, filling her, long and thick and hard.

She whimpered, clinging to the desk. It was unlike anything she'd imagined. She was certain there was no way she could take more of him inside her, but then her sleek inner heat would not only yield but thrill to him, both stretch and embrace, ease yet tighten hungrily around him. She was a velvet glove, custom-crafted for him. She'd been made for this man, she marveled, designed to sheathe him.

With one final, strong push, he thrust himself in to the hilt, the silky hair on his muscular thighs rasping against her silky bottom, and she cried out from the fullness of it. It was pain yet pleasure, it was too much, yet just exactly right. She was full of him, part of him, her body melting around him, adhering to him, making them one. It was raw, it was fierce, it was incredible.

Then he began moving! Easing out, inch by incredible inch, leaving her hot and empty and aching.

Filling her back up just as slowly. Driving himself into her sleek heat.

Cian stared down at Jessica's pretty, silken ass as he worked himself in and out of her. Bloody hell, she was tight and hot and slick.

And virgin. He couldn't believe it. He was stunned that this incredibly passionate, beautiful, smart woman had never lain with another man. He'd never have guessed it. He'd thought her an experienced woman.

But not Jessica. She'd come to him untouched by any other. And though it wouldn't have mattered to him how she'd come, the fact that he was her first man, that he was the only one she'd *chosen* to accept, with the countless men who had undoubtedly tried to get where he was right now, filled him with an intense possessiveness, gave him a primal, masculine thrill.

The need to spill his seed in her had been riding him merciless as a Harpy since he'd pumped that first inch inside. He'd damn near exploded when he'd pushed through her maidenhead.

He stared down at her, bent over the desk, her delicate spine arched, the paler skin of her full breasts crushed to the desk, the generous plump mounds spilling out the sides, her small, dainty hands stretched above her head, fingers clutching the wood, her lush, sweet ass thrusting up to meet him, he watched himself pump into her. It was the most exquisite, sensual sight he'd ever seen.

He thought of his prison, to maintain control. He needed her to find her pleasure before he took his.

Gritting his teeth, he began mentally reciting the parameters of his hell. *Fifty-two thousand, nine hundred and eighty-seven stones.*

He wanted to give her so much pleasure that each time she looked at him, her body would remember what he could make her feel, and begin hungering for it. *Twenty-seven thousand two hundred and sixteen of them paler gray than the rest.*

He wanted to be her every sexual fantasy, as well as her man and her rock and her best friend. *Thirty-six thousand and four more rectangular than square.*

He slipped one hand in front of her, between her woman's mound and the desk, found her silken nub with his thumb and began playing it, rolling his pad over it, lightly, gently. *Nine hundred and eighteen stones have a vaguely hexagonal shape.* Then faster and more firmly. Then backing off again, lightly, gently, rubbing slow circles all around her clitoris, without actually grazing it.

"*Oooh* — Cian, that feels so good!"

He eased out of her slowly, thrust back in powerfully. Teasing her nub with alternately slow and gentle, then frantic friction, he slid two fingers over her slick, swollen mound, pushing between her lips, to feel where they joined, where the thick, rock-hard shaft of his cock was entering her. Where they became one. *Ninety-two stones have a vein of bronze running through the face. Three are cracked.*

Jessi writhed deliriously beneath Cian's sensual assault. One of his big hands was on her behind, firmly cupping a cheek, holding her still; the other was between her legs from the front, delicately, expertly working her clit, backing off until she was ready to scream, resuming again just when and how she needed it. She gripped the edge of the desk, quivering uncontrollably, as if being shocked by little sizzling erotic pulses.

Her orgasm ripped through her so suddenly and intensely that she cried out, a long, wild half-sob, half-scream. She pressed the back of her hand to her mouth and lay whimpering helplessly beneath him, shuddering with wave after wave of pleasure, taking all he was giving her, convulsing as he milked every last ripple of climax from her with his pounding, with his clever, relentless hand.

Her hot, sleek warmth quivering around him was too much! He couldn't hold it and stopped trying. Dropping forward, Cian covered her, gathering her back against his hard, muscled chest, and growled close to her ear, "You're mine, Jessica. Do you ken that? *Mine.*" He gave her two more powerful pumps of his cock and exploded in hot intense spurts inside her.

The inexplicable feeling of the *rightness* of him coming inside her, coupled with the pad of his thumb deliciously abrading her orgasm-sensitive clit and his possessive words, kicked Jessi right back into another orgasm. *You're mine, too, Highlander* was her last fierce thought, before they slipped down to the floor and dozed for a time beneath the desk in a sated, entwined stupor.

Cian sat on the floor near the fire, leaning his shoulders back against an ottoman, watching Jessica, entranced.

She was sitting cross-legged on a plush lambskin rug before the briskly crackling fire he'd just topped with sheaves of fragrant heather. Her jade eyes were sparkling, her short dark curls were softly tousled, and she had a velvet crimson throw tucked about her hips. She was talking animatedly, gesturing with her hands. And he had absolutely no idea what she was talking about, he couldn't hear a bloody damned word.

She was naked from the waist up and her pretty, high, round breasts quivered and bobbled with each gesture, her rosy nipples gently swayed.

The warm glow of the firelight highlighted chestnut strands in her raven curls he'd not seen before, and kissed her creamy skin with a brush of gold.

It was all he could do to keep his hands off her, but he knew that if he pushed her too far this night, he'd not be able to have her on the morrow, and the next and the next. He had to pace himself with her, though it was killing him. His palms itched with the need to caress her lush, sweet curves, to take her beneath him again and again.

He stretched out his legs and leaned back on his hands, keeping them well behind him, forcing himself to be contented for a time just savoring the exquisite vision before him.

Jessica St. James: half-nude, all woman, and glowing from his bedplay.

He'd known the moment he'd first glimpsed her that it would come to this. That he would have her this way. As certain as his vengeance, she'd been his destiny.

After they'd slipped beneath the desk and drowsed for a time, he'd stirred, roused her, and scooped her into his arms. He'd carried her here, before the fire, laid her back on the plush creamy sheepskin, and made love to her. Slowly, gently, showing her that he was more than a great big territorial brute, that there was tenderness in him too. He wanted her to know all the facets of him: ninth-century war-laird and sorcerer, and simple man and Druid.

They'd drowsed again, then stirred again, and begun talking lazily of small things, lover's things: favorite colors and seasons, foods, and places and people.

But suddenly her gaze turned serious and she leaned forward. "How did it happen, Cian? How did you end up in the mirror?"

He leaned forward, too, unable to resist the full, soft breasts swaying toward him with her movement. He ran the pad of his finger beneath the lush curve of one beautiful, silken-skinned mound. "Och, woman," he said softly, "you show me Heaven and ask me to revisit Hell? Not now, sweet Jessica. Now is for us. No grim thoughts. Only *us*."

Cupping her breasts with his big hands, he ducked his head and slicked his tongue across one of those rosy nipples before catching it in his mouth with a husky, sensual purr. It hardened instantly against his tongue. He teased it lightly with his teeth, scraping it across the edge, then pressed it with his tongue against his palate, suckling deeply.

"Us," she repeated breathlessly, clutching his dark head to her.

It was the most incredible night of Jessi's life. It surpassed all she'd ever imagined that special night would be. It was searing. It was intimate. It was filled with sounds of passion that she was sure must have rung out from the stone walls, echoing sharply down the winding corridors of the vast, ancient castle. It was hushed and conspiratorial. It was raw. It was tender. It was perfection.

He'd taken her wildly, roughly on the desk, calling out to and laying claim upon the kindred wildness within her.

He'd made sweet, painstakingly slow love to her before the fire, cupping her face with his hands, staring into her eyes, caressing her so tenderly and seemingly reverently that she'd had to turn her face away from him to hide an inexplicable burn of tears. As he'd moved, sure and deep inside her, she'd felt as if he'd been making love to her soul.

He'd rolled over onto his back and raised her high above him, muscles bunching and rippling in those powerful, tattooed arms, then lowered her, inch by delicious inch, onto his hard, straining erection.

He was a phenomenal lover! He never went completely soft. Even after he came he was still hard. Once she'd rued his being Terminator-tough. But she wasn't about to waste a single breath complaining about him being an unstoppable sexual machine. (Though, come morning, she might waste a few breaths complaining if, as she suspected was going to be the case, she could hardly walk!)

After their third intense, erotic bout, stretched on a velvety chaise, with her riding both of them to a brain-melting, panting orgasm, he bundled them up in soft woolen throws collected from various chairs, and they slipped out through the French doors of the library and onto a stone terrace beneath the pearly radiance of a half-full moon.

He stood behind her and pulled her back into his embrace, resting his chin on the top of her head. She was cocooned by the spicy, erotic man-scent of him. Mixed with that scent was a subtler one: the smell they made together. It was intoxicating to her — the scent of their lovemaking — sweat and kisses and come.

He held her like that in silence for a long time, staring out at the night, gazing at the mountains beyond.

And she watched the sky, brilliantly splashed with sparkling stars, marveling.

College was a lifetime away.

She could no longer remember the Jessi who'd so tightly scheduled her entire life. The one who had a coffee cup stuffed way in the back of her cupboard that said: *Life is what happens to you when you're busy making other plans.*

She'd finally stopped making other plans.

And *this* was Life.

Here and now.

She realized then, much to her astonishment, standing there beneath that wide-open Highland sky in the arms of her sexy Highlander, that she was no longer in such a hurry to finish her PhD. In fact, hanging out in Scotland and doing a bit of casual, unstructured digging around these mountains could probably keep her happy for a long time. Especially if Cian MacKeltar was around to carry her tools and keep her company.

And although she knew she would probably never be able to comprehend her mother's lack of matrimonial staying power no matter how hard she tried, she suddenly completely understood Lilly's desire for babies, and her unceasing, constant love for all her children: halves, steps, and wholes alike.

It was a complex emotion Jessi'd never felt before, because she'd never met a man whose children she'd wanted and whose last name she'd tried on for size:

Jessica MacKeltar.

For the first time in her life she wondered what kind of babies she would make with a man. What kind of children they could bring into the world together, she and this big, fierce, handful of a man. They would be something — that was for sure!

Jessi knew what was happening to her.

It terrified her even as it elated her. She suspected she was glowing every bit as luminescent as the moon above her.

Falling in love could do that to a woman.

22

"We're coming in now," the deep Scottish burr of one of the MacKeltar twins warned through the double doors of the library.

Jessi flashed Cian a cheeky grin. "Guess they got tired of waiting."

"Aye, 'twould seem so, lass," he replied, running a finger down the inside of the silvery glass. She mated the pad of her index to his.

She would be *so* glad when he was finally free of that damned glass!

It had reclaimed him directly from the shower. In the early hours of the morning, they'd finally ventured from the library and wandered down corridor after corridor, peeking into various chambers, looking for a bathroom.

They'd found one befitting castle and king, with a fabulous shower sporting multiple pulsing heads and a reclining bench. They'd made love yet again, soaping each other slippery, sliding and bumping and grinding beneath the steamy spray. Then the powerful, muscled dark Highlander had dropped to his knees, pressed her back against the wall with his hands on her thighs, and, at a time when she would have sworn herself incapable of more pleasure, had kissed and licked and nibbled her to another shuddering orgasm.

She'd learned over the long, sizzling night that the forbidding man Cian MacKeltar showed the world wasn't the same one that took a woman to bed.

That man — the lover — dropped barriers, opened himself, gave in small ways she'd never have suspected. That man watched every flicker of her eyelash, learning what pleased her, what made her smile. That man teased with the playfulness of a man who'd had seven sisters he'd obviously adored.

That man had disappeared while she'd been kissing him, leaving her alone in the shower, bereft and kissing air.

She'd fisted her hands with a fierce, hurt scowl.

It had been a bad moment, eased only by the thought that in fifteen more days he would be free of the stupid glass *forever.*

She'd decided, as she'd finished rinsing off and stepped from the stall, that in retrospect, they were lucky Dageus had taken their SUV. Things couldn't have worked out better.

They were now in the highly secure castle of Cian's descendants, and she was pretty sure that — although his descendants seemed as bristly and testosterone-laden as he was — they would nonetheless do all in their power to keep him safe from Lucan until after the tithe was due. (And when it was all over, she was getting a sledgehammer and smashing that damned mirror into a thousand tiny silvery pieces. Who cared that it was a relic? It had held Cian captive for eleven centuries and she wanted it dead.)

Not once during her harrowing day yesterday had she imagined she might be starting this day — a gloriously sunny Highland morning, at that — having made hot, passionate love all night with the man of her dreams, in pretty much the safest place they could hope to be, with two other Druids present to stand additional guard between her and Cian, and any threat that might come to pass.

"Are you decent?" a woman's voice called, pushing the door cautiously ajar.

"Nay, but we're clothed," Cian purred.

Jessi laughed. He certainly wasn't decent. The man was shamelessly *indecent.* He was an animal in bed. And out. A great, big, hungry, uninhibited animal.

And she *adored* it.

Gwen hurried into the library first, trailed by Chloe. Their sexy husbands brought up the rear. Jessi studied the twins with interest this morning. She'd been too tense and worried about Cian last night to look at them much. Now she examined them at a sexually-induced-endorphin-drugged leisure.

They were magnificent men, with identical, chiseled Celtic features, golden skin, strong noses, and chiseled jaws dusted by the same dark shadow-beards.

Though they were twins, there were significant differences.

Dageus's long black hair was free this morning and spilled in a sleek fall of midnight silk to his waist. Drustan's stopped about six inches past his shoulders. Dageus's eyes were tiger-gold, Drustan's sparkled like shards of silver and ice. Though both had powerful physiques and stood well over six feet and several inches, Dageus was leaner, ripped with muscle; Drustan was slightly taller, broader, and packed with it. Both were extraordinary men, but Jessi was willing to bet all Keltar males were. All those dominant-male, exceptional qualities that shaped Cian so uniquely were still there, present in his descendants, centuries later. There was simply something extra in their blue blood, programmed into their regal genes.

Gwen smiled warmly at her. "We thought you might like some clean clothes. Chloe and I rummaged through our closets and brought you a few things. We had a few other items taken to the Silver Chamber for you."

Surprised and delighted, Jessi pushed to her feet. Clean clothes! The morning just kept getting better and better. As she hurried across the patterned rugs, Dageus and Drustan hastened past her, their fascinated gazes locked on the mirror.

"What make you of the runes on the frame, Dageus?" Drustan asked.

"I doona ken the language, do you?"

"Nay," Drustan replied.

Jessi accepted the small pile of clothing, forgetting about the men for a moment. Gwen and Chloe hadn't just brought "a few things," they'd brought her everything she needed. There was a pair of low-ride, button-fly Paper Denim & Cloth jeans that she could never have afforded herself, a delicate pink tank with a lacy scooped neckline, and a matching, soft woolen cardigan. They also brought panties, socks, boots, and — wonder of wonders — a bra! She wasn't going to sag prematurely after all. She fingered the plain white spandex appreciatively.

Gwen stepped closer and said in a low voice so the men wouldn't overhear, "I know it's not very pretty, but it's the only one I had that I thought might fit. I wore it when I was pregnant."

"Oh, it's perfect," Jessi said fervently. "It's a bra. I couldn't be happier. Thank you. Both of you." She smiled at them.

"If you're going to be staying with us awhile," said Chloe, "we can go shopping. Or if you need to stick close to the castle, we can order some things off the Internet."

Jessi blinked, feeling humbled by the two gracious women. Just like that, they'd accepted her. She'd burst into their home, unannounced and uninvited, they didn't know the first thing about her, yet they'd made her welcome. They'd brought her pretty clothes. They cared that she had a pretty bra. "Thank you," she said again, with heartfelt sincerity.

"There's a half-bath just down the hall to the left, by the great hall, if you'd like to change there."

Nodding, Jessi hurried off, looking forward to wearing clean clothes again.

When she returned to the library, the MacKeltars were seated near the fire.

They'd moved the Dark Glass from where it had been slanted against the bookcase, to the wall next to the mantel, facing them.

Cian stood, his powerful jean-clad legs widespread, his palms braced on something at the outer edges of the glass — she guessed a stone wall on each side — staring out into the library.

He was wearing the black *Ironman* T-shirt again, and the muscles in his tattooed arms rippled beneath the short sleeves with his slightest movement. She'd had those arms around her in just about every way imaginable last night. She was greatly looking forward to more of the same tonight, or whenever he could be freed next. An ottoman was propped at the base of the mirror to keep it from sliding on the polished wood floor.

On a nearby coffee table was an appetizing spread of iced scones, assorted fruits, cheeses and pastries, and three gently steaming carafes.

"The white carafe has coffee, the silver is

cocoa, and the ivory one has hot water for tea," Gwen told her.

Jessi hurried to the table, gratefully poured herself a cup of coffee, and reached for a lightly iced scone, before taking a seat and joining them.

Commandeering a few scones into his mirror, along with the entire pot of cocoa — much to the amazement and delight of both Chloe and Gwen, who made him send it back out and resummon it again — Cian brusquely explained their situation to his descendants, amid swallows of creamy chocolate and bites of pastries.

Jessi had heard it before, and he didn't add any detail to it now. No one could ever accuse the man of TMI — too much information. He advised them that he'd been bound to the Dark Glass by a sorcerer named Lucan Trevayne eleven centuries past, thereby securing immortality for himself.

"So, that's what its purpose is!" Dageus had exclaimed.

Cian had nodded and continued, telling them he'd been kept hung on one of Lucan's walls or another for the past 1,133 years. That several months ago something had happened in London that had taken down all the wards protecting Lucan's property while he'd been out of the country; a thief had stolen Trevayne's prized collection; and that the mirror had been transferred from merchant to merchant for several months before ultimately ending up in Jessica's hands.

He advised briskly of the tithe sealing the Unseelie indenture, that it was due in a mere fifteen days, that he must remain free of Lucan for another fortnight, until past midnight on Samhain, and that he was formally petitioning their aid to help him do so, and to keep "his woman" safe.

She loved hearing those words! *His woman.*

"What then?" Drustan asked the same question Jessi had broached when she'd heard Cian's story. "Once the tithe is missed and the indenture broken? What plan you then?"

Cian dropped his head down and forward, resting the top of his head against the inside of the glass. When he raised it again, his whisky eyes glittered with feral fury. "Then I will have my vengeance on the bastard who trapped me."

The room was silent a moment.

Then Dageus said, "You said the gold tithe must be paid every one hundred years in the Old Way of marking time?"

Cian nodded. "Aye."

"And that 'twas Lucan Trevayne who originally paid it?"

"Aye," Cian replied.

"Hmm," Dageus said. He paused a moment, then said softly, "Vengeance can be quite the double-edged sword, eh, kinsman?"

Cian shrugged. "Aye. Mayhap. But in this case, 'tis necessary I wield it."

"Are you certain of that?"

"Aye."

"Some blood is best not spilled, ancestor."

"Doona be thinking you ken me, Keltar. You don't."

"You might be surprised."

"Doubt it," Cian clipped. "And you doona ken Lucan. He must die."

"Why?" Dageus countered. "Because he imprisoned you? You seek vengeance for the slight? Is that vengeance worth everything to you, then?"

"What would you ken of the price of vengeance? What would you ken of the price of anything?"

"I ken many things. I broke the oath of the standing stones and went back in time to undo my twin's death. For a time I was possessed by the thirteen souls of the Draghar —"

"Christ, you used the stones of *Ban Drochaid* for personal gain? What are you — mad? Even *I* gave that legend wide berth!" Cian sounded astonished.

"Appears to be the only thing you gave wide berth," Drustan said pointedly. "Are you, or aren't you, a sorcerer, ancestor?"

Jessi bristled. Cian was a good man. She was about to open her mouth and say so, but Cian said coolly, "I have done sorcery. It appears your brother has dispensed with the occasional Keltar oath, as well."

Right. So there, Jessi thought. Nobody was perfect. She wasn't quite sure she'd followed whatever it was Dageus had done, but it'd sounded pretty bad.

"Dageus did so of love. You've told us neither how you came to bear such extensive protection runes tattooed across your body, nor how you ended up in that mirror."

" 'Protection runes'?" Jessi echoed. "Is that what your tattoos are, Cian? I've been meaning to ask you if those runes are a language. What are they for?"

It was Chloe who answered her. "They hold the repercussions of meddling with black magycks at bay," she clarified helpfully. "I've been reading about them lately."

"Oh." Jessi blinked, wondering what black magycks Cian had been messing with. She decided there was too much going on at the moment to press him on the subject. Later, when they were alone, she would ask him.

Right now, Cian was holding Drustan's gaze, his lips curved in a mocking smile. She wasn't sure she liked that smile. It was cold. It seemed doubly so after the wickedly heated ones she'd seen curving his sensual lips mere hours ago.

"Nor do I plan to discuss it," Cian growled. " 'Tis of no consequence. What is — is. What's been done, cannot be undone. All that matters now is stopping Lucan."

Dageus began, "Not necessarily —"

"Och, aye, 'necessarily,' " Cian cut him off. "I've not yet told you, Keltar, but Trevayne recently located several pages from the Unseelie Dark Book. He's been hunting it since the ninth century. Are you familiar with the Unseelie relic?"

Dageus's golden eyes narrowed and he stiffened. "Blethering hell!"

"Precisely," Cian said flatly.

"He's seeking the Unseelie Dark Book?" Drustan exclaimed. "Think you he might actually find it?"

"Aye, he will. 'Tis but a matter of time."

"Wait a minute," Jessi interjected. "What is 'the Unseelie Dark Book'?" Although Cian had mentioned it once before, she'd been so preoccupied with her own worries that she'd not absorbed what he'd said.

"Do you know who the Unseelie are, lass?" Drustan asked.

Jessi gave him a dubious look. "Um . . . fairies?" Oh, that just sounded abjectly silly. Even for a girl who now believed in sorcerers and spells and Druids.

But no one else in the room seemed to think so.

Matter-of-factly, Gwen said, "We call them 'Faery,' Jessi, but they're actually a race of beings from another world, an incredibly advanced civilization known as the Tuatha Dé Danaan. They came to Earth thousands of years before the birth of Christ and settled in Ireland."

Jessi sucked in a breath. "Oh, God — I read about the Tuatha Dé Danaan in the Book of Invasions! They were one of the mythical races, along with the Fir Bolg and the Nemedians. Supposedly they came down from the sky in a cloud of mist and fog. You're telling me they're real? That they actually *did* invade Ireland?"

"Aye. They're real, though they didn't

invade Ireland — initially they were welcomed there amongst her people," Dageus said. "It wasn't until much later that bitter dissension arose. They arrived long before the Book of Invasions purports. And here they remain, though they are now hidden from us. The Tuatha Dé is divided into two courts. The Seelie are the Court of the Light Fae — the ones whom we Keltar serve. The Unseelie are the Court of the Dark — to be given wide berth. Though separate, they are inseparably bound. Some say the Seelie created the Unseelie, others say that the Seelie themselves mutated over time. No one knows for certain. Indeed, 'tis rumored they may not even be of the same race. But all the legends agree that where goes one, so must the other. That they are like the Roman Janus heads of yore — two faces, sharing a single skull."

"So they came to our world — oh, that's just so weird! — and brought these Dark Hallows with them?" Jessi asked.

Dageus nodded. "The Unseelie brought the Dark Ones. The Seelie brought the Light Hallows. Both courts have their own relics of power. According to ancient lore, long ago in their past, the horrific Unseelie were somehow 'contained' by the Seelie.

Though they are here with us, in a manner of speaking, sharing our world, as are the Seelie, the Unseelie cannot leave wherever it is they are being held. 'Tis written in ancient scrolls that shortly after the Tuatha Dé's arrival on our world there was an uprising and some of the Unseelie nearly broke free. In the skirmish, their Hallows, including the Dark Book, were lost. Men and Fae alike have been searching for these relics of power for thousands of years. Allegedly, the Dark Glass was originally used to keep one of the Unseelie's mortal mistresses imprisoned. Over time, it has transformed, as many Unseelie things do, into something else. A thing with multiple purposes, or so 'tis said. See that band of black that rims the perimeter?"

Jessi nodded.

" 'Tis said that one day, if enough tithes are paid, the Dark Glass will go full dark, and on that day it will become a different thing entirely, a sentient thing."

Jessi shivered. She looked at Cian. "Did you know that?"

He shook his head. "Nay. But 'tis yet another reason to prevent the tithe."

"No kidding. How creepy!"

"All the Unseelie Hallows are, as you

say, 'creepy,' lass," Cian said. " 'Tis their darkness, the chill of them."

"Is it cold inside the mirror?" she asked, recalling how icy the blackness at the edge was.

He shrugged one powerful shoulder. "Aye, lass. At times I feel it more than others. 'Tis naught to fash yourself over." Directing a concerned gaze toward the twins, he said, "Lucan managed to get his hands on *three* of the Dark Hallows. The thief stole the amulet and box, as well, along with my mirror. I doona ken if Lucan has been able to recover them yet. They may still be out there."

"Och, Christ," Drustan swore softly. "And in some unsuspecting fool's hands!"

"Exactly," Cian said.

"So what's in this Dark Book?" Jessi asked. "What makes it so dangerous?"

"According to what the Draghar knew of it," Dageus said, "it contains spells to open realms, spells to harness time, spells even to unmake worlds. Worse yet, in addition to every manner of Dark enchantment, allegedly therein are also the True Names of the most powerful of the Fae — the Seelie and Unseelie royalty."

"I thought you said 'twas not easy to sort through all the memories the Draghar left in you," Drustan said carefully, searching Dageus's eyes.

Dageus said dryly, " 'Tis not. It's like having thirteen thousand-chapter books in my head. In there somewhere is a memory of every last time one of them took a piss. I know of the Dark Book because they wanted me to hunt for it while I was hunting for other tomes in my efforts to escape them. 'Twas much in their minds." His lips curved in a mocking smile. " 'Twas not I alone who sought my freedom; they wished greatly to escape *me*. Among other desires they had."

"What about the True Names is so scary?" Jessi asked. How bizarre to think that Dageus had the memories of thirteen other people in his head. She wondered if it ever gave him a headache.

"He who knows a Tuatha Dé's True Name," Cian said from within the mirror, "can command that Fae, even unto its own destruction."

"I thought the Faery were supposed to be immortal," she protested.

"Mostly they are, lass," Cian told her. " 'Tis rare for one to die, nigh impossible to slay one, but it can be done. The Fae possess unfathomable power. In the hands of the wrong man, the Dark Book could be used to harness that power. An unscrupulous man could unleash complete chaos, destroy not merely this world but countless others. Though the Dark Book is written in complex ciphers, and though 'tis rumored these ciphers actually change from opening to opening of the Book, Lucan broke several of the codes in the past when he obtained rubbings. It took him many long years, but he managed it. I've no doubt he can do so again."

"Where do you think the Dark Book has been all this time?" Chloe asked Cian. "Hasn't it been missing for thousands and thousands of years?"

"Aye. Lucan and I believed that a clan was either appointed or stumbled across it long ago and appointed themselves its guardian, much as the Keltar guard the lore," Cian said, his gaze dark. " 'Twould seem that recently, something happened to these guardians, because the person Lucan spoke with told him the Book had surfaced for a brief time and been glimpsed by several people, all of them now dead. This person — who was also killed a few weeks before the mirror was stolen — had been able to obtain a rubbing of the cover and a few of the pages therein before it vanished again."

"So, people have actually *seen* the Book recently!" Chloe exclaimed.

"Aye."

"Do we know for sure it really was the Dark Book? The real thing?" Gwen asked.

Cian nodded. "I glimpsed the rubbings of the pages. Lucan was free with what he did in his study. I think in part because he hoped to incite my interest and elicit my aid, for I was always the better sorc— er . . . Druid."

"And who ended up stuck in a mirror?" Dageus murmured.

Cian bristled, eyes narrowed, nostrils flared.

Dageus shrugged. "I was merely saying."

Cian and Dageus glowered at each other. Then Cian snorted dismissively and continued. "The Book itself is supposedly so potent that continued exposure to it alters a man, and not for the better. Even the mere rubbings of the pages pulsed with Dark power. Those were no normal sheets of parchment. There is no doubt in my mind 'twas the real thing. There is also no doubt in my mind 'tis inevitable that Lucan will get his hands on it, and sooner rather than later. Obtaining the Dark Book has always been Lucan's ultimate goal, and he will stop at nothing to attain it. I've watched his power and knowledge of Dark Magyck grow over the centuries. He adheres to no rules. He has no sense of honor. I ken the way his mind works. I am the only who can stop him."

"There are two other Keltar Druids here, kinsman," Drustan said stiffly. "I'm fair certain we may be of some aid."

"You've no bloody idea what you're talking about. The mirror makes Lucan immortal, unkillable by your means. You would be of no use. Or are you ready to begin tattooing yourself, kinsman?" Cian said silkily.

Drustan gave him a scornful look.

"I thought not." The look Cian shot back at him was just as scornful. "A man does what he must. Or he's no man."

"What he 'must' is debatable. 'Twould not necessarily come to that," Drustan replied icily.

"Och, aye, it would, you bloody fool. Leave Lucan to me. Stay out of it."

"I cannot believe this Trevayne is so much more powerful than we."

Cian's smile dripped dark amusement. "Ah — and *there's* the vaunted Keltar ego! I wondered when I'd see it. I made the same mistake. Believed I was so much more powerful. And I was. Yet here I am.

And I didn't see it coming. I will deal with Lucan. You've but to grant us sanctuary here until the Feast of All Saints. I will need to lay additional wards when next I am free. Permit that. 'Tis all I ask."

Dageus had remained silent while his brother and Cian argued. But now he cocked his head, his golden eyes shimmering strangely. "Now I understand," he said. "So that's why you plan to do it. It made no sense to me. Especially after last eve."

Was it her imagination, or had Cian suddenly gone tense? Jessi eyed him intently.

Her Highland lover's shrug seemed a bit overdone when he said, "I've no idea what you're talking about."

"Aye, you do."

"You can't deep-listen to me, not with my guards up, and I've not let them down since we met. You're good, but you're not that good."

"*Yet.* And I doona need to be. I understand this tithing business."

"Mayhap the knowledge you acquired from those evil Draghar of yours is inaccurate, Druid," Cian said coolly. "I'm sure even they made the occasional error."

"Nay," Dageus said just as coolly. "This I learned from our tomes in the underground chamber while searching for a way to be rid of the thirteen. And I know you've read them too."

"What?" Jessi said, staring from one to the other, sensing the deadly undertow in the ocean of things they weren't saying. "What are you two talking about?"

"Doona do it, kinsman," Cian said abruptly, low and intense. "Leave it. Man to man."

"Nay, 'tis too big a thing to continue speaking around. She has the right to know."

" 'Tis not your decision to make."

"I wouldn't *have* to make it if you hadn't made the wrong one by not telling her."

" 'Not telling her' what?" Jessi demanded.

" 'Tis naught of your concern. Stay the bloody hell out of it," Cian snarled at Dageus.

"Nay. Not after what transpired between the two of you last eve. She has a right to know. Either you tell her, or I will. 'Tis the only mercy I'll grant."

"Cian?" Jessi implored questioningly.

He gazed at her a long silent moment. A muscle in his jaw leapt. He turned abruptly in the mirror.

And disappeared into the silver. It rippled behind him and went flat.

Jessi stared at the looking glass in disbelief. What could be so terrible that, after the incredible intimacy they'd just shared, he would turn his back on her and walk away?

"What's going on?" She turned a plaintive gaze on Dageus. There was a sinking sensation in the pit of her stomach, and she knew, just *knew,* she was about to hear something that was going to make her wish she'd cut her ears off instead.

When Jessi heard Cian murmur a short chant, she knew what was coming and a cry of alarm escaped her. The jeweled blade that had slain the room-service assassin whipped out of the glass and lodged in a wall — behind and a hairsbreadth to the left of Dageus's temple.

"Doona answer her, you bastard," came the savage growl from the silvery glass.

"Harm any of mine and I'll break your blethering mirror," Drustan said very, very quietly. "Were I not certain you missed deliberately, I'd have done it already."

Another savage sound rumbled within the mirror, rattling the glass in its frame.

"What?" Jessi repeated weakly. "Tell me what?"

Dageus sighed, his chiseled features grim. "All Tuatha Dé bindings, lass — whether Seelie compacts or Unseelie indentures — must be periodically reaffirmed by gold. The Keltar Compact, for example, was forged in purest gold, and need only be reaffirmed if something within it is changed, or if 'tis violated by a party to the agreement. But Dark Arts run counter to the nature of things and require higher and more frequent tithes. As Cian said, the Dark Glass must be paid every one hundred years, on the anniversary of the original date of binding, at midnight."

Sorrowful gold eyes locked with hers, and that sinking sensation became a pit of acid in her stomach.

"Cian was bound on Samhain, lass. If the tithe is not paid by he who initiated the indenture — in this instance, Lucan — at precisely midnight on October thirty-first, the indenture will be violated, and all the years that Cian and Lucan have lived that were not theirs to live, will be called due. At once. In a single moment."

Silence blanketed the room. It lay there, heavy, suffocating.

"Wh-what are you s-saying?" Jessi stammered.

"You know what I'm saying, Jessica,"

Dageus said gently. "Cian came back to Scotland for one reason: to die. That's his vengeance. That's his way of keeping Lucan from getting the Dark Book and ending things for once and for all. When the tithe is not paid, they will both die. It's all over. The immortal sorcerer will be slain, without so much as a drop of blood spilled. All Cian must do is stay out of Lucan's hands until twelve-oh-one on November first. And he's right, 'tis truly the simplest, most effective way to end it. Quite tidy, indeed. Drustan and I can then track down the Dark Book and attempt to either restore it to its guardians or protect it ourselves."

Jessi gaped at Dageus. Abruptly, everything Cian had told her since they'd met — and she now realized it was precious little — tumbled through her mind, and she apprehended it all in a vastly different light. She shook her head, pressing a hand to her mouth.

Now that she knew the truth, it fit together so neatly that she was stunned that she'd not guessed at it before.

Not *once* had he ever spoken of any moment beyond his "deadline." Not even when she'd asked what he intended to do once the spell was broken. There'd never been a "God, it'll be so good to be free again!" There'd never been any mention of something he might like to do once he'd killed Lucan — maybe see a movie, have a feast, travel the world and stretch his legs a bit. In fact, there'd never even been any mention of him *killing* Lucan at all. And why would there have been? He'd never planned to actually physically "kill" him.

No new beginnings, he'd said.

He'd known all along he wasn't going to be free in fifteen days.

He was going to be *dead* in fifteen days.

Precisely two weeks and one day from today, Cian MacKeltar — the man with whom she'd just spent the most amazing, scorchingly passionate, dazzling night of her life — was going to be no more than a one-thousand-one-hundred-and-sixty-three-year-old pile of dust.

She turned numbly toward the mirror. Her own horrified reflection looked back at her. Cian was nowhere to be seen.

The coward.

Her face was pale, her eyes enormous.

"Oh, you son of a bitch," she breathed.

Right before she burst into tears.

Quod not cogit amor?
(Is there anything love couldn't make us do?)

    — MARTIAL, C.E. C.40–104

23

Jessi stood at the open window of the Silver Chamber, staring down through the dreary day at the misty castle grounds.

Cian was striding across the vast, manicured expanse of front lawn. He'd removed the braids from his hair and it was slicked wetly back from his regal face in a long dark fall. The sky was leaden, the horizon of mountains obscured by dark thunderheads. A light, drizzling rain was falling, and patches of fog clung, here and there, to damp thatches of grass, gusting in drowsy, dreamy swirls as Cian sliced through them.

He was wearing only a plaid, slung low around his hips, and soft leather boots, despite the chill in the air. He looked like a magnificent half-savage ninth-century Highland laird out surveying his mountain domain.

God, he was beautiful.

He was bleeding.

Blood trickled down his rain-slicked chest, slipped between the ridges of muscles in that sculpted stomach that, only the night before last, she'd tasted with her tongue, covered with kisses.

Freshly dyed tattoos covered the right side of his chest and part of his right arm, the tiny needle pricks still beading with a wet sheen of blood. More mystic runes climbed up over his right shoulder and, as he turned down a cobbled stone walkway, she could see that either he or one of the twins had branded a fair portion of his back crimson and black, as well.

Protection runes. *They hold the repercussions of meddling with black magycks at bay,* Chloe had said.

She was so absorbed in watching him that she didn't hear the door to the bedchamber open and someone slip in until Gwen said softly, "He's transmuting the soil, Jessi. He saw you up here and sent me to find you. He asked me to ask you not to watch."

"Why?" Jessi said tonelessly.

Gwen drew a deep breath and exhaled slowly. "It's Dark Magyck, Jessi. It has some ghastly side effects, but even Drustan agreed that it was necessary, and believe me, if Drustan agrees to any kind of Dark

Magyck or alchemy being used on Keltar land, there's a *really* good reason for it."

A faint, bitter smile curved Jessi's lips. There was so much love and pride in Gwen's voice for her husband. She knew she would have felt the same about Cian in time — if she'd been given the time. But he'd never had any intention of giving her more than a few weeks from the very first.

"It will neutralize Lucan's powers if he comes here," Gwen told her, "and Cian is convinced he will."

"If the bastard comes here, can we kill him?" Jessi said fiercely. "If the wards have neutralized him?"

"No. The glass keeps him immortal, just like Cian, Jessi. He can't be killed. The wards will only inhibit his use of sorcery on Keltar land. He won't be able to work spells and he won't be able to enter the castle proper. Cian is doing the most intense warding around the perimeter of the castle walls. It's why he wants you not to watch. Apparently, if anything is dead within the castle grounds, his wards will raise it until he, well . . . er . . . inters it again with a ritual burial somewhere else."

"Let me guess. Without his protection runes, those reanimated dead things might turn on him?"

"He didn't say. But that's kind of what I guessed too. And in Scottish soil, God-only-knows-where people and things are buried. This country's had quite the turbulent past."

Jessi shivered and fell silent again. Sorcerers, spells, and now dead-things-walking. She shook her head. How strange and terrible her life had become.

In the past forty-eight hours, she'd soared to the greatest heights she'd ever known, only to plummet into the deepest abyss. She'd been blissfully, idiotically thinking she'd found her soul mate, only to discover that said soul mate was not only going to die in two weeks' time, but she was going to be forced to occupy a front-row seat to the spectacle.

Dageus and Drustan had confined her to the castle. She was not allowed to leave unless and until they said otherwise. They believed that if she left, Lucan would either try to use her to get to Cian (frankly, she wasn't sure he'd care — why care about her body when he'd not cared about her heart?) or kill her outright if he got his hands on her. She bought into the killing-her-outright part, which meant she had to stay put if she wanted to survive.

Which meant she had to watch her Highlander die.

"Dageus and Drustan are trying to find another way, Jessi," Gwen said softly. "Some alternative to get Cian out of the glass and defeat Lucan."

"If Cian knows of no way, then do you really think they'll be able to find one? Nothing against your husband and his brother, but Cian is the only one here that seems to know anything about sorcery."

"You can't give up hope, Jessi."

"Why not? Cian did," she said bitterly. "He's ready to die."

Gwen sucked in a breath. "It's the only way he knows to stop Lucan, Jessi. At least right now it is. Let my husband and Dageus work on it. You'd be amazed at what the two of them can accomplish. But don't hate Cian for this. Oh, he was wrong not to tell you — you'll get no argument from me there. I'd be devastated too. And furious. And hurt. And devastated and furious and hurt all over again. But I think you need to ponder *why* he didn't tell you. And think about this, too: you're twenty-something years old, right?"

Jessi nodded. Below her, Cian was entering a small copse of rowan trees, moving with sleekly muscled, animal grace through gossamer milky-white tendrils of fog. "Twenty-four."

"Well, he's lived, let's see — forty-seven-point-one-six times that long — almost fifty times as long as you have, trapped inside a looking glass. Living not even a mere reflection of a life. For more than a thousand years he's been by himself, imprisoned, powerless. He told us a bit last night, after supper, while you were sleeping. He has no physical needs in there. He has had nothing with which to pass the time. Lucan never gave him any word of his clan once he'd incarcerated him. He'd believed, for the past millennium, that Lucan had wiped out his entire family, that the Keltar line had been destroyed. It's why he never thought of looking for any descendants; why it didn't occur to him that Dageus might be a Keltar when they met. The only companion he had in that mirror with him was his bitter regret and his determination to kill Lucan one day. The opportunity finally presented itself. Is it really a wonder to you that he might be willing to die to take down his enemy, rather than continue living in such a hellish fashion? It's a wonder to me that the man didn't go insane centuries ago."

Tears burned the backs of Jessi's eyes. And she'd thought she'd cried herself out yesterday. She'd wondered the same thing

— how he'd stayed sane. But then she'd realized he was a mountain.

Yesterday had been the most awful day of her life. If she could have collected together all the tears she'd ever cried, beginning with that first wailed protest at the shock of being born, through childhood pains, adolescent indignities, and womanly hurts, they'd not have made a drop in the bucket of tears she'd wept yesterday.

When Dageus had explained to her what Cian meant to do, she'd raced from the library as fast as her feet had been able to take her. She'd tried to flee the castle, as well, but Dageus had caught up with her and stopped her, gently rerouting her upstairs to the chamber they'd readied for her.

She'd locked herself in and collapsed across the bed, weeping. Eventually she'd sobbed herself into a deep, exhausted sleep. The worst of it was, the whole time she'd been crying, hating him for making her care about him, knowing he was going to die, and not telling her, every ounce of her had nonetheless ached to go back downstairs and sit as close to his damned mirror as she could possibly get. To regain that intense, tender intimacy they'd just shared. To touch the glass, if she couldn't touch him. To settle for anything at all.

To beg for crumbs.

She'd thought of what Gwen had said, herself, yesterday. She'd had the occasional lucid moments in her self-pitying and furious delirium.

Yes, of course she could see how he would not just be willing to die, but might actually be ready to embrace death after an eternity in a cold stone hell all by himself.

Understanding didn't make it any better.

She'd read once, in one of those magazines like *Woman's Day* or *Reader's Digest*, about a nurse who'd fallen in love with one of her terminal patients, a man who had no more than ten or twelve months left to live from some disease or another. The article hadn't been her cup of tea, but she'd gotten sucked into it, victim of the same morbid fascination that made rubberneckers of people passing the scene of a gruesome car wreck splashed with blood and strewn with body bags. She'd thought how incredibly stupid the nurse had been to let it happen. She should have transferred his case to someone else the moment she'd started liking him, and fallen in love with a different man.

At least the nurse had gotten nearly a year.

Her terminal patient had a mere four-teen days.

"Go away, please," Jessi said.

"Jessi, I know we don't know each other very well —"

"You're right, Gwen, we don't. So, please, just leave me alone for a while. You can tell him I won't watch. I promise." And she meant it. She would respect his wishes. Moving woodenly, she closed the window, flipped the latch, and let the heavy damask drape fall over the mullioned panes.

There was silence behind her.

"Please go, Gwen."

A few moments later there was a gusty sigh, then the chamber door *click*ed softly shut.

Lucan threaded his fingers through his hair, smoothing it back from his temples. His palms were hot, the flesh singed, his nails blackened.

No matter. In a moment, the lingering traces of Hans's misfortune would be gone.

He stepped over the charred body dis-passionately.

It smelled and needed to be removed from the pub.

Wending his way through the posh, paneled bar with its high-backed wooden booths cushioned in tufted leather upholstery, Lucan murmured a series of spells beneath his breath, concealing from the pub's animated patrons both the man he'd just scorched to a cinder, and his true appearance.

Centuries ago, tattoos had taken what remained of his face, including his ears, eyelids, lips, and tongue, making him far too memorable to observers. Even his nails had been removed and tattooed beneath. His eyes had changed shortly after he'd finished scoring the final black-and-crimson brands inside his nose. He'd ceded his dick and testicles long before his tongue, his eyelids in advance of those sensitive inner nasal mucous membranes, though by then he'd suffered no pain. People often had a strongly unfavorable reaction to the face of a sorcerer.

He shouldn't have agreed to meet Hans in a pub. Lately, several of his employees had displayed a preference for public meeting places.

As if that made any difference.

Cian MacKeltar had indeed returned to the Highlands. As Lucan had known he would. The bastard wanted to die in Scotland. As Lucan had known he would.

According to his late employee, the castle the ninth-century Highlander had once lived in was now occupied by Christopher and Maggie MacKeltar and their children.

But it was not *that* castle and its occupants that concerned him.

It was the other one. The one he'd not known existed.

A second castle had been constructed on a distant part of the MacKeltar estate at some time during the sixteenth century, years after he'd quit paying attention to that rocky, barbaric little corner of the Highlands. It was currently occupied by twin Keltar males.

With old names.

Dageus and Drustan.

Who the fuck were they and from beneath what fucking rock had they crawled?

It was in that castle, or so Hans had suspected, that the mirror was being kept. A man and a woman fitting Cian and Jessi St. James's description had been seen in a store in Inverness. There Hans had encountered the confusion typical of the aftereffects of Voice, but he'd managed to obtain the information that a heretofore unknown Keltar, one of the twins, Dageus, had driven off in a vehicle with a large, ornate mirror in the back of it. The employee had recalled the mirror because "that tattooed guy" had been obsessive about it not getting broken, rearranging it three times and padding it with blankets before permitting other items to be loaded in with it.

Lucan had not anticipated this.

He'd expected Cian to head for the hills. To be in the wide open. He'd expected to be facing one MacKeltar, not three; two of them complete unknowns. In a castle that was probably warded to the fucking rafters.

He frowned over his shoulder at the crisply blackened remains of Hans. It would remain concealed by his spell for a few moments more. Then one pubgoer or another would take note of the grisly corpse on the floor, women would scream, and men would mill about, gaping, readying their stories for watercooler chats in the morning. Law enforcement would be rung. Lucan quickened his pace, pushing his way through the boisterous after-work crowd.

It was damned inconvenient for Hans to be dead right now.

There were other matters to which Lucan would have liked him to attend. He'd not killed him — oh no, not he — he'd brooked no quarrel with Hans. The power within him was occasionally wont to act with a will of its own. It was part of being such a great sorcerer. The vessel of his tattooed body was no longer sufficient to completely contain his greatness. Magic sometimes overflowed, leaked out, and someone got burned. Literally. Lucan chuckled dryly.

Surely he was the greater sorcerer by now.

Fourteen days.

His crimson eyes lit with mirth and he was taken by a sharp bark of laughter, struck by the sheer absurdity of the thought that he — Lucan Myrddin Trevayne — could die.

Impossible.

As he quit the pub and stepped into the chilly London evening, he considered his next step. A cry of shock and horror chased him through the closing tavern door into the drizzly night beyond.

He would return to his residence and take another stab at securing a connection with the St. James woman. He'd been attempting regularly to reach her again, but either she was not logging into her account, or he was missing those windows of opportunity when she was.

Women were weak links. There was always something in them begging to be exploited. He just had to find it. Exploit it.

He would punish the Keltar for this. Wasting his time. Taking him away from his true purpose. His destiny.

Only this morning an unusual man with long coppery hair and shimmering copper eyes had sought him out, claiming to have knowledge of the ciphers in which the Dark Book was written. The man had dripped a deep-seated arrogance that could only have been born of some kind of power — either his own, or close association with someone who made him feel fearless. Lucan's first instinct had been to eliminate the man. From time to time an apprentice petitioned mentoring, or a rival sorcerer dispatched a spy. Lucan never suffered such fools to live. He didn't trust anyone who'd managed to learn of him, penetrate the layers of his many identities, and locate him.

But then the man had told him he'd actually lived among the Fae for a time, he'd been familiar with the runes on the Hallows, and he'd spoken a tongue he'd alleged was that of the Tuatha Dé themselves. He'd also displayed an intimate knowledge of the Seelie and Unseelie courts. It had been enough to stay Lucan's hand.

Whoever, whatever, the man was, he

needed him alive until he'd stripped from him what knowledge he possessed. It took time to perform a ruthless deep-probing. And until the Dark Glass was secured, such critical matters had to be suspended. He'd been forced to allow the man to leave, telling him he'd get in touch.

Oh yes, Cian would be punished. For delaying his plans, wasting his time, and tying up his resources at such a crucial hour. The men Hans had been searching with in the Highlands, those who'd been watching the airports and others he'd been preparing to ward around the Highlander when he found him, if necessary, all were men who could have been following the latest lead on the Dark Book.

He wondered how the arrogant Keltar would like spending the next thousand years hung in a deep, dark cavern, flush to a stone wall. He'd only kept the mirror in his study for the amusement it had given, and because, on occasion, he'd needed his captive to perform some deed he'd not yet possessed the power to do himself. But once he had the Dark Book, he would never need the Druid again.

And then Cian MacKeltar was going to rot in the deepest, coldest, blackest hell Lucan could find for him.

24

Under ideal circumstances, Jessi might have spent days brooding. Weeks, even. When she was hurt, she preferred to hole up and lick her wounds alone.

But circumstances were far from ideal, and days were precisely what she *didn't* have. As for weeks — she had two. Period. By the time she finished licking wounds, she would have a much bigger one to tend.

And then she would despise herself for time wasted.

Cian had either finished placing his wards, or the mirror had reclaimed him again. She knew because, a little while ago, she'd heard people out on the lawn, laughing and talking. She'd pushed aside the drapes to find diffident rays of late-afternoon sunlight trying to push through thick gray clouds and several castle maids standing about, hands on hips, eyes sparkling, flirting with a handful of well-muscled gardeners who were trimming hedges on the still-damp lawn.

She'd been startled to realize how late in the day it was. She'd passed most of it staring into space, trying to mull through thoughts hopelessly muddied by emotions, and decide if Cian was a callous bastard who'd just wanted to have sex before he [insert word she refused to say, even in her mind] or if he cared for her at all.

She could argue the case both ways.

You fit me here, woman, he'd said.

And when she remembered him saying those words, and the look on his face as he'd said them, she believed him.

Especially when she remembered it, coupled with the way he'd made love to her in front of the fire. And again later, in the shower. She could have sworn she'd felt a part of him bleeding into her through his hands, that he'd been cherishing every last cell of her being with his caresses.

Yet there was a cynical part of her that said a dying man after a millennia-old blood-vengeance might say just about anything to get: a) somewhere safe so he could *have* his vengeance; and b) hey, what about a little great sex along the way with the big-boobed babe?

Bottom line was, the big-boobed babe had finally realized that she wasn't going to get anywhere sitting in her room alone, groping blindly through her thoughts.

So she decided to go find him, and grope blindly through *his* thoughts — assuming he would cooperate — and see what might come of it.

It ended up being far more than his thoughts she groped.

Cian stood in the library, near the fire, and finished plaiting the last of the braids into his hair.

He slipped the remaining tricolored bead around it, compressing the soft metal between his finger and thumb, molding it to the end. A sorcerer did not risk any other elements on his body when working dark alchemy. He gathered his arm cuffs from the mantel and refastened them around his wrists.

The warding was now complete, the castle grounds protected. There hadn't been as many dead things in the soil as he'd expected, likely due to the lesser, ancient wards he'd discovered, and removed, before sowing his own.

Keltar soil was clean earth, strong and potent. His wards had intensified that potency to a nearly palpable degree. Indeed, as he'd walked over it, returning to the castle proper, he'd felt the power of his wards humming beneath his heels.

None of Lucan's sorcery would be of any avail to him on the castle-proper portion of the estate now.

Upon completing his task, he'd washed up and hurried to the library to advise his descendants that the job was done. He'd found the twins and their wives cozied up to a crackling fire.

There was not a single place he could look in the book-lined room that did not bring to mind intoxicatingly sensual, carnal memories of his night with Jessica. Their bodies had come together with every bit of the explosive passion he'd known they would.

The entire time he'd been laying wards, he'd kept his thoughts tightly focused on the task at hand. But now they burst free of his tight rein and turned hungrily, desperately to his woman.

"How is she?" he asked.

It was Gwen who answered. "Furious. Hurt."

"And hurt. And furious," Chloe added.

"What did you expect?" Drustan said stiffly. "You seduce her and doona tell her you're dying? Have you no honor, kinsman?"

Cian said nothing. He'd not explain himself to Drustan, nor to any man. Only one woman's opinion of him mattered, and even that wouldn't have stopped him. He'd done what he'd done and didn't wish it undone. Undone, he'd not have gotten his night. And though Jessica may think him a thousand kinds of bastard, he would have another night with her, and another still.

As many nights as he could beg, borrow, or steal from her until he was naught but dust blowing on a dark Scots wind.

"Where is she?" The mirror still hadn't reclaimed him. It had been imperative he lay the warding, but now that 'twas done, he wasn't about to fritter away another precious moment of his time free of the glass.

As Gwen opened her mouth to reply, the library door eased open and Jessica poked her head in.

Her broody jade gaze fixed on Gwen. She didn't see Cian at first.

Faded blue jeans cased those sexy legs that had so recently been wrapped around his ass, her ankles locked in the small of his back, while he'd pounded into her. They hugged low on her hips, revealing the creamy sun-kissed skin of her belly, upon which he'd spilled drops of his seed. A soft, dainty, lacy-woven pale green sweater was

461

buttoned over her heavy, round breasts.

It seemed an eternity since he'd touched her.

"I was wondering where — Oh!" The words died on her tongue when she saw him. "There you are."

Cian assessed her with the instincts of a hunter born for the kill. He'd slammed up against that sleek cool wall inside her skull so many times he no longer bothered trying to read her that way. He read her body instead.

So that was the way of it. The same way it was for him. Mindless, thoughtless need. It had her by the balls too. So to speak.

He devoured the space between them in a few aggressive strides.

Her eyes widened. She wet her lips and they parted — not in protest, but in instinctive preparation. Her eyes dilated, her legs moved slightly apart, her breasts lifted. Christ, he felt just the same way.

He saw her — he needed her.

He closed a hand on her shoulder, opened the door, backed her out into the corridor, and yanked the door shut behind them, dispensing with the MacKeltar with a single slam. Just like that, they ceased to exist.

There was only Jessica.

The corridor was long, high-ceilinged, lit by pale yellow wall torches and the fiery glow of a crimson sun sinking beyond tall mullioned windows. He backed her across the hall, pushing her up against the wall. He could feel the heat rolling off her, knew it was coming off him too. He could smell her arousal, could smell his own. What was between them was quite simply a force of nature.

As she hit stone, she gritted, with a little *oomph* of breath, "You son of a *bitch!*"

"You said that yesterday. I heard you then." If he'd had enough time — like a lifetime — to do things differently, he'd never have given her a reason to call him such a thing. If only he'd met her when he'd been but a score of years, or nay, if they'd been betrothed at birth, grown up together, hand in hand in the Highlands, his life would have been so different. He would have been a deeply contented man, and on that snowy night Lucan had knocked, he'd have been in bed with his wife. With a babe or two nearby. A sorcerer's spells and enchantments would have held no lure for him. Nothing would have, not beyond this woman. He would never have accompanied Trevayne to Ireland, would never have ridden beside him for Capscorth on a sweet spring day, only to usher in the night with the blood of an entire village on his hands.

"You ruthless bastard!"

"I know." There was no denying it. What he'd done was wrong. He should have told her from the beginning. He should have given her the choice to decide whether she was willing to give any part of herself to a man condemned to die.

"You heartless prick!"

"Aye, woman. All that and more." He'd known who she was all along. He'd known from the moment he'd first laid a hand on her, back there in the office of her university, when he'd swept her behind him to protect her from Roman.

He'd felt it right then, in the marrow of his bones.

That thing he'd waited so damned long to feel, that had never come. He'd thought thirty years so unbearably long to wait. He'd never have imagined it might take him 1,133 more years to find her, and then he'd only get twenty days into which he'd have to cram a lifetime. Och, aye, he'd felt it that night. His hand had closed on her upper arm and his entire being had hissed a single, silent word.

Mine.

He'd blinded himself to the truth, all the while determinedly pursuing her, because if, at any moment, he'd admitted she was his one true mate, he might have wavered in his resolve. And he was a man who never wavered. He decided. He committed. He paid for what he purchased. For this sin, he had no doubt he would pay with his soul.

And consider it worth it.

"I can't believe you lied to me!"

"I know." Knowing she was his mate, knowing she would live on after him, and undoubtedly find a husband and make a family with some other man, he'd tried to burn himself into her, to conquer some small corner of her heart.

He was supposed to have been her man. *He* was supposed to have been the father of her children. Not some twenty-first-century asshole that would touch her breasts and kiss her soft mouth and fill her up and never be good enough for her.

Not that he was good enough for her. Still, it was supposed to have been him.

"I *hate* you for this!"

He flinched, hating those words. "I know."

"So what the hell do you have to say for yourself?"

He clamped her face between his hands

and stared into her eyes. "Fourteen days," he hissed. " 'Tis all I've left. What would you have of me? Apologies? Self-recrimination? You'll get none."

"Why?" she cried, tears springing to her eyes.

"Because I knew the moment I saw you," he ground out savagely, her *"I hate you"* still ringing in his ears, "that in another life — a life where I *didn't* become a dark sorcerer — you were my wife. I cherished you. I adored you. I loved you until the end of time, Jessica *MacKeltar.* But I doona get to have that life. So I'll take you any fucking way I can get you. And I'll not apologize for one moment of it."

She went motionless in his arms. She stared up at him, her lovely green eyes wide. "Y-you l-loved me?"

He inhaled sharply. "Aye." Staring down at her, something in him melted. "Och, lass," he relented, "I will rue for all eternity every moment of suffering I've caused you. The entire time I'm burning in Hell, I'll regret each tear I made you weep. But if Hell were the price for twenty days with you, I'd condemn myself again and again."

She sagged back against the wall, her lashes fluttering down, her eyes closing.

He waited, watching her, committing

every last cell of her face to his memory. From her tousled raven curls to her thick, dark lashes staining sooty crescents on her cheeks, glistening with a sheen of unshed tears, to her dainty, crooked nose to her luscious, soft lips to the stubborn thrust of her chin. He was going to die remembering it. He felt as if he'd been born already knowing her face. That he'd been watching, always waiting to see it coming at him from just around the next corner.

But it hadn't come.

And he'd stopped believing in the Keltar legends of a true mate.

And he strayed into Dark Magycks.

"Mine," he whispered fiercely, looking down at her.

Her eyes fluttered open then. In their jade depths he saw pain, rawness, and grief, but he also saw understanding.

"You know what the sad thing is?" she said softly.

He shook his head.

"I think that if you'd told me the truth from the beginning, I'd just have slept with you sooner."

He winced, as time-lost-never-to-be-regained sliced like a knife through his heart. Then he realized that she'd just granted him an absolution he could never deserve.

She'd said, *Even knowing, I would have anyway.* Wee woman, heart of a warrior.

"So take me, Cian. Take me as many times as you can." Her voice broke on the next words. "Because no matter how many times we get to have, it's not going to be enough."

"I know, love, I know," he said roughly.

He wasted no more time. He took her. Cupping her face between his big hands, he kissed her, sliding his hot velvety tongue deep. Threading his fingers into her silky curls, he cradled her head delicately, tipping her at just the right angle.

Jessi melted against him. *You were my wife,* he'd said. *I loved you until the end of time. Jessica MacKeltar,* he'd called her, as if he really *had* married her in another life.

She'd wanted such words. She'd neither expected nor been prepared for them. The moment he'd said them, she'd realized that it would have been kinder if he'd not said them at all. If he'd let her think him a callous prick, let her hate him.

But his words would keep her from ever being able to hate him. They'd ripped her open, ruthlessly exposing her heart. Her anger had dropped away as if it had never been, leaving only a desperation akin to his: to have whatever she could have of him, for so long as she could have it. Because she felt it too. As if they were supposed to have made a direct hit, to have had a full, long, crazy, wild, passion-filled, child-strewn life together, but somehow they'd come at each other from the wrong angle, and missed what could have/would have/should have been.

If she thought about it, it would tear her into little pieces. She refused to drown in sorrow. She would drown instead in the exquisiteness of this moment. There would be time for grief later. Too much time. A freaking lifetime.

But now, her man was kissing her. Now, his powerful hands were hot on her bare skin, slipping beneath her sweater. Now, he was gripping her by the waist, and lifting her against him.

She wrapped her legs around him and locked her ankles behind his back, as he backed her into the wall, kissing her passionately.

She had now.

And she wasn't going to waste a single precious moment of it.

Gwen smiled over her shoulder at Drustan as he followed her to the door.

Shortly after their ninth-century ancestor had risen without a word and stalked from the room with Jessi, Gwen had realized it was nearly dinnertime. And a good thing, too, as she'd completely forgotten lunch in all the fuss today and her stomach was growling hungrily.

But upon Cian's departure, Dageus and Drustan had promptly gotten into a heated discussion about him. It had taken her a good ten minutes to regain their attention and propose they move their conversation to the dining room.

Now, opening the door, she began to step out into the corridor.

"Oh, my," she said faintly.

She retreated right back into the library and gently closed the door. "Um, why don't we just, um, stay here in the library for a little while. Who wants to play Pente?" she said brightly. "I'm not as hungry as I thought I was." She turned and butted nose to ribs with Drustan.

He caught her by the shoulders. "Why, lass? Is aught amiss? What's out there?" Drustan stepped back, staring down at her, perplexed.

"Nothing, nothing at all."

He raised a dark, slanted brow. "Well, then, let's be off —"

470

"Oh no, not just yet." She beamed up at him. Backing herself flush to the door, she draped herself casually against it. "Let's stay here. Another half hour or so should, be, er, just about right." She blinked, looking uncertain. "I hope."

Drustan cocked his head, studied her a moment, then began to reach behind her for the doorknob.

Gwen sighed. "Don't, Drustan. We can't leave just yet. Cian and Jessi are out there."

" 'Out there'?" Drustan said blankly, stopping midreach. "So? Will we not fit past them in the corridor?"

"I'm sure we could if we tried. I'm not sure we'd want to," Gwen said meaning-fully.

He regarded her expectantly.

She tried again. "You know, they're *out there*."

Drustan continued to regard her expec-tantly.

"Oh, Gwen," Chloe cooed excitedly, "do you mean *out there?*"

Gwen nodded.

"Ha!" Chloe exclaimed. "I *knew* that woman wasn't stupid."

"Wait a minute. They're out there?" Dageus said disbelievingly. "The two of them are *out there* in the corridor? I put over a hundred rooms in this castle, and they're bloody out there in the bloody corridor as if they couldn't find a door to a chamber? 'Tis not as if I concealed them — there's only one every few bloody paces or so. Is it so much effort to turn a door-knob?"

A muscle leapt in Drustan's jaw, his eyes narrowed. "Lass, are you telling me that Cian and Jessica are tooping in that corridor? Is that why you closed that door?"

Blushing, she nodded.

"You saw this? Nay, that was a stupid question. Of course you did. What, exactly, did you see, lass?"

"Me? Oh, nothing." She folded her arms over her chest and stared off at a point somewhere east of his elbow.

"Gwendolyn?" He crossed his arms and waited.

"Okay, so maybe I saw a little," Gwen admitted, "but he has her up against the wall and all I saw was his butt, and I closed my eyes the minute I saw it."

"You saw my ancestor's arse?" Drustan said frostily. "His *bare* arse? Had the man any clothing on at all?" He began reaching past her again, for the doorknob.

She waved his hand away. "Oh, for heaven's sake, Drustan, you saw him when he left. All he had on to begin with was his plaid. What do you think?"

Drustan's nostrils flared. "I think the man's a blethering savage."

"Aye," Dageus agreed.

"Oh, you two should talk," Chloe said, laughing. "And Dageus, need I remind you of some of the places you and I —"

"Case argued and won, lass," he said hastily.

"I hardly saw a thing," Gwen assured Drustan. "It's not like I held the door open and stared or anything, even though he is a MacKeltar." She blinked. "And he certainly was every inch a MacK—" She broke off hastily, looking abashed, and feigned a sudden fascination with her cuticles. "What I meant was just that you MacKeltars are a fine-looking lot of men, Drustan, and he *is* related to you, actually, he precedes you in the gene pool, which might explain . . . Oh, dear, I should probably just shut up now, shouldn't I?" She pressed her lips together.

"That seals it," Drustan said calmly. "I'm going to have to kill the man."

It was Dageus who put things back into perspective. "You doona mean that, Drustan, nor could you if you did. So long as he's bound to the mirror he can't be killed. But doona fash yourself. The poor bastard will be dead in a fortnight anyway and he'll ne'er toop his mate in our corridor again."

Drustan winced and a bleak expression entered his eyes. He stared down at Gwen a moment, then gathered her gently in his arms and held her.

Dageus pulled his wife close, as well, remembering a time when he'd not believed he had much more time with his mate himself.

Half an hour later, it was a somber foursome that peeped cautiously out into the corridor before attempting to go to dinner again.

Jessi awoke late at night, alone, in a bedchamber.

She and Cian had eventually become cognizant of where they were — and just how public it was — and had stumbled from the corridor into a nearby bedchamber.

She stirred in the great big, down-filled, canopied bed, nestled in a warm mound of velvety blankets. She pushed a hand through her wrecked curls; she didn't need to see a mirror to know she had major bedhead. At the edges of her consciousness a terrible reality knocked, seeking entrance to her thoughts, but she refused to grant it an audience. Now was now. Later would come soon enough.

She smiled. She'd fallen asleep in bed with her Highlander's strong arms wrapped around her, spooning her backside to his front side, with one of his powerful legs draped over hers.

A perfect memory, she committed it to a special corner of her mind where each moment she had with him would be immortalized. These memories she would make with him now would have to last her a lifetime.

She pushed herself up and slipped from the bed, dropping barefoot onto the floor. She dressed swiftly and hurried for the door, wanting to be with him every possible moment.

But when she ducked her head into the dimly-lit library — the castle had been put to bed along with its occupants hours ago — the mirror wasn't where she'd last seen it, and a stab of blind panic made her chest feel dangerously tight.

"We moved it, lass," a soft voice cut through the darkness.

She jumped, peering into the dim room. By the soft red glow of the embers of a dying fire, she could make out a man's shape in an armchair near the hearth. Stacks of books surrounded him on both sides and he was paging through another.

"Drustan? Dageus?" By voice alone she couldn't tell them apart.

" 'Tis Dageus, lass. Why can't I deep-read you, Jessica?"

Jessi shrugged. "I think it's because I was injured when I was young and I have a metal plate in my head. When Cian uses his Voice-spell on other people, it feels itchy inside my skull."

He was silent a moment, then snorted with laughter. "Och, 'tis too perfect. 'Tis also exactly what it feels like — a smooth, cold, hard barrier. It must shield you from magyck somehow. You said 'other people.' Has he ever tried to use Voice on *you?*"

"Yes," she said. "It doesn't work."

Dageus gave another soft laugh. "Despite how bloody powerful he is, Cian can't deep-listen to you, either, can he?"

"I don't think so. He told me none of his magyck works on me."

"Good," he said slowly. "That's very good."

She thought that an odd thing to say and began to press, but he spoke again swiftly. "Are you all right, Jessica?"

She shrugged again. What could she

possibly say? *I'm both happier and more alive than I've ever been and I feel like I'm dying, too? And I suspect before this is over, I'll wish I was.* She said instead, "Where is the mirror?"

"We moved it to the great hall at his request. When I built this castle I buried four wardstones beneath the entry: east, west, north, and south. They are massive stones and I spelled them myself. He sensed their potency and asked that the mirror be hung on the landing of the stairs. 'Twill grant him the greatest protection. He is determined Lucan not be able to reach the Dark Glass." He paused, and she had the sense Dageus was not pleased with his ancestor. "He will have his vengeance, lass, no matter the cost."

She already knew that and was in no mood to discuss it. There was a bitter stew bubbling inside her, but she was not yet ready to ladle deep down into it. She would taste the richness first. She nodded briskly. "Thank you." She slipped from the library.

Twenty minutes later, Jessi had what she needed.

While she spread the comforters and throws and pillows at the base of the mirror on the wide expanse of landing in the great hall, Cian stood framed in the mirror, watching her every move. When she was cozily scrunched into the blankets, curled on her side, facing the mirror, she smiled drowsily up at him.

"Good night, Cian."

"Good night, Jessica. Dream sweet, lass."

"You too."

He was kind enough to not remind her that he neither slept nor dreamed while in the mirror.

And Jessica made a sleepy entry in a mental diary.

Memory/Day Fourteen: We said good night tonight like a married couple who'd been together for years and years.

So what if he was in a mirror and she was sleeping on the floor.

It was still a fine memory.

25

Days sped by on winged feet.

Jessi'd always thought that was such a cliché: time speeding by on winged feet; time flies when you're having fun; or as Cian had once put it so simply — time is of the veriest essence.

Yes, it was.

Suddenly all the clichés in the world were true. Each and every one made perfect sense to her. Those love songs on the radio that had once made her roll her eyes and tune the dial to Godsmack instead now reduced her to sappy sentimentality in moments. She'd even caught herself humming the maudlin melody of a country-music song the other day and she'd never liked country music.

Last year she'd read *The Stranger* by Albert Camus in French for extra foreign-language credits. Not her cup of tea, though it had given her food for thought, including the existential contention that death made brothers of all men.

Jessi now knew the truth was that love made brothers — and sisters — of all people. As different as they were, love was that common, defining ground, making everyone the same giddy, delirious fools for it in a thousand and one ways.

Like countless women before her, from tender teens to wise seniors welcoming a second wind, Jessi began keeping a diary to forever capture her memories.

Memory/Day Thirteen: Today we kissed in all one hundred and fifty-seven rooms in the castle (including closets, utility rooms and bathrooms!).

Memory/Day Twelve: We had a midnight picnic of smoked salmon and cheeses and three bottles of wine (my aching head!) on the castle grounds beneath a star-drenched sky and, while everyone else slept, we swam nude in the garden fountain and made love on all three tiers.

Memory/Day Eleven: We chased the cooks from the kitchen and made chocolate-chip pancakes with raspberry jam and whipped cream.

What they'd done with that raspberry jam and whipped cream had had very little to do with eating. The pancakes, that was.

But not all of the memories were good. She couldn't hide in some of the memories. Some of them slapped her in the face with truth.

Memory/Day Ten: Lucan Trevayne came today.

Lucan stood at the line of demarcation between Keltar-warded land and Trevayne-warded land, staring up at the castle. He toed arrogantly up to it, though he didn't care for the feeling at all. The Keltar's power hummed in the earth beneath his feet, trying to push past the invisible boundary, butting up against his own wards.

It had taken him all night and the efforts of a dozen well-trained men to secure this portion of land, enough for him to accomplish his aims. By the light of a pale moon, while the castle slept, they'd spelled the soil, from the sleek black limousine readied behind him for a swift departure, up to the circle of estate Cian had claimed for himself.

Now he stood approximately two hundred yards from the castle proper, waiting. The Highlander hadn't wasted time and resources warding more than the immediate grounds, nor had there been any reason to. Lucan was effectively barred from the castle by this meager yet insurmountable perimeter, as Cian had known he would be.

So long as he did not cross that boundary, Cian couldn't use sorcery on him. So long as Cian did not cross it, Lucan couldn't use sorcery on him, either. As they were both immortal and self-healing, they couldn't harm each other with anything else. They'd mastered long ago the exact wards that neutralized the other's power. This was the only way reclusive sorcerers were ever willing to meet, toe-to-toe on neutralized ground. Cian would not cross the line, nor would Lucan, unless a temper could be provoked, and they were both too smart for that.

Though he was immortal and could not be physically slain, he could be bespelled. If he were fool enough to stray onto Cian's warded ground, the Highlander could trap him and cocoon him in a mystic stasis, as helpless as a fly in a thick, sticky spider's web.

Eventually, Lucan might figure out how to break free, but he had very little time left to take chances with. And he'd never been willing to wager on the outcome of a battle of spells between him and the Highlander.

The situation at this second Castle Keltar was far worse than he'd imagined. He could feel the potency of two Keltar Druids in this new castle, about whom he knew nothing but for this — their power was as old as their names. They were strong. Not like Cian. But also not like any other Druid he'd ever encountered.

He'd arrived yesterday afternoon and swiftly gotten the lay of the land: There was no way he was going to be able to get inside that castle without help.

Which was why they'd spent the night warding, why he was standing here now.

His wits would have to serve him again, as they had so well eleven hundred and thirty-three years ago.

"Trevayne." Cian's nostrils flared as he spat the word.

"Keltar," Lucan spat it back, as though the vilest of viles had passed across his tongue — a tongue so heavily tattooed it was blackened with dye.

That tongue had spoken such sordid spells and lies that it should have rotted from the dark sorcerer's mouth, as his soul had rotted from his body so long ago.

"You don't look ready to die to me," Lucan taunted.

Cian laughed softly. "I've been ready to die for over a thousand years, Trevayne."

"Really? I have pictures of your woman. She looks like quite the fuck. I'm going to find out once the tithe is paid."

"The tithe will never be paid, Trevayne."

"You're going to watch us together, Highlander. I'll push her up against your mirror and —"

Cian turned around and began walking back toward the castle. "You waste my time, Trevayne."

"Why did you come out, then, Keltar?"

Cian turned around, walked back to the line and toed it. He stood so close that their noses nearly touched. The width of a hair kept them separate and safe from each other, no more.

Lucan saw movement behind the Highlander. The woman had just stepped out onto the top stair of the elaborate stone entryway. Precisely as he'd hoped.

"To look into your eyes, Lucan," Cian said softly, "and see death there. And I saw it."

He turned sharply again, heading for the castle. He looked up at the entrance. "Go back inside the castle, Jessica. *Now,*" he called sharply, seeing her on the stairs.

"What does *she* think of all this, Keltar?" Lucan called after him, making his voice loud enough to carry clearly to her ears, as well. "Is she as eager for vengeance as you?"

Cian made no reply.

"Tell me, is she as ready for you to die as you are, Highlander?" Lucan called.

Cian broke into a sprint toward the stairs.

"I don't believe you want to die, Keltar," Lucan yelled after him. "I know I don't. In fact, I'd do virtually anything to stay alive. I think I'd agree to *anything at all* to pass that tithe through the Dark Glass at midnight on Samhain." His voice rang out, carrying clearly across the lawn, echoing off the stone walls of the castle.

Cian reached the stairs and loped up them. Turning Jessica by her shoulders, he steered her back in the castle and closed the door behind them.

Lucan didn't care. He'd accomplished what he'd come for. His final words had not been meant for the Keltar at all. They'd been meant for the woman who'd stood on the steps so foolishly betraying her emotions, her hands anxiously fisted, her eyes deep with grief.

It would take time. He had no doubt it would take more days than he would bear well, and others would die, victims of his displeasure, in the interim. Though he could not read her, in fact, had smashed up against that strange smooth barrier once again, he'd read her body. There was no greater fool than a woman in love.

"Think on that, Jessica St. James," he whispered. "And let it begin to eat away inside you."

Many hours later, long after Lucan Trevayne had gotten back in his sleek black-windowed, black limousine and gone, Jessi sat staring at the computer screen in the darkened library.

She pressed her palms to the cool surface of the small library table beneath the softly illuminated portrait of an eighteenth-century MacKeltar patriarch and his wife, keeping her hands well away from the keyboard and the mouse.

It was four o'clock in the morning and the castle was silent as a tomb. It had begun to feel like one to her too.

She hadn't been the only one affected by the dark sorcerer's visit earlier in the day. It had cast a somber pall over all the MacKeltars.

Cian alone had been grimly satisfied by it. *He comes begging. He knows I've won,* he'd told her.

Won, her ass. Dying was not winning. Not in her book.

Lucan Trevayne was evil. *He* was the one who should die. Not Cian.

She raked a hand through her curls, staring at the display. Lucan Trevayne was, in fact, utterly terrifying. She'd had no idea what to expect of Cian's ancient enemy, but even if he'd warned her, nothing could have prepared her for what she'd seen.

He hadn't even looked human. The plate in her head that shielded her from compulsion and deep-listening indeed shielded her from all magic, for, while Gwen and Chloe had seen nothing more than a handsome man in his forties, Jessi'd seen the dark sorcerer's true appearance.

He'd been so heavily tattooed that his skin had appeared rotted in places. He'd moved with sickening reptilian stealth. His eyes, if they could be called that, had been fiery crimson slits. His tongue had flickered blackly as he'd spoken.

But far worse than his grotesque appearance had been the chill and suffocating sense of pure evil that had emanated from him, even from so far across the lawn.

Not so far that she hadn't been able to clearly hear every word he'd said.

She'd tried to stay in the castle as Cian had ordered.

But when they'd gone toe to toc, when she'd seen her man facing off with that twisted . . . thing . . . out there on the lawn, she'd burst from the castle, unable to stop herself.

Her every instinct had demanded she do something — anything — to help Cian, though she'd known there was nothing she could hope to do. Not against something like Trevayne. At that moment, she'd understood much of Cian's conviction. It wasn't just horrific evil that rolled off the ancient sorcerer, it was horrific power too. Not nearly as great as Cian's, but now that she'd seen him with her own eyes, she had to concede the possibility that once Trevayne had the aid of the Dark Book, he might genuinely be unstoppable.

I think I'd agree to anything at all to pass that tithe through the Dark Glass at midnight on Samhain, the sorcerer had said.

Jessi wasn't stupid.

She knew he'd been baiting her.

Problem was, he had the right stuff on his hook.

Cian's life.

She buried her face in her hands, massaging her temples. The instant he'd said it, some terrible, weak-willed part of her had wondered how she could possibly contact him, if she wanted to.

The answer had come swiftly: E-mail. Of course. Myrddin@Drui.com. She'd had the means to contact him all along.

After a moment, she raised her head and returned her gaze to the display.

Her laptop battery was dead and she had no adaptor, so she'd waited until she was certain the castle was asleep before leaving her makeshift bed on the landing, winding down the echoing stone corridors, and booting up one of the three computers in the Keltar library.

She had over a hundred new E-mails.

Forty-two of them were from Lucan Trevayne. He'd been trying at periodic intervals to reach her again since that night in the hotel. His earlier efforts had no subject line. The more recent E-mails were captioned with blatant taunts: *Do you love him, Jessica? Are you ready to watch your Highlander die? You can save him. Would he let you die? Would he give up on your life? Buy time, Jessica, live to fight another day.*

Such a juvenile ploy. And so damned effective.

All she had to do was open an E-mail to open communications. She had no doubt that back at his residence in London — or perhaps no more than a few miles down the road, somewhere between the castle and Inverness — Lucan was monitoring a computer, waiting for the moment she did so.

Waiting for a mere "yes" to keep Cian alive.

At what cost?

Her stomach felt sick.

You can see him as he is, can't you, lass? Cian had asked, as he'd steered her back into the castle.

She'd nodded, tears threatening, for she'd known exactly where he was going.

I am the only one who can stop him, Jessica.

Yup, right where she'd thought he was going.

I am all that stands between that monster and that monster gaining unlimited power.

I don't need a crash course in ethics, Cian, she'd snapped. She'd instantly regretted her tone and words.

They had so little time left. She'd sworn to herself that she would not make a moment of it ugly, that she would not vent her rage and frustration and grief on him. That she would save her ugliness for later, when she'd already lost all she had to lose.

That now, she would give her strong, determined, noble Highlander the only gift she had to give him: perfect days and perfect nights.

A small perfect lifetime in no time at all.

I'm sorry, she'd said softly.

Nay, lass, 'tis I who am sorry, he'd replied, drawing her into his arms. *'Twas I who should have told you from the —*

Don't! She'd pressed her finger to his lips. *No regrets. Don't you dare. I have none.*

A lie. They were eating her alive. Regret that she'd not slept with him that first night in the hotel room, knowing what she now knew. Regret that she'd not stayed that first night in Professor Keene's office and summoned him out then, and gotten to have more time with him.

Regret that she was such a coward.

That she couldn't say "Screw the world! Let them fend for themselves against Lucan. Let somebody else save everybody's ass. Not my man. What about *me?*"

She bit her lip, hard, staring at the screen. Reached for the mouse. Pulled away. Reached again, her finger hovering above it. Even without contact, she could feel the chill.

Her choices: lose Cian by letting him die to kill Lucan, or lose Cian by betraying him, by allying with his enemy to keep him alive.

Either way, she'd lose him.

And if she kept him alive, he would surely hate her. "I can't do it," she whispered, shaking her head.

A few moments later, she powered down the computer and left the library.

As the door closed behind her, from deep in the shadows, concealed behind a velvety drape, Dageus watched the display go dark and sighed.

Earlier that day, after Lucan had gone, Jessica had cornered Dageus as he'd been hurrying — unnoticed, he'd thought — in the back entrance to the castle, in an attempt to avoid contact with Cian, as he'd been doing for several days now, unwilling to risk his powerful ancestor trying to deep-read him.

Dageus, do those ancient people, the Draghar inside you, know anything? Is there any way to save him? she'd asked, her face wan, her jade eyes dark with grief.

He'd drawn a deep breath and given her

the same answer he'd given Drustan when, a few days ago, his brother had asked him the same question.

Nay, lass, he'd lied.

26

Memory/Day Nine: Cian and I were married today!

It wasn't anything like I used to imagine my wedding would be, and it couldn't have been more perfect.

We wrote our own vows and had a private ceremony in the estate chapel. When it was over, we scribed our names in the Keltar Bible, on thick ivory parchment edged in gold.

Jessica MacKeltar, wife of Cian MacKeltar.

Drustan, Gwen, and Chloe stood as witnesses, but Dageus wasn't feeling well, so he couldn't come.

Cian is my husband now!

We had a wedding breakfast of cake and champagne and honeymooned a long, rainy day away in a big four-poster bed before a roaring fire in a magnificent, five-hundred-year-old Scottish castle.

His vows were beautiful, so much better than mine. I know the MacKeltars thought so too, because Gwen and Chloe both caught their breath and got teary-eyed. Even Drustan seemed affected by them.

I wanted to say the same thing back to him, but Cian refused to let me. He got really funny about it. He placed his hand on my heart and mine on his — it was so romantic — and he said:

If aught must be lost, 'twill be my
    honor for yours.
If one must be forsaken, 'twill be my
    soul for yours.
Should death come anon, 'twill my life
    for yours.
I am Given.

The words gave me chills through my whole body.
God, how I love the man!

Memory/Day Eight: We decided on names for our children this morning. He wants girls that look like me and I want boys that look like him, so we decided to have four, two of each.

(I'd settle for one. So, if anyone's listening up there: I'D SETTLE FOR ONE, PLEASE.)

Memory/Day Five: Damn the man — he asked me not to be there when it happens!

Jessi didn't see it coming. The conversation began innocuously enough. They were lying in bed in the Silver Chamber, Cian stretched on his back, Jessi sprawled, blissfully sated, on top of him. Her breasts were pillowed against his hard chest, her legs were parted across one of his thighs (and every time he moved the slightest bit she got a delicious residual tingle from the orgasm she'd just had), and her face was pressed into the warm hollow where his chest met his neck.

They'd been making love for hours, and had just been laughing about how they wanted to go raid the kitchen, but neither of them had the strength to move.

As their laughter died, there was one of those long moments that stretched uncomfortably. They'd been occurring more and more often of late, as there were so many things both of them were being excruciatingly careful not to say.

"What if we broke the mirror, Cian?" she blurted into the strained silence. "What would happen?"

He cupped the back of her head, threading his fingers into her curls. "The glass is but my window, or door, if you will, on the world, Jessica. The actual Unseelie prison I inhabit exists in another realm. I would be trapped inside that Unseelie place, with no way out. Then, when the tithe was not paid, both Lucan and I would die. He in your world, I in a windowless broch of stone."

She shuddered, hating that image. "If you knew that breaking the mirror was a sure way to keep Lucan from passing the tithe through, why didn't you do it before you ever came to Chicago?"

"Och, lass, prior to meeting you, I had no one to summon me out, or I might have. I attempted to persuade the thief to release me, but he thought he was going mad and crated the mirror up. After that debacle I concluded mayhap 'twould be wiser to let time and distance separate me from Lucan. Trevayne searches constantly for relics of power and has many contacts. I knew not which merchants might have ties to him and feared if I continued showing myself word might get back to him and he would succeed in reclaiming the mirror before Samhain. Then, once I'd met you I had to be able to leave the glass in order to protect you. 'Twas why I was so concerned it not be broken, so you would not be left defenseless." He paused, then added softly, "There was also the small fact that I never wanted to live more greatly than I did the moment I saw you, lass. For over a thousand years, life had meant naught to me but vengeance. Then the moment my vengeance was at hand, life suddenly meant everything. 'Twas a bitter pill to swallow."

Jessi was choking on the bitterness of that pill herself. As each precious day slipped by, as Drustan and Dageus continued to shake their heads and say they'd still not found a way to save him, so, too, did her grip on herself slip.

Cian might have accepted his death as a necessity, but she never would.

Each night, at some point, she ended up in the darkened library, sitting in front of the computer, her hands clenched in her lap. The past few nights she'd not even dared to turn it on.

Because each day she was weakening. Ethics? What were ethics? She wasn't even sure she could spell the word. Wasn't in any dictionary she knew.

"What if it was broken when you were *outside* it?" she pressed.

"The same. 'Tis not the mirror I'm actually reclaimed back into, but that place in the Unseelie realm. When whatever hours of my freedom I was allotted that day expired, I would be returned there again, with no way out. Again, as the tithe could no longer be paid at Samhain's end, we would die."

"Oh, for God's sake," she cried, pulling away from him. Sitting up, she punched the mattress with a fist. "I'm surrounded by magic! The three of you are Druids. On top of that, you're a sorcerer and Dageus was possessed by thirteen ancient, evil beings! Don't any of you know a spell or enchantment or *something* that can undo this stupid indenture?"

Cian shook his head. "One would think so, but nay. The Keltar were chosen to protect Seelie lore, not Unseelie. Though some of us are wont to dabble with things best left alone, we ken very little of the ways of Dark Magyck, even less about the darker half of the Tuatha Dé Danaan."

"There has to be another way, Cian!"

He sat up and grabbed her by the shoulders, his whisky gaze fierce. "Och, Christ, lass, do you think I wish to die? Doona you think if there were any other way to stop Lucan that I would seize it? I love you, woman! I would do anything to live! But the simple fact is, 'tis my very life that keeps Trevayne immortal, and nothing but my death can take that away from him. In time, he will find the Dark Book. He cannot be permitted to have that time. 'Tis not merely our lives at stake, 'tis the lives of many, 'tis the very future of your world. I can stop him now. Before long, no one will be able to."

"And you can't live with that," Jessi said, unable to keep the note of bitterness from her voice. "You have to be the hero."

He shook his head. "Nay, lass. I've never been the hero, and I'm not trying to be one now. 'Tis but that there are things a man can live with and things he can't." He took a deep breath, exhaled it slowly. "I told you I was tricked into the mirror and that much is true. But I didn't tell you that I wanted the Unseelie Dark Glass too."

Jessi went very still. "Why?" Was he finally going to tell her what happened to him so long ago?

"Lucan and I were once friends, or so I thought. I later learned he was naught but subterfuge and deceit from the beginning."

"Didn't you do that deep-listening thing to him?"

Cian nodded. "Aye, I did, for my mother cared naught for the man. But when a surface probe yielded nothing, I didn't push. I arrogantly thought myself so superior in power and lore that I didn't deem Lucan a significant threat. I couldn't have been more wrong. I didn't know that he'd sought me out deliberately to get the Dark Glass. Or that he was born a bastard, sired by an unknown Druid father on a village whore, and had been shunned all his life by other Druids. They refused to teach him, refused him entrance to their inner circle.

"What lore Lucan had managed to acquire before we met had been gained through violence and bloodshed. For years he'd been systematically capturing and torturing lesser Druids for their teachings. Even more powerful ones had begun to cede him wide berth. But he couldn't overwhelm and take captive a Druid who knew the art of Voice, and he needed that art desperately.

"He learned of me somehow and came to Scotland, to my mountains where, isolated from so much of the world, I'd not heard of him. I learned later all of Wales, Ireland, and much of Scotland had heard tales of this Lucan 'Merlin' Trevayne. But not I. He befriended me. We began to exchange knowledge and lore, to push each other, to see what we could do. He told me of the Scrying Glass and, before long, he offered to help me get it if I would teach him the art of Voice first."

"The Scrying Glass?" Jessi repeated.

"Aye." He smiled bitterly. "Lucan lied about what it was. He said 'twas used to foretell the future in fine detail. That with it one could alter certain events before they ever happened. 'Twas an enticing power to me. Especially since I'd begun to wonder what my own life held. I'd begun to doubt there was a Keltar mate for me. After all, I was nigh a score and ten, quite old for a man to have never been wed in my century."

"A Keltar mate?"

" 'Tis legend that there is one true mate for each Keltar Druid, his perfect match, his other half, the one who completes him with her love. If he finds her, they can exchange the Druid binding vows and bind their souls together for all time, through whatever is to come, beyond death, unto eternity." He paused briefly, his gaze turning inward. "If, however," he murmured, "only one of them takes the vow, only that one will be forever bound. The other remains free to love another, if he or she so chooses."

Jessi's breath caught in her throat. *How does a Keltar Druid recognize his mate?*

Am I yours? she wanted desperately to ask. But there was no way she was asking, because if he said no, it might just kill her. Then his last comment penetrated. "Wait a minute — do you mean that if only one of them takes the vow, that person's heart is forever bound to another person who might never love them back, not just in this life but through all eternity?"

"Aye," he said softly.

"But that would be awful," she exclaimed.

He shrugged. " 'Twould depend on the circumstances. Mayhap, one might think it a gift." He resumed his tale briskly. "I agreed to the bargain. I taught him Voice, and we rode out one morning for a village in Ireland where the Dark Glass was being guarded in the center of a veritable fortress by a dozen holy men and a band of warriors a thousand strong.

"Trevayne had given me an ancient sleep spell to employ upon our approach. Our plan was to render the guards unconscious, ride in and take the mirror, then ride out again. I saw no reason to distrust him. He'd demonstrated the spell several times himself, and it had merely made the subject slip into a deep slumber. He'd deferred the task to me because he wasn't strong enough to affect the entire village, and I was. I'd done my best to teach him, but he simply wasn't good enough at Voice to compel more than a handful of people in the same room with him. Though the art of it can be taught, the power that infuses it is something a man is either born with — or not. His power lay in other areas."

"Oh, God," Jessi breathed. "Tell me this isn't going where I think it is."

He nodded, his gaze distant, far away and long ago, in ninth-century Ireland. "It caused only slumber when Lucan used it, only because he lacked the power to invoke the Spell of Death. I didn't. Though I didn't know it, along with all the other 'talents' with which I'd been born was a horrific one that appeared so rarely in our bloodline that I'd never given it any thought. I believed 'twas a sleep spell I'd worked right up until that final moment I knelt in the inner chamber beside the Dark Glass and touched the holy man who lay sprawled on the floor. I think he'd tried to break the glass rather than let it be taken, but my spell had been too potent, too quick.

"He was dead. And as I sat there, even then not fully comprehending that I'd been betrayed, not able to fathom what Lucan might be after, he wove the dark binding spell around me. He had the chant, the gold, the man to ensorcel, and I'd just spilled the blood of innocents for him.

"The next thing I knew, I was looking out at Lucan from inside the Dark Glass.

"As we left the village, he gave me a view, to ensure I saw what I'd done. With one spell, I'd killed not only those guarding the glass but the entire village of Capscorth. Men, women, and children, all dead where they'd been standing; hundreds upon hundreds of them, lying in the streets, as if a plague had ripped through their world. I was that plague." He closed his eyes, as if trying to shut out the terrible vision he'd seen that day.

"But you didn't *mean* to," Jessi defended. *Damn* Lucan! She knew Cian — somewhere inside him he bore the weight of each and every life he'd taken so long ago. "It's not like you rode in there intending to kill anyone!"

He opened his eyes and smiled faintly. "I ken it, lass," he said, "and in truth, I no longer hate myself for what transpired that day. There are things a man can change, and there are things a man lives with. I live with it."

He cupped her face and gazed into her

eyes. "But what I cannot live with is putting into Lucan Trevayne's hands the kind of power that would make him unstoppable. 'Twas a village then. With the Dark Book, he could destroy entire cities, even a world. Only my death can prevent that." He paused. "Sweet Jessica, you must cry peace with this, as must I. I have no choice."

"I can't," she cried, shaking her head, blinking back tears. "You can't expect me to."

"Lass, you must promise me something," he said, his voice low and urgent. "I've been thinking much on this. I doona want you there when the time comes."

Jessi felt as if she'd been punched in the stomach. She opened her mouth, but nothing came out. She'd deliberately refused to let herself think that far ahead, to let her mind linger over the details of the night it would actually happen. To the night she would stand before a mirror and watch her Highlander age more than a thousand years in a single moment.

And disintegrate into a pile of dust.

"We'll spend what time I can be free together that day, then you will go elsewhere with the others. Promise me this," he pushed. "Drustan has pledged to break the mirror once it's done, so none can ever be taken captive again."

"That's not fair, Cian, you can't —"

"I can, and am. 'Tis a dying man's last request," he said roughly. "I want you to remember me as a man, lass, as *your* man. Not as a prisoner of Dark Magycks. I doona want you to watch me die. Promise me you won't, Jessica. *Promise me and mean it.*"

Jessi was no longer able to hold the tears at bay. Hot and wet, they scalded her cheeks.

As she stared at him through the tears, a lifetime of hopes and dreams, of wishes and desires, of love and family and children she would never get to have, flashed before her mind's eye.

It was too much.

When she spoke again, her voice was low and fervent. "I promise you, Cian MacKeltar, that I will not watch you die."

When he drew her into his arms to kiss her, she closed her eyes and counted her blessings for the privacy of a steel-plated mind.

For, though she'd pledged him the promise he'd sought, she'd not meant what he'd meant by it at all.

27

SAMHAIN
TWENTY-NINE MINUTES
TO MIDNIGHT

"That's it, Jessica. The wards are down. You ken what that means?"

Taking a slow, deep breath, Jessi nodded. "Yes," she replied softly. "Lucan will be able to enter the castle now, but he won't be able to use sorcery."

"Doona make the mistake of thinking you're safe from him, lass. He can still harm you in the way of any man. I want you to wear this."

He fastened a sheath snugly to her forearm, then slipped a plain-handled dirk into it, tip to her elbow, handle at her wrist. "Don your sweater over it."

She obeyed tensely.

"Do this." He made a twisting motion with his hand. "Drop it down."

She mimicked his movement, surprised

by how well it worked, smoothly guiding the handle into her palm.

He helped her resheathe it. "He's desperate, Jessica. 'Tis the only reason he's agreed to this. Doona think he's truly agreed to it. Expect deceit. Expect last-minute treachery. It *will* come."

She glanced up at him sharply. There'd been a strange certainty in his voice when he'd said the last: *It will come.* As if he knew something she didn't.

"But you said yesterday that you thought he would pass the tithe through the glass and go away," she protested anxiously. "You said you thought he'd focus on finding the Dark Book before he would come back and try to take the mirror from the Keltar. That's the whole point, isn't it? To buy a little more time. Right?"

He stared down at her a long, pensive moment. "I'm but advising you to be on constant guard, lass. Constant," he repeated. "Watch yourself. Doona let your defenses down for even a second. You've no way of knowing what might happen from one moment to the next. Remember that. Be prepared for anything. *Anything.*"

"You're starting to worry me. What do you think —"

"Hush, lass," he cut her off. "I must go.

Time is short and we doona wish him to see me. He believes you act alone. He must continue to believe that. But doona fear, I will be watching over you."

Halfway down the corridor, he turned back. "*Constant guard,* lass," he hissed.

Jessi swallowed. She tensed her wrist, feeling the weight of the blade. "Constant guard, Dageus," she echoed. "I promise."

Twenty minutes to midnight.

Jessi shivered as she hurried down the corridor. Five days ago, when she'd promised Cian that she wouldn't watch him die, she'd possessed great determination but little hope.

Later that night, however, her circumstances had changed drastically.

After the mirror had reclaimed Cian, she'd left the Silver Chamber and hastened to the library to open communications with Lucan. She'd been sitting at the computer, her inbox open, about to click on one of his E-mails, when Dageus had stepped from behind the drapes, catching her in the act. He'd told her he'd been in the library a few nights ago, and knew she'd been receiving E-mails from Trevayne.

As she'd gaped up at him, half expecting to be dragged off to some medieval dungeon for punishment, he'd further shocked her by saying, *How bad do you want him to live, lass?*

Figuring she had nothing left to lose at that point, she'd told him, in no uncertain terms. *I'd do anything. Even make him hate me.*

He won't hate you, lass, Dageus had assured her. *If aught, he'll hate me.*

She was counting on that. Not that he would hate Dageus, but that he would eventually forgive her for helping his enemy pass the tithe through to keep him alive.

I thought you said you didn't know of any way to free him. Why would you do this?

Why would you? he'd countered.

Because I believe there has to be a way to get him out of there, that we just need a little more time to find it.

I believe there's a way to get him out of there, too, lass, he'd replied after a brief pause.

Really? Her heart had soared at those words.

It was one thing for her to believe it; she was desperate enough to cling to any hope and she knew it. But if a Keltar Druid believed it, it was more than just possible, it was *probable*. No, it was an eventual *certainty*. There was no way Dageus and Drustan would run the risk of Trevayne ever getting the Dark Book, which meant they had to be convinced they could ultimately free Cian, and reasonably quickly after the tithe was paid.

It had been nearly impossible to conceal her change in spirits from Cian. Especially today — on what he'd thought was their last day together — but she'd managed. Dageus had been insistent she discuss their plans with no one, even going so far as to say he wouldn't help her at all if she failed to convince Cian that she believed tonight was his last night alive. *He believes 'tis the only way, lass,* Dageus had warned, *I fear he will become difficult if he suspects we plan to stop him.*

Though acting the part had nearly killed her — thank God, she'd not had to actually *live* it! — she'd been convincing, unwilling to jeopardize her only chance to save him.

E-mail Trevayne, Dageus had instructed her that night. *Tell him you'll help him get in the castle to pass the tithe through. But the Keltar keep the mirror.*

She'd done it. At first Trevayne had refused, offering myriad alternatives, all of which she'd rejected at Dageus's behest.

512

But late last night, twenty-four hours from the zero-hour to the minute, Trevayne had finally agreed.

And now — Jessi paused at the back door, inhaling sharply — he was here. Making her skin crawl. She could feel him *through* the wood of the door, cold, dark, rotten, and much, much too close for comfort.

And about to get closer.

He'd accepted her deal only when she'd pledged herself as his hostage.

You must let me use you to get in and out of the castle.

Eyes wide, she'd stared up at Dageus. Nostrils flaring, he'd shaken his head curtly. But the dark sorcerer had refused to come onto Keltar-warded land any other way, and Dageus had finally nodded.

How do I know this isn't a trap? Trevayne had typed.

How do I? she'd countered.

There'd not been much to say after that. It had been the bottom line, really. They were both risking all. And they knew it.

She glanced at her watch.

It was eighteen minutes to midnight.

Dageus had been adamant they give Trevayne barely enough time to get to the mirror and pass the tithe through. *I doona want him to have a single moment with you during which he doesn't have to keep moving. Once it's over, I'll show myself and we'll get him out of the castle.*

It was now or never.

She braced herself for Trevayne's hideous appearance.

Whatever happened from this moment forth, she would betray no fear, no weakness. She was Jessica MacKeltar, wife of Cian, and she would do him proud.

The bastard she was about to let in Castle Keltar had held her husband imprisoned for eleven hundred and thirty-three years and, though she'd never thought herself a violent person, she'd plunge her concealed dagger into Trevayne's heart in an instant if she thought she had a snowball's chance in hell of killing him.

She slid the deadbolt back and turned the doorknob.

"Lucan," she said coolly, inclining her head.

"Good evening, Jessica," Trevayne replied with a cordial smile. Sort of.

When he took her arm, Jessi barely suppressed her revulsion.

Dageus stood in the shadows of the corridor off the balustrade that overlooked the great hall, listening intently. Upon leaving

Jessica, he'd loped up the back stairs, taking turn after turn, wending a circuitous route to his current position, all to avoid passing Cian's mirror.

His brother, Gwen, and Chloe were safely ensconced in a chamber two corridors down. Until a few hours ago, he'd had to conceal his plans from even them so none could inadvertently betray it to Cian by thinking about it in their powerful ancestor's presence.

'Tis too dangerous, Drustan had growled.

'Tis the only way, brother, he'd replied.

The Draghar knew this for a certainty?

Aye.

Too many things could go awry, Dageus. You have no way of controlling what happens.

Dageus hadn't bothered arguing. It was a long shot and he knew it. He was doing little more than setting the stage, and hoping his instincts about the actors involved would prove true.

Drustan had been reluctant to agree, until Dageus had assured him that no matter what happened, Trevayne would not pass the tithe through. That he would stop him himself if necessary. But not until the last possible second, he'd added in the privacy of his mind.

A few dozen yards away, mounted on the wall of the landing, high above the great hall hung the Unseelie Dark Glass.

It was flat silver.

He imagined his ancestor inside it. Was Cian stretched out on his stone floor, arms behind his head, staring up at the stone ceiling, waiting for death?

If so, he knew the mere waiting was killing his ancestor a thousand times over. 'Twasn't in a Keltar's blood to accept death. Especially not once he'd found his mate and given the binding vows. Dageus knew. He'd been in far too similar a position himself.

Indeed, it was the similarity in their positions that had given him this idea to begin with.

He glanced at his watch. Fifteen minutes to midnight.

Expect deceit, he'd told Jessica. *Expect last-minute treachery. It will come.*

What he'd not told her was that 'twould come not from Lucan but from him.

Cian had been listening to the clock in the great hall below him chime the passing hours all evening.

'Twas now but mere minutes to midnight, and he was as prepared as he would ever be to draw his final breaths. He'd conjured a perfect mental vision of Jessica's face in his mind hours ago, and he intended to die holding it there.

It was jarred slightly by the sound of approaching footsteps. She'd promised not to watch, he'd thought, stiffening.

Then he jerked ramrod straight and pushed up from the floor as another sound reached his disbelieving ears.

The hated sound of Lucan Trevayne's laughter.

Nay! 'Twas not possible! There was no way the bastard could get inside Castle Keltar! Not without someone helping —

"Och, Christ, nay, lass," he whispered. "Tell me you wouldn't. Tell me you didn't."

But he didn't need to seek visual confirmation of what he'd just heard to know she had. And the truth was, he couldn't blame her. He'd not have let her die, either. He'd have moved mountains. He'd have battled God or Devil for his wife's life.

She'd betrayed him.

He smiled faintly.

And in so doing, she'd honored him beyond measure. His Jessica loved him enough to break all the rules for him, enough to damn the whole world just to save him.

He'd have done no less for her. He'd have kept her alive by any means possible.

"Highlander," Trevayne's voice rang out triumphantly in the great hall, "you're mine for another century."

His smile faded. Unfortunately, her actions changed nothing. "Over my dead body," he murmured. Which, as he'd always known, was the only way.

Jessi gazed up at the landing, high above the hall where, for the past two weeks, she'd slept every night unless Cian had been free to sleep in a bed with her.

Framed in the mirror, he stared down at her as she stood arm in arm with his enemy. He closed his eyes briefly, as if trying to cleanse the image from his vision. Then he said softly, "Call me out, lass. You doona wish to do this. You must let me stop him."

Jessi glanced at the tall grandfather clock in the alcove to the left of the staircase. Five minutes to midnight.

Biting her lip, she shook her head.

"Jessica, you're not just keeping me alive, you're letting him live. We've been through this. You must summon me out."

Spine straight with resolve, she shook her head again.

When the mirror blazed brilliantly and the hall was suddenly skewed by that odd sense of spatial distortion, for a moment Jessi simply couldn't make sense of it.

Then Dageus stepped from the shadows behind the balustrade and she realized he must have murmured the chant to release Cian — the chant she herself had told him that first night in the library — softly enough that only Cian had been able to hear.

But why?

"Dageus — what are you — why did you — *oh!*" she cried. He was moving protectively toward the Dark Glass, making his intentions all too clear.

She was too stunned by Dageus's betrayal to register the danger she was in until it was too late.

Lucan dropped a silken cord over her head and had it cinched tightly around the slender column of her throat, the choke handles twisted before she even knew what he was doing.

"You son of a bitch, let her go!" Cian roared, bursting from the mirror.

Rather than releasing her, Lucan turned the choke handles just a bit.

Jessica went stiff and still. She understood the use of those handles, she was familiar with the garrote as an ancient weapon. One twist and she was dead. She didn't dare move even the few inches necessary to try to use the dagger Dageus had given her.

Expect anything, he'd said.

Now, she thought bitterly, she knew why.

Three minutes to midnight.

Lucan had his wife hostage, a garrote about her neck.

"Get back in the mirror, Highlander. Return to it willingly and I'll let her live. Move. Now."

Cian stretched his senses. He should have felt it earlier, but he'd had no reason to suspect anything. Aye, the wards barring Lucan from the castle were down.

But the wards preventing Lucan from using sorcery were still up. Which meant Cian could use a spell on the bastard and Lucan wouldn't be able to counter it.

He opened his mouth, and just as he did, Lucan hissed, "Say one word in sorcerer's tongue and she's dead. I won't give you the chance to bespell me. If I hear one wrong syllable, I'll snap her neck."

Cian closed his mouth, a muscle working in his jaw.

"And that goes for you too," he barked

at Dageus. "Either of you start a spell and she dies. Get back in the glass, Keltar. Now. I'm coming up to pass the tithe through."

Centuries of hatred and fury filled Cian as he stared down at the man who'd stolen his life so long ago and was now threatening his woman.

Vengeance: 'Twas what he'd lived and breathed for for so long, he'd nearly lost his own humanity.

'Til his fiery, passionate Jessica had come along.

Once he'd hungered for nothing more than to see Lucan Trevayne dead. No matter the cost. In truth, it hadn't been so many days ago that he'd hungered for it above all else — twenty-six days ago, to be exact.

Now, staring down at his ancient enemy holding his woman captive, something inside him changed.

He no longer cared if Lucan lived or died. All that mattered was getting the bastard's hands off his wife long enough to save her. Nothing else. Just that his woman live. That she see another dawn, be granted another day. She was his light, his truth, his highest aspiration.

Love for her filled him so completely

that, in the space between one heartbeat and the next, eleven centuries of hatred and lust for vengeance were burned out of him as if they'd never been.

Trevayne was no longer his problem. Only Jessica was.

A quiet resolve, an unexpected serenity filled him, unlike anything he'd ever felt before.

"I would have bargained with the devil for you, too, lass," he said softly. "I'd have done anything too. I love you, Jessica. You are my one true mate, lass. Never forget that."

"Back in the glass, Highlander," Lucan snarled. "Or she dies. I mean it! Now!"

"You want to pass the tithe through, Lucan? Fine. Be my guest. I won't stop you."

In one smooth, fluid motion, he turned, lifted the mirror from the wall, spun about, and tossed it into the air, casting it end over end, out and over fifty-odd stairs, down to the hard marble floor below.

"Catch."

For the second time in her life, events unfolded for Jessi as if in slow motion.

With Cian's admission that she was his one true mate ringing in her ears, she watched the only thing that could keep him alive plummet to virtually certain destruction.

She knew why he'd done it. To save her. Trevayne could not both hold her and go after the mirror. Cian had forced him to choose.

Her husband knew his ancient enemy well. Of course he'd go after the mirror. Survive now, live to kill another day.

The rope slackened around her neck as Lucan released the handles and lunged forward.

She tugged the garrote from her throat and dropped it to the floor, watching, heart pounding.

If, by some miracle, Lucan managed to actually catch the man-sized looking glass, she wouldn't be surprised if the ancient mirror shattered merely from the impact of him stopping its fall.

Eyes huge, she tipped her head back and up. Cian stood at the top of the stairs, staring down at her. Love blazed in his eyes so fiercely, so intensely, that it took her breath away.

She stared at him, drinking him in. She knew she'd never make it up the stairs in time to touch him. To hold him. To kiss him just one last time.

Lucan was almost beneath the glass.

Almost.

She caught her breath and held it. Miracles sometimes happened. Maybe he'd reach it, shove the tithe through, and they'd all live to fight another day.

Mere inches from Lucan's outstretched hands, the mirror crashed to the floor. One corner of the ornate golden frame struck marble with the sharp report of a gunshot.

The Dark Glass shattered into thousands of silvery, tinkling pieces.

To Jessi, it seemed as if the entire universe froze but for those glittering shards of silver cascading across the floor.

Her husband's life lay in those pieces.

When the clock began chiming the midnight hour, her pent breath exploded from her lungs on a soft sob.

One. Two.

She raised her gaze from the floor, stared up at Cian. The Dark Glass was broken now, beyond repair. The tithe could never be paid again. She'd lost him.

Three. Four.

Dimly she was aware of Lucan, frozen, looking all-too-humanly bewildered, standing next to the twisted frame, in the midst of the shattered glass.

Five. Six.

She felt the same. Bewildered. Disbelieving. Devastated. She'd begun the day with so much hope, only to end it with none.

Dimly she was aware that the other MacKeltar had, at some point, joined Dageus behind the balustrade and everyone seemed rooted to the ground, transfixed by the scene before them.

Seven. Eight.

There was a silent request in her husband's eyes. She knew what it was.

She'd promised not to watch him die. To remember him as her man, not a prisoner of Dark Magycks.

Nine.

It was a promise she'd always meant to keep. Just not this way. Dear God, just not this way. "I love you, Cian," she cried.

Ten. Eleven.

Her promise kept was all she had left to give him.

Tears spilled down her cheeks when she squeezed her eyes shut.

Twelve.

28

It was Lucan's laughter — *after* the twelfth chime — that made her eyes snap open again.

Jessi gaped blankly at the dark sorcerer who was still, mystifyingly, standing there.

Then up to the landing beyond. Her heart lodged in her throat.

Cian was still there, too!

How could that be? The glass was shattered — it was after midnight on Samhain — and the tithe hadn't been paid.

They should both be dead!

They should be dust. Little piles of it. Why weren't they? Not that she *wanted* them to be. At least not one of them.

"Oh, God," Jessi breathed, "who cares? You're still there! Oh, God, Cian!" Inhaling sharply, she broke into a sprint for the stairs, for her beloved, living, breathing husband!

"Jessica, love, watch out!" Cian roared.

Lucan had spun around and was heading

straight for her, slipping and sliding over slivers of glass.

"Blethering hell, Cian, he's mortal now," Dageus roared. "Doona kill him. We need to know where the Dark Book is!"

But his warning came too late. For both of them.

As Lucan lunged for her, she slid the blade that Dageus had given her down her sleeve, into her palm.

She raised her hands to fend him off, and the blade slid into the front of Lucan's chest at the same moment the tip of a jeweled dirk pierced through him from behind, driven straight through his heart by the force of Cian's throw.

Then she was backpedaling away from the falling sorcerer and Cian was racing down the stairs toward her and taking her in his arms, turning her away from the gruesome sight.

She heard Dageus shouting down at Lucan, "Where's the Dark Book, Trevayne? Blethering hell, tell us what you know of it!"

Lucan Trevayne whispered, "Fuck you, Keltar."

And died.

"Oh, my God, you're alive. I can't believe you're alive!" Jessi couldn't seem to stop saying. Nor could she stop touching Cian, kissing him frantically, desperate to assure herself he was really there and wasn't going to disappear, or turn to dust at any moment.

"Aye, love, I'm alive." A string of curses spilled from his lips and he scowled down at her. "You tried to barter with the devil himself for me, you crazy woman. Bloody hell, doona you *ever* risk your life for mine. Ever! Do you hear me?" Burying his hands in her dark curls, he pulled her against him, slanted his mouth over hers, and kissed her hungrily.

"You would have done the same for me," she said breathlessly when he let her breathe again. As a matter of fact, he'd said so much on the day of their wedding. *Should death come anon,* he'd said, *'twill be my life for yours.* So what if he'd refused to let her say the same. She made identical promises in her heart. *I am Given.*

"Not the point," he growled. " 'Tis what a man does for his mate."

His mate. Jessi stared up at him, a sudden, stunning realization dawning. "Oh! The wedding vows you said that day *were* the binding vows you told me about, weren't they? You gave me the binding vows and wouldn't let me give them back! Didn't you?" She thumped him in the chest with her palm. "You tricked me!"

"I refused to let you be bound to a dead man, lass," he said grimly. "Nor was I willing to miss the chance to pledge my heart to you forever. Even if it meant I would have to be reborn again and again, and serve as naught but your protector from afar, while you loved another. To ken you were alive and well would have been enough." He paused a moment. "Not that I wouldn't have done all in my power to steal your heart from whoever the bloody bastard was," he added in a fierce growl. "I would have."

Tears of joy misted her eyes and she laughed aloud. Oh, yes, she could see her ferocious Highlander doing battle for her heart. He'd easily have won it in any lifetime. "But you didn't die, so don't try to stop me now," she said softly, taking his hand and putting it over her heart, pressing her palm to his. Speaking with quiet reverence, she echoed the words he'd given her that day in the chapel.

The moment the vow was said, the final pledge echoing in the stone hall, emotion crashed over her so intensely, her knees buckled. Love for him filled every ounce of her being. It was the most incredible sensation she'd ever felt. They were inextricably linked now, for all eternity. Cian caught her and crushed his mouth to hers, kissing her passionately. She clung to him, savoring the strength of his hard, powerful body against hers, the raw, carnal heat of his kiss.

"But wait a minute," she said, frowning up at him a few minutes later, "*how* are you still alive? I don't get it. What just happened?"

It was Dageus who replied. While she and Cian had been otherwise occupied, he and the other MacKeltars had hurried down the stairs and joined them in the great hall.

Now he guided them all away from the fallen sorcerer and the three couples moved to stand near one of the hearths.

"I didn't quite tell you the truth, lass," he said. "The truth was, we could find no way to free him. Our only hope lay in trying to void the Unseelie Indenture. The Draghar believed that, much as a Seelie Compact can be voided by an evil deed, an Unseelie Compact could be voided by a selfless act. Not broken, breached, nor violated. *Voided.* Both parties released from the binding and returned to their normal state."

"Believed?" Drustan exclaimed. "You told me they knew."

"They believed it very strongly," Dageus amended hastily, slipping an arm around his wife and drawing her close.

"Wait a minute," Chloe protested, "wouldn't the fact that Cian had been willing to die to stop Lucan from getting the Dark Book have counted as a selfless act?"

"Nay," Dageus said. "A selfless act cannot be tainted by personal motive. Cian was driven for centuries by hunger for vengeance. 'Twas in his voice every time he spoke of Lucan, of dying in order to kill him."

Cian nodded. "Aye, 'tis true. I didn't want to die. I never wanted to die. I wanted Lucan dead, and there was only one way I could accomplish it. Though I wanted to keep him from getting the Dark Book, I hungered for revenge even more."

"But he was ready to die for *you,* Jessica," Dageus told her softly. " 'Twas what I was wagering on. That he would die for you selflessly. At the moment he threw that mirror, there was no thought of vengeance in his heart at all. There was only the desperate, pure self-sacrifice of unconditional love. And it voided the dark indenture."

"You had no way of knowing 'twould work," Cian growled.

"You're right. I didn't. But I was once in a like position, kinsman." Dageus gazed down at Chloe. "I thought it safe to wager on your feelings for your mate."

"You shaved it damn close. Mere seconds!"

Dageus arched a brow at Cian's rebuke. " 'Twas our only hope."

"You placed my woman in danger."

"At least you *have* her," Dageus pointed out. "Christ, doona be tripping all over yourself trying to thank me for saving you, kinsman."

"You didn't save him," eternal-physicist-and-human-calculator-of-odds Gwen pointed out matter-of-factly. "Not really. You just set up the circumstances. He saved himself."

"Bloody good thing I didn't do this for thanks," Dageus said dryly.

"Doona be looking to me for thanks. You put us all at risk," said Drustan.

"*I'll* thank you, Dageus," Jessi said fervently. "Thank you, thank you, thank you. I'll thank you a hundred times a day for the rest of your life if you want me to, and I'm sorry I hated you there for a minute when I'd thought you'd betrayed me."

Dageus nodded. "You're welcome, lass. Though you might have kept the hating me part to yourself."

Chloe beamed up at her husband. "I'll thank you too. I think you did a brilliant job of setting up circumstances, Dageus."

He dropped a kiss on her nose. Chloe was his greatest fan, as he was hers, and would always be.

"Speaking of setting up circumstances," Drustan said slowly, "I've had the oddest feeling since the two of you arrived at Castle Keltar. Verily, I've felt it a few times prior to your arrival too. Almost as if — nay, 'tis foolish." He shook his head.

"What, brother?" Dageus asked.

Drustan rubbed his jaw, frowning. " 'Tis probably naught. But I've been suffering the strangest feeling that there's more going on around Castle Keltar of late than meets the eye. Has no one else been feeling this?"

"I can't speak for Castle Keltar, Drustan, but I think I know what you mean," Jessi said. "I've felt it a few times lately too. There's been this word on the tip of my tongue since this all began. I keep getting close to it, but it's the darnedest thing — just when I think I have it, it melts away."

Her brow furrowed and she was silent a long moment. Then "Aha! I think I've got it!" she exclaimed. "Is this what you mean? Synchro—"

"—nicity," Queen Aoibheal of the Tuatha Dé Danaan murmured, her iridescent eyes shimmering.

A collision of possibles so incalculably improbable that it would appear to imply divine intervention.

The corners of her lips lifted in a faint smile. She smoothed them. She'd been employing a mortal form so much of late that she was beginning to mimic their expressions.

Humans were forever attributing the meddling of the Fae to the divine. As well they should, for handling so many threads, subtly altering the weft and weck of the world, truly required something of the divine.

They were here now.

Her players, her pieces on the board. More than pawns, less than kings.

The catastrophe that had occurred in the seventeenth century hadn't taken place after all, not since she'd rearranged events to get the Keltar's underground chamber sealed. The one in the twentieth century hadn't come to fruition either, for the same reason. Nor had the other two, though for different reasons.

"J'adoube," she whispered. *I touch. I adjust.*

Seven times now she'd prevented the extinction of the purest and most potent of the Druid lines.

And positioned the five most powerful Druids that had ever lived precisely where she wanted them. Where they could ally her.

Where they could save her.

There was Dageus, possessing far more knowledge than any one Druid should have: all the knowledge of the Draghar, the thirteen ancients. The memories she'd left in him were doing things to him he wasn't admitting. Not to Drustan, not to his mate.

There was Cian, possessing far more power than any one Druid should have: the genetic fluke, the unexpected mutation born once in a bloodline. The things Dageus and Cian could do together if they put their minds to it worried even her.

Then there was Drustan: compared to his dangerously endowed kin, modest of power, modest of knowledge, yet superior in a way they could never be. Dageus and

Cian could go either way, good or evil. Drustan MacKeltar was that unique kind of man whose name lived forever in legends of men — a warrior so pure of heart that he was beyond corrupting. A man who would die for his beliefs, not just once but ten thousand times over if necessary.

As for her other two chosen, she would be seeing them soon.

Below her, in Castle Keltar's great hall, the humans stood talking, oblivious to her presence. Blissfully unaware that a little over five years in their future, their world was in chaos, the walls between Man and Faery were down, and the Unseelie ruled with an icy, brutal hand. The Shades were feeding again, the Hunters were enforcing compliance, calling death sentences for the slightest infraction, and the exquisite Unseelie Princes were indulging their insatiable appetite for mortal women, brutally raping, leaving mindless shells.

And she?

Ah, that was the problem.

Her gaze shifted inward from the tableau below.

Though her race could move at will through the past, they could not penetrate a future that had not yet occurred. If one attempted to go forward beyond one's present existence, one encountered an oppressive white mist, nothing more. If one went too far back in the past, one encountered the same mist. Not even the Tuatha Dé Danaan understood time. They knew how to traverse only the simplest facet of it.

She'd sifted back countless times now, from five and a half years in Earth's future — her present — delicately altering events while trying not to change too much. Concealing from all, even those of her own court, that she was temporally displaced while doing it. Worlds were fragile; one could destroy an entire planet inadvertently. She already carried the weight of such an error. It was a heavy burden. As did her long-ago consort, though the unfathomably ancient Dark King cared nothing about the blood of billions.

She'd been alive for over sixty thousand years. Many of her kind wearied of existence long before that.

Not she. She had no wish to cease. Though the loss of Adam Black to his mortal mate grieved her, and she'd considered undoing that as well, she'd learned that there was a human element that was highly dangerous to meddle with. Love's power was violently unpredictable; it affected events in ways her Tuatha Dé mind had failed to anticipate on more than one occasion.

She could not hope to predict what she could not understand. There were times when she suspected human love harbored a power more elemental and greater than any her race possessed. It infused things with strength in impossible excess of the sum of its parts. Indeed, it had been the matching of each Keltar below with his mate that had tempered them, given them cores of steel, and made her Druids into allies worthy of a queen.

The room below fell into a sudden hush. The silence drew her gaze back to the small group of men and women.

Dageus, Chloe, Drustan, Gwen, and Jessica were all staring at Cian, who had a startled expression on his face and was gazing directly up at her, where she stood beyond the balustrade.

She stiffened. Impossible! She wasn't even truly there, but a projection of herself, concealed by countless layers of illusion, beyond an impenetrable Fae veil. Not even the most adept of Sidhe-seers would be able to isolate her formless form within the dimensional deception she'd created!

Ah, yes, this Druid had power beyond any other.

"What is it, Cian?" Drustan said, glancing over his shoulder in the direction Cian was looking. "Is aught amiss? Do you see something, kinsman?"

Aoibheal stared at the Highlander, her lips tightening. She smoothed them again. Waited for him to betray her presence.

No, no, no, it was not time yet — it could too drastically alter things — it could destroy what chance they had!

She'd attained a tenuous balance of possibles at best. She needed more time.

She held his gaze, used her human eyes to convey a mute plea. *Say nothing, Keltar-mine.*

The ninth-century Highlander regarded her silently. After a moment he inclined his head in the barest nod, then turned and glanced at Drustan.

"Nay," he said. " 'Tis nothing, Drustan. Nothing at all."

Dear Reader:

Though the MacKeltars tried to persuade Cian and Jessi to remain at Castle Keltar, Cian had had enough of stone walls surrounding him, and hungered for the great wide-open.

With the aid of her contacts at the Manhattan museum at which she used to work, Chloe arranged the sale of Cian's ninth-century, jewel-encrusted wrist cuffs and *skean dubh,* making Cian a wealthy man.

After a quick trip back to the States — where Lilly St. James bestowed her ecstatic blessing upon them and insisted upon a second wedding attended by the entire extended St. James clan — Cian and Jessi set off to tour the British Isles, so he could see the future he'd missed, and she could indulge her passion for the study of the past.

Cian used his unique "talents" to clear his wife of all blame in the matter of the missing mirror and attendant events, and Jessi plans to one day finish her PhD, but right now she's too busy living life to worry about planning it.

The two of them were last seen, a little bit tipsy and a whole lot in love, dancing slow and sweet to an old Scots ballad, in a tiny pub in the northern Highlands of Scotland.

On a different note, a great many of you have written to ask whether there will be more Keltar and Fae stories in the future.

Yes. More of both are in the works. I have no intention of ending the Highlander series for some time to come.

Thanks to all of you for loving these Keltar Druids as much as I do.

All my best, and happy reading!

Karen

SOURCES

Astaire, Lesley, Roddy Martine, and Eric Ellington. *Living in the Highlands.* London: Thames & Hudson Ltd., 2000.

Bahn, Paul. *Archaeology: The Definitive Guide.* New York: Barnes & Noble Books, 2003.

Ellis, Peter Berresford. *A Brief History of the Druids.* New York: Carroll & Graf Publishers, 2002.

Green, Miranda J. *The World of the Druids.* London: Thames & Hudson Ltd., 1997.

Kennedy, Maev. *The History of Archaeology.* New York: Barnes & Noble Books, 2002.

Konstam, Angus and Richard Kean. *Historical Atlas of the Celtic World.* New York: Checkmark Books, 2001.

Melchior-Bonnet, Sabine. *The Mirror, A History.* London: Taylor & Francis Group, 2000.

Montgomery-Massingberd, Hugh and

Christopher Simon Sykes. *Great Houses of Scotland*. New York: Universe Publishing, 2001.

Pendergrast, Mark. *Mirror Mirror: A History of the Human Love Affair with Reflection*. New York: Basic Books, 2004.

Renfrew, Colin and Paul Bahn. *Archaeology: Theories, Methods, and Practice*. London: Thames & Hudson Ltd., 2000.

What Life Was Like Among Druids and High Kings. New York: Time Life Books, 1998.

ABOUT THE AUTHOR

Karen Marie Moning graduated from Purdue University with a bachelor's degree in Society & Law. Her novels, which have appeared on the *New York Times* and *USA Today* bestseller lists, have won numerous awards, including the prestigious RITA Award. She can be reached at www.karenmoning.com.